ALSO BY

MAURIZIO DE GIOVANNI

IN THE COMMISSARIO RICCIARDI SERIES
I Will Have Vengeance:
The Winter of Commissario Ricciardi

Blood Curse:
The Springtime of Commissario Ricciardi

Everyone in Their Place:
The Summer of Commissario Ricciardi

The Day of the Dead:
The Autumn of Commissario Ricciardi

By My Hand:
The Christmas of Commissario Ricciardi

Viper:
No Resurrection for Commissario Ricciardi

The Bottom of Your Heart:
Inferno for Commissario Ricciardi

Glass Souls:
Moths for Commissario Ricciardi

Nameless Serenade:
Nocturne for Commissario Ricciardi

IN THE BASTARDS OF PIZZOFALCONE SERIES
The Bastards of Pizzofalcone

Darkness
for the Bastards of Pizzofalcone

The Crocodile

COLD
FOR THE BASTARDS
OF PIZZOFALCONE

Maurizio de Giovanni

COLD
FOR THE BASTARDS
OF PIZZOFALCONE

*Translated from the Italian
by Antony Shugaar*

Europa Editions
8 Blackstock Mews
London N4 2BT
www.europaeditions.co.uk

This book is a work of fiction. Any references to historical events,
real people, or real locales are used fictitiously.

Copyright © 2014 by Maurizio de Giovanni
Published by arrangement with The Italian Literary Agency
First Publication 2019 by Europa Editions

Translation by Antony Shugaar
Original title: *Gelo per i Bastardi di Pizzofalcone*
Translation copyright © 2019 by Europa Editions

All rights reserved, including the right of reproduction
in whole or in part in any form.

A catalogue record for this title is available from the British Library
ISBN 978-1-78770-161-8

de Giovanni, Maurizio
Cold for the Bastards of Pizzofalcone

Book design by Emanuele Ragnisco
www.mekkanografici.com

Cover image: ton koene/Alamy Stock Photo

Prepress by Grafica Punto Print – Rome

Printed in Italy at Arti Grafiche La Moderna - Rome

For Caterina, Emiliano, Delia, Ludovica.
For the whole wonderful future they have
in their eyes and in their hearts

COLD
FOR THE BASTARDS
OF PIZZOFALCONE

I

And then, all of a sudden, you feel it, the cold.

It hits you like a baseball bat, with the force of recognition.

You feel it while you're still on top of her, your face scant inches away from hers, as you stare into her dull, glazed eyes.

The cold. A prickly sensation on your bare skin, powerful and determined as if there were nothing else, as if nothing else had ever existed.

You perceive it with all five senses, the cold, you see it in the steam that billows out of your mouth, you hear it in the wheeze of your heaving breath, you inhale it like a whipcrack through your nostrils, you even taste it on your parched tongue. And you touch it on her body.

You leap to your feet, as if you'd only now realized where you are and what you've done. You look around, lost, as your rage gradually subsides, giving way to your mind: a distant voice that struggles to the surface, clear reason that tries to make itself heard. Hurry. Hurry.

Move fast, even though it might all be pointless. No noise arrives from outside. That's the way it is, when it's cold out. People shut themselves in their homes, where it's nice and warm, dulling their brains until they're dumber than ever, watching TV or gazing at their computer, exchanging comments with random strangers about the sole, incessant subject of the day: My goodness it's cold, how cold it is, so chilly, Signo', can you believe how cold it is? And they say the temperature is going to drop even more, I'm climbing under the covers and staying in bed till summer.

Stupid. They're all stupid. And they think that everyone else is as stupid as they are. But not you. You're not stupid.

You take one last look around. Her room. Her few scattered possessions. A doll or two, panties and undershirts. A mess. Nothing of yours, not a trace of your presence. Good. You back out of the room. The front hall, the kitchen door. The big bedroom, on your right; from where you are now, there's no sign of him. You crane your neck, leaning forward a matter of inches, holding your breath, choking back the clouds of white vapor that spring rhythmically from your lips. For a moment you wonder whether he's gotten up out of bed and is waiting for you right behind the doorjamb, a long knife in his hand like in one of those American movies, with the predictable plot twist that comes as no surprise to anyone.

But no, there he is. You can just see his fingertips, sheets of paper, the screen of his laptop. A pen in one hand.

You stop. You think to yourself that he'll start writing again, slowly, or give some other sign of life: a cough, a sigh. The faint light of the naked lightbulb hanging from the ceiling; the little electric heater on, the electric cord wrapped in insulating tape for all the times he must have tripped over it, absentminded as he is.

Absentminded as he *was*.

Suddenly, a voice from within: Get moving, every extra second could prove decisive. Hurry. Get busy.

You heave a sigh and you step into the room. You can't seem to keep your eyes fixed on him, his head resting on the desktop, his arm dangling in the empty air.

I need something to drink, you think to yourself, gulping empty-mouthed. Something with a kick. Some wine. No, hard liquor. Something that burns as it slides down your throat, something that warms up your belly and makes your head spin.

I wonder if they have anything to drink in here. Of course, they must have *something*, poor as they are, miserable wretches, to buck up their hopes of making their way in a city that doesn't want them.

They're deadbeats.

Or maybe you should just say: They're dead.

It's colder inside than out, you think to yourself. Like in some damned freezer. Or a morgue. You wipe your trembling hand across your forehead. Maybe you have a fever. Maybe this is all just a nightmare, the kind that you have and, while you're in it, you say to yourself: When am I going to wake up out of this damned nightmare? Maybe soon you'll open your eyes and there you'll be, under the covers, with a smile on your face as you realize that it's over.

That it's all over.

The voice, the voice in your brain: Hurry up. Look around. What can give you away? What can possibly show that you were ever here?

You have no alternative but to start with him, reconstruct every gesture, every movement. Start over from him and his head.

His damned head, with that strange, absurd hollow where the nape of the neck once curved out into the back of the skull, at the base of the cranium, now damp and dark as if someone had poured paint over it, over his shoulders: Ha ha, what a funny prank. And the shirt collar, soaked in black blood.

The reddish reflection of the electric heater seems like the light of hell.

Your eyes scan the floor and at last they glimpse what they needed to see. The little bronze statuette. You lean down and pick it up.

You're surprised. It had been so light, earlier, when rage was driving your arm, when the wave of destructive fury was rushing through your veins. Now it seems incredibly heavy, a solid ton of metal moulded into the foolish image of a woman with a sash over her shoulder, a trophy from who knows what insipid evening out with music from the Sixties and young men on the prowl for willing females. You look at it as if you'd never seen it before.

Symbols. His head, her face.

His head, the head you just split open, so full of ideas, of stubborn determination to study and discover, the head you lashed out at: two, three, five blows, even though the first would have done the job, with that damp sound of a cracking walnut that you heard.

Her face, so pretty—that perfect nose, those lips so full and red, rich in promise—swollen in your grip, unrecognizable and puffy, shattered like her life.

Symbols.

Right, you think, as you slip the statuette into the pocket of your heavy jacket. Shattered and broken in the only hopes you ever had to escape from the shit you were born into and where it would have been better for you to remain. His head, her face. You didn't do it intentionally, but if you'd had to choose, that's the way you would have chosen. Those were all they had to pin their hopes on, their tickets to a better life.

Or straight to hell.

A frenzy washes over you. You need to get out of here.

You go back to the front hall. Now you're fully lucid, your mind is clear as a brisk morning with a north wind, as cold as the chill in the air. You don't shut the door, you leave it slightly ajar: someone might hear the noise and take a look, and then all would be lost.

Better to take the stairs than the elevator, it's harder to figure what floor you're coming from. You could walk pressed up against the wall, in the shadows, but after all, who's even going to see you? It's late, and in this cold no one's going out unless it's absolutely necessary.

From a couple of apartments, as you descend the stairs quickly and silently, you can hear the sound of the TV.

The front entrance: you're out of the building.

The biting cold wind slices through the air and slams into you. You pull up your lapels to cover your face, even though the alleyway is deserted. You need something to drink, you need warmth. Every step is a good step, it takes you farther away from that morgue, from those rooms full of death. You're shaking, your hands are shaking, and so are your legs. Your back is numb and tingling with tension. The weight of the statuette in your jacket pocket reminds you that it's all true.

You see the sign glowing outside a bar. The great thing about this despicable city is that any time of the day or night, there's always someone ready to welcome you in for a drink, something to eat, a smoke, as long as it's to relieve you of some money.

You step inside. In a corner, there are some customers playing the video poker machines. Sitting at one table, three young men and a young woman. There's a stench of rancid food and stale sweat, but at least it's warm in there.

You sit down, you take off your jacket, freeing yourself of the dead weight of the bronze statuette. You lay your hands side by side on the café table, and you wait for them to stop shaking.

You order something to drink, and a little something to eat, just to keep from sticking out like a sore thumb.

Unnecessary precautions, you decide, because the tall, lanky waiter with a sleepy expression doesn't even look in your direction.

The music blares out in dialect from the stereo's speakers. The video poker players are staring at the machines' displays, eyes wide open. The four young people at the table are laughing loudly.

Finally back in the normal world. Invisible again. Now everything's all right. Everything's fine.

So you drink. And you drink some more.

But the cold won't go away.

II

Corporal Marco Aragona made his entrance with a sort of dancer's vaulting leap.

"Ladies and gentleman, a very heartfelt good day to you. Have you all seen what a lovely day we have, this fine morning?"

His greeting dropped into a weary, resigned silence. Lieutenant Lojacono raised his almond-shaped eyes from the file that lay before him and shot his young colleague a malevolent glare. Pisanelli, the veteran deputy captain, shook his head with a sigh.

Aragona persisted, raising his voice with an unmistakably offended attitude: "Here we go again . . . always ready to circle the wagons, aren't you? Do you mind telling me what the hell has gotten into you all? You don't even respond to a bright good morning around here?"

Ottavia Calabrese leaned out from behind the oversized screen of her desktop computer: "You're absolutely right, Marco. *Buongiorno!* A fine good morning to you. Even though I have to say, it doesn't seem like such a fine day to me. Last night the temperature dropped below freezing, and this morning, when I took the dog out for his morning pee, there was a layer of ice on the sidewalk."

Aragona smiled and rubbed his hands: "My sweet lady, good mother that you are, what on earth could be wrong with a fine, cool winter's day? In the town where my parents live it snows every year, but everyone's cheeful and contented all the same."

A man with broad shoulders and a bull neck who sat reading a newspaper at a desk off to one side grumbled: "What they have to be cheerful about in the snow and the cold, I'd honestly like to know. Cars slam headfirst into walls, old people slip and fall and break legs and arms, and you can't stay outdoors."

Aragona threw his arms out in Francesco Romano's general direction: "Well, that's no surprise, Hulk, to hear a complaint out of you. It would be different if I'd even once seen you, I'm not even saying laugh, but so much as smile in the past few months. Why don't you try and see a glass half full at least once. The cold stirs up your energy, makes you feel like getting moving. Maybe even like doing some work, which strikes me as a rare commodity around here."

Alessandra Di Nardo, who sat at the last desk at the far end of the squad room, broke off her work cleaning her regulation handgun and addressed Aragona with feigned brusqueness: "I hope you don't mind if I point out that, like always, whether it's hot out or cold, you're always the last to arrive, so you don't actually feel all this desire for hard work. Also, may I enquire, what on earth is this getup? Where did you get that sweater?"

Aragona made a show of being offended and patted the lobster-pink turtleneck he was wearing under his jacket: "It astonishes me that you of all people, the only young woman in this old folks' home, should fail to appreciate the beauty and style of a color that brings a little cheer to the season. What's more, this sweater costs . . . "

Lojacono and Ottavia finished his sentence for him in a perfect chorus: " . . . as much as everything the rest of us, put together, are wearing."

"Exactly. Because you're all old-school cops. Old-school cops like you are something you don't even see in the cop shows from the Seventies. The profession adjusts to go with the times, it evolves, and you're all still clueless. That's why . . ."

Now it was Alex and Romano's turn to finish his sentence for him: " . . . I'll be the first to get a promotion and get the hell out of this . . . "

Aragona, waving his hand like the conductor of a symphony orchestra, finished up: " . . . shithole of a police station here in Pizzofalcone!"

The door behind him swung open and Commissario Palma appeared. Everyone lowered their eyes to the work they'd been doing, except for Aragona, who hadn't noticed a thing and therefore indulged in an exaggerated bow that displayed his hindquarters to his superior officer.

Palma gave him a slow, ironic burst of applause: "Bravo, bravo, Aragona. My compliments for your early-morning routine. Now, if you don't mind, I'd like to know how we're going to spend the day here at nursery school."

The corporal darted hastily to one side, grabbed his glasses with blue-tinted lenses that had slid off his forehead, and with the other hand brushed back his Elvis-style quiff—which he cultivated for its two-fold function of concealing a spreading bald spot at the top of his head and adding a useful inch or so of height to his stature—and promptly sat down at his desk.

Palma glanced down at the sheets of paper he held in one hand, as if seeking comfort from them. Even first thing in the morning he had the usual weary, rumpled appearance, accentuated by the perennial five o'clock shadow of whiskers, the loosened knot in his tie, and the rolled-up shirtsleeves. His hair, too, dense and tousled, contributed to the general impression he gave of untidiness and overactivity.

"Now then," he began, looking back up and around the room, "I've put together a work order. Pisanelli can supervise this project: let's dig through all the cold cases, the unsolved murders, in other words. Let's figure out whether there's anything else we can do, otherwise we'll just archive them with a brief report."

Romano closed his newspaper and muttered: "Papers and files, there's just no end of papers and files. If I'd known this was what it was going to be like, I'd have taken a job at the city recorder's office."

Ottavia addressed the commissario in a worried voice: "Dottore, are these orders from headquarters? Are they trying to tell us something?"

Lojacono, who was staring at his superior officer with an indecipherable expression, added: "Does it mean, for example, that they're thinking about eliminating the precinct again, the way they were at first?"

Pisanelli broke in: "No, not that again? Haven't we shown that we know what we're doing? Are we going to carry that burden of original sin forever?"

He was referring to the notorious story of the Bastards of Pizzofalcone, as they were called and remembered by every policeman in the greater region: former colleagues in the precinct who had been tangled up in a very serious case of corruption when they'd set out to sell a shipment of narcotics that they'd confiscated in a raid. There had been a tremendous scandal and the small but historical police station had come very close to being shuttered once and for all. In the end the top officials had decided, on a provisional basis, to keep the precinct open and operating for a probationary period.

Giorgio Pisanelli, along with Ottavia Calabrese, was one of the few survivors of the arrests and early retirements that had come on the heels of the scandal, and he was especially sensitive to the matter: if things went south, he'd feel responsible for it, in spite of the fact that he, like his female colleague, had had nothing to do with that miserable chapter in the precinct's history.

Aragona cut him off, making a show of his insufferable optimism: "Maybe it's just a matter of clearing out stacks of old documents, don't you think? They wouldn't dream of closing us down: without us, without the new Bastards of Pizzofalcone, who would they gossip about in the other barracks?"

Pisanelli whipped around and glared at him. Generally speaking, he was the very picture of tranquility, but the sound of that nickname, the Bastards, made his blood boil: "Aragona, I've told you a thousand times: you don't know as much as you think you do. They broke the law, and they'll pay the price, but the people in the quarter, who wouldn't have any protection from the criminal element if we weren't here, aren't to blame for that. We need to keep the lights burning in here and clean up the precinct's image, we're capable of doing it, so—"

Romano interrupted him, bitterly: "Sure, nice cleanup. You know they just sent us in to finish this place off, don't you? Remember, every one of us has a blot on their record. Which means we're all likely to pull some other boneheaded move. Just forget about it, go on."

Palma took the reins: "You're all complaining pointlessly. Worse than pointlessly. All we need to do is go back through the old cold cases, nothing more than that. It's a project that we'll set aside, obviously, as soon as anything new comes up. All right then, Giorgio, you coordinate with Aragona and Romano to get out the old files and start going through them—"

The sound of the phone ringing cut him off. As always, it was Ottavia who answered, and after a brief exchange, she hung up and said: "That was the switchboard from police headquarters. They just received a call, and apparently something serious has happened at number 32 Vico Secondo Egiziaca, just a short walk from here."

Lojacono had already stood up from his desk and was putting on his coat.

"I'll go."

Palma nodded and added: "That's fine. Di Nardo, you go with him. You can get a little fresh air for your handgun."

III

The minute Lojacono and Di Nardo had walked out the door and Palma had gone back into his office, Romano slammed a fist down on his desk.

"Dammit. They get to do the real work, and we're just sitting at our desks like a bunch of accountants."

Ottavia, who had practically leapt out of her chair at the unexpected noise, said: "Come on, Francesco, the commissario would never play favorites and—"

Aragona interrupted her: "No, no, little mother, you're always justifying anything that your Signor Commissario does. But the Incredible Hulk over here has a point, anytime there's anything important going on, Palma sends the Chinaman; and as far as that goes, Calamity Jane enjoys special treatment too. I'd like to know how we're supposed to get promotions by writing up reports on cases dating back a century that never got wrapped up because your partners on the force were too busy dealing drugs."

Pisanelli glared at him grimly: "Aragona, since I'm supervising this project, I'm sorely tempted to assign you some dusty case file that hasn't seen the light of day in a good solid decade. What do you say to that?"

Ottavia Calabrese tried to soften the tone: "Listen, all of you, I'm sure that the commissario isn't playing favorites at all. It's just that Lojacono has the most experience. He proved he knew what he was doing with both the Crocodile case, when he was still back at the San Gaetano police station, and the death of the notary's wife. Come to think of it, Palma assigned you to work alongside him, Marco, so—"

Romano was having none of it: "All I see happening is that Lojacono is getting more and more experience and the rest of us never see the light of day. I'm going in to see Palma, and I'm going to ask him if—"

The sound of a cough from the door to the room put an end to the argument. Everyone swung around. Standing at the door was a middle-aged lady, rather nicely dressed, who was waiting for someone to notice her presence.

"Excuse me, Signora, can I help you?"

In response to Ottavia's invitation, the woman took a step forward and entered the office, uneasily. From the ink spots on her hands, which anxiously clutched at the handles of her handbag, Pisanelli deduced that she must be a schoolteacher. He also noticed her rotund physique and her diminutive stature, only slightly elevated by a pair of low-heeled shoes.

"Yes. I would . . . I'd like to file a criminal complaint. Or, rather, I should say: I'd like to . . . make a report, that's better, I think. A report."

Romano stood up: he had no intention of letting the second opportunity of the day to work on a real-life case instead of a pile of old documents slip through his hands.

"You can tell me all about it, Signora. I'm Officer Francesco Romano, warrant officer."

She flashed a strained smile which, nonetheless, did make her look a little younger.

"*Buongiorno*, I'm Professoressa Emilia Macchiaroli. I'm a teacher at the Sergio Corazzini Middle School, not far from here. Can I . . . could we speak here?"

"Why, of course, Professoressa. We're all colleagues here."

The woman looked around and ran her tongue over her lips, still clearly ill at ease.

"Well, you see, I don't even know if I did the right thing. I thought it was the right thing to report . . . Or, I don't know if I should say, report this matter . . . I tried to persuade the mother to . . . but for some reason, she just wouldn't. Not that that's uncommon, for a mother it's hard to believe such a thing, and of course the girl's an only child, which as you know only makes it worse. On the other hand, I said to myself, what if it turns out to be true? There are lunatics, attention-seekers, make no mistake, with all the filth people see on TV, but then one time out of a hundred, it might actually turn out to be true. And then, certainly, we all know about the boy who cries wolf, just for fun, and the one time that there really is a wolf, no one believes him. Not that I'm an alarmist, in any way, shape, or form, but then you can't just let things slide without speaking up. Don't you agree?"

Aragona stared at her, openmouthed. Pisanelli concealed his face behind a police report. Ottavia struggled to focus on her computer screen. Romano wondered to himself whether the woman really expected an answer. Since in fact she seemed to, he decided to stick to generalities: "Well, of course. And to be specific, Professoressa, exactly what would we be talking about here?"

"Ah, sex abuse, of course. You see, I teach Italian Literature. To tell the truth, they have different names for the subjects these day, but those of us who went to school in the old days tend to stick to tradition, am I right? That is, it's really all a question of imprinting: if I get used to a certain terminology when I'm young, then it stands to reason—"

Aragona couldn't help but weigh in: "Please, please, Professore', try to stick to to the subject. Otherwise, our colleague can't make heads or tails of it all, and neither can any of us. And if we can't understand, we can't very well help you either."

Professoressa Macchiaroli blinked rapidly, as if astonished to have been interrupted: "Why, of course, and that's what I'm doing, I'm explaining, aren't I? Let me say it again, I teach Italian Literature, which means I'm basically the homeroom teacher for the whole class. Naturally, the kids write essays and papers, they do research projects, and I read what they write. Of course, they usually write to show off what they've learned: Literature, History, Elements of . . . "

Aragona rose to his feet: "Professore', if you teach the kids the way you come in here to lay out your situation, I can hardly be surprised that the levels of educational achievement are plunging in this country. Let me implore you, could you just tell us why you've come in today?"

With a glance that by rights ought to have incinerated Corporal Aragona, Romano tried to set things right: "Professoressa, what we're trying to understand is whether you are here to file a criminal complaint."

"No, officer, not a complaint. I believe that a complaint implies the outright certainty that a crime has taken place: and I can't be certain of that fact, nor is there any way for me to be. All the same, I do believe that one of my female students is being sexually abused. And if I want to have a clear conscience, then I have no alternative but to inform you to that effect."

Silence descended over the room. Palma appeared in his office door, his curiosity piqued by the conversation, and asked: "How old is this student of yours? And who do you think is molesting her?"

The woman turned to face the commissario, leveling her calm pale blue eyes in his direction.

"She's twelve. Martina Parise, Class 2B. And the abuser is her father."

IV

Vico Secondo Egiziaca was, in fact, just a short distance from the police station. It took less than three minutes for Lojacono and Di Nardo to walk over there, hugging the walls to ward off the chill in the air, overcoat collars turned up, eyes narrowed to defend against the cutting wind, breath billowing out in clouds of vapor.

Alex inhaled deeply.

"What can I say, Lojacono, I just like the cold. If you want to warm up, all you need is to get out and move a little. Whereas when it's hot out, there's nothing you can do: you can strip down to your underwear, but it's hot all the same, so there's nothing to be done but shut the windows and turn on the air conditioner, and everybody knows how bad that is for you."

"I don't see what there is to like about a wind that's strong enough to tear your ears off. Di Nardo, you're just trying to provoke me. When it's cold out where I come from, it's the same temperature as when it's hot out here. It's like Lapland this morning. Getting out from under the blankets was straight-up trauma. Well, here we are."

It hadn't been necessary to look for the street number: outside one of the apartment house doors stood a squad car with its emergency lights flashing, and next to the car a young man in uniform hopping from foot to foot to keep from freezing.

Lojacono walked over to him: "We're from the Pizzofalcone police precinct."

The young man in uniform tilted his head in the direction of the stairs, while cupping both hands in front of his mouth: "Look who finally decided to show. Ciccolletti, police headquarters. Upstairs. Third floor. Guy and a girl. No doorman, just in case you thought of looking for one. My partner's upstairs, expecting you. We put in a call for forensics, by the way."

His excessively casual manner rubbed Lojacono the wrong way; the Bastards of Pizzofalcone, an indelible stain of infamy. Staring into the officer's eyes, he hissed: "Ciccoletti, you're speaking to a lieutenant. So get your fucking hands away from your mouth and stand still and at attention, or I'll warm you up with a hail of fists. You read me?"

"Sorry, lieutenant. It's just that it's so damned cold this morning, and the wind is blasting down here. We've been waiting for you, we got here first thing, and—"

Lojacono turned away and strode through the front door. Alex followed him, but only after giving the uniformed officer a look that betrayed a blend of sympathy and further reproof.

The apartment building, like nearly all the other buildings in the neighborhood, had seen better days. It was an old building, subject to strict zoning requirements, and therefore intact in its crumbling façade while at the same time victim to horrible attempts at modernization of the interiors. As they climbed the stairs, Lojacono noticed the flaking walls, the ceramic tiles that had been replaced by other tiles of an entirely different color, the occasional crack that had been repaired amateurishly with raw mortar, unplastered and unpainted. The wooden apartment doors were all different, and here and there anodyzed aluminum front doors with several doorbells hinted at the subdivision of old apartments that had once been much larger and occupied by a single family. That description applied to the doorway on the third floor where they were headed. The main doorway led into a sort of entryway flanked by two interior front doors, at the moment both open.

Waiting for them on the landing was a second uniformed officer. He was older than the one waiting down in the street, and perhaps that was why he took a more formal attitude. He raised his hand to his visor.

"Good morning, my name's Stanzione. Are you the officers from Pizzofalcone? They alerted me by radio."

Alex nodded: "Right, that's us. I'm Officer Di Nardo, he's Lieutenant Lojacono. What can you tell us?"

The man turned and spoke directly to Lojacono. Certainly, in part because of his rank. But also because he's a man, Alex decided resentfully.

"The murder took place here, in the apartment on your right. Two kids, a man and a woman: she's on the bed, he's sitting at the desk in the next room."

Alex insisted, in a flat tone: "Who found the bodies?"

Hesitantly, Stanzione replied to Lojacono again, as if the lieutenant were some sort of ventriloquist and Di Nardo nothing but his puppet: "One of the young man's colleagues, and he's pretty upset. He's in the neighbors' apartment . . . two . . . two people who live next door. They made him an espresso, the lucky guy."

Without taking his hands out of the pockets of his overcoat, Lojacono examined first the aluminum door facing the landing and then the door that the uniformed officer was pointing to; no sign of breaking and entering in either case. He took a step into the apartment: the interior was illuminated by the light coming in from the window of one of the bedrooms and from a naked lightbulb dangling on a wire from the ceiling.

Alex, beating the lieutenant to the question, asked Stanzione: "Did you turn on the light?"

"No, why would I? I didn't touch a thing. I walked in,

looked around, and left. I'm not some green rookie, you know."

Lojacono concealed a half smile, picking up on Di Nardo's unmistakable and justifiable hostility, and then took the opportunity to ask: "What about the doors, how were they when you arrived? Open, ajar, shut . . . "

"Open, lieutenant, both of them. And so was the door to the other apartment."

Alex had stepped into the first room, lit up by the lightbulb hanging from the ceiling. Lojacono caught up with her and found her standing by the bed, which filled almost the whole room.

Sprawled on her back on the mattress was a young woman, her legs spread slightly. She was wearing an open jacket and a torn blouse, which partly left her flesh uncovered. She wore no bra. A very skimpy pair of panties were rolled down to the height of her left knee. A pair of jeans lay on the floor.

Though gray and in disarray, the young woman's body was very beautiful.

Lojacono leaned over to observe more closely: the face was swollen around the nose and mouth; on the neck there were a couple of reddish stripes. When he turned to look at his partner, he saw that she was staring at something on the wall. In a photograph blown up to large scale, the victim was smiling happily in bright sunlight, wearing a swimsuit, with a clear blue sea stretching out behind her. The contrast was horrifying and grim: a photograph, an inanimate object, full of life; a body, made of flesh and blood, drained of life.

The lieutenant walked out of the room, leaving Alex frozen to the spot.

Opening onto the tiny front hallway was another door that led to a larger room, at the center of which was a second corpse, slumped over a desk. A man, seated. His torso was pitched forward, one arm dangling loose, while his head and the other hand, still gripping a pen, rested on the desktop.

Lojacono stepped closer, taking care where he put his feet. The corpse was displaying the nape of its neck to him. The shirt collar had turned dark, drenched in blood as it was; the cranium presented a deep depression at the base. The man's clothing must have soaked up all the blood, because there wasn't a spot of it on the floor.

The policeman circled around the desk and found himself face-to-face with the victim. The dead man was young, not much older than twenty, maybe in his mid-twenties. Death had stamped an odd expression on his face, something approaching a taut, strained smile, which revealed his upper teeth; his eyes were partway open and staring into the empty air. There were no signs of a struggle, he must have been caught off guard.

In the front hall, the lieutenant found Alex squatting down to look at something on the floor, beneath a small side table. The woman looked up and pointed downward.

"What would you say that is?"

Lojacono crouched down beside her.

"It looks like a cell phone with a pair of earbuds. Hard to see clearly."

Alex started to extend her hand, but Lojacono stopped her: "Leave everything where it is for now. The forensics squad will be here any minute, and we can let them get it out. That's when we can examine closely. For now, let's go talk to the people who found them."

V

Professoressa Macchiaroli seemed to have experienced a stunning transformation, which might have been a result, mused Palma, of her growing confidence that she had done the right thing by speaking to them. The commissario had thanked her and told her she could go, assuring her that they would check out her suspicions, with the greatest possible discretion, naturally. Her only reply came in an utterly chilly tone, and as she spoke, she kept her tight grip on the handles of her handbag, which she had never once released: "Don't you worry about that, Commissario. I'm willing to take full responsibility, I'm certainly not afraid to have anyone know that I took steps when I learned that one of my female students was ill at ease. You should be discreet only if it serves a good purpose, to gather information: often, when talking to strangers, young people tend to clam up, and you can't get another word out of them. It's happened to us other times, you can't get them to talk no matter how hard you try. But if you need me, you can always find me at school."

Opinions differed in the squad room. Aragona had a theory all his own, which he considered to be the final word on the matter: "If you ask me, that girl's just been watching too much TV, and she mentioned something in an essay that she'd seen in some stupid series so her teacher came running to tell the cops."

Romano nodded: "Probably you're right. Around here, there's a thin line between fantasy and reality. A father can't stroke his daughter's hair without being lynched as a child molester."

Pisanelli started rifling through the papers in the folder open on the desk in front of him: "I don't know about that. Professoressa Macchiaroli is an experienced teacher, this isn't her first year teaching. She didn't strike me as the sort of person who gets carried away by excitement or mindless zeal. I'm sure she's seen more than her share of young female students. If she thought it was worth coming in, she must have had a good reason."

Aragona snickered mockingly: "Well isn't that nice, old folks standing up for each other. The decrepit, experienced cop happens to believe the word of the decrepit, experienced literature teacher. Let me tell you something, chief: just like you coming up with your conspiracy theories about unexplained suicides, she comes up with her own theories about child-molesting fathers. Who can say, maybe it's just a matter of psychological compensation: the schoolteacher dreams of being raped by someone and you're secretly yearning to commit suicide, so the two of you just fantasize about it happening to other people."

The unexpected reference to what everyone else considered a harmless obsession on Pisanelli's part plunged the office into silence. The senior policeman was convinced that a series of suicides that had taken place in recent years within the bounds of the precinct had actually been murders, and he continued stubbornly investigating his theory, gathering data, testimony, and photographs. He did so outside working hours and bothered no one, so his colleagues tacitly agreed to look the other way and limited themselves to the occasional wisecrack when Pisanelli wasn't around.

Ottavia broke the awkward silence: "Aragona, you really can be a jerk sometimes. I'm tempted to tell you to go to hell, I have to say. You have no right to judge what Giorgio thinks and says. I'm pretty sure that when you're his age, you won't have achieved a fraction of what he's done."

Romano, too, even though he was personally in favor of ignoring the schoolteacher's report, reacted angrily: "You're an idiot, Arago'. An authentic cretin. You just freely launch into two-bit psychological analysis, but you don't have the slightest idea what you're talking about."

Aragona threw his arms wide: "Well, gosh, what did I even say? It's not like I insulted anyone, did I? Chief, did I hurt your feelings? I was only kidding."

Pisanelli forced a semblance of a smile onto his face: "Don't worry about it, Marco. Trust me, I have no intention of committing suicide. Sooner or later you'll understand; in fact, all of you will see that I'm right. You just assume that I have a fixation, that I'm wasting my time, but I don't embezzle a minute from my job, I wouldn't dream of it. Plus I have my own reasons for digging into these cases. To come back to the schoolteacher, though, I was just saying that certain things shouldn't be overlooked or dismissed, that's all. Sometimes they might seem like trifles, but then it turns out—"

Romano interrupted him: "Sure, you bet, the others are investigating a multiple murder and we're stuck with the fantasies of a middle-aged woman? Why doesn't the commissario just send Lojacono to the school?"

"I told you before that no one's playing favorites, Francesco," Ottavia retorted, archly dignified. "And I also think that if there's even the shadow of doubt that a little girl is being molested, we ought to—"

Palma appeared in the door to his office: "Unless there's something urgent on the agenda, guys, I'd like you to check out this report about the little girl. It seems worthwhile to at least take a look, no? Better to make certain. Romano and Aragona, why don't the two of you check it out?"

Aragona tried to put up some resistance: "But listen, boss,

that woman's just an old nutcase. Can't we at least wait until there's a formal complaint before swinging into action? There have to be more important things we could be doing."

"Of course there are, Aragona. Like I was telling you not long ago, there are old cases to wrap up. I'm almost tempted to assign you the whole lot of them, with all the police reports to be transcribed. A nice little intellectual task that will keep you with your ass glued to a chair for six months, give or take. What do you say?"

Aragona was already on his feet, overcoat in one hand. Romano got to his feet to follow him out, emitting a low muttering gurgle.

Palma turned serious: "Guys, stop your bellyaching. A cop is a cop, and it's a cop's duty to look into every report he gets with the same amount of attention. I don't want any complaints going to headquarters about the way we comport ourselves, is that clear? If they decide to shut down this precinct, I can't have that being on account of any of our shortcomings. We're all in agreement, right?"

Aragona snapped to attention, raising two fingers to his forehead like an American Marine: "Yessir, chief. Don't worry. We'll distinguish ourselves famously, at school, and we'll bring home a first-rate report card."

"Aragona, you're an absolute idiot."

VI

As soon as he entered the apartment that shared an entrance with that of the victims, it became clear to Lojacono why Officer Stanzione had been so vague in his use of pronouns to refer to its occupants.

It didn't even slightly resemble the apartment where the double homicide had taken place. Immediately beyond the front door there opened out a large room, illuminated by a set of French doors that led out onto a balcony. The furnishings were rather garish, with pink fabrics, lace, toy stuffed animals scattered here and there, and spindly lamps perched precariously on teetering bases.

Sitting at a steel-and-glass table was a skinny young man wearing glasses. He kept brushing his long, silky bangs out of his eyes. His lips were trembling; on his cheeks, two ruddy patches betrayed the intensity of his emotion.

Standing next to him was an odd-looking young man, wearing a sort of ankle-length tunic that was decorated in garish geometric patterns. He had long hair, tied up in a ponytail, and he was barefoot. His eyes were hazel-colored and lightly made up.

Standing off to one side, as if embarrassed, was a third young man, short and dressed in black, with a couple of ostentatious piercings on his ears and nose.

Stanzione, who had accompanied Di Nardo and Lojacono into the apartment, said: "Lieutenant, this is the young man who found the corpses and called 911."

Lojacono waited for the officer to point to one of the three young men, but nothing happened. He finally turned to Alex and said: "Di Nardo, will you explain to this officer that he needs to be more specific, or do I need to draw him a diagram so he can understand that I'm looking at three young men?"

The young man sitting at the table raised one trembling hand, like a student who knows the answer to a question but lacks the nerve to speak up.

"I am. I'm the one who . . . who found . . . I mean, I called the police, or I called *you*, I guess."

He was clearly in a state of disorientation. His voice was faint to start with, and it lurched into a falsetto that he tried to conceal with the occasional fit of coughing. Lojacono scrutinized him for what struck him as a reasonable period of time.

"What is your name, sir?"

The one wearing the tunic broke in; he had a deep voice and a strong Pugliese accent.

"Renato, don't answer him. These guys will trip you up at every turn. Didn't you notice? This guy didn't even tell you his name."

Officer Stanzione snarled: "Oh, nasty thing, don't you dare, you hear me? It's already a mystery to me why you aren't in prison, the way you look. Speak respectfully!"

"You don't scare me, understand? I'm not afraid of you, officer. If anything, you're in our home with no warrant or just cause. You should just be grateful that we allowed you in without asking to see your badge, but instead you continue to show no consideration, in spite of the trauma that we've just suffered."

That was more than Stanzione could take. Red-faced, he strode one step forward, shouting: "You piece of shit faggot, I'll break that makeup-smeared face of yours in half—"

Alex grabbed Stanzione by the wrist with surprising strength, catching the officer off guard: "Shut your mouth, you idiot. Don't you realize that this guy could file a complaint against you, and he'd have every right?"

Lojacono raised both hands in a peacemaking gesture, and in his turn took a step toward the young man in the tunic, strategically placing himself in front of Stanzione: "I apologize, sir, and I'm sorry. These are difficult situations for anyone, trust me. No one ever gets used to this kind of thing. I'm Lieutenant Giuseppe Lojacono, from the Pizzofalcone police precinct. My colleague is Officer Alessandra Di Nardo. There's no need for me to introduce the other officer because he was just leaving. He'll rejoin his colleague downstairs in the street where he can wait for the forensic squad to arrive, isn't that right?"

The officer realized that he had better obey and, with a truculent glare, left the room. At least for the moment, the fact that he had left the room helped to lessen the tension.

The young man in the tunic blew a puff of air upward to get his bangs out of his eyes and introduced himself: "Pleasure to make your acquaintance. I'm Vinnie Amoruso and I live here with my friend, Paco Mandurino."

He pointed to short man dressed in black, who nodded his head.

Lojacono turned and spoke to the one who had found the dead bodies: "What about you? What's your name, and how did you happen to be in the apartment across the way?"

The young man opened his mouth, closed it again, heaved a deep breath, and then said: "My name is Renato Forgione. I'm a friend . . . a colleague and a friend of Biagio's. Yesterday he didn't show up on campus, and I waited for him all afternoon. His phone wasn't picking up, or maybe it was turned off, and this morning . . . Oh my God, I'm going to throw up again . . . "

As if seeking protection, as he uttered these last words he looked up at Vinnie, who was gently patting his shoulder. He ran a hand over his face, looked at Lojacono again, and went on: "We talk all the time, we work together, we're working on projects together at the university. I was worried, he's not the kind of guy who just vanishes . . . he never disappeared like that, it was a strange thing. So I came here. The door was ajar, I went in, and then I found . . . I found them . . . Excuse me—"

He stood up and rushed into the bathroom.

Lojacono asked Amoruso: "Did you know the two victims?"

The young man had loosened his ponytail and now he was toying with the clasp: "We still can't quite believe it, Lieutenant. I mean, who, who could have done such a thing? In any case, their names were Biagio and Grazia Varricchio, they were brother and sister. They were Calabrians, from a town near Crotone. He was the older brother, a fine young man, a colleague of Renato's, a researcher, with a degree in biochemistry, I think, or maybe it was biosciences, something of the sort, I don't understand much about it. He'd been living here for some time, longer than us, and when is it we moved in? Two years ago?"

The one dressed in black, who still hadn't uttered a word, broke in: "Two years and ten months, Vinnie."

Amoruso raised a hand to his mouth in exaggerated surprise: "Oh, *mamma mia*, already so long? The two of us study law. We're in no hurry to graduate, I will admit that, but we know enough to defend our rights."

Lojacono resumed: "You said that he'd been living here for some time; what about his sister?"

Vinnie shook his head, decisively: "No, his sister only moved in a couple of months ago."

Once again, Paco broke in: "Seven months ago."

Vinnie shot him a harsh and irritated glare, very briefly, and then turned his eyes back to the lieutenant: "If Paco remembers it so clearly, then it must have been seven months."

In the meantime, Forgione had returned from the bathroom, pale as a rag and every bit as rumpled. Alex took advantage of the opportunity to weigh in, beating Lojacono to the punch. In a rush she said: "You said that the door was left open. Are you talking about the door to the landing or the inner door to the apartment?"

"The front door of Biagio's apartment. Vinnie answered the door on the landing."

Turning her gaze to Vinnie, Alex kept up her questioning: "Didn't you notice that the door was open? Didn't you hear any noises, no shouts, nothing?"

Vinnie replied without hesitation: "Yes, Signorina, we did, but not yesterday evening. Yesterday afternoon. There certainly had been an argument. One of the voices was Biagio's, the other voice belonged to a man I'd never heard before, and they were speaking in dialect. Then we heard someone leave and Paco looked out into the hallway. But the door was shut."

Lojacono looked at the young man dressed in black: "Are you certain?"

Paco nodded: "Absolutely certain."

"And you didn't see the person who left?"

"No, he was already gone."

Upon hearing this account of the quarrel, Renato had opened his eyes wide and his lips had started trembling again. Alex and Lojacono exchanged a glance, then Di Nardo looked hard at the young man: "And you have no idea who the other man might have been? Biagio didn't say anything to you?"

Renato said nothing.

Lojacono tried reframing Alex's question: "Signor Forgione, did you know if Varricchio was expecting a visitor?"

Forgione didn't even seem to hear him, and kept his eyes glued on Vinnie. All right then, let's give Vinnie a try, the lieutenant thought to himself.

"Were they speaking in dialect? Did you hear them argue in dialect?"

Vinnie nodded his head: "I couldn't understand a word they were saying. It's not like I was trying to eavesdrop, they were just shouting so loud. I don't think Grazia was there though, or if she was, she sure wasn't saying anything."

Forgione turned slowly to face the two police officers.

"Yes, Biagio was expecting a visitor. He'd mentioned it to me in the past few days. More than expecting it, he was fearing it."

Lojacono persisted: "Do you mind telling me who he was expecting?"

"His father. He was expecting a visit from his father, from his village back home."

Alex broke in.

"You said that he was afraid of that visit. Why?"

Renato said nothing for a few seconds, running one hand disconsolately across the glass tabletop. When he looked up to answer, he had a profoundly sad expression on his face.

"He hadn't seen him in almost seventeen years. His father represented a part of his life that he'd done his best to forget. The idea of a confrontation with him was something that scared him more than anything else in the world."

His words were met with silence. Paco and Vinnie seemed to be trying to find a way to comfort their friend. It was Lojacono who interrupted the lengthy pause: "Why hadn't he seen him in such a long time? Had they argued, was there a separation, some problem with money?"

"No. Biagio's father was in prison, for sixteen years. He got out about a year ago."

"And do you know why he had been sentenced to prison?" Alex asked.

Renato turned toward her and answered in a whisper: "Murder."

VII

Sergio Corazzini Middle School was in a marginal area, a borderland. Come to think of it, Romano mused as he walked over to it with Aragona, the whole neighborhood was a marginal borderland: a continuous but jagged line that separated two different worlds, opposites that were in perennial social ferment.

He shot a quick glance at the vendors' stalls in the little street market that swamped the sidewalks, forcing passersby to walk in the street at the risk of being run down by speeding scooters, which shot past without paying the one-way signs any notice. The intense chill in the air had done nothing to discourage routine business; after all, people have to eat even if it's cold out, but the vendors kept an eye on their merchandise from the shelter of the apartment building atriums, bundled in their overcoats and with woolen caps tugged snugly down around their ears, ready to pounce at the slightest display of interest from a potential customer.

The borderline.

Purse-snatchers zoom in at top speed, on foot or two of them on a motorcycle, illegally souped up, scanning the crowd for the weak, the distracted, the hesitant, yanking and grabbing anything they can only to vanish in the maze of alleyways they know only too well, safe from pursuit in seconds.

The borderline.

Major banks with streams of men in jackets and ties and women in skirt suits coming and going, pursuing deals worth millions and international transactions, faces serious, brows furrowed. They gesticulate with headsets in their ears or else clamp cell phones between shoulder and head as they search for their poorly parked cars: two wheels on the sidewalk in a handicapped zone, after all, it's just for a minute.

The borderline.

Illegal street vendors, dozens, hundreds of illegal street vendors. Africans, with sheets spread out on the pavement and an array of counterfeit designer handbags, and hand-carved wooden animals. Asians, standing at stalls selling portable radios, battery chargers and cases for cell phones, barometers, tripods for video cameras. Slavs, selling vintage objects from their homeland or, perhaps, fished out of dumpsters in the night and repaired to the best of their abilities. And then, Italians, touting bouquets of flowers, pairs of socks, brooms, pairs of shoes, T-shirts emblazoned with phrases in dialect and sky-blue banners and scarves, eagerly buttonholing passersby, even grabbing their arms, whiny and intrusive, as annoying as mosquitoes, and then, later, all standing in line, Romano thought bitterly, to get their dole checks, all of them angrily demonstrating outside the windows of government buildings, chanting em-*ploy*-ment, em-*ploy*-ment, em-*ploy*-ment, as if they didn't earn a cent by selling merchandise in the market, as if they didn't earn a cent by working as carpenters and plumbers and installing dish antennas, for cash, under the table, without receipts: Dotto', I can save you money.

The borderline.

The hundred, thousand, ten thousand lawyers, their ties loosened to one side, or else teetering on five-inch high heels, leather satchels bulging with incomprehensible documents, hurrying up and down the stairs of the courthouses in an attempt to speed up a verdict that's endlessly delayed and they know they won't get paid until it's handed down. Years and years of study, dozens of internships, conferences, ridiculous lists of publications, master's degrees and other post-graduate certificates of all kinds, and all for miserly fees: Counselor, I'm a cousin of that old friend of yours, can't you save me a little money?

The borderline.

Magistrates, fearful, intimidated by high-placed connections boasted but impossible to verify: you never can tell. Notaries, worried by the stagnation of the real estate market, by the cost of living that no one can afford anymore, by the fog of uncertainty around contracts that their bigger clients increasingly seem to come up with. Businessmen, appalled by the specter of bankruptcy, cruising like ravenous sharks in search of cash to cover the check that's going to be deposited against their account tomorrow morning. Loan sharks, not as confident as they once were because there are more and more borrowers out there who will never pay them back, and you can break all the legs and slap all the faces that you want, but they still can't pay, the miserable losers, and they don't even bother to run away: they've lost all hope, do what you want to me, I don't care anymore. Profiteers, who are busy transporting money that doesn't exist from one country to another, from one mutual fund to another, from one void to another.

The borderline.

All together now, with indifference and resignation, everyone bearing their own invisible cross, everyone crushed by a nameless destiny, everyone with their own private borderline: two million islands in a single, vast archipelago without bridges or ferryboats. Everyone together, out in the street, shivering in the bitter cold, hopping and pounding their feet, clapping their hands together, covering their ears, dreaming of the luxury of still lying abed, back in the warmth of their home, snug under their blankets and with the comfort of sleep to ward off the despair of the morning awakening, instead of being out there, facing the perils of that miserable jungle.

Dreaming they could get back into bed to avoid being forced to cross it, at least today, that borderline.

Aragona, who hadn't once stopped chattering away about how the cold wasn't as damp where he came from, and therefore much more tolerable, while Romano replied only intermittently with monosyllables, pointed to the sign outside the school.

Professoressa Macchiaroli, tracked down by the custodian, joined them in the atrium, not far from a small electric heater that was barely powerful enough to warm itself. From the courtyard came the shouts and laughter of children in the midst of a volleyball match during their hour of phys ed.

"*Buongiorno*. Welcome. I'm glad to see you. I confess that I'm struck by such a prompt response. I was sure my words would fall on deaf ears. So it's not true what people say, the police aren't indifferent to the plight of ordinary citizens, it's not true that unless there's a dead body they won't even bother to answer the phone. On my way back from the police station, I felt sure that you had just taken me for an old madwoman who had become fixated on some imaginary situation, and that you weren't going to waste your energy on me."

Aragona, who was still convinced that Professoressa Macchiaroli was an old madwoman who had fixated on some imaginary scandal that wasn't worth the time they were wasting on it, rocked from one leg to the other, uneasily. Could that old witch read their minds?

"And I even thought that one of you might say: the others get to investigate, oh, I don't know, a double homicide and we're stuck chasing after the fantasies of a middle-aged woman."

A shiver ran down Romano's spine. He decided it was time to cut short this interview: worst case, they'd just spent some time out in the cold.

"Would you care to tell us how you came up with this idea, Professoressa? Did you talk to the girl?"

A grimace was etched on the woman's face: "If only it were so simple, you know? All too often, my dear officer, children will say one thing and then, before you know it, the exact opposite. We're used to it, we teachers, and when they confide in us we tend to take what they say with a grain of salt, especially when it comes to certain topics. But it's quite another matter when the information reaches us, so to speak, in an involuntary manner; when that's the case, then you can rest assured that it's not some kind of retaliation against parents or classmates, that there's no intention of committing mischief. Because sometimes that's what's going on."

Aragona looked around without bothering to conceal his boredom in the slightest. At last, he could no longer contain his impatience.

"So, do you have any evidence about this case you came to tell us about? Can we take a look at this evidence, if so?"

The schoolteacher sliced him into pieces with a sharp glance.

"I thought I'd already explained at the police station just a few hours ago, officer. If I'd had any proof, I'd have come in to file a criminal complaint, not just a simple report. But that's my fault, at my age I should have long ago recognized that there are people in the world who are slow on the uptake. Please, follow me to the teachers' lounge."

As they were following Professoressa Macchiaroli up the stairs, Romano shot his partner an irritated glare and whispered: "The less bickering we do, the quicker we can get back to the police station. Do you really have to play the idiot? You just don't know how to keep your trap shut, do you?"

Aragona ignored the scolding.

"We're wasting our time, I know that and so do you. All this zeal is pointless: the woman's a fool, an attention-seeker, plus she's homely as a toilet. Let's wrap this up and get the heck out of here."

As if she'd overheard, Professoressa Macchiaroli stopped in front of a closed door and hissed: "Then again, if you think it's a waste of time to find out more, we can say goodbye immediately. But in that case, I'm not sure why you bothered coming over in the first place."

Romano nodded.

"That's right. So tell us more, please."

The schoolteacher opened the door and gestured for the two policemen to follow her. Sitting at a long conference table were other teachers; a couple were reading the paper, a few more were correcting papers or taking notes. When the three of them entered the room, everyone looked up curiously, but Professoressa Macchiaroli made no move to introduce them. She opened a small locker and took out a handful of official forms folded in half lengthwise, shot the two policemen another glance, and left the room. Romano and Aragona followed her out, after an embarrassed farewell to those present, who made no reply.

The minute they were back in the hallway, Professoressa Macchiaroli explained: "These aren't things I discuss with my colleagues. Maybe it's really nothing at all, but if what I suspect should turn out to be true, then we're dealing with a deadly serious situation. Now I'm going to take you to see the principal, whom I informed before coming to see you at the police station this morning."

As they walked down the hallway, which was crowded with kids changing classrooms, going to the restroom, or buying drinks from vending machines, Romano thought to himself that the more widely held the fear that a crime may have taken place, the less likely that it's the figment of someone's imagination. If Professoressa Macchiaroli had spoken about it with her direct superior and the two of them had decided it was worth contacting the police, then it would be a mistake to underestimate the seriousness of the matter.

The principal got up from her desk and came to greet them, and Aragona's attention was focused instantly. She was a young and very attractive woman, with long chestnut-brown hair and big lively eyes. Her slender figure was sheathed in a soft woolen dress, which highlighted her breasts and left her long and shapely legs uncovered well above knee-length.

A smile was stamped on Aragona's face that, in Romano's opinion, only multiplied manyfold his usual already idiotic expression.

The woman introduced herself.

"I'm Tiziana Trani. Thanks for coming, I'll confess we weren't expecting you."

Aragona held on to her hand and gazed at her with a look that was meant to be alluring, except that it was hidden behind blue-tinted lenses.

"Why would you think such a thing, Dottoressa? We aren't the kind of police officers who turn up their noses at useful tips from citizens. We immediately realized that it was necessary to come here and get to the bottom of the matter. I'm Corporal Marco Aragona, enchanted to make your acquaintance."

Romano couldn't believe his ears. That scoundrel really had no shame.

"I'm Romano. We don't want to take you away from your work, Signora, so if you'd be good enough to tell us what you know about this situation, we'd be grateful."

"Of course. Please, have a seat. Professoressa Macchiaroli can tell you all about it."

Professoressa Macchiaroli laid out on the desktop, one beside the other, the official forms she'd taken from the locker, smoothing them out with one hand: classroom essays, at a glance; certain passages had been underlined in red pencil.

Then the woman put on a pair of eyeglasses that she wore around her neck on a thin chain.

"These are three classroom essays that the student Martina Parise wrote during the current school year. The subjects of the essays vary, of course: the first is about changing seasons in the city, the second has to do with immigration and integration, the third, from just a few days ago, is about personal relations. The last one was assigned specifically to verify certain suspicions aroused by the reading of the first two: with the principal's approval, naturally."

Principal Trani nodded her head.

"That's right, Professoressa Macchiaroli had come to see me after reading the first essay, but we wanted to get more evidence before taking any concrete steps. Go ahead and read."

Romano took the first sheet of paper from Professoressa Macchiaroli's hands, noticed the round and precise handwriting, and read the part underlined in red.

> . . . so the seasons in the city don't differ very much, except in the cold and the heat. Especially at home. I always want to get out of the house, even if the weather is nasty, because certain situations are hard to take, especially if every time I go to bed there's someone who insists on petting me and kissing me, and won't let me sleep.

Romano handed the sheet of paper to Aragona, in silence. He felt a faint sense of embarrassment, as if he'd accidentally walked into the ladies' restroom.

"Well, it's not like it gives us that much information. That is, it doesn't tell us a name, and it just talks about petting and kissing . . . 'Every time I go to bed . . . ' It might just be someone wishing her sweet dreams . . . There's no reference to rape or anything like that. It really seems like an overabundance of affection that annoys her, more than anything else."

Professoressa Macchiaroli handed Romano the second sheet.

> . . . and I don't understand what kids are complaining about when they're sent to orphanages or into foster care. They don't understand how important it is to be alone, to be able to get far away from your parents. I'd be fine if I never had to deal with my father, with his fixations, like lying down next to me in the bed, with that bad breath of his. If only I could sleep in one of those big dormitory rooms, where the girls all sleep together and there are no fathers and at the very most they might see their fathers once a month.

This time, Romano had no comment. He handed the sheet of paper to Aragona, who read it and emitted a faint sigh of surprise.

Principal Trani broke the silence: "After that, Professoressa Macchiaroli and I discussed the matter again. It still seemed insufficient to justify calling the mother: you can imagine, you don't want to destroy a family's harmony just because of a hunch, and we certainly didn't want to run that risk, did we, Emilia?"

"We did not. We're educators, and we should never forget the immense responsibility that comes with the job. So we wondered what would be best in this situation, and, as I've already explained, we decided to assign an essay on a more specific subject: maybe the fact that Signorina Parise wasn't an experienced writer might have led her to put down certain details that could be read in more than one way. We hoped that what would emerge was a picture of a happy domestic setting, and then we'd be able to set aside our concerns."

"So what happened?" Aragona asked.

Instead of answering, the schoolteacher pushed the last essay across the desk, toward Romano. She did it with just one finger, as if she found it disgusting just to touch it.

I don't understand why. He can see how he disgusts me, that I move away every time he comes near me, but he keeps doing it anyway. He can't seem to stop himself. I shut my eyes and try to think about other things. I dream of climbing out the window and being able to fly, up, up, all the way to the clouds, and from there into the sky, to heaven. I wish I could die, that way I'd never have to feel those hands all over me, everywhere. I wish I could die.

Romano realized that he was trembling. He heard the blood rumble in his ears, while deep inside he felt that unpleasant familiar sensation building up inside of him, the run-up to those bursts of uncontrolled rage that had ruined his career and his personal life. It was as if a new driver had taken over the steering wheel of his mind. It wasn't as if he lost mental lucidity, it was more a matter of a change in his point of view: it suddenly seemed natural to him to set aside all forms of rational behavior and just follow his most destructive instincts.

Doing his best to control himself, he handed the sheet to Aragona, who read it quickly and murmured under his breath: "That damned pig."

Principal Trani had her eyes trained on Romano, as if she had guessed at the conflict now boiling up inside of him. She went on talking in that calm voice of hers: "We summoned the girl here, to my office. Aside from the matter of possible sexual molestation, we were also worried about the suicidal impulses manifested in the last essay."

Romano was having difficulty breathing: "What did she say to you?"

Professoressa Macchiaroli replied: "Oh, she's a tough one.

Silent, but strong. She's one of the leaders in a class of special students, all girls who are the daughters of respected professionals and businessmen, very wealthy people. She comes from a middle-class family, but the other girls still follow her . . . "

She fell silent and looked over at the principal, as if she had remembered that it was Principal Trani's responsibility to describe the case. And the principal didn't have to be asked twice.

"We asked her to explain what she had written. She replied that she had just been speaking in generalities, that she'd merely been letting off steam, that she'd simply made it all up . . . Still, though, she was clearly hesitant, we could tell that she had changed her mind, that she was afraid now. So we suggested that we might give her mother a call to talk it over, but she told us not to, in fact, she begged us not to."

Aragona snapped.

"What do you mean, she made it up? Here it is, written as clear as day that people are putting their hands on her. You can't just make this stuff up, at age twelve!"

Principal Trani nodded her head.

"That's exactly what we said to her but, as her teacher explained, she's a tough one. She claimed that when she wrote the essay, she had just imagined a character, another self who was being molested in that way. She told us: give me a bad grade if you like, but don't tell anyone else. We still tried to talk to her mother, very cautiously, but the signora cut the conversation short, she didn't want to hear what we had to say."

Romano asked: "And at that point?"

Emilia Macchiaroli took off her glasses.

"And at that point, I came to see you."

VIII

Lojacono nodded at Alex and she stepped away to put in a call to the police station: the information that they now had was sufficient to activate Ottavia Calabrese's research, constantly connected as she was with the central mainframes and with the other police units, as well as the internet, of course. It was astonishing how quickly necessary information could be obtained, or just useful tidbits to move an interview forward, thanks to this prompt assistance.

While he was waiting, the lieutenant took advantage of the opportunity to find out something more about the victims, their neighbors, and the young man who had stumbled upon the crime.

He started with Vinnie.

"What was your relationship with Biagio and Grazia? Did you spend a lot of time together, did you socialize, did you have friends in common?"

Vinnie shrugged.

"No, not really. Biagio was a pretty reserved kind of guy, he kept to himself. He never went out, he stayed at the university where he either studied or wrote, or at least, we never saw him doing anything else. Grazia, on the other hand, went out a lot. I couldn't say what she got up to. *Buongiorno* and *buonasera*, in other words, was all we said to each other. And the only mutual friend we had was Renato."

Lojacono turned to look at Forgione, who was gradually regaining his natural color, even if from time to time he'd shoot glances at the door as if he expected to see his colleague with the shattered skull come walking into the apartment. The young man didn't wait to be asked.

"The reason we know each other is because this apartment, by which I mean both units, belongs to me. That is, to my family. To my father, to be exact. And I was in charge of finding tenants among the students from out of town."

Vinnie gave an ironic little laugh.

"Tenants, if you want to call them that. Paco and I pay rent, but I don't think Biagio and Grazia did. Am I right?"

Renato blushed.

"Biagio and I had been studying together since we first entered the university. At first he was staying at a boarding house with a bunch of other people, we'd see each other at my house, then the other apartment here became available, and I offered it to him, among other things because his sister wanted to come and see him, and . . . "

Paco commented: "And taking her in cost him dearly, as you can see."

His words astonished everyone. Up till then, after all, the young man dressed in black hadn't had much to say, and now he prompted a shrill exclamation from Vinnie.

"Paco! What are you talking about, have you lost your mind?"

Lojacono didn't want to scare the young man, but then he had no intention of dropping the matter, either.

"How did you happen to come to that conclusion?" he asked matter-of-factly.

Paco turned to look at his tunic-wearing friend; he was probably already regretting what he'd said, but he couldn't retract it, at this point. He replied in a low voice.

"Don't you see the way things worked in there? Nobody had it in for poor Biagio, that's for sure. The argument was about her, yesterday. And that guy, her boyfriend . . . one time, downstairs by the street door, we caught the two of them smacking each other, for real. Don't tell me that the thought hasn't occurred to you, too: Biagio would still be alive, if his sister had just stayed home in her shithole town."

Renato and Vinnie had no particular reaction, they just limited themselves to dropping their eyes. Lojacono let a few seconds go by, before, more or less, asking everyone: "So who is the girl's boyfriend? Does anyone know his name?"

Slowly, Renato looked up.

"Biagio never talked much about him. For that matter, he never talked much about his family, either. I think his name was Nick, I know that he wants to become a singer. To make ends meet he works as a waiter in a pub, I don't know which pub though. Every once in a while I know that he performs there."

Vinnie added to that information, shooting grim glances from time to time at his partner, who was now looking out the window.

"We caught a glimpse of him a couple of times, including the time that Paco remembers so well. An odd guy, with a huge head of rasta dreadlocks. Cute, though. Nice piece of work."

He'd uttered the last sentence while staring at Paco, as if spitting the words at him. Paco didn't even seem to notice.

Alex, clutching her phone, had left the building in search of better reception. As soon as she appeared in the street, the two uniformed officers had stopped talking and had given her a hostile glare, which she had calmly ignored. Over time, she'd gotten used to certain idiots, slaves to prejudices and ignorance, though that didn't make them any less annoying.

The fact that Vinnie and Paco were homosexuals had been clear to her even before she focused on the way they were dressed and how they moved, even before hearing them speak. She'd perceived it from the electricity that sparked between them, the complicity that bound them together, the way they occupied physical space. And she had understood it from the small surge of pride, empathy, and jealousy that she herself had felt. A sensation that was becoming increasingly common with her. The frustration at her inability to be herself, incapable of looking life in the eye and telling everyone who cared to listen exactly who she was and what she felt.

Because Alex Di Nardo, newly minted police officer, was a homosexual, too. A lesbian, she thought to herself as she punched in the number for the police station and waited for the call to go through. The right word is lesbian.

She'd discovered it when she was just a teenager, at boarding school. It hadn't been a phase, and it wasn't just a product of circumstance. It hadn't been the result of a romantic disappointment, a boy who had dumped her, or a rape or some rough sex. She chuckled bitterly to herself when she heard religious throwbacks on TV talking about homosexuality as if it were a disease. The disease, her disease, was the fact that she lacked the courage to say it out loud.

And for that matter, as that idiot Stanzione had so clearly shown, they were still a long way from being able to count on universal understanding. There was always someone snickering, elbowing their neighbor in the ribs, putting on a show of distaste. There were even those who stated, in no uncertain terms, that a lesbian was a pervert, a sad excuse for a woman, a freak of nature. Someone who, out of a defect, a vice, a perverse taste for sin, befouled an honorable surname with the foul stench of shame.

That is what her father would no doubt have said, had he ever found out. And he would have retreated into one of those horrible, persistent silences that sometimes lasted for days and months. But actually, in that case, the silence was likely to last forever. The news might even kill him, the General. The man without foibles or faults. The soldier without hesitation or doubt, who had gone out on international missions and had come home loaded down with decorations, the infallible marksman—in fact, to get closer to him, she, as a young girl, had developed a love of guns. Her adored, admired, worshipped, hated father.

It was his face that she saw before her when she gave in to her lusts and went out to get herself a little sneaky sex, perhaps with young married women on the prowl for the forbidden in out-of-the-way clubs. It was his face that she imagined when she was seized with the desire to shout out over the rooftops that she liked women. It was his face that she pictured to herself when it became clear to her that she didn't even have the strength to go out and live on her own, finally leaving behind her the oppressive atmosphere of a home as somber and tidy as the chapel in a funeral parlor. A temple consecrated to an all-powerful god, now retired, where the officiant tending to the shrine and the holy rites was his wife and her mother, a mute priestess, deprived of any and all individual free will.

Just the one daughter, Papà. A girl, and a lesbian, to boot.

Perhaps the reason her mother never answered back was a sense of guilt: guilt for never having produced a male in the image and semblance of the General himself. If you only knew the truth, Mamma, maybe you'd feel a sadistic twinge of vindication, at least: after all, you didn't get me entirely wrong.

At last, Ottavia answered. Alex reported in to her on the victims, their father, the neighbors, and the young man who had first found the dead bodies. Her colleague never interrupted with pointless questions, she took notes quickly and efficiently. Ottavia knew her job and did it well. She wasn't her type: too much of a heterosexual, too maternal, too romantic, and too sensitive. But they could have been friends.

Her colleagues in that cesspool where they had tossed her after she'd accidentally fired her pistol inside the police station where she used to work previously were turning out to be much better than expected. The Bastards of Pizzofalcone—the subject of wisecracks and the butt of jokes told by policemen all over the city, misfits rejected from all the other precincts—actually turned out to know how to do their jobs, in the end. And she was a member of that team.

Certainly, they all had their shortcomings: but then, who doesn't? Romano, with his outbursts of rage. Lojacono, who had been accused, back home, in Sicily, of conveying privileged information to known Mafiosi. Aragona, as irritating as a mosquito and remarkably skillful at sidestepping every opportunity to keep his mouth shut. Pisanelli, obsessed with suicides, and of course, even Ottavia, with that son of hers, about whom no one really knew anything much and because of whom Ottavia was occasionally forced to hurry out of the office on her urgent way home. They all had their crosses to bear, crosses of various sizes, some small and others large, penitences none of them would ever finish paying. Each had her or his own, and perhaps each carried a small portion of each of the others' burdens.

Ottavia assured Alex that she'd call her back, unless she and Lojacono had already returned to the police station by that point. Alex imagined that Ottavia would immediately charge off down the online information trails leading to and from the names she'd just supplied her with, while Pisanelli would start making phone calls, asking and receiving nuggets of intelligence from the myriad of friends and acquaintances he had in that quarter. They both left the office only rarely, those two, but they were as valuable as an entire operations control center.

She ended the phone call and noticed that her fingers were strained, numb, had almost lost all feeling. The phone slipped out of her hand and fell to the ground. She bent over to pick it up, but someone else beat her to the punch.

She looked up and found herself staring into a pair of warm, luminous eyes, the color of cherrywood.

"*Ciao*, Di Nardo."

It was the low, intense voice of Rosaria Martone, the chief of the forensic squad.

The woman Alex had fallen in love with.

IX

Romano broke the silence, teeth clenched: "You did the right thing by reporting this to us."

He now felt a burning sense of guilt, after having read the passages from Martina Parise's essays that were marked out in red. He hadn't believed that story when he'd first listened to it at the police station, he still hadn't believed in it when Palma had ordered him to check it out, he'd continued not to believe it when Professoressa Macchiaroli had accompanied him and Aragona to see the principal, leading them through the hallways of the building like a couple of troublesome pupils.

But now he thought that the caution both women had displayed was, if anything, excessive; that they ought to have intervened earlier. He also felt great pity for the young girl, whom he imagined to be reluctant to accuse her father, perhaps terrified at the thought of how he would react. And by extension, he felt within him a powerful, dark rage toward a father who had dared to place his lustful hands on his own God-given child.

Aragona, too, was churning with impatience. He'd already forgotten his firmly held opinion that the matter was a complete waste of department time and energy. To say nothing of his disagreement with Palma, now a thing of the past. Now what mattered most to him was projecting an image of himself as a tireless and determined guardian of the law, and making a strong impression, if possible, upon the school principal whose lovely legs were, alas, concealed beneath her desk.

Heading straight toward Principal Trani, he removed his blue-tinted glasses with the notorious, contrived gesture he'd stolen from a policeman he'd watched on television.

"Wouldn't it be best, at this point, to push a little harder with the mother? I mean, I get it, you have to be careful not to ruin the family harmony and all that, but it seems to me that what's written in that essay is pretty unequivocal."

The woman disagreed.

"Yes, we know that. But if the young woman refuses to confirm the things she wrote in that essay, if she continues to insist that she simply made them up, what do we do then? We are educators, we're supposed to oversee our students' learning experience, not pry into what's happening with their families. We've found ourselves faced with a case that tests our consciences so we decided to turn to the experts."

At the sound of the word "expert," Aragona sat up straight in his chair and dropped his tone of voice by a good solid octave.

"And you did the right thing, my dear Signora. I believe that the best thing to do now is to talk to the girl again."

Principal Trani's face lit up with gratitude.

"We were hoping you would say that. But I wouldn't tell Martina who you really are, she'd curl up like a porcupine and we wouldn't be able to get another word out of her. We could introduce you as a pair of administrative investigators from the school board: you heard about these essays and you asked to talk with her."

Romano was baffled, and he would gladly have throttled the life out of Aragona.

"I don't know if that's a good idea. You see, Signora, there are specialists who are trained to draw a great deal of information out of a conversation with an adolescent. I think it might be best to inform the family court and have a lady psychologist who's in regular rotation on this sort of issue assigned to the case. We don't have any of the professional skills required to—"

The principal exchanged a worried glance with the schoolteacher and interrupted him.

"No, no, I'm not going to let that happen! We've already had experience with that sort of approach, in other situations involving . . . pathological issues, shall we say, and the outcome was by no means what we'd hoped for. The students refused to talk, and your specialists came up with nothing. So they decided there was nothing they could do, and matters were left just as they'd been found. The students were worse off than when we started. If you have no intention of proceeding, so to speak, without headlights, then we thank you for your time and interest but, in that case, we'd rather take Parise's last answer at face value and accept that she just made it all up."

Aragona coughed gently and gave Romano a sidelong glance.

"Well, maybe we could give it a try anyway. Let's talk to the girl and try to figure out whether or not it's work proceeding with the mother. Doing nothing at all after what I just read goes against my instincts."

Romano felt as if he were surrounded. He had a moment's hesitation, then said: "All right, let's talk to her. But I continue to think that it might be better to turn to a genuine professional in this sector."

Principal Trani got to her feet, clearly relieved.

"It'll only take a few minutes: it's just a matter of finding the key to bring out the truth. And maybe it'll turn out that she made up the whole thing. Emilia, if you'd be so kind, go call the girl."

Once the schoolteacher had left the room, silence fell. Romano felt uneasy: the situation had taken an anomalous twist. He'd never been the sort of officer who was a stickler for standard procedure, but this time he felt that it might be best to stick to the rules. All the same, he couldn't allow that young girl to be subjected to certain indignities, if indeed that was what was happening. Aragona, for his part, had already made up his mind that the molestation was a reality, and his romantic notion of the heroic policeman meant that it was up to the two of them to solve the case then and there, not turn it over to some ineffectual bureaucrat who'd let the culprit off the hook, just because of some trivial quibble.

Not five minutes later, they heard a light knocking at the door. Professoressa Macchiaroli entered. Behind her was Martina Parise.

She was slender and attractive, of average height for her age, rather well dressed in a sweater and a pair of jeans which Aragona's eagle eye immediately pegged as bearing an expensive trademark. Her features were pleasing and her smooth chestnut hair hung to her shoulders. She didn't seem a bit surprised to see the two men sitting in the principal's office. Her large hazel eyes darkened momentarily. She bit her lower lip, but her face turned expressionless again almost instantly.

The principal was the first to speak: "Ciao, Martina. We asked you here because these gentlemen have read your esssays and wanted to ask you a question or two. You see, they work in a . . . supervisory office, and from time to time they happen to read things written by the very best students."

Romano caught the ball at the first bounce.

"That's right, Martina. Congratulations, you're quite the writer, those are some first-class essays. Listen, the part about your family, the situations you write about—"

The girl interrupted him with great determination.

"I just make up the character I write about. I explained it to my teacher and to the principal, too. That's not really my family, at all."

Her tone had been decisive and conclusive. Romano, who had no familiarity with adolescents, fumbled, unsure of what to say next. Unexpectedly, Aragona came swooping in to the rescue.

"Exactly, that's just what we wanted to talk to you about, because your character, the girl who's narrating the story, is great. We like her. Do you think we could use her in a TV series? What do you think?"

Everyone turned to look at the young police officer, in stunned surprise. Romano struggled to remain seated. Martina bit her lip again, curious in spite of herself.

"A TV series? For real?"

The policeman nodded, removing his blue-tinted eyeglasses with his usual sweeping gesture. Not even in the presence of a twelve-year-old girl did he know how to restrain himself.

"Certainly. It's a gripping, profound character, and it tells us a great deal about the malaise afflicting young people today. For instance, and this is what my partner wants to know, what's going on in the family? Can you tell us about it?"

Martina shot a fleeting glance at Professoressa Macchiaroli, who nodded encouragingly.

"She's . . . she's a young woman about my age, who attends a school a lot like this one. She would be fine, she'd be happy, if only . . . in other words . . . "

Aragona, by now fully inhabiting his part, perfect follower of the Stanislavski method that he was, pressed her.

"Could you finish your sentence: If only what? Because you surely understand that, from the point of view of television production, what counts is the drama, the challenges facing the protagonist. What does she lack, in order to achieve happiness?"

"She lacks . . . her father. Or actually, no, she doesn't lack him, she has a father. Unfortunately. Because her father bothers her. Her father is a horrible man."

Romano tried to delve deeper into the concept: "That is, your father . . . her father doesn't love her?"

Martina turned to look at him. Her pupils seemed to dilate. "No, he loves her. He loves her a little too much, honestly."

"What do you mean, too much?"

Martina's eyes welled over with tears. Her voice dropped until Romano had to make a real effort to hear what she was saying: "He gets in bed next to her, at night. He caresses her, but not the way a father ought to do with a daughter. He touches her. And sometimes he wants her to touch him back."

She seemed even younger than her age to Romano. After a long minute of silence, Aragona said: "And does she want someone to help her? Is she hoping, I don't know, for a hero to come to her rescue, to rescue her from . . . from this situation?"

Martina murmured: "Yes. She really wishes that could happen."

Romano nodded. Then he exchanged a glance of understanding with the principal, who smiled at the young woman: "All right, Martina. Thank you. You can go back to class now, Professoressa Macchiaroli will accompany you."

Once they were alone, Aragona said: "It all seems very clear to me. What do we do now?"

Romano looked into the empty air. After a moment's reflection, he looked at Principal Trani and said: "Let's talk to the mother."

X

In the victims' apartment, Alex observed in fascination as the men from the forensic squad moved around the corpses as if they were onstage. It looked like a ballet, a ballet being danced around death itself. A choreography in which the dancers followed a preestablished trajectory without ever brushing against each other.

Aside from the director of the squad herself, there were six people there: three who reported directly to Martone, and three others from the violent crime analysis unit, responsible for inspecting the corpses and taking traces to be analyzed in the laboratory. They were all dressed in white, silent and focused, skilled at moving from place to place without ever touching a thing.

Lojacono materialized next to Alex. He too was keeping his eyes on the technicians from the forensic squad, following their mute dance.

"I told the three young men in the other apartment not to leave. The one in the tunic objected, and said that he had a class at the university. He's one determined guy."

"Very determined, and also rather jealous, I don't know if you picked up on that."

"Yes. Jealous of the young woman, not the young man. That's an odd twist."

"What do you mean? If you're jealous, you're jealous. Male, female, what difference does it make?"

"Of course, of course. I wasn't saying any different. I just meant that the couple isn't in perfect harmony, nothing more than that. They looked like a couple of cats with their hackles raised. Not that that necessarily means anything, don't get me wrong."

Alex went on.

"I was thinking about the doors. The main door, the one that leads into the shared front hall, was shut; Forgione said that he'd had to ring the bell to get in. While the door to the victims' apartment was left ajar. Which means that, in theory at least, the only possible access to the scene of the murder would have been through Vinnie and Paco's apartment."

"Maybe someone left the apartment and only pulled the main door to the landing shut behind them. The only thing we know for sure is that there are no signs of breaking and entering: either the murderer had the keys or else someone let them in."

Rosaria Martone's voice, from behind, made them both start: "Good work, Lieutenant Lojacono. Now you're trying to put us out of a job."

The man turned around: "Dottoressa, what an unexpected honor: none other than the director in chief, in person, for the little precinct of Pizzofalcone."

The woman smiled at him: "Not for you, of course, no disrespect intended. These two young people invited us out. A double homicide isn't something that happens every day, even in a city like this one. Let's just say I'm mixing business with pleasure."

As she uttered the last part of the sentence, she had turned her eyes toward Alex, who was well aware that she'd blushed and therefore turned to look into the room where the young murdered woman lay sprawled on the bed.

"She was raped, wasn't she? Maybe she put up a fight, tried to defend herself."

Martone followed Alex's gaze and the ironic expression of her bronzed face turned sad.

"Maybe so, maybe not, we can't say yet. In summer, when the flesh is bared, it's easier to tell if there are marks of violence on the skin, but when it's cold like this, people are bundled up to the neck, and that makes it difficult. Certainly, the torn blouse and the position of her legs both suggest rape, but still . . . As you know, there are murder scenes that would seem not to leave the shadow of a doubt, whereas the reality is entirely different. There are perverts who like to have fun with the victim, postmortem."

"So we won't know till after the autopsy is done?"

"No, Lieutenant, not necessarily. Do you see that instrument, that sort of lamp? It's called a CrimeScope. It emanates light at various wavelengths, and it allows us to identify fingerprints, fibers, hairs, and biological substances, such as semen, for instance."

"What about the clothing? Will a specific analysis be done in the laboratory, too?"

"Yes, but first we'll finish our investigation here, with photographs shot both with side and direct lighting; we're actually almost done, and my colleague has already informed me that there don't seem to be any traces of seminal fluid. So then we'll take the clothing and transport it to the laboratory for the specific analysis you were just mentioning."

Alex insisted on the theory that the young woman might have tried to defend herself.

"But she might have scratched him, right? I don't know, there might be material under her fingernails, or . . . "

Rosaria smiled, and her voice dropped even lower.

"There might be, it's true. Unless it turns out that this was consensual: there are some women, you know, who enjoy a fake rape, and there are some men who let things spin out of control. In the meantime, we need to reconstruct the sequence of events of the two murders."

Lojacono agreed with Martone.

"Yes, that's fundamental. But she's still wearing her jacket, so she might have just returned home, or been about to go out—"

Alex completed her reasoning for her: "The fact that he was at the table in one room and she was lying on the bed in another suggests that the first murder took place without the second victim realizing it or being present. In any case, one thing is certain: they didn't kill each other."

Rosaria ran the back of her hand over her cheek.

"She was unquestionably a beautiful girl, look at her perfect figure. And look at the picture on the wall: a gorgeous smile. A body and a face like that would be enough to drive someone crazy; people kill for much less. If I were you, I'd look into her lovers, and there must have been quite a few."

"We'll certainly be sure to do so, Dottoressa. All suggestions are more than welcome, coming from an expert like you."

Lojacono turned to gaze at Alex in astonishment. In general she was extremely reserved, and spoke only when spoken to: that ironic wisecrack wasn't her style.

Martone took it in stride; in fact, her face took on a look of wry complicity.

"Wait, weren't we on a first-name basis, Di Nardo? No need for formality among women and cops."

Alex blushed again, and then, as if it had suddenly occurred to her, she said: "By the way: earlier, Lojacono and I spotted something under the console table by the front door. An object with earbuds, maybe it's a cell phone or a digital music player. Did you find it?"

"Let me go ask."

A short while later, Martone was back with a transparent plastic bag.

"Is this what you were talking about? Cute, isn't it?"

It was a cell phone with a shattered screen. From the pink plastic case, which ended in a pair of long bunny ears, extended a wire connected to a pair of earbuds.

XI

The principal hadn't yet managed to track down Martina's mother.

While they were waiting, Professoressa Macchiaroli informed Romano and Aragona about the Parise family with her usual garrulous mix of information and personal comments.

"They certainly aren't rich, but then they aren't poor either. I'd call them a normal middle-class family; it wasn't that long ago, in fact, that they would have been considered well-to-do. It's paradoxical, don't you think? Before the financial crisis a family that lived on the salary of a bank clerk could get by without difficulties. Nowadays, three people can't survive to the end of the month on even two salaries. And yet people who are on fixed incomes, now that the blush is off the rose of the so-called gig economy, ought to have an advantage, right?"

Now watch, Aragona is going to heave a sigh of annoyance, Romano told himself.

And in fact, that's just what he did.

"Sure, Professore', but maybe you could save the macroeconomic analysis for some other time, what do you say? Instead, why don't you tell me: what does the girl's father do for a living?"

Professoressa Macchiaroli made no effort to hide her resentment: "Well, that's what I was just telling you, officer: he's a bank teller, in a small branch office in the city center. An ordinary white-collar worker; I remember that during one parent-teacher meeting the mother told me that she'd had to come in alone because the bank manager had refused to give her husband time off."

"What about the mother?" asked Romano.

"She's employed in a boutique selling women's fashion, in the hill district. She told me, again, during a parent-teacher meeting, that the rent is a tremendous expense, that it eats up nearly all of her husband's salary, so she was forced to find this employment, even though she has a diploma as a corporate secretary. All the same, she's in the sales sector."

Aragona snickered.

"This whole cornucopia of words to tell us that the mother works as a salesclerk in a clothing store? One thing I find interesting though is this fact that, in all of your parent-teacher meetings, instead of talking about how the kids are doing at school, you just tell each other about your lives. Now I understand why there are always miles of cars parked in front of the schools, blocking traffic."

As if he hadn't heard a word that Aragona had just said, Romano continued speaking to Professoressa Macchiaroli.

"We'll need the addresses of the bank branch and the store, as well as the family's home address, of course. We'll start examining every angle of this story, and if anything comes up, we'll let you know."

The principal disconsolately waved the receiver in the air: "I'm afraid the Signora isn't answering. Maybe she's busy. Emilia, give the gentlemen whatever they need: we've pushed this far, we can't stop now."

To reach the shop where Martina's mother worked, Romano and Aragona took the funicular railway. Maybe it would have been more convenient to go back to the police station and get a car, but the truth was that neither of them was dying to run into Palma. They would have been forced to admit that he had been right, that the case was worth looking into, and that they had therefore been wrong.

Among other things, Romano still wasn't entirely convinced of the approach they were taking, and he expressed his concerns to his partner as they teetered, barely maintaining their balance, among the rush-hour crowd that was packed into the car.

"We'll just introduce ourselves and say: My dear Signora, we have every reason to believe that in your home, while you were peacefully sleeping, this, that, and the other thing are probably happening. She'll look at us and reply: Excuse me, but who are you? And just how do you know these things? Who told you? How dare you? And what if I simply call the police?"

Aragona was doing his best to avoid the forced proximity to the armpit of an enormous woman, sweating profusely in spite of the biting cold, who was holding on to the handrail. He put on a grimace of disgust and replied brusquely: "Then what do you suggest? That we just head back to the precinct and say: Dear Commissario Palma, call the family court, that way, in a couple of months, once they've cleared their desks of the poker tournament they no doubt now have underway, one of those five-hundred-euro-a-session psychologists might even make up their mind to give the poor kid a call and invite her in for a chat. And in the meantime that swine of a father of hers can go on wallowing in his filth."

He hadn't moderated his tone of voice at all, and in fact the fat woman now opened both eyes wide, her interest clearly piqued.

"Oooh, Jesus, and what kind of filth is this father inflicting on the poor girl?"

Aragona gave her a hard look and, jammed in as he was by the crowd, answered her with what little breath he was able to muster.

"Signo', these are police matters, so why don't you mind your own business. And take a shower, while you're at it, because you're killing us all with your armpits hanging open like that. Trust me, you can let go of the handrail, because with the figure you have on you, you couldn't fall over even if you were riding all alone on the funicular."

The shop was a luxurious boutique with four plate-glass display windows looking out over the main thoroughfare of the quarter. The clothing on display was expensive, and yet Romano and Aragona spotted at least a dozen customers inside, along with just four salesclerks, and a man who was probably the proprietor.

They decided to wait until there was less of a crowd, but after ten minutes, no one had left the shop. At that point they agreed that Aragona should go in alone, to keep from arousing suspicion, while Romano would wait in a café at the corner. Just a few minutes' exposure to the cold had been enough to chill the two policemen to the bone.

The interior of the shop, compared to the exterior, was piping hot; Aragona decided that that was why the customers were lingering at such length. He looked around to try to figure out which of the four salesclerks was Martina's mother and, thinking he had spotted some vague resemblance to the girl in a petite woman with chestnut hair and large dark eyes, he got in line and waited until she was free. When it was his turn, he asked: "Would you happen to be Signora Parise?"

"No, I'm afraid I'm not. What a pity. Are you sure I can't help you?"

Flattered, Aragona swept off his eyeglasses: "Maybe we could come up with something, if we tried. But right now, I'm afraid I really have to speak to Signora Parise. Would you mind pointing her out to me?"

The woman made a coquettish grimace of feigned disappointment.

"If you insist . . . Antonella! This gentleman wants to talk to you."

The woman who turned around caught the officer by surprise. Her appearance was as different as could be from her daughter's. She was tall, she had red hair pulled up in a bun, green eyes, and a spectacular body sheathed in a warm brown dress. She looked no older than twenty-five. She walked over, with a vaguely uneasy expression.

"Yes, tell me how I can be of assistance."

"I need to talk to you, but it's a confidential matter. Could you step outside with me for five minutes?"

"I'm . . . I'm actually working, I was just assisting that woman and—"

Aragona interrupted: "It's about Martina."

Antonella stared at him. There was an inscrutable expression on her face, a blend of apprehension but also grief and sadness: she had the eyes of a suffering mother.

"Wait for me outside."

She walked over to a coworker and pointed her to the customer she had been serving, then went up to the man at the cash register, an impeccably groomed and elegantly dressed man in his early fifties, and whispered briefly to him. A hostile look appeared on his face, then he brusquely nodded to the woman, who grabbed her overcoat and hurried out of the shop.

Romano was waiting for them at a table in the back of the café. When he saw them come in, he got to his feet and extended his hand: "*Buongiorno*, Signora. My name is Francesco Romano, and this is Marco Aragona, in case you haven't been properly introduced. Sit down, make yourself comfortable. Can I get you something to drink?"

Signora Parise sat down, rigidly.

"An espresso, thanks. So can I ask what this is about?"

Her voice had just the faintest hint of concern. Romano, too, noticed how little she resembled her daughter. The officer decided to create the least threatening atmosphere possible.

"Today, at her school, we had the opportunity to make your daughter Martina's acquaintance. You seem too young to be her mother."

A glint of fear appeared in the woman's eyes, though she proceeded to put on a strained smile as she ran her long fingers through her hair.

"I was . . . very young when she was born. I was just seventeen. I'm twenty-nine now."

"And you look much younger than that, believe me. My compliments."

A waiter arrived with the espressos.

"Please, don't keep me on tenterhooks. What has Martina done? What did she say?"

Romano seized the opportunity.

"Why, what might your daughter have done or said?"

The woman started to get up: "Unless you immediately tell me who you are, I'm going to have to put an end to this conversation."

The two policemen exchanged an uncertain glance. Then Romano said: "Signora, don't be frightened. Our job is in fact to ensure that nothing bad happens, or if it's happening, to make sure it stops. We're both officers from the Pizzofalcone police precinct, but we're here to speak with you on a completely informal, friendly basis. The principal and the Italian literature teacher contacted us. They're worried about Martina. But I think you already know all about that."

Romano and Aragona expected her to react with anxiety, anguish, or else indignation. Instead, Antonella drew a deep sigh and focused on the espresso demitasse, as if she thought she could find answers in it.

"So it's come to this. We've reached this point. The police, no less."

Aragona spoke softly: "Signora, you have no reason to be angry with the teachers: they're mothers, too, it's only human for them to worry. We read the essays that your daughter wrote and . . . we believe it's perfectly legitimate to ask some questions, to be frank."

The woman said nothing, still holding her head low.

Romano added: "On the other hand, it certainly happens sometimes that kids with overactive imaginations dream up things that don't match up with reality. Maybe that's what happened with Martina, perhaps she just felt lonely and she invented a parallel life. And it might be that she hasn't even told you about any of these things."

Signora Parise suddenly raised her head, and Romano found himself under the cold fire of those green eyes. Then she said: "There you go, officer. Bull's-eye. Maybe she never even told me about any of these things. Or maybe she tried, but I refused to listen."

Aragona was confused.

"But why would you refuse to listen?"

"Because these things are false, that's why. Otherwise I would have come directly to you, and at a dead run. Or else I'd have killed him with my bare hands. But none of it's true."

"How can you be so sure?" Romano asked her.

The woman's face had turned pale, strained. Her features had tightened, and two lines around her compressed lips gave the policemen a preview of what she would look like as an old woman.

"Because I know my husband. He's a simple, good-hearted man, and Martina and I are all he has in the world. He isn't a pervert, he isn't a madman, he isn't a maniac."

Romano leaned forward. From the very beginning, he wished he'd never had anything to do with this whole matter, but now that he was in it, he wasn't willing to be dismissed out of hand.

"Then why in the world would your daughter have decided to dream up anything of the sort, can you tell me that? And what's more, describing certain scenes in an essay she was assigned to write for a class."

Signora Parise's lower lip began to tremble.

"I don't know. I don't know. My daughter and I talk all the time. I don't know why she felt the need to . . . I can't even bring myself to say it. But I do know, and I know it for certain, that there's not a word of truth to it. I won't dignify this nonsense with a police report, in fact, if anything, I'm tempted to sue the school for excessive zeal, but since it's also clear to me that they had only the best of intentions, I'll just pretend the two of you never came to see me."

She stood up and started out of the café. Aragona only stopped her when she had her back to the little café table.

"Signora, wait a second. Maybe you can explain something to me that I don't understand, and maybe I'm crazy. But how can you bring yourself to sleep peacefully, to come here to work, to walk down the street, to shop for groceries and cook dinner with the knowledge that maybe, just maybe, there's someone in your house that's molesting your daughter? She's no more than a little girl, for fuck's sake. Don't you understand that?"

The woman stood motionless, like a mannequin, then her shoulders bowed forward. At last, they heard her voice: flat, low, steady.

"Sometimes, I bring her with me. I bring her with me when I have to come back to work here, in the afternoons. I bring her with me, so I don't have to leave her alone at home."

And then she hurried out of the café.

XII

The waltz of the dancers in white around the corpses had almost come to an end when the assistant district attorney Laura Piras burst onto the scene of the double homicide.

As usual, she was in a hurry, with the look of concentration on her face that always gave whoever was talking to her the constant sensation that they were wasting her time.

As usual, she was moving quickly and yet, it had to be said, gracefully.

As usual, she was dressed in a dark suit—jacket and trousers—a sober uniform that however wasn't able to conceal the soft curving lines of her body, curves that focused the gazes of all the men in the room upon her.

As usual, she immediately took command of the situation.

And, as usual, at the sight of her, Lojacono felt that mixture of disquiet and pleasure that he was growing to recognize so easily.

"Here I am. I'm sorry I'm late, I was at a hearing I couldn't leave. All right then, what do we have here? They told me that they were a young man and woman. Ah, *ciao*, Lojacono. So we meet again. And on such a delightful occasion."

Her voice, ironic and warm, accompanied the sensual effect of the Sardinian accent that made its cadence so distinctive. Behind her was Stanzione, who had accompanied her upstairs.

The officer said: "This way, Dottoressa. You see, the young woman is in the bedroom, while the young man—"

Lojacono interrupted him in a chilly tone: "Stanzione, who said that you could leave your post at the front door? I thought I had made myself quite clear. Get back downstairs immediately or I'll be forced to file a report."

He hadn't raised his voice, but everyone in the room froze. The uniformed policeman pointed to Piras: "But I just accompanied the Dottoressa upstairs. We were the first to get to the scene, after all, and—"

"If the lieutenant gave you a job to do, I suggest you do it. I can take care of myself, never fear."

Repressing his rage, Stanzione gave a brusque salute and left the apartment. Piras put on a faint grimace of astonishment.

"Wow, this looks fun. It appears that I missed the party. Well, Lojacono, bring me up to speed."

"They're almost done surveying the murder scene. I'll tell you everything we know so far."

Lojacono provided the prosecuting magistrate with a detailed account, from the location of the corpses to the interview with the next-door neighbors and the young man who had stumbled upon the crime scene.

The woman followed everything he said attentively, chewing her lower lip and nodding; she twisted the ends of her hair with one hand. Lojacono found her irresistible.

When they had finished, Alex came over.

"*Buonasera*, Dottoressa. Excuse me, Lojacono, but Ottavia called from the police station. When we get back there, she wants to talk to us, she seems to have come up with something new."

Piras scrutinized the young woman.

"*Buonasera*, Di Nardo. Well, how do you like things in Pizzofalcone?"

Alex exchanged a slightly confused glance with Lojacono, but then replied confidently.

"I'm very happy to be working here, Dottoressa, thanks for asking. It hasn't been long, but we're a good team, we work well together. And of course, the lieutenant is a genuine maestro."

Lojacono was surprised, he hadn't been expecting such a wholehearted endorsement from his partner. He bowed ever so slightly: "I learn from you, too, every day, Di Nardo."

Laura smiled.

"*Mamma mia*, so much honey I feel sticky. In any case, I'm glad to hear that things are on an even footing over there, I was one of the people pushing to keep the police station open after what happened with the Bastards."

Rosaria Martone came over, pulling the pair of latex gloves off her hands.

"Oh, *buongiorno*, Laura. So you made it. We're done here, we'll talk later when we have our written findings."

The magistrate greeted her cordially and said: "You don't miss a single one, do you? Have you developed any theories yet?"

"If I'm honest, no. There are so signs of a struggle, not even around the young woman, who at first glance would seem to have been the target of an attempted rape. Next to the bed there are some objects on the side table that ought to have been knocked to the floor but weren't, and are still sitting there. Of course, the murderer might have put them back, but that doesn't square with the clothing scattered around the floor."

Lojacono said: "As for the young man, there are no signs of a struggle anywhere around him either, he even still has a pen in his hand. They must have caught him by surprise, which is pretty odd, unless, I don't know, he had the music turned up high or something like that."

Martone added: "What's more, there's no murder weapon to be found. Someone hit him at least three times on the same spot with a blunt heavy object, but we found only faint traces of blood and hair under the chair. The blunt object must have been taken away."

Laura turned her gaze from the bed, where the young woman's corpse lay, to the desk, over which the second victim lay sprawled. As often happened when she was deep in thought, she was humming a soft melody under her breath.

"All right. Seal the place up after the morgue attendants have left. I have a feeling that this crime scene still has something to tell us. Rosaria, I'll call you tomorrow. But don't forget: absolute top priority. There were already three reporters and two television news crews downstairs. They're going to put pressure on us, especially considering the age of the victims."

Martone said farewell and headed off, accompanied by Alex. The magistrate spoke to Lojacono: "We have the details of the two victims, the person who found the bodies, and the neighbors. We still need to find the father, to dig into the argument, and her boyfriend, who might very well have played a role in all this mess. But, tell me, how are you doing? And your *family*?"

The ironic reference to Marinella, the daughter who had come from Sicily to live with Lojacono a few months earlier, didn't escape the lieutenant.

"Fine, thanks. She busts my chops, exactly the same as her mother, and she's a little too independent: she inherited that from yours truly. Anyway, she's happy, and she likes it here. To use her words, it's all 'fantastic' and 'spectacular.' Now she's even started school."

"How about you, are you happy?"

Lojacono pondered the question, as if the answer was incredibly complicated.

"Yes. And relieved, too, because the thought that she was living in Palermo with that lunatic ex-wife of mine didn't do a lot of good for my peace of mind. Only, now, I just feel an extra burden of responsibility. She's turning into a woman, you know, and I can't tell what she's thinking at any given moment, the way I used to."

"Still, that shouldn't stop you from living your life. For example, it seems to me that you and I have a rain check on a dinner together. You think you'll have an evening free anytime soon?"

When they had first met, they were both convinced that their hearts were frozen solid, and yet they had also immediately realized that there was an attraction between them, something that Lojacono had even struggled to ignore. But it often happened that his mind, allowed to wander freely, off leash, so to speak, found its way to Laura's soft, curving figure, a figure that he had been able to observe one evening when she had driven him home, in her car, in the rain. On that occasion, he felt certain, something meaningful would have happened, if Marinella hadn't been there waiting for him, in the atrium of his apartment building, drenched and shivering, having run away from her mother's home to come live with him. Since that night, he and Laura had seen each other for work, and they'd talked on the phone occasionally, just to pass the time of day, but they'd never again been alone together since that night.

"Of course, I will. I want to find the time and I will. I just need to work out the timing with Marinella."

"Don't you think she can take care of herself? She can eat something, watch a movie, and go to sleep. Or else you could find a babysitter, if the idea sets your mind at rest."

Lojacono started laughing.

"Stop mocking me. Once you're a father, your daughter will always be a little girl, right? Don't fret, I promise I'll take you out for dinner soon. As for the case at hand, the matter of the father and the boyfriend, we've set Calabrese on their trail, and I hear that she already has some news for us: that woman knows how to make her computer work for her. And Pisanelli, too, is bound to come up with something. He knows every stone in the quarter."

Piras turned serious again right away.

"Excellent teamwork, for a ragtag group of cops that no other precinct in the city seemed to want underfoot. You know that you're still the subject of considerable controversy, right? There are still people who insist that the Pizzofalcone precinct should be closed. And we're talking about very influential people."

"I know. We all know. But the truth is, we're doing just fine. In some cases, certain defects, combined with other defects, actually become virtues. Two negatives make a positive."

"And now you're spouting algebra. Are you and Di Nardo going to be working this case together?"

Lojacono looked over at his partner, who was saying goodbye to Martone at the front door.

"Yes, I expect we will. Palma likes to stick to that rule, whoever gets the first call on an investigation works it through to the end. I'm happy about that, Alex is a good cop."

"And considering the way she's talking to our mutual friend, maybe I won't have to be jealous of her, either."

Lojacono was baffled.

"What do you mean?"

Laura lowered her voice and gave him a wink.

"Don't you know? Rosaria likes girls. And your friend Di Nardo seems perfectly comfortable with her."

Just a few yards away, Rosaria Martone was saying: "Well? How long are you going to make me wait for this second date?"

They'd gone out together a few weeks earlier, after a blizzard of texts and phone calls that Alex had experienced in a furtive and secretive manner, with an overriding sense of guilt. They had gone out for dinner on the other *lungomare*, or waterfront, the less famous, more intimate one. Rosaria had reserved a corner table, secluded and secure from prying eyes, and in silence Alex had loved her for it, because she had been considerate and sensitive enough to think of that—Rosaria who was unafraid, Rosaria who proudly showed off her inborn self, Rosaria who didn't lurk in the shadows.

Little by little, during their dinner together, helped along by a couple of bottles of chilled white wine and the gentle sea breeze, Alex had been able to relax. Later, on a tree-lined street that overlooked the calm waters and the silvery wake of the full moon, they had kissed. At first hesitantly, and then with the steadily mounting flame of a deep and immense lust. Hands had sought out flesh, and they had felt like a couple of desperate teenage girls.

Rosaria was more experienced and uninhibited, but Alex had a blazing fire within her that had been smoldering, starved of air, for far too long. It was she who had been the first to find her new friend's pleasure, brushing her with feverish knowledge exactly where Rosaria was expecting her. Then Alex, too, had experienced her own climax, over and over again, too many times to count, repaying each orgasm that she received.

I want a bed, Rosaria had said. Maybe not this time, but when you ask me for it. Yes, Alex had replied. I'll ask you for it. And at that very instant, she wished she could say: Now, now, now. But at home she had told her parents she was out for dinner with her colleagues from the precinct, and she knew perfectly well that neither the General nor her mother would sleep a wink until they heard her key turn in the lock.

The two women had left each other beaming, overheated, and happy. That was the last evening of the fall that still held a bit of the warmth of summer. After that, the cold had come, and Alex had slipped back into the nightmare of her uncertainties, a slave to the thousand little slaveries she had grown up in, crushed by her inability to be all that her father wanted.

Still, Rosaria had reached out to her over and over again, guessing at her taboos and her fears, making it clear that she was willing to wait.

She felt something different and very powerful. This wasn't just another of the many flings she'd indulged in: in some strange way that young woman, so slender and delicate, strong and determined, overwhelmed her. But Rosaria needed to give her the time to emerge from her shell. She desired Alex, with every ounce of her being, but she also feared she might run away, terrified at the thought of being herself.

They had called each other, back and forth, constantly, but still it had taken two dead bodies before they actually saw each other again. It wasn't exactly a suitable circumstance, but Rosaria hadn't been able to resist and had spoken to her.

Alex remained silent for a good long time. Her heart was pounding in her ears. She could sense Lojacono and Piras's eyes on her. It was at least in part to put an end to that uncomfortable silence that she finally answered: "The day after tomorrow. Let's meet the day after tomorrow, in the evening."

XIII

When Alex and Lojacono left the apartment building, once they had completed the lengthy ritual of inspection of the scene of any and every murder, the sun had already set.

The cold slapped them in the face, leaving them breathless. The victims' apartment was unheated, and it hardly seemed imaginable that it could be even colder outdoors. But it was. Lojacono decided that the North Pole must offer, more or less, the same delightful weather.

There was still a squad car parked in front of the apartment house entrance, but it wasn't Stanzione and Ciccoletti's car; they'd clearly been relieved at the end of their shift and now they were snug and cozy in the warmth of their homes, mulling over the challenging day they'd just had, ruined by their run-in with the Bastards of Pizzofalcone. Their lucky successors, who had the heater going full blast, didn't even bother to greet Lojacono and Di Nardo, doing no more than to wave their gloved hands from behind the rolled-up windows. Nor did they bestir themselves when, out of a couple of panel vans parked just beyond the barrier constituted by the squad car with its flashing rooftop hazard lights, there emerged three women and two men, looking chilled to the bone, warmly bundled up to their eyes and armed with TV cameras; the two policemen preferred to pretend they were deep in a romantic conversation, eyes locked. Lojacono sent them a silent curse.

One of the female reporters walked up to the lieutenant and

stuck a microphone under his nose, clutching it with a gloved hand.

"Good evening, we're going out live, this is live: you're one of the investigators handling the double homicide on Vico Secondo Egiziaca, aren't you? Tell our viewers, have you come to any conclusion? Do you have any leads?"

"Talk to police headquarters," was the terse answer she received.

Lojacono tried to move past her, but the reporter must have been accustomed to pursuing reluctant interviewees, because with an agile sideways leap she was instantly blocking his way again. The lieutenant shoved the microphone aside with a brusque gesture, so at that point the woman tried to play the card of female solidarity, aiming the mike directly at Di Nardo.

"Is it true that both murders were committed with tremendous savagery? We have heard a description of a cranium shattered and crushed and the rape of a young woman."

Only the police had had access to the crime scene, aside from the three young men who had been questioned, and all three had been prevented from leaving the apartment. Alex wondered whether it was Stanzione who had leaked those details. She replied, with some annoyance: "Didn't you hear my partner? We aren't making any comments."

The reporter waved her hand toward the cameraman, and once the little red light had flicked off, she snapped: "What the fuck, don't you have even a speck of fellow feeling for people who are just doing their job? Hours and hours in a fucking panel van that's cold as a meat locker and you can't give us so much as a word?"

Now Lojacono was really irritated.

"Fellow feeling, huh? Fellow feeling, you call it. There are two dead bodies upstairs. And for all we know, their friends and family are listening to your bullshit. Fellow feeling."

He made his way through the crowd and walked off, followed

by Alex, while the two men in the squad car continued their conversation, focusing their utmost attention on making sure they saw nothing.

After a walk that lasted several minutes, leaning into the wind and wordless, they arrived at the police station. The glass door shut out the chill behind them, and they found themselves suddenly immersed in a tropical clime.

Guida, the uniformed officer who was almost always on duty at the front entrance, snapped to his feet.

"*Buonasera*, Lieutenant! What do you think? I fixed the heater. It works now."

Officer Guida felt a strange three-part mix of emotions toward Lojacono, one part reverential fear, one part unconditional devotion, and one part holy terror. The day of his arrival in Pizzofalcone, the lieutenant had in fact upbraided him forcefully for his slovenly manners and his rumpled, down-at-the-heels uniform, recalling him to values and standards that he seemed to have forgotten. That episode had reawakened a sense of pride in Guida, and in his bald cranium a determination had arisen to win his superior officer's approval, whatever the cost, in order to convince him that he had misjudged his underling.

In the context of projects designed to achieve this objective, since Guida had overheard Lojacono's muttered complaints about the cold, the officer had armed himself with screwdriver and monkey wrench and had spent half the morning in the boiler room, until he had managed to reproduce what he naively believed to be an approximation of the genuine Sicilian climate. The result was that it now felt as if they were in the middle of the Amazonian rain forest in the heat of the summer.

Lojacono gasped like a fish, and quickly stripped off as many layers of clothing as he could.

"Guida, have you lost your mind? Lower the temperature, otherwise when we go outside we'll catch our deaths. I can't imagine why the glass doors haven't shattered: there must be a twenty-degree difference between indoors and out."

A look of dismay appeared on the officer's face.

"Oooh, I'm sorry, lieutenant. I'll take care of it right away, at your orders! It'll take a while to let the heat subside, the boiler's been going full steam since this morning, and—"

Alex chuckled, as she was unbuttoning her overcoat.

"Nice. If they don't shut us down for prior violations, they'll do it for the heating bill."

In the office, the situation was only slightly better, thanks to a window left slightly ajar, letting in an icy draft. Pisanelli, directly on the trajectory of that draft, felt as if half his body was in the Arctic and the other half in Cambodia, and he wryly claimed that he was quite comfortable, *on average*. The aged deputy chief informed Alex and Lojacono that the commissario had been summoned to police headquarters—apparently the double homicide had made quite an impression in the higher reaches of police administration—but would be back soon.

Ottavia confirmed that report.

"He asked us to wait for him to get back before discussing the case. He wants to hear your report before briefing you on what we've managed to put together here."

Lojacono threw both arms wide.

"The only thing we know for sure is that there are two dead kids, and it wasn't a pretty death for either. In any case, the forensic squad has completed its investigation, and Piras dropped by as well."

At the far end of the office, Romano and Aragona were deep in conversation: they seemed to be in disagreement about something.

Alex's curiosity was piqued.

"Hey, you two, why all the mystery? Are you planning a surprise party?"

Aragona was about to deliver a retort, but Romano grabbed his arm and squeezed it tight.

"No, it's nothing. We were just discussing a crosscheck we completed."

Before Alex had a chance to reply, the commissario entered the room, busy trying to unwrap the long scarf he wore around his neck.

"Ah, so you're all here. Excellent. *Mamma mia*, it's freezing outside and boiling in here, it's enough to give you a heart attack. It's like a Swedish sauna and accompanying ice bath."

Lojacono huffed: "That Guida, I almost liked him better when he was a slob and a slacker. Well, Commissario, what did the high muck-a-mucks want?"

Palma had laid his jacket and overcoat over the back of a chair, and now he was rolling up his shirtsleeves, as was his habit.

"The usual. They don't trust us. They tried to get me to say that we're not up to handling such a major case, that we'd rather hand it off to someone with more experience and dodge the responsibility. Television news crews and radio reporters have lunged for this thing like a dog with a bone: big-city violence; dangerous streets and now people aren't even safe in their homes; the usual criminal element; the Bronx comes to Italy, and so on and so forth."

Ottavia looked at him with a hint of concern.

"Well?"

"It would serve the purposes of plenty of people if we were to admit we weren't up to the job, which would mean that other investigators who are dying for the chance to preen in front of the news cameras would finally get their chance. The idea is that everyone would feel reassured if the case could be put into the hands of *real* investigators, *skillful* and *competent* ones, instead of the Bastards of Pizzofalcone."

Aragona's eyes opened wide: "Did they really say that, chief?"

"Not in so many words. But they were acting all solicitous: Palma, are you sure you can handle this? Palma, don't worry, we can take it off your hands. Palma, no one could say a word against you, don't sweat it, after all, with the human resources you've been given . . . "

His imitation of the self-important, falsely confidential tone of the police chief brought smiles to everyone's lips, in spite of the uneasiness they all felt. The stain, the scarlet letter. When would they ever be able to scrub it away?

"So what did you say to them?" asked Pisanelli.

"What was I supposed to say? I listened to them with respect and attention and didn't say a word. Then I said no, thanks, we don't need anything, and we certainly don't want extra help. That my team is very competent and capable of handling any emergency. That this is a police station, in a precinct like all the others, and that if anything happens in our precinct it's up to us to take care of it."

The commissario's words dropped into a strange silence. Everyone was staring at some inanimate object or other—tables, chairs, computers—avoiding the eyes of their colleagues. They felt a blend of powerful sensations: pride, self-awareness, even fierce determination, but also fear, a sense of inadequacy, and anxiety. Each of them was hoping that Palma was right. And each was afraid that he wasn't.

Only Aragona, his face transfigured by an ecstatic smile, as if he had just beheld an apparition, exclaimed: "Bravo, chief! Bravo! We'll make them spit out those insults, we'll make those sons of—"

Palma raised his hand.

"Arago', don't you dare, remember, we're talking about our superior officers. I actually did ask them for a little help: to shield us from the media, which will keep us from having to waste time on that. The department spokeswoman told me not to worry, that she'd take care of it. She knows her business, but she'll only be able to stave them off for so long. As for the rest of you, do me a favor, and don't breathe a word. They're going to try to interview us, try to wangle information out of us: so no one say a thing. To anyone."

Lojacono asked: "What do you mean, 'she'll only be able to stave them off for so long'?" Palma stroked the short, bristly beard on his chin; when he was at a loss, that's what he always did, Ottavia thought to herself.

"What I mean is that unless we come up with something fast, they're going to take the case away from us. This is too big. Two kids whose father has a prior murder conviction; the small network of university students from out of town; and what's more, the young woman was attractive, we've all seen her on the internet. A lot of leads to chase down, in other words. We need to pin down something fast, be able to say that we're following a lead."

Alex spoke up from the back of the room.

"Well, then, we'd better come up with this lead, hadn't we?"

Palma agreed.

"Why don't you start by telling us everything you know."

XIV

As he woke up, he felt a terrible chill. It was very cold. He looked around, in the dim light, without recognizing the room. There was a strong, bitter smell, and he had the impression that his torso was damp. He touched his chest. His fingertips sensed a sticky substance. He realized that he had vomited in his sleep.

He reached his hand out on the side of the bed and hit something that produced the sound of glass. A familiar sound. He'd drunk himself stupid, and then he'd passed out.

Freedom. Freedom. This isn't what he'd been dreaming of, he thought. It wasn't this.

His mind strayed to the whore, a black woman he had picked up on the street the night before; luckily he'd had the presence of mind to make sure she left, otherwise she would certainly have rolled him, taking wallet and cash. Instinctively, he patted his pocket and felt the familiar bulge of his wallet. He'd paid her what he owed her and seen her out the door. Good work, you were smart for once. At least you've learned a thing or two.

When you're behind bars, he thought, you dream constantly of freedom, you think you can perceive it in its concrete form. As if it were a cool breeze, or the memory of a taste. And you give it a first and last name, as you draw up the list of things you'll do when no one can tell you, with a long piercing whistle, that your hour of exercise in the yard is over and it's time to head back to your cell.

For the first ten years in prison, he had thought of his wife *and children. Then he had come up with the idea of the black whore and he had cultivated that fantasy. It had come to him when his wife had fallen sick and had stopped coming to see him in the visitors' room, to keep him from having to look at Death, riding on her back, eager to carry her off.*

A black whore, he kept telling himself, there, behind bars, is just a piece of life. You have your fun, you pay her, and you send her away. She's not a real woman, she has nothing to do with the woman who stood beside you in real life, with the mother of your children.

A black whore doesn't resemble that girl dressed in white who shone in the June sunlight, a thousand years ago.

You can't confuse a black whore with the smiling woman who greeted you when you came home from work, and at the mere sight of her you felt like taking her in your arms even before you had a chance to wash your hands.

You don't hold a black whore by the hand for a solid hour while she gives birth to a ten-pound baby boy, all the while smiling at you nevertheless, even through the pain and suffering.

You don't caress a black whore while she sleeps, thinking that your life depends on hers.

You don't even recognize a black whore, because all black whores have the same face. You fuck them and you send them away, and that way you're free to practically drink yourself to death.

Outside there was no sound of traffic. He tried to remember where he'd wound up, in what corner of that absurd city, but his memory was too tangled up.

He got up and went over to the window and his back twinged in a stabbing burst of pain to which his head responded with an immediate, terrible pulsating ache in his temples.

He felt like an old man. In prison, the difference in age didn't matter. Young or old, they were all behind bars, brothers in sorrow, strangers in flesh and soul. Now though he felt like an old man.

An old man is a sad thing, he thought, as he looked out at the pitch darkness outside the smudged dirty panes of the windows in his room. Unless he has a family.

A family. He saw in his mind's eye the young woman in the white dress in the June sunshine: back when she was still alive, then he had a family. But now she was dead. She had died without him. She had died while he was still behind bars.

A family. A wife, of course, but also children. What's left to a man, if they take his family away? There was someone in prison, maybe a professor, who spoke as bright and clear as mountain air; he had murdered his wife and her lover, and never regretted having done it, far from it. Well, the professor had explained the meaning of the word "proletarian" to him: someone who is poor, extremely poor, a man whose only wealth is his offspring, from the Latin proles, *meaning offspring, posterity, in other words, his children.*

Proletarian.

He'd had two children when he'd gone into prison, and when he got out there was only one waiting for him, his daughter; then she too had abandoned him. What else was he supposed to do? He'd gone to fetch her home. That's what.

He thought that he had two children, but instead he found himself face-to-face with two strangers. His son, that young asshole, had even gone so far as to threaten him: Beat it, or I'll call the police and have them throw you back behind bars. I brought you into this world, he had replied to the boy, and I can send you straight back out of it. And the girl, the girl who bore his name, the girl who was so similar to her mother when she had danced all in white in the June sunshine—the girl was just as rotten as the boy. Just so she could chase after her lazy good-for-nothing boyfriend, she'd started waving her bare ass around for all to see. Offspring. Nice offspring that he had.

Then a guy reacts without thinking. Then a guy gets himself into trouble he can never get out of.

God, what a terrible headache. He dragged himself back to the bed, in his eyes the vague recollection of a broken, intermittently flashing neon sign: a fifth-rate pension over by the train station.

He didn't have much left from the money he'd had when they released him from prison. Maybe back home he could find work in the fields, again; that's not a job that can change much in sixteen years. Even though everything else in this world seemed to have gone insane, he thought, people everywhere tapping on the cell phones in their hands, flat, gleaming television sets even in the bars and cafés, cars that all look identical.

He didn't have much money left, but he did have a little. His wife—before dying far from him, *what a prank you played on me, what a miserable prank, to die like that*—had even set aside some money and had hidden it in their usual place, the jar under the old shoes in the cellar. When he had found that money, old banknotes rolled up tight, whose value he couldn't even place yet, he hadn't been able to withstand the emotion. He had broken down crying like a fool. It wasn't much, but it was still a message that came from the afterlife.

Now you're dead and I don't know how to live. Ain't that grand.

He grabbed the bottle. There was enough left to send him back into a dreamless sleep. This evening, or this morning, it all amounted to the same thing, *I don't want a black whore. I don't want anyone near me. Even if a black whore is warm, at least.*

And she's cheap, too, when all is said and done. But no cheaper than the bottle that you use to die a little bit.

To die a little more.

XV

Once Alex and Lojacono had finished their detailed account of what they had seen and heard on Vico Secondo Egiziaca, and had answered their colleagues' questions, a sort of grim blanket descended over the squad room. Now everyone had the corpses of those two kids in their mind's eye: years and years in regular contact with murder scenes did nothing to make the image any less heartbreaking.

Palma kept nodding his head, as if following a flow of thoughts known only to him.

"All right then, the weapon that was used to kill the young man couldn't be found, but it's certainly a heavy object. And the young woman, in all likelihood, was suffocated or strangled. The best evidence suggests a man, and a reasonably powerful one, too."

Romano shook his head.

"Not trying to contradict here, but I've seen women capable of knocking a horse to its knees with a single punch. What's more, the young man was taken by surprise, from what we were able to determine; even a young girl could have smashed his skull in with a hammer. As for the sister, well, maybe she was attacked from behind. I don't think that these elements can point to a solid conclusion concerning the murderer's strength."

Aragona chewed thoughtfully on the arms of his eyeglasses.

"I'm curious about the state in which the young woman's bedroom was left. Alex said that Martone is of the view that, if there had been a struggle, then the items on the side table by the bed would have been knocked to the floor, which therefore means that the murderer—male or female as the case may be—would have gone to the bother of putting them back where they'd been. But that strikes me as highly unlikely: first a murderer kills two kids, and then tidies up? Why should he?"

Pisanelli picked up a sheet of paper.

"All right, now it's our turn to add some information to the story. After Alex called in, we both got busy. Ottavia learned some very interesting things, and in a moment she'll tell you more about those. On the other hand, I talked to a friend who runs the most powerful real estate agency in the quarter. Now, the apartment that the Varricchios occupied belongs to the father of Renato Forgione, who is Biagio's colleague and who found the bodies. Everyone with me?"

Lojacono nodded.

"That's what the young man told us."

Pisanelli continued scanning the notes that he held in one hand.

"And in fact, that's the way things stand. Renato's father, Professor Antimo Forgione, is a famous biotechnologist who teaches at the university: a self-made man, from a poor family, who grew up in a small town in the provinces. Now he's a respected luminary, and he delivers lectures around the world. He's a specialist in the metabolism of the very elderly, and he's loaded with money."

Aragona couldn't contain himself.

"Why don't you ask for his phone number, Chief, because that sounds like the doctor for you."

Pisanelli was the only one to chuckle at the line.

"Maybe you have a point, he might be able to help me. But there's no doctor who can do a thing for the disease you're suffering from. Stupidity is incurable. In any case, Dr. Forgione owns a number of apartments in the district and even in the same building, including the one where the victims' neighbors live, as you already know."

Alex confirmed the detail.

"They seemed to be friends of young Forgione. Or at least, on familiar terms."

Pisanelli read aloud: "Vincenzo Amoruso, age twenty-four, from Foggia, and Pasquale Mandurino, same age, from Metaponto. Both their names are on the lease as tenants: it's all properly registered, nothing under the table. The professor does things by the book. The rental units, my friend informed me after checking it on the land registry database, were legally subdivided, properly permitted and approved by the city office in charge."

Palma asked Lojacono: "So are these two young men a couple or just roommates?"

"They seemed pretty tight."

Alex interrupted, confidently: "They're a couple. And Vinnie, at least, is pretty jealous of his partner, I got that from a couple of glances and one sarcastic reply."

Lojacono was uncomfortable.

"We can't say that for certain. We got the impression that—"

Aragona cocked an eyebrow.

"And who was this faggoty jealousy directed at? The owner of the apartment, or the dead man?"

Alex glared at him.

"Neither one nor the other. Vinnie, who's the more effeminate of the two, was jealous of the fact that Paco know about the young woman's movements. Jealousy, as you seem not to know, comes out of love, and you can feel it toward anyone."

Ottavia stepped in to put an end to the quarrel before it could degenerate any further.

"The most significant fact, in any case, has to do with the two kids' father, Cosimo Varricchio, age fifty-five. But the whole story of that family is interesting."

"Four hours on the computer and the phone: Giorgio and

Ottavia did an excellent job of reconstructing everything outside of the scene of the murder," said Palma, with a hint of pride.

"Thank you," the deputy chief replied. "Let's hope it comes in useful. In any case, the Varricchio family is from Roccapriora, in the province of Crotone, inland. A town with a population of three thousand, and most of the inhabitants are farmers. Seventeen years ago, on a Saturday night, Cosimo goes to the bar in the town piazza to waste some time, while his wife, Annunziata, known to her friends as Tatina, remains at home with Biagio, aged eight, and Grazia, who was three. In the bar, an argument gets started and then degenerates, over some trivial matter. Everyone was drunk, and Varricchio starts trading punches with an older fellow, a field hand just like him. He knocks him to the floor and turns to leave, but the other guy, according to the testimony of more than one witness, insults his wife: apparently Tatina was the prettiest girl in town and all the men were mooning after her."

Romano was interested now.

"Huh? Why would you insult a girl, just because she's pretty?"

"You've got me there. But the fact remains that Varricchio turns around, goes back, breaks the leg off a chair, and starts pounding the guy on the floor with it until he kills him."

It was if someone had dropped a bomb. Aragona was taken aback: "And nobody tried to stop him? In a bar in the main piazza of a small town in Calabria? You said that there were witnesses."

Ottavia narrowed her eyes: "Thirty-one people, to be exact. The carabinieri were very meticulous, when they got there. But they got there too late. No one had had the nerve to intervene. It seems that Varricchio had flown into a blind rage."

Palma hugged his arms to his chest.

"All right, so he served sixteen years and seven months in prison. If he'd had a better defense lawyer, he would have been given a shorter sentence: he was drunk, he'd been actively provoked, and he had no weapons on his person, but that's how it went. He's been out for less than a year, right, Ottavia?"

"That's right. In the meantime, his wife, the beautiful Tatina, even though she had been courted and pursued by many different men, remained at home, a good little homemaker, with her two children, doing her best to raise them right. She did all the jobs she could think of: ironing laundry in people's homes, cleaning house, anything as long as it was honest work. Then she fell ill and died, six years ago, still a very young woman. The report from the carabinieri makes it very clear: no extramarital relations, a tireless worker, much loved. The whole town attended her funeral."

Lojacono had taken on the meditative demeanor that made him look even more Asian: hands with both palms planted on the surface of the desk, slanted eyes narrowed to two slits that barely made it possible to glimpse his pupils. He asked: "What about the kids?

"With her savings, the woman had taken out a small life insurance policy, naming her children as beneficiaries, which took care of basic necessities and allowed Biagio to finish high school. Even though everyone insisted and advised her, Tatina had refused to let him quit school: the boy was a good student, a first-class student. He graduated with excellent grades and came here to study at the university, doing odd jobs to pay his way. Giorgio learned that last detail from his friends."

Pisanelli threw both arms wide, almost as if excusing himself for his excessively vast network of contacts.

"The students from out of town, both because they need the work and maybe because they're suited to it, are the best source of manpower for cafés and businesses in the area. I've asked around, and I found the proprietor of a restaurant where he worked. He had only the highest words of praise, he said that Biagio was tireless."

Ottavia went on.

"At the university he also got to know Renato Forgione, from what I hear in the department's administrative office, a very good student, with an excellent academic record. They made friends and graduated together. Apparently, Forgione gave Biagio a big hand up, financially speaking: he didn't ask him to pay rent, with his father's approval, of course, and now and then he even paid off his debts."

Alex nodded her head: "He must have been very fond of him, that much was clear. Forgione was devastated."

Ottavia sighed.

"They were both first-rate students, and apparently after they graduated all the schools came courting them, and so did a number of corporations. But they both decided to stay at the university and they started working with Renato's father. From the information we've been able to gather so far, there's nothing fishy about the young man's life. He was all study and research, not especially sociable or open, a couple of female friends in the past, and always in the university context."

"What about the sister?" asked Romano.

"That's the point. The whole time he was at the university, Biagio sent home money to help defray his sister's expenses. She had gone to live with an uncle and aunt. Apparently, she was the spitting image of her mother as a young woman, but just, let's say, more outgoing. All the boys and young men in the town, and even the neighboring towns, had been buzzing around her since she turned sixteen."

"So, you're saying she was a bit of a slut?" Aragona insinuated, with a wink.

Alex elbowed him hard in the ribs. Ottavia glared at him.

"No, not the way you're talking about. She was pretty, she was sunny, she was intelligent. After graduating from high school, though, she decided not to continue her studies, even though her aunt and uncle had offered to help. She preferred to remain in her hometown, or at least that's what the carabiniere I spoke to told me. A really kind and helpful gentleman."

Aragona, massaging the rib that had taken the blow from Alex's elbow, muttered: "If I could go back in time, I'd join the carabinieri, instead of the police. Then I'd find a town like that one, where the girls are beautiful and the only job is to meddle in other people's business."

Ottavia made a dismissive gesture.

"He's a senior, veteran carabiniere, a lance corporal who's been there forever. It's a small town, everyone knows everyone else. In any case, Grazia had a motive to stay put."

Alex's curiosity was aroused.

"What motive was that?"

"Love. She stayed in Roccapriora as long as the boy she had fallen in love with stayed there."

"Which means till when?" asked Palma.

Ottavia consulted the notes that she had taken on the computer: "I have here that she left last April."

"So her father had already been released from prison."

"Yes, he's been out a few months now. According to the lance corporal I spoke to, Cosimo immediately went back to the family home, a short distance outside of town, which had been sitting empty since Biagio left to attend university and Grazia went to live with her uncle and aunt. Then he demanded that his daughter come back to live with him. An argument ensued, because she didn't want to, and it even seems, though there was no solid confirmation, that Varricchio beat up his brother-in-law, his late wife's brother, because he'd taken up for the young woman. In any case, the brother-in-law chose not to press charges."

Romano asked: "Do we know who the boyfriend is?"

"Domenico Foti, age twenty-two. In town, everyone knows him as Nick Guitar; on his social network profile, he calls himself Nick Trash."

XVI

You're a piece of shit. You're a tremendous piece of shit. Because you have the money to be in here in the first place, sitting at this table with your young woman, ordering anything you please and even complaining at having to wait for a couple of minutes, you just think you're so much better than I am.

But you're a piece of shit. No more and no less.

Not just you, don't get me wrong: everyone in this place is a piece of shit.

For that matter, it's a place designed to appeal to the smug young sons and daughters of the wealthy neighborhoods of town, the kind of place that's fashionable for two or three years, no more, after which nobody goes there anymore. At that point, the proprietors rest on their laurels, the fading glow of past glory, hoping for a return to a popularity that's never going to come back, and then they finally shutter the place. For people like us, for people who don't have a rich Papà who cheats on Mamma and then salves his conscience for the fact by spreading money around to everyone in the family—for someone like us who just works in the place—it's fundamental to understand when the time has come to move on.

Things are fine here for now. No doubt, I have to put up with some humiliations, people like you, my dear piece of shit, as you complain about slow service and leave me a one-euro tip. I hate you and everyone like you, but the ones I hate most are the ones who leave a one-euro tip. Better to leave no tip at all than a one-euro tip. That at least seems honest: I didn't like having to wait, so I'm not giving you anything at all. But a one-euro tip is an insult. Sometimes, it's an unforgivable insult.

I still can't seem to let these things slide off my back. And maybe I never will. But that's okay. It's the anger that feeds my music. It's with that anger that I manage to survive and make sure my dream survives, too.

It's easy for you, you piece of shit. What problems do you have in life? What problems have you ever had? It's not like you were born in some tiny shithole town in the middle of nowhere, some burg that's not even mentioned on maps, stuck in the middle of the most overlooked and downtrodden region of all of Europe. They throw you a lavish birthday party every year, and your Papà buys you a new car, and your Mamma buys you the latest pair of shoes, the finest brand. And if you're ever lucky enough that they get divorced, you'll just get twice the swag.

Instead I have to stand here and serve you, and listen while you lecture me, with that shrill little faggoty voice of yours, just so I can nourish a dream that might never come true.

I can take my little revenges, though. For instance, I can spit in the beer you ordered from me. For instance, by exchanging hot glances with the slut you brought in here, who stares at my junk and my pectorals every time I pass by your table.

And for that matter, that's only natural, seeing that you're a homely piece of shit, no matter how much money you may have. It's only natural that she should look at a man who could finally give her a proper appreciation of the meaning of the verb "to fuck."

I could wait until she gets up and tells you, excuse me, I'm going to the restroom, and then follow her downstairs and take her into the supply closet and give her five minutes of paradise and a point of comparison. In fact, that's exactly what I used to do, at the beginning, until I realized I was running too big of a risk. There aren't many places in this town where they give you a steady salary, on top of the tips.

There are times, you piece of shit, when I wonder how long this is all going to have to continue. How many sandwiches, how many beers am I going to have to serve. How many floors am I going to have to mop, at night, while you sleep peacefully in your bed and your slut goes around cheating on you with guys like me.

Because that's the way women are, you piece of shit. They swear their undying fidelity, they tell you how much they love you. They even follow you when you leave town and move away: it's just to be close to you, they tell you, but it's actually so they can keep an eye on you and then have their own fun. If we were friends, you piece of shit, and I consider myself lucky that we never will be, I'd tell you to steer clear of love in general, because love will just drag you down with it. I even wrote that in my last song, another song that, along with the other hundred or so that I've written, might never have the honor of gracing a stage in an auditorium.

Love drags you down.

She used to gaze at me as if I were God Almighty, back in the village. All the guys swooned over her, but she only had eyes for me. I could have told her to walk naked down the main street of town and she'd have done it, but even so, she would still have belonged to me, and me alone. Whereas you, you piece of shit, you can't even begin to imagine how pretty she was. Not one of these little sluts—these little whores in your oh-so-respectable city, made up and dressed to the nines and accessorized to the tune of thousands and thousands of euros—can even hope to come close. Even the cheapest glad rags, if she wore them, looked like a custom-made evening gown, stitched by some world-renowned designer.

Because she was beautiful, you know that, you piece of shit? Just beautiful.

Sometimes I would gaze down at her, after making love with her in the grass, and I'd ask myself what on earth could be better than this; I never came up with an answer. Now, if I try playing the things I wrote back then, they seem like pieces written by someone else.

Sometimes, love needs a place to live, you know that, you piece of shit? A physical location, a street, a zip code. If you move it from there, then love sickens and dies, unless it's treated in time.

I left my hometown because I believed that certain things couldn't change. I left because I thought that if I stayed there I'd die, I'd suffocate, but instead what happened is that I died here. Because love, if you take it away from its home, can no longer breathe.

I remember when I found her there, waiting for me outside the door of the club, right here, not thirty feet from the table where you're drinking with such gusto that beer I spat into. She was waiting for me to finish my shift, smiling as if she'd just jumped out of a cake. God, she pissed me off.

I was here to work. I was here to meet someone who could help me cut a record. I was here to build my future and hers, too. And there she was, standing proud and smiling in the pouring rain. She didn't understand that I needed to have her far away, to guard the heart that I had given her, not right here, to bust my balls.

There she stood. And there she was again, night after night, because she thought I was fucking all the girls I could here, in this city, that I had come here to have fun where she couldn't find out about it, not to work. The times I was able to get a gig singing, ramshackle clubs that paid just a few euros, she would swoop in like a hawk, and instead of watching me perform she'd survey the other women, monitoring their every movement.

You can't imagine, you piece of shit, the constant arguing, the obsessive fixation that she turned into. She'd gone to live with that brother of hers, who was born an old man, that useless creature who knows nothing about real life because all he can think about are books, and she'd done it for one reason only, to torment me.

Then she started looking around a little.

Do you understand, you piece of shit, just the way this superficial and absurd city of yours can treat a woman who comes from a tiny, godforsaken little town, especially if she's beautiful enough to take your breath away? Someone who's got it into her head that her man is cheating on her every night, someone who wants to take revenge?

It didn't take her long to get busy. She could have done it behind my back: busy as I was, I might not even have noticed. But maybe there was no fun to it, if I didn't know.

You know, she said, I've been offered work as a runway model. What kind of runway, I asked her. Like at an airport? Runway, don't you get it, she replied. Run-way mo-del. A fashion runway, like the ones you see in magazines. So then I asked, who offered you this work? Some guy on the street. What do you mean, some guy on the street?

So it turns out that while she was on her way to buy some groceries, some guy in an SUV pulls over and stops her: just like in some dumb American TV show. Excuse me, Signorina, can I steal just a second of your time, just a moment? And she, bumpkin that she is, ignorant country girl, who has no idea that in a city like this one you should never stop and talk to someone on the street, just smiles and says: Sure, I'm all ears. With the face she has. With that body, you understand, you piece of shit? Sure, she says, I'm all ears.

And it turns out that this guy has a modeling agency, surprise surprise. That he'd noticed her walking down the street: You know, Signorina, I really want to compliment you on your natural grace. Oh, Signore, what a coincidence, that's actually my name, Grazia. Ah, how funny you are, can we relax and switch to the informal? Why, of course, my pleasure. Natural grace indeed. Fine firm ass, is what he meant to say, I really want to compliment you on your fine firm ass.

Ah, now you get mad, she says to me. When you play your guitar, or stroll from table to table smiling at the girls, putting on a show like a guy who puts out for money, I'm not supposed to say a word. But when someone offers me a job, oh no! and there's nothing wrong with me working, is there? It's not like I'm going to be a prostitute or anything, I'm just showing off nice clothing to other women, after all. But then I'm suddenly a slut, is that it?

You try and explain to her that it's not the same thing at all. You try and explain that for an unexperienced young woman it's dangerous to frequent certain circles in a place as complicated as this city. You try and explain that the runway presentation is just the first step, then come photographs and after that, who knows what else.

You're so selfish, she screams at me. I feel like doing certain things. Just the same as you, I have no doubt.

That was when I hit her the first time. I'd never touched her before, not to hurt her, anyway. I don't know where it came from, but there it was. She looked at me for a whole minute, hand on her face, tears streaming silently down her cheeks. That image was what inspired my song, "Tears on Your Face," which might have been the best piece I've ever written.

She wouldn't answer the phone for two days. I had to go to her apartment, and then that idiot brother of hers wouldn't let me in: I knocked him out of the way with a quick smack of the back of my hand. I took care of everything the way real men like me take care of things, you piece of shit. Real men. Not like you.

She promised me she'd never do it again. That I had it backwards, that I didn't understand, that she'd stop for my sake, even if there was nothing wrong about it.

It all seemed too easy to me. I thought she'd put up more of *a fight. It smelled fishy to me, so I took the day off work, I told them I wasn't feeling well, and I set out to follow her.*

She was still going, you bet she was. She was going, bright and cheerful, then she'd come downstairs out of that place with five or six other whores, all of them worse than her, and she'd head home. I went in, I made friends with the doorman, and I got him to tell me what they wore on these runway presentations.

Underwear, and that's all. Can you imagine, you piece of shit? Underwear. A thong, a bra.

My woman striding back and forth in a thong and a bra, with that body of hers that turns your brain and your heart inside out, those endless, perfect legs, those arms, the belly she has.

Underwear.

And I'm not sure it's just women who go to see those runway presentations, is it? There are salesmen and businessmen who are there to select the items, the lines to manufacture and market. That filthy pig of a doorman even offered to put me in touch with one of the girls. You just give me ten euros, I'll talk to her and get you her phone number. I pointed to the picture of her and the filthy pig exclaimed: Ah, the Calabrian girl! She's new here, and she's spectacular. But she's a tough nut to crack, she doesn't put out. You're going to have to spend at least fifty euros. I don't even know why I didn't break his nose for him, the filthy pig.

When I saw her in front of me that night, I lost control. I took her into the back of the shop, and God only knows how I managed to keep from murdering her. God only knows. She took off running, in tears, and since then she never showed her face around here again.

I'm here to work, you piece of shit. Strictly to work. And I wanted to construct a future for me and for her. But now I don't know anymore if she's the one I want at my side. Now she's no better in any way than the little slut sitting by your side, who secretly watches me when you're turned away. What good is a girl like that, to me?

A girl like that doesn't mean a thing to me.

As far as I'm concerned, a girl like that can just die.

XVII

Pisanelli ran his hand over his eyes. He was tired. His shift had been over for hours, his and everyone else's. But they needed to plan out their next steps in the investigation, and they couldn't stop now.

Lojacono, on the other hand, seemed carved out of stone; he wasn't moving a muscle.

"Has the father been contacted?" he asked, calmly.

Ottavia shook her head.

"No. He's not in his hometown. He told a friend that he was coming here."

"Did he tell him why?"

"To go get his daughter. He wanted her to come home with him."

There were a few seconds of silence, broken only by the whistling of the icy wind as it rattled the windowpanes. Finally Palma spoke up.

"The girl must have had other ideas, and that's the reason for the quarrel that the two young men overheard."

"Probably," Alex agreed. "But it seems that she wasn't there for that argument. Vinnie and Paco heard two men arguing in dialect, but they didn't see anyone. What's more, they don't know Cosimo Varricchio."

Pisanelli toyed idly with a pen.

"Maybe it was just the television turned up loud, sometimes that happens. It strikes me that this whole thing with the father is a little contrived."

Ottavia disagreed: "Let's not forget that he's a violent individual, with a prior conviction for murder."

"He beat a man to death over a trifle. It seems reasonable that he might have lost control," Aragona added.

Romano snapped.

"What the fuck are you talking about, Arago', what do you know about it? Are you saying that if a guy made a mistake once, he's bound to make the same mistake again? What, is he branded for the rest of his life? What we're talking about here is a father that you're saying murdered both his children, I mean, can you imagine? These aren't crosses you can lightly put on people's backs to bear. Not even when you're a bunch of loser cops gossiping in the local bar."

That disproportionate reaction to what Aragona had said created a sense of awkwardness in the office. It was clear to everyone that Romano was defending himself, not the victims' father. In the past, because of his inability to control his temper, he'd grabbed a suspect by the throat, winning himself a suspension, followed by a transfer away from the Posillipo police station. And that wasn't the first time such a thing had happened.

Palma tried to buffer the tension.

"Of course, of course. We certainly shouldn't jump to conclusions. Let's take the fight into account and try to figure out who was yelling and why. Let's track down this father, if nothing else, we're required to inform him of what's happened. And let's find the young woman's boyfriend, too, so we can figure out when the last time he saw her was. Ottavia, do we know where he works?"

"Yes, luckily we can turn to the social networks: people post everything imaginable these days. He's a waiter in a trendy bar in the center of town, the Marienplatz, a place that stays open till all hours. The bar is closed today. We should be able to go talk to him there late tomorrow morning, when they're busy cleaning the place up. Unfortunately, I don't seem able to track down a home address."

Lojacono listened attentively, while Alex took notes.

"So this young man is from their hometown, too, isn't he?" asked the lieutenant. "What's the place called . . . Roccapriora? Which means he would be just as capable of arguing in dialect."

Palma nodded, wearily.

"Yes, but for now we're strictly in the field of suspicion and innuendo, for the moment we have no solid evidence. All right then, we need to get busy. Lojacono, Di Nardo, of course we're all at your disposal, any logistical support you may need. I believe that the survival of this precinct may largely depend on the outcome of this case."

Lojacono furrowed his brow; this was the first time in hours that there had been a crack in his impassive demeanor.

"No pressure, though, right, boss? If we do manage to crack the case, though, credit will be due to all of us. The information that Ottavia and Giorgio manage to put together saves us lots of legwork and time. Aragona, too, plays a fundamental role: his presence here at the station definitely gives us plenty of incentive to stay out on the street in spite of this cold."

Everyone laughed. Aragona objected.

"Why, I'm the one who has to find the culprit for you every time, because you're all rotten old fossils with decaying synapses!"

Palma turned to Romano.

"By the way, what did you turn up with the young girl? Did you go by the school?"

Romano exchanged a rapid glance with Aragona.

"Yes, yes. Most likely, just as we imagined, the schoolteacher is a bit of an alarmist. We met the principal: she and Professoressa Macchiaroli let us read several passages of certain essays she wrote that could easily lend themselves to suspicious interpretations."

Ottavia snickered.

"Boy, it's easy to see that you don't have children. We've been referring to the principal for years now as the academic director and class writing exercises have become 'short essays.' You ought to keep up with things."

Aragona shot her a grimace.

Palma pressed on.

"Well, so what impression did you get?"

Aragona put on a wary, watchful face. In the rest of the room, the tension had subsided, and the others were still discussing the double homicide in low voices; the group's slackened attention allowed the young officer to remain vague.

"Well, boss . . . maybe it's worth the trouble to check out a couple more details on this matter. Tomorrow, unless there's something more important on the agenda, we could do a short informal investigation of the girl's parents."

Palma scrutinized him.

"Listen, men: if there's anything, anything at all, tell me about it right away and we can get the family court involved. There are certain matters here that only specialists can handle. In any case, I'm in agreement, first let's make certain: the last thing I want to do is ruin people's lives over a bunch of fantasies. Just be cautious, though."

Romano scratched his cheek.

"All right, chief. Just one last quick check."

Palma looked at him, as if trying to decipher his expression. Ordinarily, Francesco was only too willing to share his doubts. It was unusual to see him being so reserved.

The dense agenda of appointments and commitments that awaited the team took his mind off that nagging thought, though. He called the room to attention, cutting through the low buzz of conversation.

"It's late, people, very late. Thanks as always for your generosity and cooperation, but now we'd all better get some rest, tomorrow's going to be a long day. Let's go home."

XVIII

Let's go home.
Walking through the deserted streets, swept by a wind that seems to have blown up out of the Siberian steppes, howling like a wolf and cold as ice.

Let's go home. At least there it's nice and warm, and we'll be surrounded by our own possessions, our own sights and sounds.

Let's go home. That way we can shut this infamous world out and forget about it.

Let's go home.

Pisanelli happened to cross paths on the landing with the Commendatore Lapiana, who lived in the next apartment.

His comb-over was out of place and he wore a stained smoking jacket under his overcoat. He must have fallen asleep and then awakened with a start, remembering that he needed to take the little mutt out for a walk; the diminutive dog was wagging her tail affectionately, on her short leash. In his other hand, the man held the scoop and the plastic bag to collect the dog's excrement.

"*Buonasera*, Commendatore. Pantera is burning the midnight oil, isn't she?"

The other man gave him a look of despair.

"Dotto', don't talk to me about it . . . But seriously, aren't animals supposed to die young? This dog is sixteen years old, and she's healthier than I am. It's just that *she*," and he nodded in the direction of his own apartment, behind the door of which was his wife, "treats her like a princess. But one of these days, when she's out doing the grocery shopping, I'm going to take a pillow and suffocate this little bitch: and I'm talking about the dog, not her owner, of course. That way, at least, I won't have to go out at night in all this cold. Because it's really cold out, now, isn't it, Dotto'?"

Pisanelli smiled and nodded his head: "I'm sorry to say it, but yes, Commendatore. Just be patient, though, your wife loves Pantera."

The mutt with the incongruous name—Panther—looked up, turning her cataract-blurred eyes toward Pisanelli, as if she had guessed that he was talking about her, and panted.

"You see?" Lapiana commented. "She understands. I know that she understands. More than *that woman* does. *Buonanotte*, Dotto'. And just one favor I have to ask you, if you're asked to investigate the mysterious death of a dog found suffocated, forget anything I ever told you."

As his neighbor headed out to brave the tundra-like weather, retracting his half-bald head into the collar of his coat, the deputy captain unlocked the door to his apartment. The heater, set to a timer, had worked perfectly, he was glad to notice, and the warmth wrapped him in its embrace.

Ciao, he whispered. Then he turned on the television set, tuned to a channel chosen at random, with the volume low but still audible; it was something he always did, to cover the sound of his own voice. To ensure that neither Commendatore Lapiana, his harridan of a wife, nor the small, ancient pooch Pantera should get the idea that Deputy Captain Giorgio Pisanelli was losing his mind.

"*Ciao*," he said again. "*Ciao*, my love. I'm home. I have lots to tell you."

He went into the kitchen to make himself a bowl of pasta. He was feeling peckish, even if he knew that he wouldn't digest his meal if he ate that late, and that he'd toss and turn all night like an omelette.

After all, he said, it's not going to be my stomach that kills me. You know that, my love. It's the unwelcome guest who dictates the countdown.

The guest. That's what he called it, confidentially, as if it were an old friend who had come to spend a few days with him. Only, this guest had been there for more than a few days, and wasn't going to be leaving, unless it was the two of them leaving together.

The guest.

As if he'd summoned him by evoking the guest's name, he was forced to rush to the bathroom. As usual, it was difficult and painful to pee; the toilet was spattered with blood. The guest. His prostate cancer.

He kept it hidden, just as he did his depression, just as he did his deranged habit of conversing with a wife who had been dead for years. Because if they knew, they'd force him into retirement, turn him into a shell inside of which a battle would play out, a battle whose outcome had already been decided. Time. It was just a matter of time.

He went back into the kitchen and plastered an off-kilter smile on his lips. He didn't want Carmen to see him looking sad.

He was positive that his wife was still there, inhabiting that apartment, as lighthearted and cheerful as before she'd fallen sick, before she'd dried up and withered away in that bed and finally decided that it was no longer worth the trouble of living. He was sure that she was watching him, listening to what he said, gently and sweetly empathetic. He was sure that she was reading his facial expressions, every single line and wrinkle on his face, the way she did when she still had eyes and hands.

Because love, Pisanelli thought to himself, is an enormous

thing. Something far too beautiful, profound, and important to depend on anything as fleeting as life.

I have so many things to tell you, sweetheart. We had an intense day, at the office. Sit down and listen to me while I cook the pasta.

He was home again.

Let's go home.

Let's leave the cold, the wind, and people's stupidity behind us. Let's go home, where everything is safe and quiet. Where there's no danger.

Let's go home, surrounded by our furniture, in the spaces that we know so well that we could move through them, blindfolded and in pitch darkness.

Let's go home. Where we're safe and sound.

The only place where we can feel calm and untroubled. And where we can pursue that destructive illusion that we call happiness.

Even though it was cold out, bitterly cold, Francesco Romano couldn't seem to bring himself to walk in through the main entrance of the apartment building where he lived. The wind was relentlessly pounding the corner of the deserted street and the baffled policeman offered the strange spectacle of a massive, scowling man with his house keys in hand. He seemed like a modern statue, of the kind that are meant to express the malaise of the contemporary individual in the face of reality.

Let's go home, Palma had said. As if that were an easy thing. As if it were comfortable.

To Francesco Romano, that home had been just one person: Giorgia, his wife. The woman who had been at his side since their time together at the university. The woman who had stood beside him throughout his career. The woman who had supported him, who had done her best to tame his spiky personality.

Do I have a spiky personality? Romano wondered. Maybe I do. If everyone says so, and if no one feels any need to fall back on euphemisms, there must be a certain element of truth to it. A spiky personality, a difficult character. And yet he was capable of being cheerful and kind, and deep in his heart he felt compassion for the weak, for those who suffer the abuse of the powerful, of bullies. That's why he had chosen to become a policeman: he detested injustice. Every time he witnessed an act of bullying, he felt the need to remedy that injustice. Does someone like that have a spiky personality? No, that just couldn't be.

If it hadn't been for those moments.

The wind strengthened, almost as if ready to engage in a test of wills with that man who dared to defy its icy breath. But he didn't budge.

Those moments. He'd read that they're sometimes described as a red veil, as rage descends over the eyes. That's not the way it was for him: those were his moments of greatest clarity and lucidity, when a force, at once extraneous and familiar, started to surge under his skin until it reached his short, powerful fingers. The moments when someone else took control of him from within, sweeping away with a single gesture self-restraint, principles, conventional behaviors, and superstructures. Those moments in which rage reigned all-powerful as queen in Francesco Romano's heart and mind.

He'd felt it, that day, as he read Martina's essays, imagining that filthy disgusting pig slipping into his daughter's bed. If he'd had that swine within reach, he might not be able to control himself again.

Romano and Giorgia had no children. They'd tried, and she in particular had always dreamed of being a mother, and he had gone along with her wishes. The tests hadn't turned up any problems. There was nothing wrong with him or with her. The doctor had shrugged and said: sometimes, two people can just be incompatible.

Incompatible. But how could two people who had grown up together be incompatible? Two people who had never lived apart for even so long as three days? Who loved each other with all their hearts?

Let me correct that, thought Romano: who *had loved each other* with all their hearts.

A car went by. From the window, a young man shouted: go home, why don't you, can't you see she's not coming? A voice slurred by alcohol, laughter from inside the car, the screech of tires as the car revved away. You too, you asshole, you're telling me to go home, too. And just where would my home be?

Because sometimes it happens at home, too. Maybe you're just having a shitty period and things are going badly at work. Maybe you're given a suspension because a criminal dares to laugh in your face and so you grab him by the throat; I'd like to see how anyone else would have handled it. And maybe you get transferred to the absolute asshole of the city, treated no differently, in terms of comments and mockery, than people who peddled confiscated narcotics.

At a time like that, it's no surprise that a guy could be irritable. Sensitive, upset. That he might react disproportionately to a perfectly normal argument.

That he might give his wife a smack in the face.

Why did you leave, Giorgia? Why didn't you give me one last chance? Why couldn't you understand that it was a very particular time for me, that I was wounded and desperate? Why can't you understand that I need you?

Let's go home, Palma had said. But that wasn't his home. Not without Giorgia.

He realized that he was colder inside than out. He'd look around for a bar that was still open. He'd drink a beer, at least one. To muster the courage to unlock that front door and climb the two flights of stairs.

Otherwise, he'd sleep in his car, and maybe he'd even die of the cold. That way, maybe, Giorgia would finally understand.

Let's go home.

That's where everything goes the way it's supposed to. That's where nothing ever changes, because there's plenty of human warmth and your imperfections are known and accepted. Because there, at least, they love you.

Let's go home.

Aragona walked up to the reception desk and said: "Ciao, Peppi'. What's the word, this evening?"

The desk clerk returned his greeting with professional aplomb.

"*Buonasera*, Signore. Everything's fine, thanks. Shall I have some dinner sent up to your room?"

The Hotel Mediterraneo, Aragona mused. It might not exactly be home, but you certainly can't argue with the cool factor of living in a first-class hotel, can you?

"Thanks, I'd certainly appreciate that. I haven't had a second all day to eat so much as a panino. The city's just deteriorating, and if it weren't for us, the thin line standing up against the swelling criminal tide . . . "

The man nodded, sympathetically.

"Certainly, Signore. And we honest citizens are only too grateful. Let me make a quick call down to the kitchen. They ought to be open, even at this hour. There's been a party."

Aragona sighed, removing his eyeglasses with a dramatic sweeping gesture: "Why, of course. People throw parties. They have fun. Blithely unaware of the dangers out in the streets. Just think, today two kids were murdered in their home. Just around the corner from the police station."

The desk clerk's eyes opened wide.

"For real? And you're investigating it, Signore?"

"That's not something I can talk about, Peppi'. These are confidential matters, what do you think? The evildoers and malefactors might follow us home, come to where we live, and even, perhaps, try to blackmail us by threatening those who work nearby. Even by threatening a hotel desk clerk."

The man ran his finger under his collar, clearly ill at ease. He looked around the deserted lobby, circumspectly.

"Really? Does that actually happen? Agreed, then, Signore. I won't ask a thing, in that case."

Aragona shot him a conspiratorial glance.

"That's right, now you're talking. *Buonanotte*, Peppi'."

And he headed off toward the elevator that he would ride up to his room, on the eleventh floor.

Living in that hotel was a luxury that he'd have a hard time explaining to his fellow officers. And in fact, they knew nothing about it. His room, with breakfast included, devoured his entire salary, but then Marco could rely on the sizable monthly wire transfer that his mother sent him from his hometown, without informing his father. It wouldn't be easy to give up the comforts that living in that commodious hotel offered him.

And then there was Irina. Irina, the lovely blonde waitress who served him breakfast on the roof garden, whose smile was enough to give meaning to his entire day. Irina, who would greet him the next morning, just a few hours away now, with those wonderful, musical words: What can I bring you, sir?

He, dark and smoldering, would take off his glasses and run his hand through his hair to make sure that the inconvenient, vulgar bald spot that was spreading at the vertex of his head would remain unseen. He'd stare at her, with an intense gaze, and in a deep and knowing voice, he'd finally utter the words that he felt certain she was awaiting with tender concern: an espresso doppio ristretto in an oversized mug.

Whereupon, Corporal Marco Aragona, tireless crime-fighter, would be ready for new, life-threatening adventures.

Let's go home.

At home, those who love us will be waiting for us. This world is tough, difficult, suspicious, a road paved with hatred and pain. Under the domestic roof, we'll find love, the sweetness of our family.

Let's go home. Because at home our family is waiting for us, the true nurturing nest, the one in which we feel protected. At home, we'll find those who understand us, who know us. The people from whom we have no secrets.

Let's go home.

Alex tried to make as little noise as possible, but she immediately spotted the glow of light from the kitchen. She pushed open the door and there was her father, in pajamas and dressing gown, sitting at the table in front of a cup of tea.

"*Ciao*, Papà. How come you're still up?"

An obvious question, and she knew the answer by heart.

And sure enough, that answer came promptly.

"Do you think there's any way I can fall asleep until I know you're home? Anyway, as you know, I'm used to it. I wish I had . . ."

. . . a penny for every . . .

" . . . a penny for every night I . . . "

. . . I went without sleep . . .

" . . . I went without sleep while on duty in my career. Have you eaten?"

"Yes, Papà, I had a sandwich a few hours ago at the police station. You know, we have a case that—"

The General raised a hand: "No. I don't want you to tell me

a thing. I said nothing about my missions for years, so now I wouldn't dream of indiscreetly trespassing on the details of your work. Just tell me . . . "

. . . whether you're all right and . . .

" . . . whether you're all right and if you need any help. That's all I want to know."

"I'm fine, Papà. And I can handle things on my own, thanks."

The General imparted a quick, proud smile.

"I know. That's the way you've always been, ever since you were a little girl. Strong and stubborn. I've tried never to meddle because I think that children . . . "

. . . grow up faster if . . .

" . . . grow up faster if their parents let them handle things all on their own. And you know perfectly well that . . . "

. . . oh, God, please don't say it, Papà. Don't say it again.

" . . . I have full and implicit faith in you. I'm sure you would never disappoint me. Isn't that right?"

I wish you were here, Rosaria Martone. With your bronzed skin, your wonderful smile. With your ravenous kisses and your blessed hands that know how to give me so much pleasure. I really would like to see you face-to-face with the General as he asks you whether you would ever disappoint him.

"Yes, Papà."

The man stood up, gratified. Before heading off to bed, he gave Alex a rapid pat on the cheek.

She shut off the kitchen light and started weeping, silently, in the dark.

Yes, let's go home.

Because there's nothing else left to do, out in the world. Because the world has finally come to a halt, and for the next few hours nothing at all will happen.

Now, yes, we can go home.

Ottavia knocked lightly on Palma's door. They were the only two people left in the office.

"May I come in? Commissario, everyone has left. I left the computer turned on so the database could update."

Palma looked up from the papers that he was compiling. He had deep creases of exhaustion around his eyes, but with that thick tousled head of hair, with his collar loosened and tie pulled low and sleeves rolled up to the elbows, he still seemed like a young man.

"Thanks, Ottavia. You were at your best today. You collected a great deal of useful information. It really was a stroke of luck to find you already here."

The woman blushed.

"You're always too kind, sir. I'm just doing my duty. It would be such a shame if the police station were to be closed."

Palma stared at her for a long time, without uttering a word. She was so pretty, so womanly. At the same time, she filled him with tenderness and something else he was too scared to delve into.

"You just can't bring yourself to speak to me in the informal, to call me by my first name, can you? I really wish you would. You're the first one in here in the morning and the last to leave at night, we see each other every day in this vale of tears: don't you think we should become friends?"

Ottavia replied with a warm, full voice that plucked at the strings of his heart.

"Maybe, little by little, I think I can do it. It's a matter of time, like for anything else. Right?"

Palma swept back his hair, uneasily.

"Yes, I guess so. I imagine it's a matter of time. We'll do our best to shake this curse of the Bastards of Pizzofalcone off our backs. And then, if they choose to shut us down all the same, at least we'll have clean consciences."

The woman gave him a worried look; he seemed even wearier than usual.

"We'll pull out of it, you'll see, sir. We're all good cops, and we know our jobs. Some of us are even outstanding cops. And deep down, after all, that lunatic Marco might have a point: It's not so bad being the Bastards. It's a sort of trademark."

Palma shook his head.

"Aragona . . . If we ever manage to straighten him out then, yes, it will all have been worth it. But now you'd better get home. It's late, I don't like the idea of you out all alone at this hour."

In Ottavia's mind's eyes, she pictured the members of her family. Her son, Riccardo, shut off to the larger world, a boy who could only repeat that one monotonous word: Mamma, Mamma, Mamma. A hammering accusation against the distance she kept, as if he could read her mind, as if he knew that he was nothing but her damned cross to bear, the one obstacle that for almost fourteen years now had been preventing her from becoming the woman she wished she could be. Her husband, Gaetano, smiling and solicitous, always thoughtfully tending to the most trivial details in order to make her happy, Gaetano who almost seemed to be taking on the guilt for Riccardo's problems. Gaetano, unaware that she, Ottavia, no longer loved him, if, that is, she ever had.

Home, she thought. If it hadn't been for the knowing, alert eyes of her dog Sid, home would have been the last place on earth she would have wanted to shut herself in that evening.

"Never fear, Commissario. I have a pistol in my handbag, and I know how to use it. What do you think, that after spending all that time in front of a computer, I've turned so soft and flabby that I've forgotten I'm a cop?"

Palma couldn't help but run his eyes over the woman's gentle but lithe curves.

"I might think anything of you, Ottavia, except that you've gone soft and flabby. Trust me on that."

Palma's voice, which had come out a little hoarse, made her start. It really was time to get out of here, she decided.

"You go home, too, though, sir. I don't want to see that you've slept in the office again. We've got some frantic days ahead of us, with this double homicide case, those two kids, and we can't afford to have a chief who's out of order, not up to snuff. So is that a promise?"

That woman really was enchanting.

"It's a promise. Well, then, *ciao*," he said, informally.

"*Ciao*," she said, just as informally, and quite unexpectedly. Then she turned and hurried out the door.

XIX

As if it were possible, the following morning seemed to be even colder than the preceding day.

On the news broadcasts, reports on weather conditions led the lineup. Experts maintained that a cold snap of this intensity hadn't been seen in who knows how many years. Opinion writers, too, hastened to put in their two cents on the subject, which happened to be the chief topic of conversation in public establishments, on the subways, and in the city's homes. Everyone was asking the same question: How long will this last?

And yet, if you stopped to think about it, the problem didn't really concern those who talked about it from the comfort and warmth of the indoors, well protected from the brutal north wind that tore the breath from your lungs and interrupted your speech. It concerned the homeless, the street vendors, the city's poor. In the last few nights, five people had died of exposure, either in gallerias, doorways, or unheated lobbies. Volunteers were doing their best to reach out, but there was only so much they could do.

The truth was, Lojacono told Alex, that the city wasn't built to ward off the cold. It wasn't used to it. Windows didn't close tight, and there were often drafts, the window and door frames weren't designed to provide a seal against escaping heat and intruding wind, the heating systems worked poorly if at all. Large facilities designed for public use, such as offices, stations, and bus terminals, weren't even heated. The cold didn't have to be asked twice and it wormed its way in through any of the hundred thousand gaps left unguarded due to the familiarity with heat, like so many gaps in a defensive fortification.

Immediately after the news about the cold snap, and before the news reports on domestic and international politics, including the various wars being waged around the world, the mass media focused on the murder on Vico Secondo Egiziaca. It seemed that there was no single piece of crime news in the country to rival it in gravity and horror, nothing worse than the story of the two young Calabrian siblings murdered with such savagery in the big city.

The two investigators had spent part of the morning filling in, with Ottavia's help, the array of information that had been gathered concerning Grazia Varricchio's father and her boyfriend.

The father seemed to have vanished into thin air. He had certainly taken the bus to the train station, but after that all traces of him had been lost. Most likely he had caught a train from there, but there could be no certainty even about that, because no one at the ticket windows remembered a traveler who matched his description: stocky, with thinning hair that was still dark, penetrating eyes that were also dark.

The friend who'd been the last to talk to him, the one he'd told that he was planning to go to the city to bring his daughter home, was a neighbor, he too a field hand, but retired now. He had answered the carabinieri's questions monosyllabically, with the customary mistrust shown by locals toward law enforcement of any kind. It was clear he was reluctant to get Cosimo in trouble, but above all it was himself he didn't want to get in trouble. Better to keep mum, or say no more than what was strictly necessary.

A little more information had emerged concerning Domenico Foti, AKA Nick Trash. A restless young man, according to one of his old schoolteachers, but no worse than any of the other students. Caught with a bag of grass in his pocket at age sixteen, he had promised not to do it again and had been punished with a good sharp smack to the nape of the neck; otherwise, a few late-night pranks in the sleepy weekends of Roccapriora. His father was dead, he had four elder brothers who had left for various parts of Italy in search of work, and back in his hometown an elderly mother and a married sister, whom he called once a week. An abiding love of the guitar. He carried his own guitar with him everywhere he went, whence the nickname of Nick la Chitarra, or Nick Guitar, which had then been replaced by *'o Parruccone*, or Bigwig, when he had grown his hair out in a spectacular set of rasta dreadlocks—dreadlocks that he was said to be sporting still. His favorite style of music was reggae, but he was happy to sing anything, as long as they let him sing.

The photographs on social media showed a handsome young man with a sad smile. In a couple of pictures, he appeared with Grazia, who had the natural gift of seeming to be posing even when she wasn't.

The right time rolled around to find him in the pub where he worked. Alex and Lojacono headed out, facing up to the wind that kept the sky clear and the air crystalline, but also swept away any warmth the sunlight might afford, no matter how brightly it shone.

The lieutenant wondered how low the temperature would drop that night, and he started worrying about Marinella, who tended, like all girls her age, to underestimate the cold when it came to choosing what clothes to wear. He was tempted to call her; he wanted to make sure that she had worn a woolen scarf to school that morning. But then he realized that Alex would overhear, and in any case his daughter wouldn't answer his call, not in the presence of her classmates.

They were in luck: the staff at Marienplatz were already setting up for the evening. They knocked at the glass door. A slovenly young woman, snapping a mouthful of gum, came to the door. She said that they were closed, and in any case they didn't serve lunch.

"We're not here to eat," Alex replied, brusquely. "We're from the Pizzofalcone police precinct, and we're looking for Signor Domenico Foti."

That didn't seem to make much of an impression on the young woman. She looked the two cops up and down and said: "Who is that supposed to be? No one here goes by Signore, and I don't know anyone named Domenico Foti."

Lojacono took a deep breath.

"Listen, Signorina, it's cold outside. Very cold. Are you going to let us in or do we need to call reinforcements and maybe shut down your establishment for three or four months?"

The girl took a step back. Inside it was pretty comfortable, even if there was an overpowering smell of cleaning fluids. Lojacono counted at least three young people busy cleaning up; a bucket and a brush left untended in a corner suggested that the gum-chewing young woman was a member of the party, too.

"All right, then, like I was saying, we're looking for a person who we're told works in this place, a certain Domenico Foti."

"And like I was explaining, I have no idea who that would be. We all know each other here, more or less, but what with shifts and rotations, there must be thirty of us or so, including cooks and bartenders. It's not like we introduce ourselves by name and surname."

"So, we understand he's a reasonably tall guy, with rasta dreadlocks," Alex explained. "A genuine mountain of dreads, unless he decided to cut his hair recently."

A glimmer appeared in the young woman's eyes.

"Ah, *Nick*. I always assumed his real name was Nicola, not

Domenico. You're in luck, he's working today's shift; he was supposed to be here already, he ought to arrive any minute. Did he get up to something? Did he beat her up again?"

Both Lojacono's and Di Nardo's antennae began to quiver. The lieutenant realized that he needed to move very cautiously at this point.

"Beat her up? He might have. Just when was the last time that it happened, exactly?"

The young woman smiled, as if she were remembering something funny.

"*Mamma mia*, he gave her a tremendous smack! It was a couple of evenings back, on the weekend. It's pure bedlam here, you know? A real mess. Anyway, in comes this girl, just gorgeous: every guy in the place had his eyes popping out of his head. To get anyone to pay attention, certain nights, you either need a girl like her or an atomic bomb."

Alex tried to cut to the chase.

"So Nick was here? What was he doing?"

The young woman looked at her as if she were an idiot.

"What do you mean, what was he doing? He was serving tables. Without a second to catch his breath. And while he's working, this girl shows up in five-inch heels, she looked like a movie star, and she goes straight over to him; any minute now, the whole room was about to get to its feet and give her a standing ovation. Instead, Nick pretended not to notice her. I was just a few feet away. It was absurd: he went on working as if she didn't even exist."

Lojacono encouraged the young woman in her evident eagerness to recount what had happened.

"Interesting, please continue."

"She grabbed him by the arm and gave him a shove; he came close to dropping the trayful of glasses he was carrying. At that point Nick let fly with an openhanded slap to her face: *whack!* You could hear the noise of it ten feet away, even with the music they play at top volume around here, so that we can't hear a thing by the time we leave at the end of our shifts. The girl put her hand to her cheek and said: You're a piece of shit. I heard her clear as a bell. Of course, everyone in the place turned away and pretended not to notice."

"And then what happened?"

"Then Nick set down the tray, very calmly, and said to me: Tatiana, fill in for me here. And he dragged her outside. It was like watching a live telenovela, is what it was like."

"And how did it end?" Alex asked.

Tatiana shrugged her shoulders, without once stopping her openmouthed chomping on that cud of pink gum.

"How am I supposed to know? After about fifteen minutes he came back in with a scowl on his face and went back to work. We never saw the girl in here again."

"And you didn't ask him anything? Like, I don't know, who she was, or—"

"What, are you kidding? I mind my own business, and if you don't, you won't last long in this place, trust me. Ah, here he is now. Nick, these two wanted to talk to you."

XX

A tall young man with dreadlocks had just appeared in the front door of Marienplatz. He hesitated, as if he'd just resisted the temptation to turn on his heels and stride away. Then he met Lojacono's eyes and walked over.

"Who are you?"

Alex and Lojacono turned toward the allegedly discreet Tatiana who, even though she'd declared her iron determination to mind her own business, showed no sign of picking up bucket and brush and getting back to work. Perhaps, with the story she'd told, she was convinced she'd now earned the right to be a spectator during the interview.

"Domenico Foti, I imagine," the lieutenant began. "I'm Lojacono and this is Di Nardo, we're from the Pizzofalcone police precinct. We need to speak with you, sir. Can we move somewhere a little quieter?"

The young man's eyes darted from one officer to the other, as if trying to gauge their intentions. At last he nodded and walked out the door, to Tatiana's unmistakable disappointment, as she turned back to her drudgework.

Across from the pub's entrance was a small café. They sat down and Lojacono ordered a couple of espressos. Nick shook his head no when the policeman asked if he wanted anything.

The lieutenant scrutinized the young man and decided to probe a little.

"Signor Foti, do you have any idea why we're here?"

"No, none at all."

Was he faking it? Even if he had nothing to do with the murder, could he really not have heard a thing, not have seen the evening news or heard anyone chatting on the street?

"We understand that you've been in contact with Grazia Varricchio, who lives on Vico Secondo Egiziaca. Is that right?"

"What do you mean, in contact? She's my girlfriend. Why?"

"Is it true that the two of you quarreled recently?" Alex butted in.

"Ah, so it's about that. Tatiana couldn't wait to tell someone, could she? It was just an argument, and maybe it got a little bit out of hand, but an argument all the same. I don't know why you would—"

Lojacono interrupted him.

"When was the last time you saw her?"

"It would . . . would have been the evening she came here. It was Saturday night. After we fight, she has to simmer down a little bit, you understand? I just wait, and in the end she calls me up and—"

Alex persisted.

"But you haven't talked since then? You haven't gone by to see her, or—"

Nick jumped to his feet.

"Listen, do you want to tell me what the problem is? If she came in with a complaint about me smacking her, well, after we left the place she punched me and scratched me, just look at this." And he pointed to red marks on his right forearm.

Lojacono stood up and put a hand on his shoulder, gesturing for him to sit down again.

"I'm afraid I have some very bad news for you, Signor Foti. Grazia and her brother were found dead in their apartment yesterday morning. They were killed."

Right then and there, the young man's expression remained unchanged. Then a look of astonishment swept over his face.

He even tried to put on a very strained shadow of a smile, almost as if he were certain that Lojacono was making some sort of strange, incomprehensible joke.

He tried to speak but couldn't do it. He stared at Alex, as if pleading for help. This isn't something you joke about, ma'am, can't you explain to this man that he needs to tell me right away that it isn't true? I get it, you're a couple of friends of Grazia's, or maybe of her brother's, and now she's going to jump out of the woodwork and laugh at me: There, you see how you'd feel, if you lost me forever?

Forever.

Lojacono and Alex waited, in silence. How they loathed that aspect of the policeman's job: bringing news of someone's death. Their faces were the ones that would appear before Domenico Foti's eyes every time he thought back to that moment.

Unless he was just acting.

Unless he had been the one who snuffed out two young lives on Vico Secondo Egiziaca.

Unless the scratches that he was still pointing to, as if paralyzed, had been the result of the last, dying, desperate attempt of the woman he had loved to defend herself.

Nick's lower lip began to quaver, and his hands—which he had placed on the table—started shaking too.

"How . . . how did it happen? What do you mean, killed? An accident? The water heater, the kerosene stove . . . it's cold out, she hated the cold. She was always complaining about the cold. What do you mean, killed?"

Lojacono sighed. He just hoped this wasn't all an act, his grief seemed so genuine.

"No, it wasn't an accident. We can't go into the details, but this was murder. A double homicide."

Nick squinted.

"The father. The father. Have you tried talking to the father?"

"No, we still haven't been able to track him down."

"She . . . was afraid of him. She thought he might come here, to this city, to take her home. He had called her, he'd threatened her. He . . . do you know about him? He was in prison, he killed a man."

"Signor Foti, where were you on the night between yesterday and the day before?"

The question had been asked by Alex in a courteous tone of voice, but it exploded like a bomb, triggering a reaction in the young man of absolute and unmitigated surprise, as if someone had just asked him to lay out the principles underlying the science of quantum physics.

He opened both eyes wide and raised one hand to his chest.

"Where was I? Wait, do you think that . . . We just had a spat, we'd argued like that a million times, at least. She was the love of my life, I adored her. I never would have hurt her, never."

Lojacono decided to reassure him. Whether he was innocent or guilty, this wasn't the moment to lean in hard.

"Please try to understand, it's police procedure. You were seen fighting just two days earlier, and we are required to follow every lead. It doesn't mean that we suspect you or anyone else. It's too early for that. But we do need to get a complete overview of the situation. I would imagine that it's in your interest as well as ours to help us break this case as quickly as we can."

Foti continued staring at them as if in the throes of a hallucination. He seemed to have plunged into some terrible nightmare and was just hoping to wake up from one moment to the next. He drew a deep breath.

"I was at home, sleeping. Which is what I'm always doing, when I'm not either working or playing music. Because I play the guitar and I sing, and every so often I even manage to get paid for it. That's why I came to this city, to see if I could get anyone to notice me. And she, Grazia, came here on my account. Oh my God."

Alex and Lojacono were all too familiar with that mental process whereby, step by step, as the mind linked events together, the scenario took on a new form and the sense of guilt was reapportioned. If I had never come here for my fucking stupid music career, the young man was thinking, Grazia would still be alive.

Unless, of course, all that was just part of his act.

"Where do you live? Could someone have . . . "

"No. No one could have. I live all alone in a basement studio apartment in the Spanish Quarter. On Via Speranzella, 18. Since I get home late at night, I needed a place with a separate entrance, as well as a place that costs next to nothing. I think rats would turn their noses up at the place, but I don't care. Anyway, I went to sleep at ten and woke up very late the next morning. Since the club was closed that day, I didn't have to go to work."

Which meant, no alibi. No witness. Lojacono decided to change the subject.

"What was your relationship with Grazia's brother like? Were you friends?"

Nick couldn't seem to make his way back into the territory of reality. He was in a state of shock.

"Who, Biagio? We knew each other from town; back there, everyone knows everyone. But when Grazia and I . . . when we started dating, he had already left. We'd run into each other, from time to time, we'd say hello, but he was a very private guy, closed to the world. He loved his sister very much, and that was something we had in common. I don't know, he might not have cared much for me. I think he would have preferred someone with a job in a bank, or even better, a university professor. But instead Grazia had fallen in love with me."

He started crying. Then he began to retch, and Lojacono

was afraid he was about to vomit on the floor, after which his shoulders began to shake as his eyes filled with tears and his face contracted at regular intervals into a grimace of grief.

He went on talking through his sobs.

"Not long ago, we spent an evening together, the three of us, at their house. We ate dinner, we had fun. Biagio asked me about my plans for the future. He even said that, if I really wanted to cut a record, maybe he could help me out with the money. We were very different, but out of love for Grazia, who could say, maybe we could even have become friends. And now . . . him, too. God, God . . . What am I going to do now? Can you tell me what I'm supposed to do?"

Alex and Lojacono exchanged a glance.

There was no answer to that question.

XXI

Sitting in a car parked in front of the entrance to a bank, like a couple of armed robbers in a poorly made American film from the Seventies; only it was never cold in the movies.

Romano realized that he had actually uttered those thoughts under his breath when he heard Aragona's tart retort.

"I don't understand what you all have against American movies from the Seventies and Eighties. That was a golden age, with fantastic actors playing magnificent policemen, not the way it is nowadays when they depict us all like the Bastards of Pizzofalcone, the real ones, a bunch of corrupt cokehounds. Back then the guardians of law and order were heroes who—"

Romano stopped him.

"Arago', you know the routine where a guy says: Oh, things could be worse, it could be raining, and then it starts raining? That's exactly what I was thinking just now: Things could be worse, Aragona could start talking. And sure enough, you started talking, right on cue. I already feel like an idiot sitting here waiting for I don't know what. All that was missing was for you to give me a lecture on film history."

"I just wanted to make my point. A cultural contribution, it's not like we have some sort of professional obligation to profess utter ignorance. And anyway, we agreed to come here and see this guy in person. To figure out whether we should proceed."

"And how are we supposed to deduce whether or not he's a goddamned pervert, from the color of his eyes? Do you think that people like that have a special complexion, or they wander around in some theatrical costume and makeup?"

Aragona made a face.

"No, but if you ask me, if his face doesn't tell us anything in particular, then there's no point continuing with the investigation. Maybe later on we can try again with the mother, maybe we can convince her to open up a little bit, otherwise we'll have to go back to the school and tell them that we weren't able to learn anything more, but that if they are willing to lodge a criminal complaint, let them go ahead, and we can hand the case over to the family court, like the commissario suggested. Isn't that how we agreed to proceed?"

Romano kept his eyes focused on the bank door. He had a shadow of whiskers on his face and he looked as if he hadn't slept the night before.

"The mother . . . the mother struck me as odd. As if she felt guilty, somehow. If she'd only told us that she didn't believe it, that we had no right to put the matter in doubt, and so on and so forth, I'd have known more or less what to think. If she'd been shocked and surprised, I'd have thought something else. Instead I got the impression that she knew something, but something . . . else. I don't know how to explain it."

Aragona wasn't certain he'd understood what his partner had just said.

"Well, I read what the girl wrote, and that's all I need to make me want to know what's going on at their house. And if I want to figure it out, I need to look this guy right in the eyes. Look out, here he comes now."

The branch office was small and the staff—the policy of frugality when it came to resources applied to everyone—was limited to a director, a well-dressed man with salt-and-pepper hair, a little older than the others, and three clerks, two women and a man: Signor Parise, in fact, Martina's Papà. Romano and Aragona had agreed to wait until the lunch break; there were too few customers to hope they could go in without being noticed.

That morning they'd asked Ottavia to do some searching on the internet; they'd also asked her not to utter a word to a soul, not even to Palma, because all they wanted for the moment was to get a clear and complete picture of the situation.

Ottavia, who was especially sensitive to the issue of child abuse, had agreed. After spending an hour searching the far corners of the internet, she'd nodded meaningfully in their direction.

"Boys, care to buy me an espresso? Once a day, I don't mind being reminded of what one tastes like. The coffee that Guida inflicts on us with his terrible moka express pot is just getting worse, if that's even possible."

At the café, she'd pulled out a few pages she'd printed out.

"All right, then, the guy is named Sergio and he seems like the illustration you'd find in the dictionary next to the definition of 'depressing.' He has twenty-one friends on Facebook, which basically means not having any friends at all, in case you miss the point, all of them old classmates from his school days who basically reply in words of one syllable to his pathetic memories of the good old days. He's a nondescript little man with photography for a hobby, an art by the way at which he doesn't particularly excel. He does lots of portraits of his wife and daughter, who are both genuinely pretty. The wife, in particular, strikes me as far, and I mean far, above average."

Aragona heaved a sigh.

"No doubt, a hell of a woman. I have to wonder why she ever married a guy like him."

Ottavia ruffled through, in search of another sheet.

"Reading and interpreting a few phrases I've culled here and there, including poems and the words of wisdom of great philosophers, I've come to the conclusion that when they got together, she was just a girl, or not much older, and that she got pregnant. There's a post in which Parise tries to strike up an exchange with an old classmate of his from the university. In it he recalls that he couldn't attend a seminar because his daughter was sick. He was twenty-four years old, he was already behind on his exams, and he never did graduate. Now he ought to be thirty-six."

"That explains a great deal," Aragona replied. "Certain choices will shape the rest of your life."

"But did anything else surface?" Romano asked. "I don't know, pornographic pictures, maniacal phrases . . . "

"No. All the photographs are perfectly normal. Martina with her mother, riding a bicycle, in the mountains, at the beach . . . I have to say, the girl doesn't laugh much: but that doesn't mean anything."

"And what's he like, physically?"

"I told you, nondescript. Average height, receding hairline, shabby-looking clothing. Just a face in the crowd. An everyman, really, just a cipher. See for yourself."

She had pointed to him on one of the printouts.

And now, there he was in the flesh, Sergio Parise, walking through the cold to the delicatessen nearby, bundled up in a heavy jacket with an old-fashioned cut, his scanty hair tossed in the wind. Romano and Aragona got out of the car and started after him.

Inside the shop there was a small crowd, but Parise must have had some understanding with the proprietor, because he picked up a package wrapped in yellow paper, already there on the counter, paid the attendant, and headed off toward the bar at the end of the street. He found a small table inside, sat down, asked for half a liter of mineral water, carefully opened the package, and pulled out a baguette—a mortadella sandwich—which he bit into, ravenously.

From his vantage point, at the counter, Romano decided that this was such an ordinary man, so excessively normal, that it was actually frightening. Thirty-six years old, too old to hope for a new life, any career possibilities or new opportunities, but still too young to give up, to resign himself, to stop bothering to look forward, to turn inward and just wait for the end to come. A flash of self-awareness shot through his mind and a disagreeable inner voice demanded of him just what he, Romano, was still hoping for from his own life. He silenced it with annoyance and refocused his attention on the little man.

The man was dressed in a nondescript manner. An ugly jacket in some vague shade of brown, a poorly ironed casual shirt, and a garish, badly stained tie. Jeans of an unknown brand, a pair of shoes made of shiny leather with rubber soles. He had to wonder if the man's wife, spectacular woman that she was, was embarrassed to be seen walking next to a guy like him on a Saturday night.

Aragona, staying true to form, was focusing on two young girls eating desserts and chatting. They must have been high school age, eighteen years old more or less. They were attractive and dolled up in a provocative manner; a section of tattooed flesh poked out of their low-waisted trousers, their young breasts were emphasized by a cunning push-up bra. They were giggling and mischievously trying to catch the attention of a handsome young man sitting not far away, listening to music on his earbuds and reading a book.

Romano was about to elbow his partner in the ribs, to remind him that they hadn't come there to hook up with adolescents, when Aragona grabbed a pack of cookies from the display case and went over to Parise's café table.

"Do you mind? Is it all right if I take a seat at your table?"

Both Romano, standing about a yard away, and Parise were startled by Aragona's initiative. The bank clerk sat there with a mouthful of food, looking around as if to find another unoccupied table to which he could point that intrusive customer but, finding none, resigned himself to the inevitable.

"Be my guest," he said, with his mouth full.

Aragona sat down.

"You know, as cold as it is out, it's practically impossible to find a seat in a café anywhere. Let me just finish my pack of cookies and then I'll get out of here; I have to be back at the office in half an hour."

Parise nodded, continuing to chew.

"Yeah, I've got about a half hour left on my lunch hour too. I work at the bank on the corner. I could eat at my desk, but it's just depressing never once to leave the office during the day."

Aragona shot him a look of understanding.

"You can say that again. All day looking at my colleagues' miserable mugs. I can't stand some of them, what would it cost them to smile, right?"

Romano, who was able to follow the conversation perfectly as he sipped his espresso, made a mental note to give Aragona a good swift kick in the ass first chance he got. All the same, he couldn't keep a faint smile of amusement from playing across his lips.

"It's not so much my colleagues," Parise replied, "there's only four of us. It's the place itself that I find depressing. A person can't wait to get back home."

"I get that. I'm a partner in a law office, not in this neighborhood; I was here to see a client. I'm not in such a hurry to get home, though, because I live alone. What about you? Are you married? Do you have children?"

A question tossed out at just the right moment; nothing suspicious about it. Romano had to admit: Aragona knew how to bring the conversation around to where he wanted.

"Yes. I have a daughter, she's twelve and a half. She's growing up, I can hardly believe it. She'll always be my little girl, to me. My wife has a job, too, and she's always tired at night, but family is family, you know how it is."

Aragona snickered.

"To tell the truth, no, I don't, but I can imagine. Personally, I prefer having my freedom. Isn't it better to have the option to bring home a different girl every night?"

Sexually tinged exchanges between men. Romano wondered what his partner was driving at, and he noticed that every so often Aragona was shooting glances at the two high school girls, to make sure that they were still there.

"No, I don't think so. I have everything I need at home. I just wish, let me say it again, that my wife didn't have to work late so often. Sometimes I have to cook my own dinner. Getting home and there's no one there to greet you, that's depressing, let me tell you. I feel sorry for you."

"No, no, I'm doing fine. Maybe it's just a phase, most likely one of these days I'll get the yearning to start a family. But didn't you say that you had a daughter? At least, if your wife's at work, you have her, don't you?"

Romano held his breath. A little too personal. Maybe, at this point, the man might retort: what the hell do you care who's at home waiting for me? He sure would have said it, if it had been him in that situation, he thought. But Parise must not have had many opportunities for conversation, because he swallowed Aragona's bait, hook, line, and sinker.

"Yes, but lots of the time her mother takes her with her. She doesn't want to . . . we don't want to leave her home alone. These are strange times, people don't feel safe in their own homes. Don't you think?"

Aragona pretended he was chewing a cookie and muttered something.

Parise went on.

"So I often find myself all alone. My wife works in a prominent clothing shop and enjoys the proprietor's unalloyed confidence; in fact, he often involves her even in the accounting. Sometimes she has to stay long after closing time. Let me repeat, I wish I could free her of this obligation, but she makes a lot of money, as much as I do and occasionally even more. Children are expensive, sacrifices need to be made."

"I can imagine. So what's your daughter like? She's still a student, right?"

This time, Romano detected a hint of wariness in Parise's voice.

"Of course she's a student, she hasn't turned thirteen yet! And I hope she'll attend university, and that unlike me, she'll actually get a degree. She's a good student, her teachers are very pleased with her. Unfortunately, with the work that I do, I miss all the parent-teacher meetings at school, but my wife goes to them and hears nothing but good things. She's a good girl, my daughter. A good girl, and a pretty one."

Was there something else in that fatherly pride? Pretty. To talk about a little girl like that being pretty.

Aragona decided to play his last card. He stared at the derriere of one of the high school girls: they were both bobbing their heads to the beat of the music pouring out of the speakers of the café's radio. The young man with the earbuds had never once lifted his head from the book.

"No doubt, fresh young girls are quite another matter, compared to mature women. You see those two, what a treat they are. They have asses that can do everything but talk."

The man followed Aragona's gaze and when he realized what he'd been looking at, he turned away all at once, with a blush.

"They can't be sixteen yet," he whispered, "you can't even look at two young girls like that!"

Aragona feigned surprise.

"What are you saying, they're eighteen if they're a day. Plus, didn't you see how they're dressed? Trust me, those girls aren't hoping for anything other than a couple of real men to ask them out."

Parise lunged to his feet, gathering up the wrapping of the panino and sweeping the crumbs into it.

"You don't look at little girls like that," he said grimly. "I have a daughter of my own, or had you forgotten? You don't look at little girls!"

And he left the premises, striding briskly.

XXII

Giorgio Pisanelli arrived at the park outside of the National Library, out of breath and running a little late. Not that he had an actual appointment, but on another couple of occasions he had missed her by a matter of minutes, and he didn't want to let that happen again.

The only thing was that with the unholy mess attendant upon the double homicide, and the sudden burst of intense attention focused on the precinct, everyone had become exceedingly nervous lately. Palma was in constant contact with police headquarters, which demanded a steady flow of information on every new development, of which by the way there had so far been none; the partners from the police station referred back to him and Ottavia as they moved around the city, requesting further information about this or that; Ottavia herself, who had always been the very picture of unruffled calm, was not only working the computer but had also started making one phone call after another, and she was reaching out to him for assistance. For instance, just a short while earlier, she had asked him to check again whether Biagio Varricchio had had any special relations with anyone at the university that they didn't know about, but it appeared that the young man, aside from a few acquaintances in the laboratory, basically socialized with no one.

He emerged from the walkway and looked around. It was cold and there was none of the colorful confusion of crowds of children. In fact, the tree-lined space around the fountain, usually populated by chatting mothers and nannies, was empty, with the exception of a couple of cats intently sparring over the narrow strip of sunlight that streaked the grass.

Pisanelli caught his breath. The veil of cold whiteness that covered the leaves and the surface of the water gave the landscape a Nordic appearance. If Santa Claus had suddenly ridden his sleigh across the sky, more than a month early, no one would have found it all that strange.

Then, out of the corner of his eye, the senior policeman noticed a movement. On one of the benches, in the shadows, a woman was seated and, with a slow and mechanical movement, was taking something out of a sack and scattering it before her, as a pair of small birds eagerly pecked.

It was her.

They had met the week before, just before the mild fall weather deteriorated into a Siberian chill. That day, Pisanelli hadn't felt like going back home, nor did he much want to linger in the office: the air was too sweet, filled with the scents of the sea, and the warm sunshine was too tempting. He had always had a special love of the little park of the Palazzo Reale, the royal palace, in front of the National Library. He liked watching the children play, the mothers gossip, the students lazing in the sun with a book in hand and earbuds in their ears. They were scenes that smacked of family: they reminded him of the time in his life when he had been happy without realizing it.

You only recognize happiness by looking backward. That's the price we pay for our constant, unswerving focus on the future: the days, weeks, and months to come. It's worth noticing, Pisanelli had once told Brother Leonardo, the diminutive Franciscan monk of the church of the Santissima Annunziata who was his only real friend: we're only happy in the past. Out of the past emerge memories of a morning, a party, a lunch, perhaps with a beloved person who's no longer with us, as in my case, or more simply of our lost youth, and sure enough, up surges a stabbing pang of regret. And yet, in that moment you're remembering right now, were you truly happy? No, you weren't. You were worrying about your mortgage, the upcoming vacation, a pair of new shoes, you didn't know that just a few years in the future you'd be looking back on this day with longing and regret.

Those were the thoughts going through the mind of the senior policeman that late afternoon full of sunshine and scents, when he had spotted her, then too intently scattering crumbs to the birds. And he had instantly recognized those eyes. Lost in the void, in the silence, empty: eyes that saw no future. And he had felt his heart lurch.

He'd never really been able to explain, when asked, why he was so obsessed with suicides. His maniacal collection of articles and accounts, photographs of the places where so many people had voluntarily taken their own lives, according to the conclusions of all the investigators involved. He'd never been able to explain the reason for what might have seemed like a perversion, a deviant aspect of his personality.

Carmen, his own beloved Carmen, hadn't been able to tolerate the pain, a cursed pincer that was consuming her from within. She'd decided to give up, to take to her heels. She had decided to die.

But wanting to die is one thing, not wanting to go on living is quite another.

He understood why someone would want to flee the suffering, he could understand that someone might wake up no longer capable of facing up to that climb up the mountainside, a climb that grew steeper and more challenging with every day that passed. That he could understand.

However the sweet sickness that saps your energy a little at a time, the hollowing out of the heart, the ebbing of desire toward the things around us, the feeling of missing someone, sheer loneliness, none of these things were as ferocious as the pain that afflicted the body, they weren't sufficient, in and of themselves, to make someone prefer death. The faces that piled up in his file folders, the uncomfortable eyes in the photo IDs or lost in their cadaverous rigidity, were merely weary. A day later, or a month, or ten years later those same people might well have found some new reason to cling to life.

Or take him, for example. He was old and sick, he'd lost the woman that he loved—he had a son, yes, but Lorenzo was an adult by now, he had his own personal interests and he lived far away, he had no need of a father, nor any need of the limp weekly phone call that they exchanged every Saturday—and yet he certainly had no interest in dying, quite the opposite. He had to go on living, and working, too, if he wanted to find out who had killed those people, deciding that they possessed a power normally allotted only to the Lord Almighty, and why.

He'd said it loud and clear to Leonardo, the only person with whom he'd ever had an extended conversation on the subject: having a mission is a good reason to go on living; your mission is to save souls, mine is to catch whoever is separating those souls from their bodies. The monk insisted on explaining to him that no one would do such a thing, that it was a matter, rather, of the victory of the pain of living over life itself, but he didn't believe the man. And he went on delving into those lives in an attempt to identify the moment in which they'd met the gaze and the hands of their executioner.

For some time now, though, he'd concluded that he would have greater chances of success in his investigation if he tried to thwart the murderer's moves, rather than trying to reconstruct his homicidal plan by poring over the police reports that had been written by colleagues who felt no need to delve deeper into the matter.

Since the suspicious cases were concentrated in his quarter,

Pisanelli pounded the pavement far and wide in an attempt to identify the potential victims in advance, people who stood out because of the fatigue they displayed as they dragged themselves through their day. Women and men who downed doses of psychopharmaceuticals, who had recently lost someone near and dear, who had fallen ill, who had been forced to declare bankruptcy or shutter their company, who had tumbled, in other words, into the coils of depression.

He hadn't had any luck so far. But he had a feeling he was on the right path.

The week before, Agnese, the woman he'd come here looking for, was dressed as she was today, only the week before it had been at least eighty degrees warmer: a light overcoat, buttoned up to the neck, beneath which hung a long heavy skirt and a pair of thick black socks. Her hair hung lifeless, concealing the features of an expressionless face. She might be any age from thirty to sixty, but she was probably in her midforties. She had dark eyes that, perhaps, in some distant past, might even have been pretty, but now seemed blind, wide-open over a panorama they could not see.

Pisanelli's attention had been caught by a man with a mustache who was telling the woman not to litter the path with bread crumbs, because they were bound to draw bugs and rats. The harshness of his scolding, and the unmistakable terror of the poor creature, incapable of retorting, had aroused the policeman's pity, and he had interceded, identifying himself and telling the man that he'd take care of the situation. Sitting down beside her, he had started talking to her in a calm and soothing voice, while the man with the mustache, standing a few yards away and observing the scene, grimaced in irritation. Only after a while had Agnese started replying to him: at first, in monosyllables, then with growing confidence and warmth.

She'd been married once. The loss of a child during the pregnancy had driven her husband away. He had left her just before she also lost her mother to a sudden illness. She was getting by on the rent money from an apartment that she still owned; she had no relatives, no job, no friends.

When he spoke to her, Pisanelli had the impression that he was sinking into a dark, deep swamp, from which it seemed impossible to escape. And yet, deep in that unmitigated loneliness, he could detect a glimmer: a desperate determination to survive.

Agnese dreamed. From time to time, in a half-waking state, she met the son who had never been born and who perhaps, precisely because unborn, had influenced her destiny. She saw him in a kindergarten smock on the first day of school; she heard him speak to her, calling her Mamma.

She had confessed this to Pisanelli the third time they met, always on the same bench, looking around, afraid that someone else might overhear. She was afraid she might have lost her mind, and that if anyone else realized it they'd lock her away in a mental institution. If that happened, then her little boy, whom she had named Raimondo, would never again be able to come see her.

Agnese was well aware that Raimondo wasn't real. But then no one's ever seen an angel, either, have they? So what was so bad about at least fantasizing, and thereby grabbing for herself a little chunk of the happiness she'd never been able to enjoy?

Happiness is in the past, Pisanelli had said over and over to himself. In memories or in regrets. He was happy that the woman had opened up to him, happy to be the life raft that could help to save her from that last, definitive shipwreck. And he'd felt further comforted in his personal conviction: people like Agnese don't want to die. They want to go on living their life, made up though it is of fragments of that which went before.

He sat down beside her. The bench was ice cold and the metal bit into his flesh through the cloth of his trousers. He carefully tugged at the tails of his overcoat to make sure he was as snug as possible.

"Ciao, Agnese," he said. "Isn't it a little too cold to be sitting here? Don't you think you should find some shelter?"

The woman struggled to tear her gaze away from the empty air in front of her. She was blue with the cold, and yet she wasn't trembling. She stared at him as if she hadn't seen him, and then, slowly and irresistibly, from the depth of her thoughts there emerged a smile.

When she smiled, it was as if she shed ten years of age all at once, and perhaps she really did.

"Ciao, Giorgio. I was expecting you. Do you see that sparrow over there? It's new. It wasn't here yesterday."

Pisanelli wouldn't have known a sparrow from a sparrowhawk, but he nodded.

"That's true. Good eye, Agnese. You're right, it's new. Are you happy?"

She lowered her voice.

"You know, I thought that maybe Raimondo might want to see me. After all, in my dreams, I can see him, but I'm not certain that he can see me. And so, maybe, he asked if he could come see me in the form of a sparrow. Because it's very strange that in all this cold, a new sparrow should show up, isn't it?"

"Certainly, Agnese. Maybe so. Who can say. Now tell me, did you see anyone today? Did anyone, I don't know, a man or a woman, approach you? Remember, you promised that you would tell me about it, if it happened."

She went back to that blank expression and shook her head gently.

The policeman reached a hand out to the twist of paper, grabbed a pinch of crumbs, and tossed them toward the sparrow, which pecked at them.

Agnese smiled. So did Pisanelli.

XXIII

Lojacono and Alex had been at the police station for half an hour now and, since Guida still hadn't managed to get the boiler calibrated to an acceptable temperature, they were close to missing the arctic weather outside the building.

"What with all these shifts in temperature, we're sure to get sick," said the lieutenant. "I already feel like I have a fever. Where are the others, though?"

Ottavia, who had brought a light blouse from home in her bag, replied: "Aragona and Romano are out looking into that matter with the young girl. Pisanelli said that he had an informal appointment; he's been going out to lunch for the past few days now. The commissario is at police headquarters again, poor thing: they summoned him to agree on a communications plan. Do you two have any news?"

Alex reported on the conversation with Foti, the young woman's boyfriend. When she was done, she commented: "I certainly had the impression that he wasn't telling the whole truth. For instance, he was very vague about his fight with the Varricchio girl. In any case, I definitely thought I detected a moment's hesitation. What about you, Lojacono?"

"Yes, maybe so. He certainly seemed upset to me. Maybe we should get back in touch with him once he's had a chance to calm down a little."

A sly expression appeared on Ottavia's face.

"If you like, I can think of a possible reason for the argument. And I don't have to get up from this desk to do it."

The two cops exchanged a glance of astonishment.

"You care to be a little more explicit?" asked Alex.

Ottavia Calabrese pointed at her computer.

"You have no idea the things you can find with this thing. I took advantage of a few moments of quiet this morning to surf their profiles and skim the network of young people in general. Did you know that for the past few months, Grazia Varricchio has been working for a modeling agency, doing runway presentations and photo shoots?"

Lojacono shook his head.

"No. What kind of agency are we talking about?"

"It's called Charles Elegance. It's located in the Centro Direzionale Office Park, Block T, Building 3. The owner is one Carlo Cava. From what I've been able to figure out by studying the website, it's pretty closely tied up with the fashion industry: wedding gowns, the collections of local designers, as well as swimsuits and intimatewear."

Alex was stunned.

"Just how did you come up with this piece of information?"

"Easy: the agency posted a photo album on the website with a sort of backstage coverage of a photo shoot, and the models were identified, though only by their initials. All I had to do was put the two letters in the search engine and waste a little time searching here and there. Look."

She turned her screen around so it faced them, displaying a series of shots in which several attractive young women were shown posing in swimsuits. Alex and Lojacono recognized Grazia instantly; she was by far the prettiest one, and she shone with a luminous glow.

"I think it's worth doing a little more digging," Ottavia went on. "What kind of runway presentations she did, how many, what sort of relationship she had with the agency, and so on. Here are the phone number and address, written on this piece of paper."

Lojacono put it in his pocket.

"The boss is right, you're a war machine. We still don't know anything about the father, right?"

Ottavia raised a finger.

"One thing at a time. Weren't you interested in finding out what the argument between Grazia and her boyfriend was all about? The young man, if you ask me, knew something about the photographs and the runway presentations, and he wasn't crazy about it. I found a status on this topic. You both know what a status is, don't you?"

Alex nodded and Lojacono shook his head. Calabrese decided to offer a brief explanation.

"A status can be, for instance, a thought, a consideration, or a state of mind that someone shares on their social media profile. Which is to say: here's what I'm thinking, and I want to tell you all about it."

Lojacono was baffled.

"Oh, yeah? And who gives a damn?"

Alex and Ottavia laughed.

"Well, it turns out that lots of people do, and in fact they're very interested, far more than you might imagine. Our friend Nick Trash, for instance, has quite a considerable following; I even noticed that certain songs of his, available as online videos, have been viewed many thousands of times, and the comments, especially those with female names, are pretty enthusiastic. It's not to my taste, but some like it, clearly."

Alex zoomed in on the topic.

"What about the status you mentioned?"

Ottavia typed for a few seconds.

"Here, read for yourself. He wrote it last Friday, two days before the murder."

A photograph appeared on the screen of Foti's face—and especially hair—and underneath it, the words: "Certain women think that all they need to do is show off their ass in a photograph to increase their self-worth. But an ass is just an ass, and it's never worth as much as a clean face."

Lojacono grimaced.

"Deep thoughts. Is that Confucius or Karl Marx?"

Ottavia laughed.

"Okay, I'll admit I wouldn't have it engraved on my front door, but still, if you ask me, the chance that this is a reference to Grazia strikes me as pretty solid."

Alex thought it over: "I don't think a guy would post something like that on the internet before murdering his girlfriend."

"Not if we're talking about premeditated homicide," Lojacono broke in. "But if it were in the heat of the moment . . . "

Ottavia shrugged.

"It's up to you two to check it out. As for the father, no news. I talked to my friend the lance corporal. It seems that no one in Roccapriora is talking about anything else. The town is crawling with journalists and every fool in town is spouting opinions into their microphones, dredging up memories, impressions, and half-baked conjectures. Once again, he talked to the friend, the field hand. He's certain that the man tried to get in touch with Cosimo Varricchio, but he's every bit as certain that he was unsuccessful. We circulated the name and photographs to the railroad police and highway patrol. We'll see what comes of it."

Palma came in; he was frantically peeling off his overcoat and jacket.

"*Mamma mia*, Guida is trying to kill us all with the heat in here. If you ask me, the police chief ordered him to do it, that way he won't have to worry about what to do with the precinct. Any news?"

Once he'd heard the report he remained silent for a moment, gathering his thoughts.

"Okay, then, we're starting to have at least a scrap of a lead.

Run on over to this modeling agency. It's a good thing that Ottavia figured it out before the press could. You have no idea: they're crucifying us, police headquarters is subjected to a constant barrage. Before long, the spokeswoman was telling me, we're not going to have any alternative, we'll have to issue a statement. We need to toss them a bone."

Lojacono nodded.

"In the meantime, we told Foti not to leave his home. Five minutes to grab a bite to eat, if nothing else to bolster our defenses against the cold, and we'll get back out on the street, boss. But what matters most is to find the father of the two victims, if you're looking for some real substance to placate the press. We have too little information about the young man."

XXIV

The trattoria "Da Letizia—Local Home Cooking" was pretty close to the Pizzofalcone police station. You could get there in ten minutes at a comfortable slow walk up through the *vicoli*. In the summer, it was a pleasant stroll, with the cool breezes caressing you gently as they dropped down the slope from the hillside to the waterfront.

But it wasn't summer anymore. Now the summer was nothing but a distant memory. Now, at the dawn of this new ice age, the gentle breeze off the hillside had become a vicious, cutting blast of wind that practically kept you from walking at all. You had the sensation that from one moment to the next, your ears were going to turn to glass and fall off, shattering on the pavement.

All the same, Lojacono managed to convince Alex to eat lunch there. The fact was that he hadn't talked to Letizia in more than ten days, and he wanted to ask her a favor, a rather personal one.

The lieutenant had met Letizia when he'd first come to the city and a lovely friendship had soon blossomed. He had entered the restaurant because he'd been caught by a sudden downpour while returning home, and as long as he was there he decided to stay for dinner. Letizia's curiosity had immediately been stirred by that man with the almost Asian features, tall and athletic, who had sat down at a small corner table and had immediately dug into everything that the menu of the day had to offer, ravenous as a wolf. And so, afraid that her regular prices might frighten him away, when she brought him the check she had offered him a substantial discount, practically half price, astonishing her staff.

But she was the proprietor of the establishment, and she could do exactly as she pleased.

Letizia's trattoria was one of those places that, while still apparently modest and unpretentiously local in appearance, become quite fashionable on the strength of the kind of strong word of mouth that makes the number of tables available inadequate to the press of requests. The food was excellent, the service was prompt, and certain dishes, the specials or reliable warhorses of the house, were the causes of devoted pilgrimages on the part of the city's more dedicated gourmets. A couple of high gurus in the temple of gastronomy, having heard rapturous praise of the food from reliable culinary cognoscenti, had come to dine there incognito and had written glowing reviews in specialized magazines and webzines, as well as dining guides.

If the quality of the cooking hadn't been reason enough, there was also another good incentive to frequent the restaurant: Letizia herself. She was an attractive woman in her early forties with a nice figure and an open, infectious laugh. She did her own shopping and took painstaking care of every detail, combing the markets and choosing the raw materials with as much attention as any mother would devote in choosing groceries for her own family. Then she got the day's cooking started, only to leave it in well trusted hands and dedicate herself to the work of being the restaurant's hostess and impresario, with a sincere and affectionate cordiality that enchanted her clientele. It wasn't uncommon, at the end of the evening, for her to get out her guitar and sing one or more of a repertoire of songs in dialect, showing off a voice that would have drawn an ovation at the opera house. The lingering customers stayed on in part because they hoped they'd be able to hear her perform.

Lojacono had no idea of the privilege he enjoyed. And for that matter, he hadn't realized what was crystal clear to everyone else, from the assistant chef to the busboy and every last waiter: that Letizia liked him, a lot. The woman, who wasn't in a relationship, was courted by any number of men, and to each of her suitors she offered a smile and a slice of Neapolitan tart, but never so much as a glimmer of hope. Lojacono, on the other hand, who was the focus of special and doting attention, hardly even seemed to notice. The corner table was always empty, in spite of the line winding out the door; on it was a card, hand-lettered, reading "Reserved," and a small crystal vase that always had a fresh flower. Letizia's mood turned dreary if too long a time stretched out since his last visit, as had been the case lately. Some form of contact with the smoldering and handsome lieutenant was still assured her by Marinella, Lojacono's daughter, with whom Letizia had established a very discreet relationship of feminine complicity. She was easily able to pry news from the young woman about her father's life, and especially about the worrisome shadow cast by Piras, the magistrate who required no excuse to call him on the phone, something that instead Letizia was cautious not to do.

When the door swung open and Lojacono and Alex stepped in, practically frozen solid, Letizia's heart leapt up in her chest. If she had chosen to listen to her womanly instincts, she would have swung over and stood right in front of him, her eyes flaming as she stared him in the face, asking him the reason for his silence and the table left empty evening after evening. Instead, she glided toward him, beaming.

"Well, well, look who's here, Lieutenant Lojacono! What foul wind brings you up here, may I ask? And for lunch, what's more. You, night owl that you are."

Lojacono, who wasn't stupid, detected the spite behind the irony.

"You're right, I haven't been around for a while, but these

have been tough days. And after all, cold as it is, I just wanted to go home and sleep. But here I am, you see? Speaking of winds, good or bad, I hope you appreciate the effort: there's a blustering north wind out there that grabs the breath right out of your mouth."

Letizia greeted Di Nardo.

"Ciao! You're a member of the team, aren't you? I saw you when you all came in to celebrate a few months ago, at dinner. Let me see if I can remember . . . Alessandra, right?"

"Alex will do just fine, thanks. I can testify that Lojacono insisted on coming here, even though we're short on time."

"Never fear, we can get the food on the table in minutes, there isn't much of a crowd in the middle of the day. Especially not in this cold. Certainly, if Peppuccio had thought, just this once, to call ahead . . . Please, sit right down."

"Peppuccio?" Alex murmured, as she sat down.

The lieutenant threw his arms wide. Only Letizia had called him that since he had left Sicily. One time, when the woman had noticed that he was particularly down in the mouth, she had asked him what friends and family called him and he, with some shyness, had told her.

Alex leaned forward.

"Let's settle on a figure: how much will you pay me to keep this from Aragona?"

Letizia came to Lojacono's rescue with two steaming bowls of rigatoni al ragú, while a waiter trailed after her with a bottle of red wine and a pair of glasses.

Lojacono objected.

"Have you lost your mind, pasta with meat sauce for lunch? You know, we have to work afterward, it's not like we can go take a nap."

"As if I didn't know you, you'll gobble it all down in two minutes, and then you'll be clamoring for more. As for Alex, here, she strikes me as one of those girls who are skinny as a rail but eat like wolves. Am I right?"

Di Nardo had shoveled the first forkful of pasta into her mouth and was already melting into a state of ecstasy.

"*Mamma mia*, Signora, this is delicious. Better than my mother's."

"That is quite a compliment. Well then, Peppuccio, what's new? Is Marinella doing well?"

"She's doing great. She just loves this city of lunatics, for her it's just a never-ending vacation. She even fits right in at school; there aren't any problems I can see."

The woman, standing beside the table, watched the two cops eat, and felt the surge of satisfaction that comes only to those who cook with love.

"She's a smart young woman, that Marinella. I knew she'd do well: it's the city that needs to worry about her, not the other way around."

Lojacono seized the opportunity. He wiped his mouth with the napkin, took a sip of wine, and said: "Listen, Leti', I wanted to talk to you about Marinella, in fact. I want to ask you a favor."

"Go right ahead."

"Tomorrow evening I have an appointment after work. As you you know, I hate to leave her alone, but I definitely can't bring her with me. Do you mind if I send her here for dinner? I'll come get her as soon as I'm done. Then, worst case, if I really run late, I'll call you and maybe she can spend the night at your place. You know that you're the only one I can trust."

Letizia hesitated, and Alex, and Alex alone, noticed that her expression had hardened. It was only for an instant, and her face relaxed immediately.

"Certainly, Peppuccio, don't worry about it. You know it's a pleasure for me. Tell her to come on by any time she likes, or bring her by yourself, if you'd prefer."

Lojacono stood up and gave her a kiss on the cheek.

"That's a load off my mind, thanks. We need to run, now, what do I owe you?"

"If you had come in alone, I'd have willingly punished you for this long absence by charging you a hundred euros for two bowls of rigatoni; but since I'm happy your likable partner's come by, it's on the house. Now get out of here, we need to get ready for our paying customers. Ciao, Alex, hurry back. It was a pleasure."

The two cops thanked her, left the restaurant, and started off downhill, hunched over in the chilly wind.

Letizia found herself thinking that, in all likelihood, this was all in preparation for Lieutenant Giuseppe Lojacono's first big date since he'd first arrived in the city, though not one that was going to feature her in the role she might have wished for.

She felt her heart sink, and yet at the same time she was surprised to feel a rush of unexpected determination: she, Letizia Piscopo, wasn't going to resign herself; some magistrate from Sardinia wasn't about to rob her of the first man to arouse her interest in a long time, far too long a time.

The war, my dear Dottoressa Piras, has only just begun.

Singing happily, she headed back into the kitchen.

XXV

Cute. They're cute.

Some of them are even very cute. But then there are ugly ones, too: it's incredible how people manage to get such a distorted view of themselves. One time, in fact, I heard that a young woman came in who tipped the scales at 200 pounds. I was told about her, because they never let her get all the way to me. They know I wouldn't have been especially courteous.

Not that I have anything against the ugly, heavens no, and for that matter, if there weren't any ugly people, how would we ever be able to appreciate beauty? The ugly are a necessary evil. For the most part, they're well aware of the way they look, and they keep to themselves, lurking in the shadows. When they can, they conceal their appearance with appropriate clothing, or else they devote themselves to intellectual pursuits.

I'm obsessed with beauty. Or actually, I should say, with elegance, which is something quite different from beauty. When it comes to elegance, I'm quite a stickler. First and foremost, let it never be said in my presence that elegance is a way of covering up ugliness. That's not the way it is. As if elegance were just a matter of dresses and shoes, as if all that were needed was a designer handbag or silk scarf to make up for an asymmetrical face or a wart on the nose.

The distorted use of words is one of the ills of our century. She's elegant, we say. Or, even worse, we say: at least she's elegant. As if we were talking about something to make up for a shortcoming, a crutch. Since I have plenty of money, some think,

I can use elegance to conceal the sweepings of ugliness under the carpet of beautiful accessories.

Elegance is quite another matter. Elegance is beauty worn proudly, a natural grace in one's movements, a fierce attitude visible in one's limbs. Elegance is symmetry. It's more, it's harmony. A classical statue is elegant, as is a Mozart sonata and a Matteo Thun sofa. A red rose is elegant, as is an Afghan hound. Elegance is the immediate sensation that you are in the presence of a possible perfection. Elegance is a trace of the presence of God in His creation.

So many women come in here, fully convinced that beauty is all that's needed. They're not entirely wrong: come to think of it, people are crude, and they're glad to settle. I see posters on the walls, magazine covers, advertisements, television commercials: tits and asses, slutty faces. The appeal isn't to the heart, to the mind, but directly to the genitalia. And so, if you so much as say to them: You know, you really have a nice ass, they immediately get it into their heads that they can become runway models, or have a top photographer take their picture, they think they have the world in their clutches, that they can win over anyone, with the scent of what they have between their thighs, they can hook some rich fat cat and drive him crazy with their allure.

And then they show up, they knock at the door, they sit down and cross their legs and look around: here I am, the queen has arrived, make way. Horrible, ignorant southern bumpkins, these women; half-baked, vulgar fishwives. They don't know that their smooth, ivory hips, their gravity-defying breasts, will soon be sagging burdens, defeated by ill-advised diets and a natural propensity to become, every last one of them, useless cellulite-ridden creatures that finally just plop down in front of the television set. Like their mothers.

Of course, I accept some of them. I mean, we have to work somehow, don't we? If I were to indulge my criteria wholly and in every decision, this place would have shut down years and years ago, and I'd be working in finance or selling vacuum cleaners. Instead, we're actually growing. Even though I can sense the uneasiness of certain customers. They confusedly realize that I'd actually welcome a different sort of request, not just: So listen, Dotto', find me two girls with big titties, because this ad is for a food shop and pictures of anorexics tend to make you lose your appetite.

There's no problem, they're perfect for their purposes. Good-looking girls, young and well nourished, and you throw some clothes on them, get them ready, and have a competent photographer do a shoot. My photographers are the best around, and when you take a look at the final product, you might even be tempted to believe that the model is something other than a small-town girl who can't open her mouth and produce an articulate sentence.

But true elegance is an absence that hovers in the air. What we do is construct a simulacrum, a pale imitation good enough for a posed picture or a stroll down the catwalk in a pair of heels so high that they determine the gait and the stride, not the girl wearing them.

No one should think for a second that things are any different in Rome or Milan. I go there every season, and what I see is atrocious. They think it's enough for a girl to weigh ninety pounds, stand six feet tall, and have a demented glint in her eyes to be elegant. There too they've forgotten the meaning of the word, and in fact the clothing has become horrible in a desperate attempt to be special. There was a time when it was the models who held up the clothing, and now it's the other way around. It's unmistakable.

Another truth that I bitterly and belatedly learned, to my regret: it's possible to lose that elegance. It's not like a surname, or the color of your eyes. The passage of time, sheer excess, the cruel blows of fortune can deprive you of proportion and confidence, two necessary components. I've seen plenty of women who were once the quintessence of elegance turn into parodies of what they used to be.

My wife, for instance, was elegant. I could sit there for hours on end, admiring the position of her hands, the way she sat on the sofa with her legs tucked up under her: a feline creature, ready to pounce. She was the epitome of elegance. Then she started drinking. Now no one could detect or even guess at the echo of a stride and a gait that once caught me and refused to let me go, not under those varicose veins and that hint of a bulging tummy.

You can miss elegance, the way you might miss a beloved person who is no longer with us, the way you can miss your own youth. I've stopped chasing after it, I've resigned myself to remembering it.

Then I saw her.

I saw her far from here, not among the lines of young women eager to do a test shot or add to their book; or even among the would-be prostitutes who are convinced that the agency is just a cover for an escort business, girls who would rather be an escort than get a university degree. I saw her on the street, no different than a thousand others: discount jeans, canvas shoes, a shapeless bag with who knows what inside it, and a pair of earbuds in her ears.

She was walking.

I came dangerously close to running into the car ahead of me, so hard was I staring at her. I slammed on the brakes, people turned to stare when they heard the screeching rubber, but she didn't, because she was listening to her music. I double-parked my SUV and hopped out; everyone behind me was leaning on their horn, freaking out, but I would have done the same thing if I'd been on the highway, if I had had to.

She was walking.

No, it's not quite right to say that she was walking: she was dancing. I know the score of the way she was walking the way a *choreographer knows the score of* Swan Lake: *muscles pulling taut beneath her skin, as she sailed through life with the certainty of someone who has charted her course.*

What's more, she was beautiful. That wouldn't have been necessary, the way she walked was more than enough, but she was also beautiful.

I stopped her without any real idea of what I was going to say to her. And she, with surpassing grace, took the earbuds out of her ears and stared at me with those immense eyes. She emanated a curiosity devoid of any mistrust.

I was completely intimidated, I felt unworthy to speak with that goddess.

All around me, the symphony of car horns went on, I wouldn't be able to stay there much longer. I asked her—or really perhaps I should say that I begged her—to take a moment to talk to me, just a brief instant. I felt like Doctor Zhivago as he watches Lara go by and fears that he might be about to lose her again.

Once again, I was in the presence of true elegance. I had it before me again, just when I was starting to think that I'd lost it once and for all. I could sweep away the fear that I'd only ever imagined it after all, the fear that it had never existed.

Even the sound of her voice was no disappointment, even though I'd feared it would be. The Calabrian accent, those broad flat vowels, bowed down upon her lips and played their part in the intriguing overall picture. She was beautiful. Ravishingly beautiful.

I managed to talk her into getting in the car. I drove a few blocks at walking speed, then I parked and we stepped into a café. I spoke to her, I told her about myself and the work I did. In my voice, I realized, was the tone of someone begging. I, who listened from morning to night to the pleas of women of all kinds, and then decreed their fate, I was begging her. I couldn't let go of that panther gait, that long graceful neck, that slender, lithe body. I couldn't let go of her.

I tried to figure out whether she needed work. I saw the thoughts pass over those dark eyes of hers like clouds above the sea.

In the end, she told me that maybe, one day, she'd drop by the agency and try out. Maybe.

She came in, and it went very well.

And so I talked to her about lighting, dresses, and shoes, handbags and jewelry, probing her yearning for luxury, but I glimpsed not a trace of that desire. I was afraid she was going to pull out.

Then, she asked me what she asked. I was on the verge of bursting into laughter at the puny nature, the petty insignificance of her demand.

Instead I kept a straight face and said: Yes, that won't be a problem. And we came to an agreement. I was happier than I ever remember being in my life.

I needed to find out everything about her. Everything. The years that she had spent out of my sight could not be allowed to remain a mystery. I asked, and she answered. She told me about her brother, her father, the man she was close to.

I immediately realized that the last two were going to be an obstacle in terms of what I had in mind for her. I talked to her at considerable length, eloquently arguing in favor of the values of freedom, of self-determination. And I told her that, sometimes, in order to do someone good, you need to conceal from them the manner, however legitimate, however fine, however gratifying and amusing it might be, in which this good is achieved.

I couldn't allow reluctance and scruples to steer her to live so far from her real self.

When she stood up and went away, her image remained in my eyes. I couldn't even begin to imagine how that moment would mark the beginning of my damnation. Because now I don't know if I'll be able to go on living without seeing her walk and laugh, dance and eat.

Now that she's dead.

XXVI

Brother Leonardo Calisi started up the steep hill, his short legs pounding furiously. Puffs of steam issued from his mouth into the cold air. With his hands plunged into the pockets of his habit, resting atop his belly, his diminutive stature and his ruddy cheeks conferred upon him an unmistakable and comical appearance that might easily have prompted a smile. But on that chilly November afternoon, a smile was fairly rare currency among the few shivering passersby.

Truth be told, he wasn't smiling either. Truth be told, Brother Leonardo was worried.

It wasn't the cold that was giving him pause, even though like so many other parish priests in the city, he was working as hard as he could to offer shelter and protection to the homeless, to whom he had even opened the doors of the convent's refectory, to the immense horror of Brother Teodoro, the cook. Nor was he preoccupied by the countless concerns of his office, since he possessed the energy and strength to deal with every conceivable difficulty: deep down, he said, everything that happens is God's will, and as such we men are obliged to accept and tolerate it.

While the sunshine was making an effort to raise the temperature at least to freezing, Leonardo had very different matters on his mind. He was thinking about his secret mission.

At night, after saying his prayers and before falling asleep, in his deeply personal dialogue with Our Lord, he compared his work with that of an agent of the intelligence services. One of those operatives capable of jumping off a speeding train onto the back of a motorcycle, like in those movies that, from time to time, in the recreation hall, his confreres insisted on watching. Only Brother Leonardo was "on a mission from God."

In spite of himself, he had to smile when he was reminded of that line from the famous comedy starring Dan Akroyd and John Belushi. There wasn't a human being on the planet more different than he from John Belushi, the beloved actor who had fallen victim to his own excessive appetites. Leonardo didn't even know what excess was, quite the opposite. He was an exceedingly moderate and sober individual: never an outburst of anger, no messy desires, never the call of the flesh. He didn't even feel the need to replace sandals with proper shoes, even though the weather had forced many other monks to make the switch.

And he never hesitated in his service to the faithful, in spite of the fact that responsibility for the parish weighed chiefly on his shoulders, with a series of heavy obligations. In particular, he was the first to volunteer for shifts hearing confession.

He turned the corner and came face-to-face with an elderly couple, assiduous worshippers at the church, who greeted him and gave every sign of stopping. But he didn't slacken his pace, doing no more than to impart a hasty benediction: if he had stopped to speak with them, and especially with Signora Caterina, who possessed an unstoppable gift of gab, the north wind would have transformed the three of them into ice statues. And after all, Brother Leonardo was in a hurry. He was in a tremendous hurry.

It was in fact the confessions that helped him in his secret mission, though that was something he certainly couldn't explain to his fellow monks, who were so dear to his heart. Their fragile consciences couldn't bear the burden of that information.

He shot a glance at a scrap of paper he had in his pocket and checked the street numbers.

Certainly, his many responsibilities filled his days, took most of his time, and the task he had assigned himself required great care and dedication. He couldn't allow himself to slip into a slipshod carelessness. One time, under great pressure as he hurried to celebrate Christmas Mass, he'd come terrifyingly close to committing a grave error that would have led to catastrophic consequences. No, he needed to remain on the alert.

He was grateful to God for having chosen him. For having shown him how lovely the world was, how wonderful life was, and for having taught him to defy sin, to protect his fellow man from the devil. In a homily that he had delivered the week before, he had cautioned his parishioners against the temptations of the Great Adversary, which so often present themselves in forms that are difficult to recognize. The devil, he had reminded them forcefully, is cunning by definition.

The malaise of this century, as Leonardo could see, as clear as daylight, was loneliness. Because of it, men and women were cast adrift and were no longer capable of stirring pity in others, because they shut themselves up in an impregnable tower of their own construction, built around their own despair. Science, in its myopic cluelessness, had even attempted to treat this scourge. As if depression, the abandonment of love, could be cured with a pill, like a migraine.

In Leonardo's view, loneliness was the product of a progressive turning of one's back upon God.

It was self-evident, wasn't it? As one turned one's back on God, one inevitably found oneself increasingly alone. Free will, originally a gift, had been polluted by the Evil One, until it turned into the most terrible of damnations, since it allowed men to choose to remain alone, in prey to anguish, and therefore falling easy victims to the cunning Horned One, who tricked them into committing the gravest of all sins, thus casting them down into eternal hellfire.

The gravest sin was suicide.

How many times, in the coolth of the confessional, amidst the odor of incense and the candles flickering under the painting of the Holy Annunciation, had he heard those words: I want to die, Father, all I lack is the courage to kill myself.

As a young monk, when the curly locks crowning his head weren't white like they were today, he had spent hours beseeching those wretched souls not to throw away the greatest of all gifts. He had tried to persuade them to listen to reason, he had even wept. And more than once, brokenhearted and eyes puffy with tears, he had been summoned to identify the remains of those who, in the end, had finally worked up the courage.

Then he had realized that his mandate, his mission, in fact, was to prevent those fragile souls from falling into the clutches of Lucifer: the tug of war between God and the devil must no longer end with a victory of the Father of Lies.

But what could he do to help, he, a poor little monk just five feet tall, armed with nothing more than a placid smile and a pair of clear blue eyes? What could he do if he relied only on the aid of the Gospel, which fewer people seemed willing to listen to with each passing day?

Leonardo found the street number that matched the address written on the scrap of paper. He went and inquired with the doorman, who was cooped up in his overheated little booth. He obtained the information he needed.

The illumination had come to him at dawn one day, ten years earlier, while he was praying and reflecting on the suicide of a young man who had hanged himself, driven by his terror at the thought of having to confess his homosexuality to his family. His face wet with tears and his heart pierced by a sense of helplessness, he had received a message from God, wrapped up in the first beam of sunlight that day.

So he'd have to do it.

He'd have to kill them before they could kill themselves.

That was the only way to rescue them from the devil's clutches: to keep them from sinning by taking their own lives.

But by doing so, would he be sinning? He had asked God that question, his heart palpitating at the thought, terrified at the prospect of languishing in hell. The Lord hadn't answered him, not directly anyway; and yet, by the light of the doctrine he had studied for so many years to such good effect, Leonardo had nevertheless come to a conclusion. He would not be punished. That which is done in the name of God, and according to His will, to help Him triumph in the daily battle against evil, is no sin. And in heaven, when the time came, many angels would flank him, clustering around him on judgment day, and they would tell the Almighty Father that this small humble soul had saved them from committing an act that would have been irredeemable for them.

It was no simple matter. The slightest error in his evaluation and he would kill someone who, deep in their heart, might still find a reason to go on living, sooner or later, even if that day were far in the future. The candidates suited to benefit from Leonardo's extreme and desperate act of mercy were only those who walked through the dolorous vale of absolute affliction, with no hope of ever escaping. Men and women who no longer had any bond to life, who sooner or later, one rainy weekday morning, while the television screen blathered away with some inane infomercial, after even their last remaining friend had failed to pick up the phone, would tug open the window or turn on the gas and put an end to an existence that no longer offered any peace.

He couldn't gain the certainty that he was right during a simple confession or with a conversation in the sacristy. He had to talk to the candidate several times, clearly understand the reasons at play, delve deep into the emotions and the memories.

He had to take his time and make sure that the person really had nothing left to live for. His own salvation was at stake. The Lord would never forgive him for the superficiality of an over-hasty act, and he would find himself peering down into the abyss of the Great Adversary.

As he was climbing the stairs, his mind turned to his friend Giorgio Pisanelli, one of God's children who was dearest to his heart.

More than once, in the aftermath of the death of Giorgio's wife Carmen, whom he had assisted in the final, atrocious period of her too-short life, he had thought that Giorgio might be a serious candidate for his services: the man had been dead-eyed, flat-voiced, the same features that Leonardo had identified all too often in others. Leonardo had been alone in knowing about the disease that the policeman refused to treat. How often he had begged his friend to see a doctor, to battle against his cancer. But his friend had stubbornly refused: Giorgio was afraid he would be put into early retirement.

Because only Giorgio Pisanelli—and that reason kept the monk from helping his friend to commit the one act that would have brought him peace—had been capable of glimpsing a consistent plan, a single hand behind the apparent suicides that were taking place in the quarter. And Giorgio had got it into his head to discover just who was behind that plan. And so he was obsessively tracking down a murderer whose existence nobody else believed in.

Giorgio Pisanelli was hunting for him.

Little did he suspect that his best friend, the one who ate lunch with him once a week at the restaurant known as the Trattoria del Gobbo, the one he confided in and who supported him in the grief and sorrow of his memories of his wife, might actually be the man he was trying to track down. And for that matter, there was absolutely nothing Leonardo could or would have done to defend himself, if his friend ever happened upon the truth. Leonardo was no murderer. Aside from the affection he felt for Giorgio, he was incapable of killing any man who had a strong reason to go on living—even if the strong reason in question was Leonardo's own capture.

But that wasn't the source of his unease, as he placed his half-moon reading glasses on the bridge of his nose to read the name on the doorbell next to the door. Pisanelli was miles from having picked up his trail, and in any case he was keeping Leonardo briefed on the developments of his investigation, so he'd have no trouble parrying his blows. No, his sense of disquiet was due to the spiritual exercises he was scheduled to undergo in just a few days' time.

These exercises were a recurring obligation, a beneficent and soul-preserving week of silence, reading, and meditation led by an aged and learned father at a Roman monastery. Usually Leonardo looked forward to these sessions with joy, because they gave his soul, worn and weary from absorbing the sufferings of so many worshippers and religious brothers whose confessions he received, a chance to cleanse itself in the presence of holy doctrine. This time, however, the exercises were landing square in the middle of the final conversations with a candidate, just as Leonardo was on the verge of attaining solid certainty that said candidate no longer had any desire to live.

He rang the doorbell. What was he to do? Accelerating the pace of events would be dangerous, because he could never, for so much as a second, allow a worm of doubt to wriggle into his heart. The doubt that he might be putting an end to a life not yet meant to be cut short.

But to delay, on the other hand—to put it all off till such a time as he might return—exposed the person in question to the perilous risk of being unable to wait, the danger that that person might go ahead and cut her own life short, thus binding herself over to the tender mercies of Satan for the rest of eternity. Who would be able to assuage his conscience, if such a thing were to occur?

The atrocious dilemma tore at him, and that was the reason he'd set aside an hour or so for that chat. He'd pretend to have happened by, purely by chance, and he'd talk to the person about this and that, seeking a word, an expression, or a sigh that might sway him definitively in one or the other direction.

He heard a dragging, shuffling step, then the door swung open.

Leonardo's face beamed in a mild smile.

"Peace and goodness, my dear Agnese."

XXVII

The Centro Direzionale office park was a grim place even on sunny days or warm spring afternoons, but on that chilly winter evening, largely deserted and with the metal shutters of the sparsely scattered shops and cafés rolled down and locked tight, it was evocative of the postnuclear landscape of some dystopian science fiction holocaust.

Alex and Lojacono had left their department-issued car in one of the underground parking structures—dimly lit, frightening grottoes where the wind moaned like a wounded wild beast. They had then climbed the stairs to the ground level: an ideal spot for armed robbers, or evildoers in general, to lurk in ambush, though it was safe to say that, with the chill in the air, it was likely the evildoers were holed up in video game arcades, or else at home with whatever company they could scrape together. Nonetheless, the two cops had each instinctively raised their hand to grip the butt of the pistol resting in a shoulder holster, a gesture that gave each a subliminal surge of comfort.

Their footsteps echoed in the silence. It had just turned seven o'clock, but it might as well have been two in the morning, deserted as it was except for the infrequent passersby they crossed paths with along the ultramodern thoroughfares of the quarter. The glass-clad skyscrapers still had plenty of windows lit up in the darkness, which meant that business was continuing as usual and Planet Earth was still inhabited; that said, no one was defying the chill of the evening, unless strictly necessary.

When they reached the building indicated on the sheet of paper Ottavia had given them, a structure of average height wedged between two steel-and-glass colossuses, they entered a vast, unheated atrium where there was no sign of an attendant. They studied the many nameplates on display until they found the one they were looking for: "Charles Elegance." Fourth floor, unit 32.

The elevator felt like a walk-in freezer; it even made the same sound as one. Lojacono, who was slightly claustrophobic, imagined the grim outcome if the mechanism were to break down in those desolate surroundings, and the likelihood that their lifeless bodies would be found frozen solid the next morning. Instead, they arrived at their destination safe and sound. They rang the doorbell.

Greeting them as they walked through the door was a good-looking, dark-haired young woman. Her welcome, as plastic as it was professional, was replaced by a crestfallen expression when she learned that they were policemen. The young woman stood up and left her desk, vanishing around a corner only to reappear a few moments later, inviting them to follow her.

The agency certainly lived up to its name. The deep pile of the dark-brown carpeting absorbed their footsteps, drowning all sound, while hidden speakers spread melodious notes that made the place seem exotic and charming. In the one room with an open door, Alex and Lojacono glimpsed two female models dressed in evening gowns, stretched out on a sofa and floodlit; a photographer was moving around them, snapping photos in rapid succession. The receptionist apologized, as if they had just stumbled upon some unseemly spectacle.

When they reached the end of the hallway, she knocked gracefully at a dark wooden doorway, more massive than any of the others. Next to the door a nameplate commanded pride of place: "Director."

They went in.

The office was illuminated by the warm light flooding from two floor lamps and a desk lamp that stood atop a massive mahogany desk. Behind the desk sat a skinny man in his early fifties dressed in a dark sweater and wearing eyeglasses. The man stood up and walked to meet the two policemen, hand extended in greeting.

"*Buonasera*, I'm Carlo Cava, I run this agency. I can imagine why you're here. Make yourselves comfortable. Can I get you something?"

Alex and Lojacono thanked him politely but declined the offer and then took seats in the armchairs to which they'd been directed. The young woman who had accompanied them to this point slipped away after being dismissed by her employer with a wave of his hand.

Now they could talk.

"Signor Cava, I'm Lieutenant Lojacono from the Pizzofalcone police precinct; my partner here is Officer Di Nardo. May I ask why you assume you already know the reason for our visit?"

"Lieutenant, I do read the occasional newspaper. And even if I didn't, plenty of my compatriots watch the television news and listen to the radio, all the more so given the fact that for the past two days this topic is all anyone in this city has talked about, with the possible exception of the extreme cold. I know what happened to Grazia Varricchio, I'm sad to say. And, of course, I know that she was one of our models, even though she had only started working with us very recently. I simply added two and two and got four."

"Why didn't you think of calling us to inform us that she had been working with you?" Alex asked.

"And what could I have told you, officer? That the young woman had taken a few pictures here, that she had been duly paid, and that not even the staff of this agency had had time to get to know her?"

Alex felt an instinctive surge of dislike for that individual and the way he spoke, in a barely audible voice, leaning comfortably against the high backrest of his chair, arms crossed over his narrow chest. The man struck her as being perfectly in control of the situation, and extremely careful not to let slip that control.

"Exactly, how long had Varricchio been working with you?" Lojacono resumed.

"Less than two months. I'd have to check to be sure, but I'm almost positive that she only did two photo shoots: one for swimsuits, which was rather successful, and another for wedding gowns, which has yet to be published. She also did a runway presentation, though not here, of course."

Alex asked: "What do you mean by 'not here'?"

"We only do photo shoots here. We prepare a set, we make use of our own photographers, or else freelancers we decide to hire for the project, and then we deliver the pictures to the client who commissioned the shoot. The runway presentations, on the other hand, are held at the fashion houses themselves, or else in hotels, cafés, or nightspots. Depending on what is needed. We receive a fee for each young woman we supply."

"So the Varricchio girl modeled for runway presentations and photo shoots?" Lojacono asked.

"A reasonable question; after all, not all the girls are suited for both jobs. There are highly photogenic women who just don't know how to do a runway presentation, and others who are magnificent on the runway but simply don't lend themselves to being photographed."

Alex was perplexed.

"Even though they're all pretty? Why is there such a difference?"

"Signorina, beauty is much more complex than people generally think. To put it in professional terms, there is static beauty and dynamic beauty. I imagine you've had occasion to notice how, sometimes, a person that you consider beautiful looks very different in a photograph; while on the other hand you may have chanced to meet someone who was stunning in photographs and found them very disappointing. Young women who have the gift of appearing perfectly lovely both to the eye and the camera lens are rare, exceedingly rare. Varricchio was one of these rare creatures."

There was something alluring about the way Cava spoke. That impression was only heightened by the comfortable warmth that enveloped the room and the scent of sandalwood that floated in the air. Alex had the sensation she had wandered into the lair of a dangerous animal.

"And how do you find these girls? Do you place classified ads?" Lojacono asked.

"Lieutenant, if we asked all the girls who consider themselves pretty or, even better, elegant, to come into our offices, we'd have to fight off a genuine state of siege. And most likely we wouldn't find even one young woman suitable to our purposes out of the whole mob. So in answer to your question, heavens, no. We have our networks, people my colleagues and employees know or have chanced to meet, professional models who have worked with us before, actresses in local theaters, announcers from various local television networks. From time to time someone may happen to come in of their own accord and we decide to give her an audition, but that's a rare exception."

Lojacono took a look around. On a number of shelves lining the walls, for the most part stacked with numbered file boxes, there were also photographs on display with the same model dressed in radically varying fashions. The cut of the dresses and the changes in the woman's face made it clear that the pictures dated back over a period of at least two decades.

Cava followed Lojacono's gaze.

"That's my wife, Lieutenant. The most elegant woman this agency has ever had the privilege to represent."

That last phrase aroused Alex's curiosity.

"Elegant. From the way I hear you use that adjective, I'd have to guess that you consider elegance to be superior to beauty. In fact, earlier you said: 'Pretty or, even better, elegant.' Why did you say that?"

The man turned in her direction, but he didn't seem to be looking at her.

"Elegance, Signorina, is far less common than beauty. Most important of all, there's no two ways about it. It's something that no cosmetic surgeon, no fitness center or gymnasium, no beautician can give you: you have it or you don't. But I realize that that's not easy to understand."

It was clear, not so much from the choice of words as from the tone of voice in which those words had been uttered, that there was a subtext to what the man was saying: Alex not only didn't possess the gift of elegance, but she would almost certainly be incapable of even recognizing it if she saw it. The police officer didn't feel even slightly diminished by that tacit judgement: she would have been far more uneasy if she'd sensed that the reptile sitting across from her found her attractive.

Lojacono tried to shrug off the sleepiness that Cava's voice and the atmosphere of the place were inducing in his body.

"So did the Varricchio girl have it, this quality of elegance?"

Cava stared at his desktop for a moment, and then looked up at the lieutenant.

"Yes. She did."

The answer prompted a brief silence. Then Alex stirred in her chair.

"Can you tell us how you found her? Is she one of those very few candidates who came in unprompted?"

"No. She was spotted by chance, she was asked if she wanted to do a test shoot, and she accepted."

"And just who is it that spotted her?" asked Lojacono.

Cava turned his face to the window on his left, through which he enjoyed a splendid panoramic view of the void that was the central thoroughfare of that block of offices. He sat that way for a few seconds. An instant before Lojacono could solicit an answer to his question, he finally said: "I did."

XXVIII

Carlo Cava's office was shrouded in silence. Something about the way he had said that it was he who had discovered the Varricchio girl had left the two policemen perplexed. Finally, Alex spoke.

"But where did you first see her? Did someone introduce her to you, did you meet in a public establishment?"

Cava continued gazing out the window, as if he expected to see someone arrive.

"I certainly don't think we frequented the same establishments, no. I just spotted her on the street."

"So, do you usually pick up your models on the street? Do you notice a woman out for a walk and just strike up a conversation?"

With some visible effort, the man tore his eyes away from the desolate panorama outside the window and focused them on Alex's face in a chilly stare.

"I get it. A person like you, officer, would think that way. You churn through the slime of everyday life. You deal with the worst aspects of ordinary people. You're not accustomed to seeking out grace and beauty. I'm very sorry for you."

Lojacono was about to weigh in, but his partner beat him to it.

"Sure, sure, I get it. Beauty, grace, and all the other bullshit you care to throw into the mix. You saw a young woman who was pretty, or beautiful, out walking down the street. She had a nice ass and you stopped her. That's what happened, truth be told."

Lojacono practically jumped in his seat. Here we go again, he said to himself. Usually, Alex was much more relaxed and balanced in the way she interviewed people. This newly aggressive edge he was seeing in his partner was not only rather unprofessional, it was also harmful to their investigations. It might lead Cava to clam up. He wasn't a suspect, and the information he was providing was invaluable. Lojacono did his best to get the conversation back on track.

"Where did it happen? And did you talk her into it?"

Cava continued to stare at Alex, his eyes inexpressive behind the lenses of his eyeglasses.

"Her ass. Staring at her ass. What an exquisite expression, officer. The same expression that her boyfriend used, according to what Grazia told me, when she told him about our meeting. Evidently, you and the boyfriend share a similar mentality." He turned to speak to Lojacono. "It was on Via Filangieri, Lieutenant. A young woman like any other, with a pair of earbuds, listening to music, and wearing absolutely ordinary clothing. Usually my eyes simply slide over people of that sort as if they didn't exist. Leaving aside how nice the ass may or may not be."

"Then what attracted you to her? Her earbuds?" Alex replied sarcastically.

Lojacono shot her a glare. Cava went on as if he hadn't even heard her.

"Because she stood out from all those girls like a princess among commoners. That was her unique quality. She looked like the only individual in color in a black-and-white movie. I was in my car and I pulled over and double-parked: I couldn't begin to describe the mayhem that ensued. I persuaded her to come get an espresso with me and we talked. I explained the way we worked at the agency, she told me that at the moment she was neither studying nor working, and that if it was a clean, honest line of work she'd be glad to consider it. And she gave me her details, her phone number and email address."

"That's it? That's all? Didn't you do a photo test?" Alex insisted, looking at him stubbornly, as if trying to convince him to turn his head in her direction.

"Of course, we did a photo test. One of our photographers took a few shots of her so we could market her to our clients, and we asked her to walk in a pair of high heels. Sometimes they can't even cover a yard in high heels, accustomed as they are to those miserable canvas shoes."

"And how did it go?"

"She was perfect. It seemed as if she'd never done anything else, all her life long. She was born to be looked at by other people. I hadn't seen anything like it, not in years and years. The photographer was practically weeping in gratitude."

"What about the payment? Did you come to an agreement in advance?"

Cava shook his head..

"She refused to talk about money until I told her that one of our clients wanted her for the swimsuit campaign, which in fact starts in the fall. It was the first client we had shown her book. He chose her, straight as an arrow, out of at least thirty candidates."

"And at that point?"

"I offered her a steady contract at substantial fees, one of those agreements that the other girls, even the ones who were established professionals, would gladly have chopped off a finger to get. She had tremendous potential, and as soon as the competition saw the photos from the first shoot, they'd be falling all over each other to try to steal her away from me. I figured the best thing would be to lock her up tight, as the phrase goes. Her reaction, though, wasn't at all what I expected."

Lojacono thought about the drafty apartment with the

broken ceramic tile and the poorly functioning electric heater. The patched blanket that he'd seen on the young woman's bed, next to her dead body.

"So what did she do? Ask for more? Demand a higher fee?"

"No, the opposite. She told me that she preferred not to take on long-term commitments. She was terrified at the thought of what her boyfriend would say, and she told me about him. She even told me that she intended, sooner or later, to get married and have children. Things that the other girls were always careful not to admit, since they know that I'd fire them if I heard that."

Alex spoke up.

"But you didn't fire her."

"No, I didn't fire her. And you know why I didn't, officer? Because I knew I'd never find another one like her. That's why. Moreover, she asked me for a pittance compared to what I'd have been willing to pay her. A sort of flat fee, for the swimsuit campaign and two runway presentations."

"How much?" asked Lojacono.

"Thirty-seven hundred euros. Not four thousand, not thirty-five hundred. Thirty-seven hundred. Exact, to the penny. And then she told me that that was all she needed."

It really was strange, they had to admit it.

Cava seemed to be painfully amused by the memory of the episode. Then he stood up, went over to a shelf, confidently pulled out one of the file boxes without the slightest hesitation, came back to the desk, and opened it, turning it around then so the two cops could see.

In the photographs was Grazia Varricchio.

Alex and Lojacono had seen her dead, a battered body sprawled on a rumpled bedcover, and they'd seen her in snapshots from the beach, smiling cheerfully into the lens of a camera held perhaps by her brother, or maybe by her boyfriend. They knew that she was pretty. But to look at her in the pictures that lay before them now was to look at a completely different person. A woman who emanated an extraordinary force of personality, capable of blotting out everything that surrounded her by her mere presence.

There were fifty or so shots, in black and white and in color. In them, Grazia appeared in a variety of outfits: a long formal dress, jeans and top, an ample country-style skirt and a straw hat. In five explosive portraits, she lay, half-naked, on an unmade bed, barely covered by the hems of the sheet. In some shots she was serious, in others sweet, on the verge of tears, feline, angry. Her deep dark eyes, her pouting mouth, her impertinent nose, the perfect oval of her face were all musical instruments being played in a duet of model and photographer. The light flowed around that lithe body with the discretion of a devoted handmaiden.

"Now you understand," said Cava. "That young woman had the world in the palm of her hand. We wouldn't have been able to hold on to her for long. My agency is the leader in southern Italy, but Grazia had much greater potential than anything we could offer. In two years, no more, she'd be on the covers of the most important international fashion magazines. She'd be working on the sets of the world's finest photographers, and then she'd be cast in movies. That's why I almost burst out laughing when she asked me for thirty-seven hundred euros."

Lojacono nodded.

"So you gave it to her."

"Right away, and in cash. In exchange, I asked her for exclusive rights for a year, and she agreed. She said that, after all, she wasn't planning to work any longer than a year."

Alex couldn't seem to tear her eyes away from a photograph in which Grazia, lying on a bed, gazed into the lens with a languid, satisfied expression, as if she'd just finished having sex. She was wonderful.

"And you didn't ask her why? Why she wanted to stop after doing just one shoot? It doesn't make any sense, does it, Lojacono? Either you don't do any, or else . . . "

Cava looked out the window again. He seemed to be chasing after a memory. Then he turned back.

"Of course, I asked her. I was looking at an extraordinary opportunity, the kind that come once in a lifetime, and I'd found her, all by myself. Do you think I was about to let that opportunity slip through my fingers?"

Lojacono's almond-shaped eyes had taken on their usual inscrutable expression.

"So what did the young woman say?"

"That if she did it again, someone would kill her."

Out in the street, the terrible cold didn't keep the cops from exchanging their initial impressions of the meeting they'd just finished.

Alex was grim.

"I don't like this guy Cava. A woman tells you that she can't take any more pictures or someone will kill her, and you don't even ask who and why? I don't believe this story, the idea that he didn't know what to say."

Lojacono was walking with his hands in his pockets and his head tucked low in the lapels of his overcoat.

"If she really had said it to him in the tone of voice that he described, gazing into his eyes . . . You heard him, he admitted himself that he had fallen under the spell of this young woman. And at the same time, he hardly strikes me as the kind of guy who would have taken it upon himself to protect her. He's not a man of action."

"I don't understand why you're standing up for him. He's just a damned sex maniac, even though he puts on all those airs like some two-bit aesthete. I'd dig a little deeper on him."

"Di Nardo, excuse me if I say it, but it strikes me that you're a little biased against that man. When all is said and done, he's been very useful to us. Let's focus on the facts, instead. As of now, the only person we know has actually raised his hands against the Varricchio girl is her boyfriend, our good old friend Nick Trash, or whatever he tells people to call him. Then there's the matter of their father. We need to figure out whether it was really him arguing with Biagio the night before."

As they got into the car, Alex shivered, and wondered why it was colder in the car than outside in the open air.

"It's probably the way you say, but I insist, Cava isn't telling it straight. For that matter, he's admitted it: he had the goose that laid the golden egg in his grip, and he didn't want to let her get away. Plus, what do you think of that strange sum? Thirty-seven hundred euros. Why was the young woman in such a hurry? Why did she need that money?"

Lojacono slowly pulled out of the parking spot.

"Yes, that's something we need to get to the bottom of. But if you're thinking of some financial motive, it seems inadequate as a motive for the murder of two people. Instead we need to figure out whether her brother had talked with anyone about anything and whether he was aware of Grazia's personal situation and her boyfriend and all. Tomorrow, let's go to the university. And let's hope that we get some results from the forensic squad."

That last observation brought Alex's mind back to her date with Rosaria the next day. She coughed, trying to cover up her embarrassment.

"About tomorrow, by the way, congratulations on having parked your daughter so adroitly at the trattoria. I don't think there are any meetings or depositions planned for that evening. So you have plans of some other sort, eh, Lojacono?"

Lojacono was clearly uncomfortable.

"No, it's just that I have certain friends coming into town: just going out for a pizza with the guys. But I don't want to leave Marinella at home all alone."

Alex snickered.

"Sure, of course. Anyway, you do understand that the Signora Letizia is sweet on you, right?"

"Oh, come on, we're just friends! You're not one of those people who don't believe in friendship between a man and a woman, are you? Letizia and I have known each other since I moved here. Don't be silly, there's never been anything between us."

"I don't say there can't be such thing as a friendship. I'm just saying she has a big fat crush on you. Believe me, a woman understands certain things in a flash. So look out, that's all I'm telling you: she strikes me as a decent person, it would be a pity to make her suffer."

"Thanks a lot. It's a full-service police station, I'll say that for the Pizzofalcone precinct: it even supplies advice to the lovelorn. Saints, poets, and navigators, forget about the Bastards."

The young woman laughed.

"For sure, Aragona ought to be here for this. He thinks of himself as a satanic policeman, you can just imagine how angry he'd be to be described as a saint. By the way, I wonder what he and Romano are getting up to with that case of the young girl. I plan to ask him."

XXIX

Romano resurfaced from the silence in which he'd been shrouded for close to a half hour.

"We're in a different film now. We've moved from an American cop show from the Seventies to a poor imitation of *Wings of Desire*."

Aragona stared at him, baffled.

"What's that? I've never seen it or even heard or it. Is it about airplanes or birds? Or angels? If it's about angels, what does desire have to do with it? Or with us, for that matter?"

Romano shook his head and went back to staring at the shop where Martina's mother Antonella Parise worked. It wouldn't be long to closing time now, and the few shoppers who were leaving the shops lining the exclusive downtown street were hurrying away to get out of the cold.

This time the woman had brought her daughter with her. Romano and Aragona had been following them since the afternoon, when they had left their building and caught the bus. Through the shopwindows, which offered a good, if partial, view of the interior, they had seen the girl pull her textbooks out of her backpack and head to the back of the store. There hadn't been much business that day, so her mother had been able to go back and check in on her repeatedly. The manager was always at the cash register, unfurling smiles for the benefit of all those who entered.

"What a fucked-up job, being a shopkeeper," said Aragona. "You lick ass until your tongue dries out, hoping people will buy something, and then for all you know the customer will make you get out everything in the shop, and then say thanks, I'll think it over, and leave without buying a thing."

Romano, who felt exactly the same way about that profession, wondered why Antonella would bring Martina with her. The girl seemed old enough to look after herself for an hour or two, until one of her parents returned home.

Unless, he had then answered his own unstated question, it was precisely the return of her husband that the mother feared most.

Martina reemerged from the back. She looked tired. There were no more customers and the four salesclerks, Antonella included, were tidying up the apparel. Romano focused his attention on mother and daughter, who were deep in a confab. It seemed as if the girl was trying to convince the woman to do something, and that the woman was resisting. After a while, Antonella, with a defeated attitude, went over to her employer, who was counting cash. There was a brief exchange of words between the two of them, and Romano thought he picked up on a knowing glance among the other shopgirls around them.

The man, careful to avoid notice, slipped a few banknotes out of the wad he was counting and furtively placed the cash in the woman's hand.

Disappearing from Romano and Aragona's line of sight for a moment, Antonella crossed the space between the two shopwindows, went back to her daughter, and leaned down toward her. Martina threw her arms around her mother's neck, hurried to grab her overcoat, and left the shop.

Aragona elbowed his partner in the ribs.

"Follow her," Romano told him. "I'll stay here to see what else happens."

The girl headed for a large building not far away, a well-known shopping center that stayed open till all hours, and featured hi-tech products, books, and records.

She was walking along, sticking close to the walls, in search of shelter from the driving cold. At a certain point she pulled out her cell phone and started talking. Aragona was tailing her from about thirty feet back. Absorbed as she was by her conversation, she was unlikely to notice him even if she happened to see him, but all the same it was best not to run risks.

Martina stopped in front of a shopwindow where a number of mobile tablets were on display; the conversation on her cell phone grew increasingly animated. Aragona looked over at the bus stop shelter, where he'd be able to get close enough to listen in without being observed. He slipped over to the shelter and listened closely.

" . . . and I said to her: you're a monster. What kind of a fucking mother are you, if you won't take your own daughter's wishes into account? Already you married a penniless bum, a guy who works all day for a few bucks in that shitty bank of his, and now you can't even . . . eh, sure I said it to her! In these exact words, I swear it! What did she do? She made the usual face of a beaten dog, that miserable expression as if I'd beaten her black and blue, and then she went to him . . . No, he gave in, right away. What is it people say? You can get more with a kiss than a . . . exactly. He coughed up the money, it's just that it's not enough for a 64G. That sex maniac isn't earning the way he used to; between the financial crisis and the cold, no one's buying a fucking thing. What do you think, should I settle for the 32G, or put the money aside and wait? After all, I got the phone last week, right? . . . Well, I can always go and take a look at it, if the handsome salesclerk is there. After all, you know it, I can't go back before an hour is up, because—"

The young woman burst into vulgar laughter. Aragona was disconcerted by this metamorphosis from the intimidated and diffident young girl he'd met at the school. Now, if he had been asked to compare this scene to a film, he would have mentioned *The Exorcist*.

" . . . can you imagine if I walked in while they were doing it? Not a chance, I'd lose everything. What? Are you crazy? Why would I think of asking him? He doesn't have two pennies to rub together . . . Oh, no, he knows perfectly well that his salary is barely enough to cover the rent. She has to take care of everything, from the electric bill to clothing, and the fees for the tennis club, no, seriously. So he's fine with letting us . . . Okay, okay, let's talk later. I get no signal inside and I'm freezing my ass off out here. *Ciao*, bitch."

Aragona let almost a minute go by, then followed her inside. He had no trouble finding her again, he knew where she was going now. And sure enough he found her chatting happily with a young man in a salesclerk's uniform, who had a pink tablet in one hand.

He felt a surge of nausea, as if he'd overeaten.

Seated in the car, parked in a strategic location, Romano continued scanning the interior of the shop, which had closed by now. Antonella's three fellow salesclerks had almost finished cleaning up, cracking jokes and laughing together. Every so often they'd shoot a glance toward the part of the shop where Romano guessed Antonella must be now.

After a few minutes, they got their overcoats and called a hasty goodnight, heading off toward the funicular railroad. Taking turns, like in a game of Chinese whispers, they shared hushed observations about something that must have been quite amusing, considering the reactions.

The lights switched off in the boutique, all except the light that could be seen through the open door to the back of the shop. From what Aragona had been able to observe the day before, when he had asked Martina's mother to come with him to the café, it must be a sort of storage area, but with a table and a sofa.

In the dim light, Romano glimpsed Antonella leaning back

on the doorframe, as if to rest her back. He could just make out her silhouette, tall, elegant, her hair hanging over her shoulders, her breasts. Then the shop owner heaved into the policeman's line of sight. He walked slowly over to the woman. Romano thought they must be talking, but the posture of her body betrayed an intimacy that hadn't emerged in the presence of the other shopgirls.

Antonella Parise lazily raised one arm and laid it on the man's shoulder, as if to dance. He pressed closer. Their bodies were one against the other. They kissed.

Romano looked around, as if it would be a problem for him if someone else saw them, or if the girl came back. But there was no one on the street. Just the wind, howling relentlessly.

The man and woman went into the rear of the shop, shutting the door behind them.

Romano remained seated in the car, trying to make sense of that scene while awaiting Aragona's return.

XXX

"Hello, Laura? *Ciao*, it's me. Are you busy?"

"Ciao! No, no. I'm not doing anything important. I was just going over Palma's notes about the progress you're making."

"Well, it's not as if we'd made any giant strides, truth be told. We're working like crazy and—"

"Sure, I get it. I'm doing my best to give Palma a hand, you know, but at police headquarters there are lots of people who—"

"Palma told us. Believe me, there's no one who could do better than he's doing. That might seem presumptuous, but I'm sure it's the truth. These things take time. We need to dig into the lives of two people, it's no simple matter."

"I understand that. Still, do your best to narrow the field just as soon as you can, we need someone to arrest, at least. Certainly, if we were to find the father, who's an ex-convict—"

"I don't like this story. We don't have any solid leads, we don't even have the findings of the forensic squad yet. Just because he's an ex-convict doesn't mean that—"

"I know that, but you have to admit that it's the most logical lead. I read the accounts given by the two neighbors, what are their names again . . . Vincenzo Amoruso and Pasquale Mandurino, about this quarrel in Calabrian dialect between two men a few hours before the murder, and—"

"That's not why I was calling you, to tell the truth. I wanted . . . I mean, I just wanted to ask you if—"

"Go on, tell me what."

"I was just wondering if you wanted to go out tomorrow night for that pizza we've been talking about. I mean, it doesn't have to be pizza, I mean, of course not, if I eat pizza my stomach is killing me later, maybe we could get seafood. Or meat, why not, you must have some incredible steakhouses over in your part of the city, I can look into it."

"Wait a second, help me understand here: Are you asking me out to dinner? Is this a date you're asking me out on?"

"Laura, please, don't go out of your way to make everything harder for me."

"Yes, the answer is yes. When are we meeting, and where?"

"I'll swing by and pick you up. I have a car, I bought it so I can take Marinella when she wants to go study at a girlfriend's house, for instance. Even though she prefers to walk, or take public transport, though I don't know how she does it in a city like this. I mean to say, if you're okay with it, it's just a beat-up old compact, but it's in pretty good condition, and—"

"It'll be fine. And as for the restaurant, it's your choice. I like everything, I'm not a picky eater. I eat plenty, too much maybe. I'll expect you at the office, I can't manage to get home in time. About nine o'clock?"

"Perfect, thanks. I'll . . . I'll be there right on time, I'll call you when I get there. Maybe by then I'll even be able to find a parking place."

"Sure. Of course."

"Because, you know, around the district attorney's office, it's impossible, unless you're Aragona and you park on some sidewalk or other."

"I remember how Aragona drives, he was my driver for a while, he's a real lunatic."

"Yes, he's a lunatic. And he's a southern bumpkin, too. But in the end, it turns out he's a good cop. The others, too . . ."

"I'll bring a change of clothes, I can't possibly go out

dressed the way I look at the end of my work day. You'd run screaming at the sight."

"I doubt that. When I see you, the last thing that occurs to me is to run away."

"Thanks, too kind. See you tomorrow."

"Till tomorrow. *Ciao*."

"Lojacono?"

"Yes?"

"Are you sure? I mean, you know that I've been waiting for this phone call for some time now. Are you sure? Because I'm not the kind of girl who's just looking for someone to—"

"I'm sure."

"All right then. Kisses."

"Kisses to you."

XXXI

I wonder why I'm thinking about kisses tonight.
We've been through so much, together. We've shared dreams and hopes. We've imagined, eyes wide open, every sort of future, even the wildest dreams.

And we've had so many victories against the slings and arrows of life, both you and I. Because not believing was hard, even for me, more than once. But then there was you, so everything struck me as different; when there are two of you, battles becomes so much easier to fight.

It seems impossible that you're gone now.

It seems impossible that I can't call you, now that I hear the wind howl and I think of how cold it is outside. I wish I could talk to you, even without feeling you at my side. It would help me.

Tonight, I'm thinking about embraces.

When you miss someone's flesh, you immediately imagine sex. But it's in the embrace itself that you lose yourself, don't you think? When two bodies are pressed one against the other, without defenses, without barrier. An embrace is such a reassuring thing.

I remember all the times that we reassured each other.

You knew me so well, so very well. Nothing of the sort had ever happened to me before. I know that I'm not easy to decipher, and yet you guessed my thoughts from nothing more than an expression.

It's a priceless sensation, to be understood. It's wonderful to *feel like you're important, to know that your state of mind, just a word from you, can change the temperature around someone.*

That's why I couldn't tolerate your betrayal.

If it had come from some other direction, I could have tolerated it, these are things that happen in life. But not from you, that I couldn't take, I never thought I would have to defend myself from you.

It was a knife in the back that murdered the finest part of me, the part that had finally opened up to a fellow human being.

Your betrayal meant that opening up, surrendering, taking off the armor that I'd worked so hard to construct, had been a mistake.

No, that I couldn't take.

To see your name like that.

To see that photograph.

I couldn't take it, do you understand that? I had to do what I did next.

Still, tonight I miss your embrace. Tonight I wish I could feel your body next to mine.

And lose myself in a long, endless embrace.

XXXII

There is one moment of the day that is unlike any other, and yet it's the same in every home. That moment is dinnertime.

First of all, dinner is different from lunch, because after lunch you have an entire afternoon and most of the evening ahead of you, still to be lived and experienced, and the many thoughts of the day still to come only serve to distract you.

It's also very different from the evening's return home, when you hurry into the bathroom or to your computer or the television set, with a hasty hello or at most a passing, grazing kiss.

But not at dinner. At dinner you look each other in the eye, you tell each other how the day went.

And if you have plans for the next day, then you talk about them at dinner.

Marinella put a fistful of pasta in to boil, while humming under her breath the refrain of a song she had heard in the street.

If there was one thing that enchanted her about that city, it was the music. Everywhere you went, whatever the time of day or night, there was music. She remembered hearing her father describe it as a source of annoyance, an absurd intrusion on his personal space, even if only an auditory one, but she actually loved it.

This wasn't the only point on which she was in disagreement with her father, concerning that city. To put it simply, she disagreed with her father about pretty much everything concerning that city.

He continued to see it as a sort of prison, a place he had been sent to serve out an unjust sentence. While the place he had come from was an earthly paradise where it was always summer, where the weather was never cold, where the air was saturated with the scent of flowers and the sea was within reach all year round, a land inhabited by cordial people who draped a garland of flowers around your neck everytime they saw you in the street, a Hawaiian lei: Aloha, Papà.

But what she remembered was three movie theaters in a radius of a hundred kilometers, a blistering heat that never let up, gossip, backbiting, and worst of all, the fact that everyone knew everything about everyone else.

When she and her mother were left there, all alone, after Lojacono had been transferred away on account of that murky accusation, a chill had descended around the two of them, even though they'd had nothing to do with it. Compared with that chill, the cold they were suffering now, in that wintry season, was nothing but a lovely springlike cool breeze. Everyone had turned their backs on them, refusing to speak to either of them; in fact, even most of their relatives had grown distant.

The reasoning was simple and straightforward: if it was true, as people were saying, that the lieutenant had passed confidential information to the Mafia, then he was a traitor and a turncoat; if it wasn't true, then he was dangerous. In either case, best to have nothing more to do with him, or anyone connected to him.

At first, moving to Palermo had seemed like a solution, but instead it had merely brought to the surface another, very serious problem: the relationship between Marinella and her mother, Sonia. A treacherous, silent battle that culminated with the daughter running away to the city where her father was serving out his sentence. At that moment, anything seemed better than those constant, unending Sicilian quarrels, fights that made the air unbreathable inside the home and out.

She'd always got along well with her father. Not that they were all that close, he wasn't much of a talker, but they did resemble each other, in personality as well as physically, and they understood each other on the fly, without any need for too much chitchat. What's more, he represented a point of reference, a safe harbor: and of course she would seek a port in the storm. It had been natural to think of going to stay with him.

Her Papà hadn't sprung any surprises on her, he was the same as he had always been. The real surprise had been the city.

Marinella had entered a world that seemed to have been waiting for her all her life. Even the things that her father considered defects, and which truly and objectively were, met with her approval: the chaos, the mess, the cheerful mischievousness, the art of getting by, the tendency to face the worst with a smile, these things too amused her.

The day before, she had beheld a scene that struck her as pure art. A guy at the wheel of a black Mercedes had turned down a narrow one-way lane, traveling in the proper direction. His car only barely cleared the walls on either side. About a third of the way along the lane, he came face-to-face with a badly dented compact car, driven by a woman who was clearly a terrible driver, proceeding up the *vicolo*, traveling in the wrong direction. Well, the guy in the Mercedes, probably guessing that the other woman would take an eternity to back up the narrow lane, had turned off in a spectacular gymkhana, wedging his way past the fruit stands and the chairs of the aged, black-clad women, so that the lucky woman driving the wrong way was able to proceed on to the main thoroughfare. In exchange for his kindness, he had received from the woman a dazzling smile, to which he had replied with a cordial ah-go-fuck-yourself.

How could you help but fall in love with a place like that, Marinella thought to herself.

Then, of course, there was the music: radios, bootleg CDs, pirated MP3 files, car radios blasting at full volume, with pounding bass lines that could be heard a hundred yards away. A cheerful cacophony, a kaleidoscopic soundtrack. You only had to choose what to listen to, ruling out, as far as possible, everything else.

The young woman asked herself how big a role Massimiliano played in the instinctive love she felt for that city. Probably a pretty big one, she had to admit.

The young man lived in the same apartment building as Lojacono. Marinella presumed that her father's choice of that building hadn't had anything to do with the fact that the young man lived there, but she was grateful to the whims of chance for that choice, all the same. Because Massimiliano Rossini, majoring in literature and an aspiring journalist, as well as the eldest son of a very likable woman from whom Marinella had borrowed sugar, salt, and pepper on three different occasions, strictly for purposes of research, was the handsomest and most charming young man in the entire northern hemisphere.

The two young people had crossed paths several times on the stairs, until one day Massimiliano, attracted by that young female tenant with a dark, almost goth edge and strange, almond-shaped eyes set above intriguing high cheekbones, had started up a conversation. Marinella felt as if she had won the lottery—for that matter, she could hardly keep on borrowing cupsful of condiments, and she wouldn't have known what other maneuvers to undertake in hopes of approaching him—and for a little while she had actually considered the possibility that he was just stringing her along, because she deemed it impossible that anyone like him might seriously be interested in anyone like her.

It hadn't been easy to get much past the standard greetings: *ciao*, how's it going. She'd talked it over at some length with Letizia, who had soon become her friend, even more than her father's. Letizia, ironic and amusing, never intrusive. Letizia, beautiful, welcoming, and comforting. Letizia—if only her mother had been like Letizia; trust her father to be such a knucklehead that he failed to notice the woman was in love with him. Instead, he was all agog over that unlikable Sardinian woman in a skirt suit.

In any case, Letizia had recommended a few minor, decisive moves that had promptly led Massimiliano right into the jaws of her trap. A refined strategy made up of failures to say hello, words half uttered, and sudden dazzling smiles after lengthy silences, from one balcony to another or else downstairs, in the lobby. And at last—on the exact timetable and in the very manner foretold by the wonderful witch, who simply ran a restaurant when she wasn't casting spells—he had invited Marinella to go out. Just the two of them. Alone.

Now the problem had taken on a different coloration, quite another degree of difficulty, passing from yellow to red. There was a towering obstacle to be overcome, and its name was Giuseppe Lojacono. The sky could fall, the world could collapse, but at eight on the dot every evening the lieutenant returned home to spend the evening with his little girl, who joyfully made him dinner; at the very most, occasionally, he might go eat at Letizia's. To tell him loud and clear that she intended to go out on a date with a young man she'd met was out of the question. To him, Marinella was still in the midst of her childhood, and any such statement would throw him into a state of panic, with a wide array of entirely unpredictable and uncontrollable reactions: he might even choose to confront Massimiliano face-to-face, and that would surely spell disaster. No, she'd have to proceed with extreme caution.

And so she had devised a complex system of interlocking

lies that called for the participation of not one but two of her female classmates and their respective mothers, standing by to field any phone calls her father might make to check up on her. D-Day was tomorrow, when Massimiliano planned to take her to the movies for the very first time. Now, during dinner, she only had to toss out the piece of news, as if incidentally, the impending and terribile math quiz that had been scheduled for that week and the nocturnal study session that the three girls would engage in, at the home of the girl who sat next to her in class. She drained the pasta, heaved a deep sigh, and walked into the dining room, driven by the worst possible intentions.

Dinner.
The perfect moment to tell the whole story.
The perfect moment to confide our innermost thoughts to our families, and receive the caring advice of those who love us.
The perfect moment to put our hesitations and scruples behind us, to just be ourselves.
The perfect moment to come out into the open.

Alex sat down at the table before a bowl of noodle soup, stifling the vomit impulse that always rose treacherously at the back of her throat. She despised noodle soup, she found the broth disgusting and she found the broth even more disgusting when paired with the tiny star-shaped noodles, and yet, for more than twenty years now, punctually, once a week, she had swallowed that junk down to the last mouthful, feeling as she did so, the General's eyes, monitoring her at regular intervals, checking up on her sound nutritional health. Every so often she would return his glance, feigning enjoyment.

Sometimes she thought of herself as a sort of latter-day Dr. Jekyll, with a monster hidden deep inside her, ready to pounce out at a single leap, to the unreasoning terror of all those around her.

Her distaste for the noodle soup was only accentuated by the terrible slurping noise her father produced with every spoonful, followed by a dull grunt of pleasure. If Alex ever decided to run away from that apartment, after shooting both her parents to death, it was bound to happen the evening noodle soup was served. About that, she had no doubts whatsoever.

The dinner proceeded in utter silence, according to the etiquette she had learned growing up: if anyone had anything to say, they could do so in the two-minute interval between the end of the meal and the turning on of the television set. She waited for that moment with utter calm, slicing with painstaking and irritating care the slab of meat that followed, anemically, the equally tasteless first course.

At last, at the appointed time and with the bothered, discontented tone of someone who is unable to get out of a distasteful duty, she informed her parents that the following evening she'd have to take part in a meeting at the police station about the double homicide she was investigaing.

She mentally begged the forgiveness of the two murdered kids for having used them in such an unfitting manner. But they were all victims, together, and they had to help each other out as best they could.

The General muttered something about the fact that the department was asking too much in exchange for the pittance of a salary, but Alex's finely tuned ear caught the undertone of pride for a daughter working to solve such an important case, a case that had been the talk of all the news broadcasts.

Alex imagined herself in bed with Rosaria Martone, in the aftermath of a dinner comprised of oysters and white wine, with brightly lit candles and the scent of incense, and she had to make an enormous effort to keep from smiling down at the apple she had just started to peel.

*

Marinella waited under her father had finished eating. He seemed more silent than usual, slightly ill at ease, but perhaps he was just tired.

She felt a surge of tenderness: there were times when he seemed so terribly old. For a moment her conscience stung her at the thought of leaving him all alone, even if only for an evening. Then she thought about Massimiliano, his dazzling smile and unruly bangs, the strong hands that gripped his backpack as he trotted down the stairs, and all her doubts were rapidly swept away.

She was about to open her mouth and begin her well rehearsed description of the math quiz, the challenge of the problems, and the importance of sufficient study time with the help of her girlfriends, when her father beat her to the punch.

"Listen, sweetheart, would you be very upset if I didn't come home for dinner tomorrow evening? An old friend of mine from the police academy, another Sicilian, is in town for a course he's taking, and since he'll be done late I don't want to invite him here for dinner, but I'd still like to see him, I haven't spent time with him in a long time. I'd ask you to come along, but I know you'd just be bored. You know the routine: memories, the old days, and so on and so forth."

Marinella was tempted to leap onto the tabletop and break into a dance, but her father might have put a negative interpretation on such a reaction.

"So where are you going to take him, Papà? To Letizia's?"

"No, he . . . he doesn't know his way around the city, it would be too hard to give him instructions to get to the trattoria. By the way, about Letizia, I asked her if you could go over there; I don't feel like leaving you all alone here in the apartment. She's expecting you at eight o'clock, but if your homework keeps you from getting there right on time, don't worry about it."

A minor stumbling block, thought Marinella, but one she could certainly get around: Letizia was on her side, it wasn't going to constitute a problem.

"All right, no sweat, after all I've got lots of studying to do: the day after tomorrow, we have the math test. I'll eat at Letizia's."

Her delight at having encountered such a soft landing where she had been anticipating a hard thump kept the young woman from asking herself about her father's mysterious evening out, something that she certainly would have done otherwise, if she hadn't had plans of her own.

She reached out for an apple, seized it, and bit into it with gusto.

Dinner.
The best moment of the day for a happy, united family.
The best moment of the day for utter sincerity.

XXXIII

For once, they all showed up at the police station at the same time, well ahead of the usual hour for the start of their shift. For some of them, like Ottavia, this was nothing new; for others, such as Aragona, the event bordered on the miraculous.

The tropical heat was not yet pounding through the building, because Guida had only just started up the boiler that steam-heated the radiators. Romano, who had no problem with the cold, stripped down to his shirtsleeves; Alex, on the other hand, kept her jacket on.

Palma looked around with some satisfaction, but on his face there was no mistaking the vein of worry that almost never seemed to subside lately.

"I'm happy we're all here, because that means we can hold a little war council all our own at the start of the day. You know the way matters stand, whether we consider it to be lucky or unlucky, nothing else much has happened in the past few days, and now the press is all over us on this case of the murder of those two kids. The truth is that we're not making a great deal of progress. We haven't flushed out the father yet, in spite of the fact that we've put out all-points bulletins with mug shots. I'm just wondering how a guy the police know so well can vanish into thin air like that."

Ottavia was disconsolate.

"Unfortunately, it happens. A couple of times a day I talk to the carabinieri in Roccapriora, who have been put on emergency alert and are keeping a close eye on the family's few friends, relatives, and acquaintances. I even dug down into a couple of harebrained escapades pulled off by Foti, the Varricchio girl's young gentleman friend, but really they were just stupid pranks, in the worst cases. So, all things considered, we have nothing to show in that connection."

"And what about Cava, the guy from the modeling agency, do we have anything new on him?" Alex asked. "He made a terrible impression—on me, anyway."

"I did a few searches from my computer at home, after you all called me when you were done with your meeting. There's not a lot to report there: he's been married to the same woman for twenty years, they have no children; she was a model and was pretty well known, but then she quit. Which is something that happens. I found an article in a scandal sheet from ten years ago or so that talked about a tremendous scene during the summer in some club near the beach. It seems she was drunk and accused him of cheating on her with another woman, also a model, but nothing else seems to have happened."

Pisanelli butted in.

"The agency is fairly well known. I asked a friend of mine who's a fashion journalist, and she told me that it's one of the biggest agencies in southern Italy, if not the biggest outright."

"Which means that it ranks about two hundredth nationally," Aragona grumbled. "Like all the other companies around here."

Pisanelli shrugged his shoulders.

"All the same, it has a pretty good reputation. I checked it out with the local courthouse and there don't seem to be any lawsuits pending against it in the labor courts, which is pretty unusual for a company in that line of work. Ironclad contracts, and everything seems to be done in the light of day, withholding and worker's comp and all the rest of it."

"Good to know," said Lojacono, "but we're not talking about tax evasion here, and Cava is no Al Capone. He struck me as a very controlled person, maybe even a little too much so, the typical behavior of people with deep-seated obsessions. The profile of the murderer is that of a person subject to outbursts of rage, moments of absolute blind fury."

"For instance, the young man who sings and plays the guitar," Romano said distractedly. "You described him as a moody, emotional individual. And since we know he hit her once, you turned him into the favored guilty party of the day."

Palma spread both arms wide.

"Look, basically we're just stumbling around in the dark, here. We're waiting for the final report from the forensic squad, we're still waiting to track down and question the father, we're waiting for someone to make a false step. We're waiting. And while we wait, time passes, and you know that statistics tell us that . . . "

Aragona finshed his sentence for him.

" . . . if the guilty party isn't apprehended in the first twenty-four hours, the odds of catching them drop precipitously."

The commissario glared at him.

"That's exactly right. And you aren't the only one who knows that, they know it at police headquarters, too, where they can't wait to lunge at us like a flock of vultures eager to take the case away from us. A couple of days, no more than that, and we'll have to throw in the towel."

"It's not over yet," Lojacono said grimly. "Leaving aside the report from the forensic squad, there are plenty of other elements still missing. We need to understand the reason for the strange sum the Varricchio girl asked Cava to give her, thirty-seven hundred euros; we need to get over to the university to figure out whether the young man, Biagio, had confided in anyone there; and most of all, we have to find the father of the two victims, Cosimo. They can't take the case away from us before we fill in the picture with those items. We'll get busy, but you have to give us cover."

Palma realized that everyone was looking at him. Beat-up bastards they might be, but at least they were a team. And they were a team that wasn't about to give up the chase.

"I'll do everything I can. But let me say it again, at the very outside we have two days. I'll ward off the blows as they come, but if we don't find anything, at some point I'll have to give in. Lojacono, make full use of all the precinct's resources, including me, if there's anything I can do. And you two," he said, turning to Romano and Aragona, "unless you have any new developments in the case of the molested girl, close the file and hand it off to the family court, so you can lend a hand."

Romano shot a glance at Aragona.

"Let us have the rest of the morning, boss, and we'll be at your service."

Palma pointed his finger at Romano.

"Agreed, you can have the morning, but then I want your report. Get on it, guys."

And with that Palma vanished into his office.

Aragona had a rapt, dreamy look on his face.

"God, I love it, when he does that."

XXXIV

Lojacono's university experience dated back to a long time earlier, and what's more, had taken place far away, in another part of Italy; Alex's own experience was more recent and had unfolded there, in that city, inside a venerable old palazzo with austere stone staircases and marble busts set in niches. Nonetheless, going back to a university campus aroused in each of them the same blend of nostalgia, cheerfulness, and the sense of being an outsider that all adults feel when they find themselves surrounded by kids and young people.

A human tide ebbed and flowed in all directions. Individuals and chattering clusters bumped into each other; apologies flew in all directions. Eyeglasses and ponytails, full beards and ridiculously wispy mustaches, brightly colored mohawks and combat boots: everyone looked different and yet everyone looked similar in gaze and gesture.

Large cork bulletin boards were stacked deep with archeological strata of announcements and ads: jobseekers and apartment hunters, offers of pets up for adoption, scooters and used clothing for sale, tutors touting their services and babysitters with their hourly rates. Clustering like swarms of bees, young people would congregate before a rumpled sheet of paper, tearing off a tab with a phone number, only to buzz off elsewhere.

Groups of students loitered, sitting on the steps of the staircase that led to the upper floors; if the weather had been any different they would have been out basking in the sunlight chatting about challenging exams and love stories; but that day the benches backing up against graffiti-covered walls were ice cold, and the only ones braving the chilly winds were the diehard smokers whom hall monitors and janitors had brusquely ejected from the atrium.

Lojacono and Di Nardo had asked Ottavia to call ahead and announce their visit, so they could be sure to secure a meeting with both Professor Forgione and his son, Renato, whom they wanted to interview a second time; the morning he had found the dead bodies, he'd been too traumatized to be fully lucid.

The two policemen had come to the conclusion that, unlike Grazia's world, multifaceted and filled with relationships that led in different directions—her boyfriend, her father, the modeling agency—Biagio's world was entirely contained within the walls of the building they were now inside.

When they reached the top floor, they emerged into a hallway along which ample windows let in streaming rays of sunshine. The throngs of the lower floors had subsided here. A woman welcomed them into an office stacked high with documents and then walked them through a second, even narrower hallway and up a short flight of metal steps to a door, on which she knocked. Lojacono secretly hoped that they'd have a guide on the way out as well, otherwise they were at serious risk of never finding the exit.

Professor Antimo Forgione, chair of the department of biochemistry in the School of Industrial Biotechnologies, came forward to greet them. He was a solidly built man, well tended and in his early sixties, with a strong resemblance to his son. He wasn't a very tall man, but his neatly brushed salt-and-pepper hair and the strong set of his jaw gave him an imposing presence, accentuated by the broad shoulders and beginnings of a potbelly that could be guessed at under the extremely well tailored navy blue blazer and regimental tie.

He gave Alex and Lojacono an open, cordial smile, with a faint hint of sadness.

"*Buongiorno.* Your colleague called the administrative office yesterday. I had a conference here in the city, but I postponed my attendance because I was eager to meet you as soon as possible. What happened to poor Biagio is a terrible thing. Here at the department we're all devastated."

The office wasn't big, and it looked lived-in and a little messy: a workplace, not a front devoted to public relations. With the professor's help, they cleared the two chairs in front of the desk of the stacks of scientific journals and graphs that cluttered them.

"Excuse the mess, things just seem to pile up at a terrifying rate. I wonder when this blessed digital revolution everyone's been talking about for years will finally get rid of all this paper. But please, make yourselves comfortable, and tell me what I can do to help the investigation. We assure you that we're willing to offer our wholehearted cooperation, and by we I mean the university, of course."

Lojacono thanked him with a nod of the head.

"Professor, rather than searching for anything in particular, we're trying to assemble as much information as we can. I'd like to get your impressions of the young man, and perhaps the names of everyone he knew and spent time with, as well as whether he had recently had any arguments, any quarrels. That kind of thing."

"Arguments? Quarrels? Biagio Varricchio? You obviously never met him. He was the kindest and gentlest person in the universe. Courteous to a fault, serious to a fault. There were times he'd come here and I, in the midst of all this mess, simply wouldn't notice that he was waiting, because he'd just stand there, next to where you're sitting now, and wait until I asked him what he wanted. No, I'd rule out entirely the idea that there had been quarrels here in the department."

Alex was taking notes on her pad.

"Had you known him long?"

Forgione furrowed his brow.

"Hmmm, let me think about that: the first time I noticed him was six years ago, during a biochemistry exam he took as a student. He was particularly brilliant. A genuine natural talent. Behind his calm and poise, he concealed a fertile and intuitive mind. There aren't many others like him, unfortunately."

"Why do you say unfortunately?"

The professor sighed.

"You see, Signorina, many of the young people who enroll in this department simply weren't admitted elsewhere. The difficulty of entrance exams for the departments of medicine, pharmaceutical sciences, or engineering means that students who were unable to get in elsewhere just enroll here, only to reapply to the departments where they were really hoping to be admitted. That means we get a lot of first-year students, but then those numbers subside with each passing year. There really aren't many students determined to devote themselves to our subjects, even though they're actually wonderful and fundamental, and offer important professional opportunities. But that's hard to get across."

"But that wasn't the case with Varricchio?" Lojacono asked.

"Biagio was here because this is where he wanted to be. I told you, it happens rarely, but luckily it does happen. He chose this as his major immediately after that exam, and I appreciated that too, because he wasn't doing it to get a high grade: this was his genuine passion. He was like a son to me."

Alex studied the professor's face: he seemed sincerely saddened.

"So are you saying that you had a closer relationship with him than with your other students?"

"Yes. You've met my son; I'm a lucky father, Renato's a talented young man and, God bless him, he's following in my footsteps: he's one of our most highly respected assistant professors. Well, Biagio was his best friend. They had been studying together ever since their second year in the department and they conducted research as a team. They coauthored several important articles for scientific journals, and a number of projects they began together were adopted by American universities we work with. It's something I'm very proud of."

"So you had an opportunity to really get to know him, then, Varricchio?"

Forgione's face darkened.

"Why, of course, he was always around the house. I wish I had a euro for every time I found him bent over his books at dawn, in my kitchen, after a whole night spent studying with Renato. He always had a smile on his lips, he was always apologizing for being in the way. A young man worth his weight in gold."

"What exactly were his duties here, in your office, then?" asked Lojacono. "What was his job? Did he teach?"

"Yes, but that wasn't his main activity. We try to make the best use of all our resources, and Biagio's strong suit was research, as is my son's. Together, the two of them were unstoppable, a force of nature. As a father I can tell you that I'm very concerned about the repercussions his death will have on Renato: he basically hasn't spoken a word in the past two days, he's in a state of shock. In any case, Biagio spent most of his time in the laboratory, working on tests and experiments on the materials that his research focused on."

"Could you be a little more specific?"

Forgione searched for something on his desktop.

"Well, he took his degree, with me as his advisor, with a very nice thesis on the bioengineering of metabolic enzymes. Rather innovative, not so much in terms of the topic as in the way he identified potential developments. Needless to say, he graduated with distinction. Ah, here it is, I've found it."

He opened a magazine on the desk, color printing, glossy paper. Under the headline of the article, "The Young Turks of Biotechnology", a photograph of a very embarrassed but still quite alive Biagio Varricchio gazed up at the policemen through the thick lenses of his glasses.

"Here, you can keep it," said Forgione. "It's published by the university, and the other students read it. The work done by Biagio and my son gained a certain degree of prestige. They're doing a research project on recombinant proteins, I hardly think it's worth trying to explain it to you, but if you like—"

Lojacono held up his hand.

"No, thanks, that won't be necessary. But, please forgive me if I insist on this point, Professor, but are you sure there wasn't any, I don't know, jealousy? Someone who might have been interested in taking over as—"

Forgione interrupted him, in a decisive tone.

"Absolutely not. Everyone does the job that they're assigned here: there are no rivalries because everyone does different things. What's more, unfortunately, we don't have much money, so there's not any real economic incentive for going to war. Our doctoral students are paid badly, without great prospects for advancement. Theirs is a labor of love, or else they do it as a way of one day getting a job in private industry."

Lojacono took advantage of the opportunity to bring up a new topic.

"Did you happen to get the impression at all recently that Biagio needed money in any particular way? That he had asked for an advance on his salary, or a loan from anyone?"

Forgione concentrated, trying to remember any episode that might line up with the theory of financial need laid out by the lieutenant.

"Not that I can think of. But I doubt it. I feel sure that if he had really been in dire straits he would have turned to me. My door was open to everyone, and all the more so for him. And then, Lieutenant, the doctoral candidates were always paid very late: he would only have had to ask for an advance on what little was owed him, and just as in other cases we would have found a way to help him out."

"And you didn't notice any changes, any shadows, in the last little while?" Alex asked.

The professor thought it over again. Lojacono noticed how he always took the questions asked very seriously; he took nothing for granted and didn't seem interested in proving that he had everything under control.

"Listen," Forgione said at last, "unfortunately, as you can well imagine, my job has become more bureaucratic than actually scientific, and these days I'm spending very little time in the laboratory. Though I do try to keep my relationship with my colleagues alive: I inquire as to what they're working on and periodically meet with them, if only for a chat . . . a good state of mind, mental freedom, and focus are all fundamental qualities in a scientist. If you want to get an answer to your question that's of any real value, you're going to have to talk to my son, but if I'm honest, I have to say, yes, in the last little while the young man had started to seem shut off and perhaps even a little preoccupied. The results of his work were still remarkable, but there had been a slight decline, and I have to say that in fact Renato was helping him, increasing his own contributions to the project. They thought I hadn't noticed, but I know my chickens."

"In your opinion, what was the cause of this impasse?" Alex asked.

Forgione shrugged his shoulders.

"I couldn't really say. But, according to my son, it was the arrival of Biagio's sister, whom I never even met, that brought a degree of . . . messiness into Biagio's life. Maybe even just a degree of activity and liveliness he wasn't accustomed to. I imagine that you're aware that Biagio occupied, rent-free, an apartment we own, and that therefore a certain procession of characters who were rather . . . particular had been mentioned to me by the building manager."

"Such as?"

"Apparently, a month or so ago, the young woman had a fight with her boyfriend in the atrium. An elderly woman who lives on the second floor was frightened by the shouting and lodged a complaint during the condominium board meeting."

The two policemen exchanged a glance: that must have been the fight mentioned by Paco Mandurino, one of the Varricchios' next-door neighbors. No doubt about it, the relationship between the late Grazia and Nick Trash had been a tumultuous one.

"Thanks, professor," said Lojacono, "you've been very helpful. Now we'd like to see where Varricchio worked. And we're going to need to talk to your son again. Maybe something will occur to him that might prove useful."

Forgione stood up.

"Why, of course. Come with me, I'll take you to the laboratory."

XXXV

Antonella Parise emerged from the funicular railway at the end of the line high atop the hill. With her tall, lithe figure, her agile step, her red hair tied back in a ponytail, she stood out in the crowd that flowed through the chilly morning air toward the various destinations of their workdays.

Romano and Aragona emerged from the shadows and came to a halt right in her path.

The woman pretended not to recognize them and tried to sidestep them, but Aragona darted quickly in front of her, barring her way.

"*Buongiorno*, Signora. We certainly seem to be in a hurry this morning. Wouldn't you have a moment to join us in an espresso?"

Parise snapped, angrily, "You have no right to go on pestering me. If you won't stop, I'll file a complaint with your superiors. Neither I nor my family have done a thing deserving of such—"

"And we'll be the first to present our apologies directly to your husband," Romano interrupted her, "since he doesn't have the slightest idea of what people think of him at your daughter's school. In fact, you know what? Let's go see him right away."

The woman said nothing, her green eyes leveled at the policeman's face. Then she turned and strode off toward the café near the funicular stop.

When they had sat down at the little café table and placed

their order for three espressos, the woman hissed: "Why can't you understand? There's nothing at all to find out. Nothing to investigate, nothing to discover. My daughter . . . she's raving, she's dreaming, she's fantasizing, but she just writes down her dreams. And that's all."

"You see, Signora," said Aragona, removing his glasses, "you don't have to convince us of it. We know that Martina made it all up."

"What? I mean, in that case, you . . . then, if so, why did you come up here? I need to get to work, I can't—"

Romano said, in a low voice: "So, aren't you interested in knowing how we came to this conclusion? Because I can imagine that you understand that the crime of which your daughter has accused her father is one of the foulest and most odious crimes known, a very grim matter that the law generally delves into without pity, bringing in psychologists and magistrates. These are long and painful procedures, and they can ruin a person's life. Or even many people's lives."

Antonella sat there silently, slowly shaking her head as if rejecting out of hand even the mere hypothesis of what Romano had just foreshadowed. A tear rolled down one cheek, and she wiped it away with a brusque gesture of one hand.

"No, I'm not interested in hearing how you figured it out. The only thing I'm interested in is having you leave me alone, and more importantly, having you leave my husband alone. He's a good person, and the last thing he deserves—"

Aragona let loose with a crude burst of laughter.

"Once again, we're completely in agreement, my dear Signora. Your husband is a good person, and this is the last thing he deserves. There are lots of things he doesn't deserve. Don't you agree?"

Romano was pretty sure that his partner had just been unnecessarily crude, and intentionally so, but he didn't feel he had the right to scold him for taking that minor satisfaction.

"We aren't interested in entering into the details of your relations," he said. "Luckily for us, that's none of our business. What does concern us, however, is the fact that your daughter is spreading the idea among the people who know you as a family that her father is molesting her. We need to understand why, in order to reassure people who might someday decide it's worth submitting a formal criminal complaint. So, either you talk to us, or else we'll have to talk directly to your husband."

For a few seconds, Antonella Parise sat there, motionless, inexpressive. Then the dam burst, and the woman opened her heart to Romano and Aragona as if they were a pair of father confessors, not a couple of cops.

My husband doesn't make much money. It's not like he doesn't make much in any absolute terms, I realize there are people who get by on far less and maybe even have more children. I've often thought that perhaps that was our mistake: if we'd had more than one child, the kids might have had their heads screwed on a little straighter.

Martina, you know, is intelligent. Really intelligent. And clever, too. She's always been a sharp kid, much more so than other girls her age. She knows how to manipulate people to get them to do what she wants; she has the gift of guessing other people's weak points and using them to her own advantage. I know, it's not very nice for a mother to talk this way about her own daughter, but it's the truth.

The parents do their best, but it's just that sometimes they don't realize that what they think is their best really isn't. For instance, we wanted the girl to attend an elite school, alongside the children of distinguished professionals and industrialists. We thought that by doing that we'd give her a path to enter fine society, and perhaps, in time, to meet someone who could emancipate her from her mediocre status.

We were wrong.

We were wrong, because the only thing we achieved was to instill in her a sense of inadequacy. She learned to act a certain way, instead of being something specific. And she developed a sense of envy.

My daughter envied her girlfriends or, actually, her classmates, from the first day of school on. She envied them their shoes, their jackets, their backpacks, their chauffeur-driven cars that dropped them off at school, the homes to which she was invited for parties. Since she couldn't rival the other girls in terms of clothing or social circles, she decided to become their leader. And she succeeded.

She started hating her father three years ago. She blamed him for what he couldn't afford to buy for her. And in the end she couldn't think of anything better to say than that Sergio is a miserable loser, unable to provide us with what we deserve. She didn't take it out on me because I'm pretty so, in her opinion, I just need to find a wealthy boyfriend and make her rich too. Her father, on the other hand, is nothing but a ball and chain, a hindrance.

In a certain sense, it was she who pushed me into the arms of Pasquale, the owner of the shop where I work. Our relationship began before he hired me; we met in the waiting room at the dentist's office where I took Martina. She calls him Uncle Lino, short for Pasqualino. He buys her fake affection and, more importantly, her silence, by giving her gifts, and in exchange, she offers him an opportunity to . . . well, it seems to me that you already understand that part.

Are you wondering if I feel dirty for what I've done? Yes, I feel dirty. But not for the reasons you're probably imagining.

My husband knows about my relationship. About six months ago, Martina told him about it, hoping that that would drive him away. She thinks that if we can just get rid of Sergio, Pasquale would leave his wife and all three of us could live together in happy luxury. That, of course, is not what would happen. It's one thing to hand a young girl a hundred euros so that you can fuck her mother without being disturbed or inconvenienced, it's quite another matter to destroy your life. What's more, everything's in his wife's name, and he'd be left without a penny to his name.

I tried to explain it to my daughter, but she's convinced that if we play our cards right, it'll all turn out for the best. The only obstacle as far as she can see is Sergio. When she tried to tell him, he started yelling that he didn't believe it and that he wouldn't believe it even if he saw it with his own eyes. He didn't even ask me to quit my job, because in that case we would have to retrench drastically: sell the car, move house . . . And things would just be worse. Better to turn away and pretend nothing's happened.

Martina's latest fixation is this thing with sexual molestation. So you're not willing to leave? she decided. Then I'll get them to come take you away. I'll get you arrested. She got the idea from a TV show in which the father is hit with a restraining order keeping him from coming within a mile of his children. Ridiculous, isn't it?

I no longer love my husband, let's be clear about that. We were just kids when I got pregnant with Martina. But that doesn't mean I'd dream of accusing him of that kind of filthy crime, not in my wildest dreams. I'd rather just go on living like this, at this point, I can't turn back time.

I know I can't.

Romano and Aragona sat there in silence, their eyes fastened to the woman's face.

They stood up, went over to the cash register and paid for their espressos, and left the café with an oppressive sense of anguish that they hadn't had when they'd gone in.

There was just one last thing to do, before they could consider the matter settled.

XXXVI

Lojacono and Alex followed Professor Forgione through a maze of hallways and staircases. The lieutenant was increasingly convinced that without an expert scout to guide them back out, they would have remained prisoners for the rest of their lives in the coils of that building.

When they got to the laboratory, they were quite impressed. The place was spacious, tidy, and spotless. Deep down inside, the lieutenant was forced to admit that often his negative prejudices against that dirty and chaotic city were proven wrong by the things he encountered in real life.

Renato was standing in front of a complicated system of test tubes and very narrow glass pipes. He was staring into the middle distance, as pale as a rag; with one hand he was tormenting the hem of his lab coat. His grief at the loss of his friend and the trauma of having stumbled upon his corpose were far from having been metabolized.

There were at least eight or ten other people in the room, and at the sight of the professor they all grew agitated. It was clear that the boss was rarely seen around there, and the general intent was clearly to make a good impression.

"Signori, *buongiorno* to you all," said Antimo Forgione. "Forgive us if we interrupt the work you're doing. As you know, the university and our institute in particular have suffered a terrible loss, that of our friend Dr. Varricchio. This gentleman and lady are from the police and they're conducting an investigation into the case. I'd like to ask you to make yourselves available to them and answer any questions they may wish to ask of you."

Lojacono appreciated the peremptory tone of that request.

"Thanks, Professor. For the moment, we're happy just to speak with your son, whom we have already met before."

The others in the room exchanged glances, heaving a sigh of relief, and silently went back to the work that they'd been doing.

Renato came over, saying hello.

The professor led them to an office that was separated from the larger room by glass walls, transparent but soundproof.

"Renato," he told his son, "these policemen want to know about the last period of Biagio's life: how he was doing, whether he was having any troubles. I told them what I could, but you were his friend. I also told them that recently you'd been covering up for his shortcomings with the work you did . . ."

The young man waffled defensively.

"Papà, come on, I told you a thousand times, that's not the way it was, he—"

The professor gently touched his arm.

"My dear boy, do you think I don't know how to judge my own coworkers? I always know what you're doing in here, and also what you aren't. For the past six months, for the most part you've been in charge of the projects assigned to the two of you. But that doesn't matter, I knew just how capable and skilled Biagio was, it was just a matter of waiting for the bad times to be over. Unfortunately, as we know, they didn't end at all."

Renato opened his mouth, and then shut it again. The hand that he raised to adjust his eyeglasses was trembling.

Lojacono and Alex were speechless. Before his partner had a chance to say something unnecessary, Lojacono took back control of the situation.

"Professor, we thank you for your time. We don't want to take up any more of it. Why don't you let us ask a few questions of our own? We'd like to spend a few more minutes with young Dr. Forgione, here, and then we'll get out of your hair."

"Let me thank you for your diplomatic approach, you want to talk to Renato alone because you think that he might find it awkward to talk with me here. But let me assure you that my son and I have no secrets between us, and—"

The young man weighed in, decisively.

"Papà, why don't you just let us talk. Biagio wouldn't have wanted me to reveal things in your presence that he had told me in confidence."

Forgione nodded.

"Yes, you're probably right. Signori, my regards. If you need anything, you know how to get in touch."

And he left the room.

Once the professor had left the laboratory, after saying goodbye to the other researchers, the young man relaxed. Alex recognized in his eyes the often debilitating effects of the influence of an authoritative father.

Renato caught her look, and sighed.

"My father is a great scientist, a fantastic man, but sometimes he just doesn't understand certain situations."

Lojacono tried to reassure him.

"Don't worry about that. Among other things, he was very helpful, and I assure you that's rarely the case. To come back to us, when we spoke with you at the apartment, we were interested in you inasmuch as you were the one who found the victims. Now we'd like to talk to you as a friend of Biagio Varricchio's, to better understand his life and his sister's life. We're going to need to track back to whoever—"

Renato waved his hand.

"I understand perfectly. Go ahead and ask: I'm as eager as

anyone to ensure that whoever committed . . . that terrible deed should be identified and made to pay for it."

Alex noticed that the resemblance between father and son become more unmistakable the moment that the young man lost his usual indecisive expression.

"The professor referred to the fact that Biagio had been somewhat distracted on the job. Can you tell us more?"

Renato gently shook his head.

"You see, our line of work involves a few initial hunches followed by lengthy, boring routines, taking measurements, rechecking them, experimenting: all to prove whether a single hypothesis is true or false. All it takes is the slightest oversight and you run the risk of taking for granted a reaction or a process that invalidates all the rest. Error lurks around every corner."

"So?"

"Biagio was always a fantastic researcher, full of brilliant hunches but especially determined and careful when it came to the successive steps, the process of verification. Recently, though, it was as if he'd lost his ability to concentrate. I had to double check his data, which delayed the completion of the research project. I think that's what my father was talking about. I was happy to do it, Biagio helped me out when I was studying, and even afterward: in some sense I was just returning the favor. It was a bad time for him."

Alex wanted to get a clearer understanding.

"So are you saying that the problem was that Varricchio's calculations, or whatever they were, had to be done over again?"

"That was part of it. Then there was the issue of how seldom he was showing up in the laboratory. He'd stay at home with his laptop and say he was working from there. But he'd stopped bringing anything back here. It was clear that he had other things on his mind."

"Had he confided in you the reason for his uneasiness?" Lojacono asked.

Renato shrugged his shoulders.

"Biagio didn't talk much, in part because he didn't have anything going on outside of the university. He used to say that he'd start going out, spending time with other people, once he'd attained the professional goals he'd set for himself. Actually, though, he was just shy, even with me, and I was his only friend."

"But you must have had some idea of your own, right?"

"You can't live with a person for ten or twelve hours a day without understanding, at least a little, what is going through his mind. The problem was his sister."

"Had he told you anything about her?" Alex persisted.

"Yes. When he was at the university, we would eat lunch together, and if we were working late, I would drive him home. In those periods of time, he had an opportunity to chat a little bit."

The young man tended to dole out information with an eyedropper. Perhaps that was typical of the work he did, Lojacono thought to himself.

"Then, do you think you could explain to us why his sister would have been a problem?"

Renato looked at him, in some surprise.

"Didn't you talk to Paco and Vinnie? Grazia had turned Biagio's life upside down. Before she came, everything was calm and quiet, there was a smooth and orderly routine. After she arrived, the place turned into a circus. Just think, when there was work to be done even after the laboratory had closed for the night, Biagio preferred to come to my house, just like in the old days when we'd study together. In fact, if I didn't see him for a while I'd start to worry. That's actually why I dropped by to see him the other morning."

"What do you mean, a 'circus'?"

"That her boyfriend would come and go, and he and Grazia were always fighting furiously. Then there was his father, constantly threatening to show up there and drag his daughter back down to the village. Biagio was terrified of him. He described him as a hulking monster, violent and capable of anything. Then there was the whole thing with the photograph."

"What photograph?"

"Grazia had brought Biagio a snapshot with her name on it that she'd had taken for a modeling agency; she was practically nude, wearing nothing but a skimpy swimsuit. Only her boyfriend happened to get a look at it, too, and he ripped it into a thousand pieces and then attacked her. Biagio, who certainly was no fighter, found himself forced to stand up for her."

Lojacono thought it over. The episode fit in with everything he'd learned when he'd questioned Foti and Cava; and the young man's reaction seemed to fit right in with his personality.

"What was Biagio planning to do?" he asked.

"He loved his sister very much. In an almost paternal way. He'd worked himself half to death to be able to study and at the same time pay for her expenses living with their aunt and uncle. I myself helped him out financially when he was in his direst straits. I think he wanted to go on helping her, but she had no other real gifts, aside from her beauty. Becoming a model, all things considered, was a pretty good idea, and Biagio was happy about it. But her boyfriend and the father would never have allowed her to do it."

"And so?" asked Alex.

"And so Biagio was in a state of crisis. His mind was accustomed to finding solutions, but now it was chasing endlessly around the problem without being able to make head or tails of it. And that was draining him, exhausting him. Sadly."

"Speaking of money, Doctor," Lojacono jumped in, "had

Varricchio asked you for any money, recently? Even a small sum, but above and beyond his usual needs."

"No. He never asked for money, maybe I didn't make myself clear. I would sense when he needed money and arrange to get it to him. The apartment, for instance: I let him have it years ago, when I realized that living in a pensione was forcing him to study in bed, by the dim light of a bare bulb. Or the grocery shopping, the household staples like laundry detergent and other cleaning supplies that I'd send around periodically. For his other needs, the salaries that we get here, when we get them, were more than sufficient for him. At least, until his sister arrived. But he never asked me for a cent."

Lojacono exchanged a glance with Alex.

"Doctor, we thank you for the information that you've given us. If we were to need anything else—"

"He was an extraordinary young man, you know? A wonderful friend. And he would have been a great scientist, the kind that really leave their mark. My father thinks that, of the two of us, I was the more brilliant, but he is completely wrong. Biagio was a shy type, and even when he was interviewed by the universitary magazine, he was very shy, but he had remarkable abilities."

"We're sure that's true, Doctor. We're sure of it," Alex murmured.

Renato stared at her. His eyes, behind the lenses of his glasses, were welling over with tears.

"He was my friend. I loved him very much. No one will miss him more than I will."

XXXVII

The principal, Tiziana Trani, hadn't expected to receive another visit from Romano and Aragona so soon. To tell the truth, she had hoped never to see them again as long as she lived, because that would mean that the ugly story of Martina Parise was a gross exaggeration.

When she found them waiting at the door to her office, accompanied by her secretary, she felt her heart lurch in her chest.

Romano greeted her.

"Please forgive us for just showing up like this, Signora, but we need to speak to you. Urgently."

The principal studied them, clearly worried. She gestured to her secretary, who left the room, closing the door behind her.

"Then it's true? Really? Oh, my God," she said as soon as they were alone.

Aragona made his usual grimace and removed his eyeglasses.

"No, Signora. It's even worse, in a certain sense. Could you summon Professoressa Macchiaroli? Maybe she ought to be present, too."

In class 2B, a sleepy hour of Musical Education was under way. They were talking about solfège and scales, or rather, the elderly teacher was, but it was a soliloquy, while most of the students were texting each other under their desks.

The whole classroom's interest was aroused by the arrival of Professoressa Emilia Macchiaroli, who knocked on the door, stuck her head in, and called Martina Parise's name in the grave tone of someone reading a funeral announcement. Before leaving the room, the girl exchanged a conspiratorial glance with two female classmates seated directly behind her.

The whole way down the hallway to the principal's office, the literature teacher never spoke to her once, and she busied herself replacing her triumphant expression with one better suited to the role of sexually molested adolescent, a grim, sorrowful look.

When she saw Romano and Aragona sitting at Principal Trani's desk, she pretended that she was astonished. Actually, she'd never believed for a second in that story about them being administrative investigators: the noose was tightening, at last. Of course, there was still a risk of that idiot mother of hers denying everything, but then she had read that it was normal for a wife to refuse to accept the truth when confronted with evidence that her husband was molesting their daughter. The investigators wouldn't believe her mother, and soon she'd be free to enjoy their new life.

In any case, the last thing she cared about was whether or not that insignificant creature, her father, was sent to jail. All she cared about was getting him out from underfoot. After all, out of her twenty-five classmates, no fewer than nineteen of them had parents who were either separated or divorced, and they were all having a high old time, battening off their fathers' sense of guilt and their mothers' abiding resentment.

The principal wasted no time on preliminaries.

"Martina, the other day, we told you a little white lie. These gentlemen aren't administrative investigators, they're from the police."

No kidding.

"What you wrote in your essays, and also what you told us

when we met here, didn't persuade them, and they decided to delve a little deeper."

Good.

The less ridiculous policeman of the two, the one with the square face, addressed her directly.

"Yes. We dug a little deeper, and now we believe that what you wrote in your essays might be true. Even if you claim you just made it up."

Well, aren't you clever.

"But we need evidence, and that's what we're missing."

So what the hell do you want, a video on YouTube?

"So there are two options: either we find the evidence, or you need to make a nice, clear, detailed complaint."

A complaint. Well, that might be cool: an interview on afternoon TV, pictures in the newspapers . . . it's just too bad that, since I'm a minor, they'll have to pixelate my face.

The ridiculous one weighed in, toying around with those horrible Seventies glasses of his.

"Naturally, without any evidence and without confirmation on your mother's part, the criminal complaint will mean transferring you to a group house, at least for the duration of the investigation."

What the fuck is this asshole talking about?

"What . . . what exactly is a group house?"

The ridiculous cop went on, beatifically.

"A small community in a place far away, run by psychologists and volunteers, where they take in maladjusted children guilty of minor crimes that don't call for incarceration, or else children who have been, as in your case, the victims of domestic violence."

So, basically, a community of losers and criminals.

"You'll have to change schools, too. But you'll be assured of an education at one of the special institutions that operate with considerable success in the more challenging parts of town.

The staff at those institutions know how to manage this type of situation."

The policeman with the square jaw shot a grim look at the ridiculous one. Maybe he didn't want him to reel off all that information.

It still wasn't over. Of course, that idiot mother of hers would provide all the confirmation she needed: she had her by the short hairs.

Martina spoke, in a low voice, gazing into the empty air, with a disoriented and pained demeanor.

"But what if . . . if my mother were to say that it was all true?"

The one with the massive jaw put on a falsely contrite expression.

"We talked to your mother this morning. She denies in the most absolute terms the idea of any molestation."

Everyone's eyes—the principal, the schoolteacher, and those damned policemen—were fastened on her. The assholes had come to an agreement.

The ridiculous one piled on: "You needn't worry. Of course, in the group house, you won't be allowed to have a cell phone, a computer, or a tablet, because it's important to avoid any ongoing contact with your original environment, nor will you be able to talk to your current classmates, but we're certain you'll make other friends, among the other girls who share your terrible condition."

Martina leapt to her feet. There was a joyous and innocent smile on her face.

"So you fell for it! Forgive me if I wasted your time, I really wanted to make sure that my story was realistic. When I grow up I'd like to be a writer and I wanted to do this experiment."

Aragona was disconcerted.

The girl gave him a sweet smile.

"Don't worry, my family is perfectly happy. Deliriously happy."

Romano shot her a furious glare.

"Listen, Signorina, do you really think you can play pranks about certain matters? Do you realize that your father could have been in serious trouble?"

Martina continued smiling.

"But Dottore, do you think that I would have dreamed of leaving my father in a mess of that kind? I just wanted to be sure that you would take me seriously. Can I go back to my class now, please? There's an interesting music lesson, and I wouldn't want to miss it."

Principal Trani heaved a sigh.

Aragona said: "If I were you, I'd think about becoming an actress, not a writer. You seem more cut out for it."

"Oh, really? Thanks. I'll keep that in mind." And she strode lightly to the door.

As her hand came to rest on the door handle, it was frozen in place by Professoressa Macchiaroli's hissing voice, which had remained silent until that instant.

"I think we'll have a pop quiz soon, Parise. I'm really curious to see how well you study in the idyllic environment you have at home."

Martina left the room without turning around.

But her ears had turned beet red.

XXXVIII

Deputy Chief Ottavia Calabrese sat down at her desk, her face hidden behind her computer screen. She had had to go out because she'd been summoned to her son Riccardo's school. Usually it was her husband who tended to that sort of emergency, but for once they hadn't been able to get hold of him.

Over time, they'd come to a tacit understanding: until Ottavia got home in the evening, anything that had to do with Riccardo fell under Gaetano's jurisdiction. The fact that Gaetano was a respected and prominent engineer who ran a company with fifteen employees—as well as the fact that in the midst of an economic downturn he earned twenty times the salary of a government civil servant like her, and that his time was, therefore, from the point of view of their family economy, far more important than hers—wasn't the kind of consideration to be brought to the fore. And, in fact, Gaetano never did bring it up.

The truth is, thought the policewoman as she signed on to her email, that Gaetano, for who knows what reason, felt responsible for Riccardo's condition. As if he possessed the absolute certainty that the mysterious gene responsible for the birth of that son secluded in a world all his own had come from him, and that as a result, Ottavia's life had been ruined.

All of it true, she fiercely told herself. All of it true.

Because it was true that one of her husband's great-uncles had been strange and mentally disturbed and that his parents and siblings had kept him hidden until the day that, at the age of twenty, he had jumped off the balcony.

It was true that in their first years of marriage Gaetano had taken precautions because he hadn't wanted children, and then he had finally given in to her demands and done her this great favor.

It was true that she had never accepted Riccardo and that she put up with him as her burden, her undeserved cross to bear.

It was a bitter irony that the boy could only emerge from his shell a little when he had her near him. That he'd sit on the floor in silence, that he'd lay his head on her legs and continue murmuring in a dull monotone that one word, *Mamma, Mamma, Mamma*: not an invocation, not a plea, not even an accusation.

Gaetano changed him, washed him, and took him to school, insisting relentlessly with the teachers on the importance of stimuli. He had taken him to a thousand doctors around the world, and he still was searching for others to contact; he read publications on the topic, he reached out to parents' associations and university clinics.

Every so often, just to wound him, Ottavia would ask him if he'd received any newsletters lately from Lourdes or Medjugorje, or whether he could rely on even more highly placed connections. Her husband would shake his head and then walk away, realizing that this was one of those moments.

It was always one of those moments, Ottavia would have liked to tell him. Always, if she was at home. Only when she went out to take the dog for a walk did she regain a piece of herself. And only at work was she truly happy.

If she had plotted on a Cartesian curve her mood over the course of the day, the result would have been a steady rise from seven in the morning until three in the afternoon, a progressive decline from three until seven in the evening, a sudden spike when the time came to bid Palma goodnight, and then a collapse until seven the following morning.

Palma, Palma, Palma. The handsome, rumpled commissario, the man with tired, kind eyes who had brought a smile back into her life, along with a deep concern, a sense of languor, a hint of uneasiness, and a grace note of hope. Palma, who had led her in front of a mirror, naked, to search for imperfections she could mend. Palma, who perhaps—though she was cautious not to get her hopes up—smiled at her occasionally in a very special way. In a way he smiled at no one else.

She shot a furtive glance around her monitor. At the others.

Romano and Aragona had returned to the office while she'd been out and, in response to her courteous request as to whether they had come to any conclusions with respect to the alleged molestation of the girl at the Sergio Corazzini Middle School, their only response had been a muted grunt. They weren't a particularly well-suited pair, but then no pair that included Aragona could be. That young man was a real piece of work, no two ways about it.

A real piece of work, the phrase almost made her laugh. Riccardo was a real piece of work, Marco wasn't, the most eccentric quality he had was the occasional blindingly garish shirt.

That very morning, her son had climbed up on his desk and had peed on the classmate sitting in front of him, who hadn't noticed a thing until he felt the stream of warm liquid on top of his head.

It had taken Ottavia fifteen minutes to get to the school and another half hour to calm her son down; he just wouldn't stop screaming and wriggling free from the hall monitors as they struggled to keep him from rushing out of the classroom by main strength. She'd spent another hour trying to explain to the principal, the teacher, and the mother of the bespeckled classmate that they had to do their best to be understanding:

Riccardo didn't always understand what he was doing. Another fifteen minutes to get back to the office, for a total of two hours wasted, while the ever attentive Gaetano continued his building inspection, his expert evaluation, or whatever the hell else it was that he was engaged in somewhere his phone was getting no bars. Ah, the delights of motherhood.

Now, though, she was finally back in the squad room, accompanied by Romano, Aragona, and Pisanelli, while Alex and the Chinaman were out on the streets, on the hunt. The door to the commissario's office was shut, as it was whenever he was out.

He must be at police headquarters again, thought Ottavia. Let's keep our fingers crossed.

The fear that the police precinct would be shuttered had been kindled in her by her pride, wounded by the unseemly episode that had swept over the old structure, and then by the desire to prove that they weren't all unworthy, her new colleagues and she herself. Now she didn't want to lose a setting where she felt fully alive, where she had goals to fight for, without that vague feeling of apathy that derived from her sense of resignation. The resignation that she could sense growing inside her every time she thought about her son.

But in order to keep hope alive it was indispensable to find at least a suspect in the case of the two murdered siblings. That's what Palma had said. She hoped that Alex and the Chinaman would be back soon with something new to contribute.

Scrolling down through the email that had come in while she was gone, she saw with a surge of joy what she had been waiting for. She'd have something to report at the meeting.

Palma said goodbye and left the police chief's office. The umpteenth meeting had ended with a big fat nothing as a result.

The climate wasn't especially favorable. There was no legacy of trust around the Bastards of Pizzofalcone. Certainly, no one had dared to use that terminology in his presence, but that was clearly the upshot. The previous successful investigations had left no lasting impression in the minds of his superiors, at least nothing capable of standing up to the brutal shove that had been given to the reputation of the police by that earlier incident of cops peddling confiscated narcotics, the regrettable affair that had caused the lasting stench. All the same, Palma suspected that that wasn't the real point.

The real point was that his colleagues were convinced they'd cleverly foisted off so much dead weight, people who were useless or even toxic, and they were extremely reluctant to entertain the idea that they'd misjudged their staff. And in particular they refused to believe that a newly minted commissario such as Palma could have succeeded in transforming that motley crew into a team worthy of the name.

A Sicilian accused of collusion with the Mafia and thefore shipped off to gather moss at the San Gaetano precinct, in a dusty office in the police station where he spent time playing solitaire on the computer, had somehow turned into a world-beating investigator; a side of beef of a cop, an oversized lunk who in Posillipo had come close to murdering a hooligan with his bare hands, had now become a disciplined and intelligent policeman; a madwoman who had fired her pistol in the police station where she worked had been transformed into a perceptive and determined officer; a sort of Harlequin clown who had avoided being kicked off the force for rank incompetence only because of highly placed connections was actually turning out to be an intuitive and sagacious investigator. And the hand-me-downs from the original precinct, the only ones that the tempest of the original Bastards had spared, a mercurial and daydreaming deputy captain and a competent and well-liked matron with an obsession for computers, long considered little more than a secretary, had managed to put together the most efficient database for criminal investigators in the entire greater metropolitan area. It wasn't easy to swallow for administrators who had decided and declared that there was no blood to be squeezed from these stones.

All the same, as Palma climbed into his car and headed back to his police station, he knew all these things, and he had stated them loudly and clearly to the police chief himself, as he advised Palma to give up the case. The police chief liked Palma, and maybe it was because he caught a glimpse of himself in him, the same youthful enthusiasm, the same stubborn determination that had driven him early in his career. He knew that he wouldn't survive a failure in this atmosphere, and so he was offering an honorable way out. But Palma was convinced he could still pull it off. His team was competent and talented, and what's more, they wanted to prove to the world that they still knew how to do their job, and do it well.

In the battle he was fighting, Palma had found an unexpected ally, Laura Piras. Well known for her absolute intransigence and rigor and for her unwillingness to brook incompetence, the female magistrate had instead treated the Pizzofalcone team with great indulgence, right from the very outset. Her opinion, fortunately, was regarded very highly, largely because she was tireless and thoroughly prepared, and because nearly all the important cases that came through that office sooner or later wound up on her desk.

In other words, the police chief and Piras for the defense, and all the rest of the city's police force for the prosecution. He was slightly outnumbered, Palma told himself. And now the press and the television news were piling on against him, too. The police spokeswoman might be fighting like a lioness, but how long could the wall of silence erected to protect the confidential nature of the investigations hold out against a story that so unsettled public opinion?

Palma shivered from the cold and from his uneasiness. They needed to come up with something, and they needed to do it fast. Anything at all. He had confidence in his team and in himself, but he had no trust in his luck. He hoped with all his heart that, for once, his luck would change and he'd be blessed with a windfall of some kind. He didn't want to lose his team. He didn't want to lose the Bastards of Pizzofalcone.

Most of all, he didn't want to lose Ottavia.

He pressed his lips together and stepped on the accelerator.

XXXIX

Palma made his entrance into the squad room just after Lojacono and Alex had returned.

The commissario seemed upset. He didn't bother to say hello, he just started talking right away.

"So here's the way things stand: they already have a team ready to replace us on the Varricchio case. The excuse is that in this fucking city the television news and the press are talking about nothing else, and the police force can't afford to be made to look like fools. I acted like a madman, I said that we're working hard and working well, that a great many people are involved and that we have to be given at least the time we need to interview them. In response they started raising their voices and saying things that I don't even want to repeat here."

If someone like Palma, usually so decorous, had begun using curse words, he must be churning with adrenaline, thought Ottavia.

Lojacono spoke for them all.

"So how did it end?"

"I just outshouted them. I told them that I expected them to give me a written document detailing exactly what missteps we had committed and how they would have done better in the same situation. Luckily, Piras was there, and she backed me up. She's monitoring the investigation as the magistrate responsible, and she reiterated her full faith and confidence in the work we're doing. They had to eat crow, and believe me, they didn't like it, but they had to put up with it, for now."

Everyone heaved a sigh of relief.

To the surprise of his colleagues, Pisanelli let himself go in a burst of exultation.

"Well done! I can just see them there, sitting in the front row, all the rival officers: they're just itching to get their hands on our territory, which is centrally located and therefore entails regular interactions with the prefect and his lady wife, the mayor and *his* lady wife, and the police chief and *his* lady wife."

"Exactly. What's more, the officials who rejected the lot of you are eager to prove that they were right and that I, the police chief, and Piras were all dead wrong. But let's not waste any more time on this piffle. Romano, Aragona: where are we with the molested girl?"

Romano broke in brusquely.

"Case closed, chief. Just as we'd imagined, it was pure fantasy; the girl was just looking to be the center of attention. We're certain about it now, believe me. And I can guarantee you that no criminal complaint will be filed."

Palma shot a contented glance at him and at Aragona.

"Excellent, once things have settled down, you can tell me the details. Starting today, the whole team is working full-time on the Varricchio case. Lojacono, Di Nardo, any news?"

Alex, leafing through her notebook, brought her colleagues up to date on the state of progress, including the visit they'd paid to the university that morning.

When Alex was done, Ottavia weighed in: "I have something, too. The medical examiner's report has come in: they were very fast, clearly they're getting plenty of pressure, just like we are. If you like, I can read it to you all."

"We're all ears," said Palma.

"All right, then: as far as the young man is concerned, 'the body presents, in the vicinity of the occipital region and the adjacent left parietal region, multiple stellate lacerations and contusions due to successive blows inflicted with a blunt object possessing a projecting edge, traces of which can be found, in negative relief, at a number of separate points on the scalp surface—'"

"Meaning someone smashed him over the head repeatedly," said Aragona under his breath.

Ottavia went on, her eyes glued to the computer: " . . . upon the removal of the pericranial soft tissues, evidence was found of a left occipital-parietal fracture, with multiple fracture lines, two of which are full-thickness lines."

"What are full-thickness lines?" Alex asked.

Romano replied brusquely.

"It means that the blows shattered his skull. Through and through."

Ottavia got to the conclusion: "Cerebral hemorrhage and locuses of multiple cerebral lacerocontusion in the left posterior and cerebellar occipital and parietal cerebral region. Area of lacerocontusion also concerning the right frontal lobe, due to recoil."

There was a detectable surge of horror in the room. To some extent, the impersonal technical language only made what had happened to the young man even more atrocious.

"The killer came up behind him," Aragona said coldly. "One blow, then another and another, as he took it out on him. Driven by blind rage, and a lot of it, in any case."

Lojacono, impenetrable as always, nodded as if he were repeating a Buddhist precept.

"That's right. And rage multiplies the force of the blows."

"Now listen to what they write about the sister," Ottavia resumed, and heaved a deep sigh. "Hemorrhagic infarct of the deeper facial tissues, fracture of the nasal septum, and a circular fracture line at the right zygomatic arch. Infarct of the suprahyoid and infrahyoid muscles, with fracture of the lesser horn of the hyoid bone. Presence of foamy hematic material in the trachea and in the greater bronchi. Examination of the osseous segments of the cervical spine showed a fracture of the left superior facet of the axis vertebra. Array of signs pointing to violent mechanical asphyxiation, with hemorrhagic infiltration of the neck organs."

By the time she got to the last few words, Ottavia Calabrese's voice had started to falter. The woman had instinctively raised her hand to her throat.

Alex's eyes were open wide.

"So you're saying that first he smashed her face in, and then he strangled her? Is that it?"

"Not necessarily," Lojacono replied. "Maybe he just put a hand on her face to make her shut up, then he strangled her. In any case, he did it with enormous violence."

Romano nodded.

"Sure, that makes more sense. It doesn't say anything about lacerocontusions, so he didn't beat her. He didn't want her to scream."

Pisanelli spoke in a low voice, as if he were in church.

"It's different from the young man. With him, it was rage, here it's desperation."

Aragona turned to Ottavia.

"Okay, but did he screw her? I mean to say, you know, did he rape her?"

Setting aside the rather abrupt, direct manner, which was certainly less than elegant, that was the question that everyone else had on their lips.

Ottavia scrolled through the document with her mouse and resumed from the point where she had stopped.

"'Overall indications of violent mechanical asphyxiation in the context of manipulation of the neck. Vascular constriction, sympathetic inhibition, and cardiocirculatory arrest. The search for elements of objective correlation to sexual violence yielded no results: perineal, vaginal, and buccal swabs; absence of any lesions, either cutaneous or of the mucosal, that can be morphologically ascribed to other parties. No signs of previous sexual relations.'"

The silence that followed was heavy as a blanket, and every bit as suffocating. Alex and Lojacono saw Grazia's beautiful body stretched out on the bed before their eyes again; the others imagined it.

Aragona murmured: "No. He didn't screw her. Maybe she put up some resistance. Then her brother arrived, and—"

Lojacono stopped him.

"No. Her brother was seated, he was writing, he even had his pen in his hand. It doesn't add up."

Alex was shaking her head.

"The rage. The extreme violence. Biagio sitting peacefully at the desk. Grazia with no signs of rape. It could have been . . . "

Pisanelli continued her sentence as if it had been his own thought.

" . . . anyone. Her boyfriend, come to ask her for an explanation of the photographs . . . "

Romano: " . . . her father, who wanted to take his daughter back home . . . "

Aragona: " . . . Cava, the guy from the modeling agency, who couldn't come to terms with the idea that she no longer wanted to pose for him . . . "

Ottavia: " . . . one of the young men: Biagio's colleague or the two young men from the apartment next door."

Palma ran his hand over his face.

"Please, let's proceed in an orderly manner and without any preconceptions, or we're just going to get ourselves confused. Any news from the forensic squad?"

Ottavia was already on the phone. After a brief exchange, she hung up.

"They're almost done. We'll have the report this afternoon."

"All right," said Lojacono. "There's time to talk to Vinnie and his friend, Mandurino, and we can just hope we catch them at home. But we also need to figure out the thing about the money, the thirty-seven hundred euros that Grazia asked Cava to pay her for the photo shoot. It's too strange of a figure not to have some meaning."

Pisanelli threw both arms wide: "I've reached out to my banker friends, and neither of the two victims had a checking or savings account in the neighborhood. And, as you know, the registry for these things has been centralized, so we can rule out the idea that either of them had any relations with these banks, which are the most prominent ones. I don't think it makes any sense for someone to go and deposit a rather modest sum, all things considered, outside of the normal banking insitutions, or to use a front or false identity. And since it seems clear to me that murder for purposes of robbery can be ruled out entirely, if the money isn't in the apartment, then it means that they went out and spent it."

"Sure, but how?" asked Palma. "But for now, let's not waste time on conjectures. Lojacono, Alex: you swing by and talk to the Varricchios' neighbors. Romano and Aragona: after lunch, head over to the laboratory of the forensic squad and get them to give you the report, which will save us time. If you have to, wait there. Take advantage of the opportunity to ask for a list of the things that they inventoried in the apartment, maybe the money was there, hidden under a floor tile. Then we can all check back later."

XL

Brother Leonardo leaned over the table, pointing at the fried potatoes on Pisanelli's plate.
"You aren't going to eat those? All right then, give them here."

The deputy captain was always amazed at the wolfish voraciousness of his diminutive friend's appetite: he was the only human being he knew who was capable of chewing with both sides of the mouth to eat faster. From time to time, from the other tables in the Trattoria del Gobbo, someone would look over to watch the funny figure of that monk who had to put a cushion on his chair to reach the tabletop, while his feet, sockless in his sandals, dangled inches off the floor.

"So, do they feed you at the parish church?" Pisanelli ribbed him. "Or is it that the bigger monks don't leave you anything to eat?"

"Don't be ridiculous," Leonardo said, as he swallowed, "I'm the parish priest. In fact, one of these days I'm going to decide to be the only one eating, while all the other monks have to stand around me, serenading me with a Gregorian chant. You can't even begin to imagine how monks singing stimulates my appetite. But believe me, it's not a matter of hunger: I just don't like seeing waste. Do you know that with all the food the rest of you leave on your plates, you could feed all of equatorial Africa for many, many years?"

"Certainly. Remind me of it this evening, that way I'll pay to send dinner to a village in Kenya. You know that I don't eat as much as I used to."

Leonardo furrowed his brow. He looked like one of those ceramic figurines they set out in yards and gardens.

"Are you all right, Giorgio? Are you feeling well? When are you going to realize that you need to see a doctor? I really don't understand why you're so stubborn about it—"

Pisanelli raised his hand.

"Hold on there. Remember your promise: We aren't going to talk about that. My health remains parked outside like a car on the street. Otherwise, no more lunches. And seeing that it's my treat, I'd like you at least to keep your end of the bargain."

Leonardo wouldn't let go of it: "You don't seem to realize the crime you're committing against God by displaying such flagrant disregard for your own life and health."

Pisanelli cut a piece of meatball and popped it in his mouth.

"Mmm . . . meatballs in ragú almost make me think you might have a point: maybe there really is a providential God. Otherwise, there would be no such thing as meatballs, or they would have been separated from the ragú in the primordial chaos. And that truly would have been a shame."

Leonardo broke out laughing, in spite of himself.

"You're the most likable blasphemous miscreant that it's been my pleasure to know, Giorgio Pisanelli of the Pizzofalcone police precinct. And to return to an earlier point, it's only normal that it should be your treat. Vow of poverty, as you know. So tell me, what good things have you been up to lately?"

"No good things to speak of, that I can say with certainty. We're dealing with the double homicide of those two young Calabrians, you must have heard about it."

"How could I avoid it? It's the talk of the town, poor creatures. Have you found out anything?"

"No, unfortunately, nothing yet. We're groping in the dark. But we're all working together. And the two colleagues assigned directly to the case, Lojacono and Di Nardo, are fine investigators. I'm confident we'll get to the bottom of it."

Leonardo shot him a sidelong glance.

"Okay, but what about you? What exactly are you working on now?"

"I'm gathering information, as usual. And I'm still on the trail of the depressives, if that's what you're trying to find out. We've talked about that lots of times before."

"And lots of times before I've told you that you keep taking on things that are none of your business. It's admirable that you should try to help those who no longer want to live, but this idea of the mysterious suicider is just absurd. Sheer folly."

The deputy captain looked out the window, where the scattered passersby were looking for an open shop where they could escape the icy wind.

"Not bad. It would make a good title for a novel. *The Mysterious Suicider*. Have you ever thought of becoming a writer, Leona'? If you ask me, you could enjoy a successful career."

"Sure, sure, you can be the funny guy, but in the meantime your colleagues take you for a madman."

"Maybe so. It may be an obsession, but it helps me to make it through the day. It gives me a reason to get up in the morning, to go to work, and to look forward to the next day. It anchors me to the here and now and keeps me from ending it all, from trying to escape."

Leonardo stopped chewing and stared at his friend. Yes, Giorgio, you still have the will to live, even if you refuse to get treatment for your disease. The Lord can rest easy, you still haven't made up your mind to consign yourself to the Devil.

"And have you made any progress on your fixa . . . on your mission? You'd told me about that woman, Agnese. Do you know that she's one of my parishioners? That is, she would be, if she ever came to church, but if you ask me she's someone who's given up, who no longer has any wish to live."

Pisanelli turned his eyes back to the monk.

"No, Leonardo. That's not right. She has suffered a trauma,

in fact, a series of traumas. She lost her child, her husband left her, her mother died. She has no job, she has no friends . . . "

"And that tells you nothing? For a woman who's still relatively young, not to have any social life is a sign that she has lost any interest in the world. She doesn't even have the comfort of faith and—"

"That's it," Pisanelli hissed, "that's where you wanted to wind up: she has no faith, so she wants to die. Listen, that's not the way it is, Leona'. A person can do without."

Leonardo replied seraphically: "All right, tell me where you see it, all this desire to live that you see in your friend Agnese. Give me a good reason not to be afraid that tomorrow, or next week, in some deeper fit of depression, she won't decide to turn on the gas or swallow an entire bottle of pills. Talk me into it."

Two friends at a restaurant, sharing their weekly lunch. A senior policeman, elderly, weary, and sick, kept alive by an absurd conviction, and a diminutive monk, a caricature who seemed to have walked straight out of a story that grandparents tell their grandkids, harmless to all appearances: no one could ever have imagined that these were the two parties, prosecution and defense, of an occult tribunal where a person's life or death was decided.

Pisanelli looked down at his hands, motionless on either side of the sauce-spattered bowl. Then he looked up.

"The sparrow," he said.

Leonardo narrowed his bright blue eyes.

"The what?"

"The sparrow, Leona'. Do you remember the first time I told you about her? I told you that I'd met her because she was feeding the birds in the park outside the National Library."

Leonardo nodded.

"Well, ever since then, I've been going to the park to make sure that she's all right. I sit down next to her, give her a smile, and she smiles back. At first, my belief that she wants to go on living was based on a mere perception. She hadn't spoken a word to me, really. I was afraid she was an ideal target for the mysterious suicider, as you call him, his next candidate."

Leonardo was feeling uneasy.

"Giorgio, listen—"

The policeman stopped him.

"No, you listen to me. I told her things, and I'm sure that she listened to me, but she almost never answered me. She just went on scattering crumbs for the birds. Then, yesterday, something strange happened. Already I was amazed that she was there, with the terrible chill in the air . . . "

"Yes, but—"

"Hold on. At a certain point she starts talking. *She* starts talking to *me*! And she tells me that a sparrow, one of those sparrows, might just be Raimondo, her son, come there to see her."

"Her son? Raimondo? But didn't she lose him before he could be born?"

Pisanelli shot a look around the room to make sure nobody else was listening in on the conversation.

"Yes. But to her, after carrying him in her womb, he was still alive."

"It's absurd, you realize that, don't you?"

"Truth be told, you're the one who insists that a life is a life, in every sense of the word, from the instant of conception on. Or am I wrong?"

"And you think that Agnese wants to go on living because the child she never had is coming to visit her in the form of a sparrow? You realize that you're going crazy yourself?"

Pisanelli slapped his open hand down hard on the table, making the utensils rattle. The other diners looked around.

"No, I'm not crazy, I tell you. All I'm saying is that we've found common ground, I'm finally able to talk with her. And however absurd you may think it is, she's finally opened up to me."

Leonardo sat staring at his friend in silence.

"You're taking on an enormous responsibility, you realize that? Maybe we could have her committed to an institution, one of those places where—"

Pisanelli clenched his hand in a powerful grip.

"No, no, Leona'. It would be the death of her. She's rediscovering herself, I'm sure of it. It's only going to take a little while longer."

The monk's eyes were full of sorrow.

"I'm leaving the day after tomorrow, I have my spiritual exercises to attend to. I'll be gone for ten days. My absence is a terrible risk, you understand that?"

Pisanelli blinked rapidly in confusion.

"Why do you say that it's a risk? Who is it a risk for?"

Leonardo withdrew his hand from the clench and now he was patting the policeman's hand.

"For you, my friend, and for poor Agnese. Two souls adrift in this cursed loneliness that is the world out there. What's more, how will you get by without these lunches of ours? You'll have to eat my share."

"Impossible, Leonardo. Impossible."

XLI

In the street outside number 32 on Vico Secondo Egiziaca, Lojacono and Di Nardo rang the doorbell for the third time on the intercom with the faded nameplate reading "Varricchio—Amoruso and Mandurino," and for the third time they waited in vain for an answer. The cold showed no sign of relenting, even in the early afternoon, and on that corner where the apartment building that had been the site of the double homicide stood, it was even worse.

Lojacono's extremities were tingling and numb: that winter, he felt increasingly sure, would never end. For that matter, the city was reacting very badly to the persistence of that bad weather, shutting itself up in an unnatural silence. You couldn't hear the usual chorus of voices, no one was shouting, the windows weren't slamming, and even the car horns seemed to have subscribed to the universal vow of silence.

They were just about to turn to leave when the street door swung open and Paco appeared, bundled in a plaid blanket. The young man scrutinized them with unmistakable mistrust, pulled the door open a little wider, and, without inviting them in, vanished into the darkness of the atrium.

"The intercom doesn't work. It never has. It rings but you can't hear the person speaking, and if you want to open the door you have to come downstairs."

Having uttered these words with a moan, the young man headed back upstairs. Lojacono and Alex trailed after him. Before entering the apartment, they took a look at the front door of the Varricchio home. At the center of the door was a warning from the judicial authorities, fixed in place with duct tape.

The temperature indoors was only slightly more comfortable than it was out on the street. They noticed that the young men had tried to seal the French doors with rags and bits of felt, but still a draft streamed through the off-kilter aperture that made the electric heater's ineffectual efforts even more useless than usual.

Paco took the blanket off of his shoulders, revealing his total black attire from the previous visit, and then brusquely inquired if they wanted any coffee. Alex decided that he wasn't being intentionally rude: quite simply that was how the young man communicated with his fellow human beings.

The two police officers politely declined the offer.

"Please forgive me if I have to waste any more of your time," said Lojacono. "We just wanted to—"

"Vinnie's not here," said Paco, "he's at the university. He has a major exam in a few days and he needed to ask a professor a few things. I'm not sure when he'll be back."

"That doesn't matter, we just wanted a few items of information that you can certainly provide as well. Then, if it proves necessary, we can always come back later."

Paco said nothing. He sat down at the table, keeping his eyes downcast. His short hair betrayed a receding hairline and incipient pattern baldness at the top of his head. Without looking up, he said: "It's just become hellish here. Reporters every minute of the day. If you ask me, Vinnie is having the time of his life, he likes to talk, talk, talk, but I hate it. They won't leave me alone. I'll have to tell Renato, if it goes on like this we'll be obliged to leave."

"We can imagine," Alex broke in. "But considering what happened, it's only normal that people want to know. You just need to be patient: the same way it started, it will end."

"Sure, but right now the situation is intolerable."

Lojacono decided to get to the point.

"Signor Mandurino, do you remember anything unusual that happened in the days, in the hours prior to the night of the murder? I don't know, anything Grazia, or Biagio, might have said . . ."

Paco looked up at the lieutenant.

"Well, as far as Grazia was concerned, it was all always unusual, the things she did . . . In other words, she didn't have a normal life. She went out at all hours of the day or night, and it was never the same, she'd shout into the phone, laughing, quarreling. And her boyfriend was no better. When the two of them started shouting in dialect, you couldn't understand a thing."

"Was he here during the last few days?"

"No. We hadn't seen him around for a while. In any case, if you ask me, he was afraid that he was losing her. And that's why they fought constantly."

Lojacono appreciated the concise manner in which the young man had described relations between Foti and the Varricchio girl.

"What about the other fight you overheard? You couldn't understand anything that time either?"

"No. The only thing I could tell for sure is that there were two men arguing and that one of them was Biagio. It was strange, because Biagio never raised his voice."

"What were the Varricchio siblings like, personality-wise?" Alex asked. "Did they get along? Did they love each other?"

Paco stared at her. Little by little, his expression softened.

"So, you see, Vinnie has an odd personality. If he likes someone, they become his best friend; if he doesn't, they become an enemy. It's just something I have to put up with. Grazia was beautiful, and she was a good young woman. But her beauty either attracted people or repelled them. Maybe it's hard, being beautiful. I couldn't say."

Lojacono and Alex waited. They knew that Paco, after his fashion, was answering the question.

"And so the boyfriend, the phone calls, the people on the street. She was forced to be cheerful and strong. But she was neither the one thing nor the other. She was only herself when she was with Biagio."

Alex was starting to get curious.

"What do you mean?"

"They spent a lot of time together toward the end. Before, Biagio always used to go to the university: I'd run into him when he came in or out, and that was all. He'd smile, say hello, he wasn't a person who talked much. We saw each other occasionally, in the evening, maybe with Renato, but that was it. Then he started working at home, much more frequently. Maybe he was working on a project that didn't require being in the laboratory."

Lojacono tilted his head to one side, as if he were trying to hear a whisper.

"And the sister, did she stay at home with him?"

"No, no. She was always out of the house, for one reason or another. But when they were together, they'd smile at each other in a very particular way, as if only they understood each other."

The lieutenant followed his own line of thought. Alex wondered what it was he was trying to understand, what he was imagining.

"How long ago did Biagio start working mainly at home?"

Paco stopped to think.

"Vinnie was studying for his Civil Procedure exam, which would mean three months ago. When he's getting ready for a challenging final exam, he never moves from this table and he's constantly asking me to fix him coffee. I would take one to

Biagio, too, who studied with the door open, the way that we do, to get a little air to circulate; it's brutally cold out now, but believe me, when the weather is hot, it's like an oven in here. And so we'd keep the windows open, in both apartments, and the front doors, too. This was orginally one big apartment, did you know that?"

Lojacono persisted.

"So Biagio stayed at home to study?"

"He would stare at the computer screen, take notes, type a little, take more notes, check books and databases that he carried with him back and forth from the university on a portable hard drive, then he'd stare at the computer screen some more, and so on. If you ask me, he was studying. What do you think?"

Alex thought that unusual way of answering questions was amusing.

"Didn't anyone ever come to see him?"

"No. I'd say not. Every once in a while he'd jump up, check the time, stick his head in, and say: if my sister comes home, tell her I'm at the university, in the laboratory. Then, a couple of hours later, he'd come back and sit back down at the computer. I've never seen anyone work so hard."

"But you never heard him talk about any disagreement, any quarrels . . . "

"Biagio quarrel? Impossible. That's why we were so scared to hear that shouting in the afternoon, it wasn't normal. Among other things, let me say it again, he almost never had anyone over, except for Renato, who worried about him and would bring him groceries, that sort of thing. It even happened sometimes that we'd have to answer the door for him because the genius, over in his apartment, had fallen asleep and didn't hear the doorbell from the landing. One time we found him sprawled over his desk, snoring. We laughed and laughed. No, he really was an easygoing guy."

"And when he wasn't around, the times that he had to go to the laboratory, did his sister bring anyone home? Or did anyone come over to see her? Did you ever happen to see anyone out of the ordinary?"

Alex thought about Cava, the chilly, remote gaze, arms wrapped around his torso as he stared out the window of his office at the nothing that lay outside. That man, she couldn't say why, gave her the creeps.

Paco tried to remember.

"No. As you've seen for yourself, we can't work the street door from up here. Each of us has their own doorbell on the landing, but the intercom rings simultaneously in both apartments, which means that if someone came to see them, we'd know it, too, and if someone came to see us, then they'd know it, too. Among other things, in here our cell phones get practically no bars, which means that just pressing random buttons on the intercom is the only way to get in the front door. Someone would always come downstairs, we never needed to establish whose turn it was. Worst case, if no one was getting up, we'd shout across."

Lojacono was concentrating.

"So let me reiterate: the intercom rings but that's all it does, and you get no service with your cell phones, so there's no way to know who's trying to get in downstairs and you have to go down to find out. And then no one ever came to see them."

"Except for Grazia's boyfriend," Paco specified, "but lately he hadn't even been coming upstairs. When it was him we knew it because he'd ring and ring, like a crazy person, and then she'd go downstairs and they'd fight in the lobby downstairs. So people started complaining to Renato's father, who owns half the building."

Alex asked: "And that afternoon, when did you hear the argument?"

"Biagio went down to answer the door, and we didn't see

who it was. After a few minutes we started to hear shouting, and after that, the door slamming. And nothing more after that until the next morning, when Renato woke us up because he'd found what you already know."

Lojacono was motionless, his narrow-slitted eyes were gazing at a generic, unspecified spot.

It was Alex who finally broke the silence.

"Signor Mandurino, what have you come to think happened? In your opinion, who could have committed these murders?"

The temperature seemed to have dropped even lower in the room. Once again, Paco stared at the tabletop.

"I don't know. Her boyfriend may have been violent, but I think he actually loved her. I don't think you could do anything like that to someone you loved. You could smack them, you could leave them. But you couldn't do anything like *that*." Then he looked up and his eyes met Lojacono's. "Something like that is because of a betrayal, out of hatred, out of fear. Not out of love. You don't kill someone out of love."

XLII

He opened his eyes again. His head was aching even worse now. The throbbing came violently, as if from outside his head: a goddamned drum pounding endlessly and without any rhythm or beat.

He'd vomited all over himself again. He felt a surge of disgust for himself, for life, for the world, for that damned city.

How long had it been since he'd gone out? He'd paid for three days in advance when he'd checked in, and so far they hadn't come knocking at his door, so more time than that couldn't have gone by.

Even if, he thought as he struggled to get up into at least a seated position, they could perfectly well have come and he might not have heard them.

Maybe that's what the drum was.

He got up, walked over to the door, and pulled it just ajar. Outside was nothing but the darkened hallway, with the dirty, ragged carpeting. From one of the rooms he could hear the dull, repetitive thumping of a bed banging against the wall. He was reminded of the black whore who had come there with him, who had steered him to this pensione. Maybe it was her. Maybe it wasn't.

He shut the door again, trying to master his nausea and his vertigo. He felt a profound loathing for that place. He felt a loathing for the black whore. But above all, he felt a profound loathing for himself.

The room reeked of his vomit, but also of mold. There was a

diseased heat, dank and oppressive, fed by a heater vent that spewed air from above. He felt as if he couldn't breathe, and he dragged himself over to the window.

He struggled to get it open; the sash was rusty and covered with dust. He finally tugged it open and the cold poured in like a ferocious beast, taking his breath away and slicing through the torpor that covered him like a blanket.

In spite of the temperature, the street was full of life; even a scooter zipped past, driven by a man bundled up like an astronaut.

He took a deep breath, filling his lungs. He liked the cold. The cold was free. In prison, what dominated was heat, the same as it was here in the room: a heat made up of too many people, a grim dreariness, unwashed flesh, and obsession. The only place you could find cold was out in the yard, in that illusion of an outdoors, of a world where if you chose to, you could go back to living or at least dream of doing so.

But instead, that's not how it went. Instead, what happened is you didn't go back to living at all. The world outside was just another prison.

Either space, or money. They'd take either the one thing away from you, or the other. You were obsessed either by the lack of the one thing, or the lack of the other. Space in prison, money outside. Otherwise, there was really no difference.

That's what he had told him: I'll give you money. You just leave her alone, let her do as she pleases, and leave me alone too. And I'll give you money.

The words surfaced again in his mind when he felt the first shudder. I'll give you lots of money.

What the fuck do I care about money? That's what he'd said to him, in his language, in that language that he too was speaking again after all this time. What the fuck do I care about money? I don't even want to know where you get your money, you who live in this miserable apartment, who don't own a thing, and with all your books and all your scraps of paper, you still live like a bum.

He had confronted him face-to-face, as if he were a man. As if he didn't still stink of his mother's milk, as if he didn't remember who he was, just who it was that he was dealing with, where he came from and why. There he'd been, an inch from his nose, eyes hard behind the lenses of his glasses, the eyes that, he hadn't been able to avoid noticing, were the same as the eyes he'd seen reflected back at him in that shard of broken mirror, the same eyes that he had narrowed against the glare of the sunlight when he'd finally found himself a free man, no longer behind bars.

He'd seized him by the throat.

Bellowing, he'd seized him by the throat.

His own flesh, his own blood. The reason why—for every day and every minute, for more than sixteen years—he'd dreamed of finally getting out.

The only factor that had allowed him to get through the endless nights. The reason he'd been able to tolerate the silence.

He hadn't dropped his eyes. And he'd kept his hands at his throat like a lamb, like a child.

If he hadn't squeezed, hadn't throttled, it wasn't because his blood wasn't boiling in his veins, nor was it because he'd remembered who this actually was. It was because in his eyes there wasn't fear. There was pity.

I'll give you money, he had said.

He breathed in the cold air one more time, and he suddenly felt like crying.

XLIII

Romano and Aragona's return from the forensic squad's laboratory was awaited with great trepidation. The third day, now, was about to come to an end and there were no new developments on the horizon.

"Damn it, that place is perfect for a murder," said Alex. "There's no doorman, and there's not a single security camera in the neighborhood, I don't know, in a bank or any other kind of office. There aren't even any restaurants or bars where a customer or a waiter might have noticed some peculiar doings in the building."

Ottavia, as usual, was staring at her computer screen: "There's nothing on the web, for that matter. Just idle chatter. A bunch of young people say that they met Biagio Varricchio at the university or else that they took exams with him, but there's no one who saw him in the last hours of his life on earth. And then down in their hometown, Roccapriora, everyone talks about Grazia, about how beautiful she was, but no useful evidence is emerging."

Palma, sitting on the edge of a desk, tried to be optimistic: "Let's focus on what we do have. The neighbor, as Di Nardo and Lojacono just told us, neither saw nor heard anyone arrive, but he confirms that there was a screaming fight in dialect, and we can take it as virtually certain that the one shouting at Biagio was his father. If we really get all the way to the final timeout with nothing more in hand, then we'll be forced to assume that it was him."

"We don't have any confirmation of that," Lojacono replied, "and there is no shortage of Calabrians in the city. Better to admit defeat than to point the finger at someone without proof. I'd like to speak to the father, primarily to get a better understanding of his relationship with his daughter. What's more, if it turns out that it was him, why he left slamming the door after him, after having it out with the young man. It just doesn't make a lot of sense."

Palma wasn't willing to abandon his point of view so easily.

"Then where is he now? Why haven't we heard from him? He must certainly have heard that his two children were murdered. And after all, you can slam a door and then open it again. Maybe he came back a minute later, pretending he was sorry, and his son sat down at his computer and then he murdered him; then he waited for the young woman to come home and then he killed her, too."

"All right, but still, it's just a hypothesis, and a pretty far-fetched one, too. Among other things, from his profile, it would seem that Cosimo Varricchio is the kind of guy who acts on impulse, not the kind who thinks things over and then comes back to crack your skull open. Unless I can see a strong motive, I have my doubts. Why should he have murdered them? Because they had failed to show him proper respect? Because they had made him feel useless, secondary? For money? For old resentments we know nothing about? I'm not saying that it's impossible, but I do want to talk to him and look him in the eye."

Romano and Aragona walked into the room, chilled to the bone.

"Ah, at last, a little warmth. Believe me, it's like a Norwegian tundra out there. Is there any coffee?"

Palma stared at Aragona with a look of resignation.

"You're thinking of coffee at a time like this? Well, what do you have for us?"

Romano set down a bundle of papers on the desk.

"They did a good job. The director, a woman who knows what she's doing, told us that she knows that this is a high-priority case. They put a rush on everything they could, but it still takes time for certain processes . . . "

"Sure, sure, okay. Just tell us what we need to know, if there is anything we need to know."

Romano grimaced.

"I'm afraid there's nothing definitive, boss. Many of the things they found are simply confirmations. There's no semen on the young woman's clothing, which means that, while we already knew from the medical examiner that she wasn't raped, now we also know that no one carried out any sexual activity, let's say, flying solo, on her corpse or on her while she was still alive. The material found under her fingernails wasn't organic in nature, so that means she was unable to dig her nails into the flesh of her attacker. Martone told me that they were able to examine this material because the necessary authorization from the prosecuting magistrate arrived immediately, something that usually doesn't happen."

"What about the blood?" asked Lojacono. "The blood near the young man, or the blood in her room?"

Aragona replied, between sips of coffee.

"It all belonged to the victims; the murderer, whoever it was, left the apartment untouched. And of course, no trace of the murder weapon, though Martone's assistant, an obnoxious guy whose name, if I remember rightly, is Bistrocchi, thinks it must have been a blunt metal object, considering the damage done by the number of blows inflicted."

There was a disappointed spell of silence. If any traces of organic substances had been found under Grazia's fingernails, or even better, drops of blood from anyone other than the victims, they would at least have had something.

"Did they find the money?" asked Lojacono.

Romano searched through the documents.

"I have a complete inventory, the description of the scene of the crime, everything. The only money was seventy-four euros in his wallet and eighteen euros and seventy cents in her handbag. In any case, that confirms, in case there was any need, that it wasn't a burglar or a robber, otherwise they would have taken that money too."

"What did they do with Cava's thirty-seven hundred euros?" Alex asked, under her breath. "They didn't put it in the bank, they didn't have it at home. Did they pay off a debt? Did they spend it on something?"

Aragona made a face.

"*Mamma mia*, this is such disgusting coffee; that Guida is a dog. Anyway, I made a point of asking Martone whether there was anything of value, anything new, in the apartment. She said there wasn't. If they'd used that money to buy anything, they didn't have it at home."

Palma heaved a sigh.

"Fingerprints?

Romano tapped his right forefinger on a sheet of paper.

"The fingerprints actually do provide a small bit of help. If nothing else, they confirm our initial conjectures. The victims' father was there. There are substantial signs of his fingerprints, obtained by means of the usual fingerprint dusting technique. They were compared with the prints that they have on file. Martone says that there's no doubt about it."

Palma didn't bother to conceal a surge of satisfaction.

"Aha. Good. Where were the prints found?"

"They were pretty much everywhere in the larger room; none in the young woman's room."

"Did they check the phones?" asked Lojacono.

"Yes," said Aragona. "The young man had his cell phone on his desk, though that was pointless, because there's no cell phone service in the apartment, from what we were told. The most recent call, incoming, dates back two days and it comes from a number belonging to Renato Forgione, his best friend. The last outgoing call is to his sister, evidently he'd been out of the apartment when he called her, the night before they were both murdered. They talked for six minutes and a few seconds, starting at 6:32 P.M."

Romano checked on a sheet of paper and looked over at his partner in surprise.

"Later maybe you can tell me how you remember it all by heart, this stuff. The young woman's phone was found under a console table in the front hall; Martone said that you spotted it, Alex. By the way, she says to tell you hi."

Di Nardo concealed the surge of emotion behind a forced cough.

"Were there any calls?"

Romano nodded: "That's the most interesting angle. First of all, the phone's screen is broken because it was hurled forcefully onto the floor; it's not like it just fell and wound up under the piece of furniture. It broke in spite of the rubber case, a horrible thing with bunny ears, they showed it to us. There were no fingerprints on it, except for Grazia's. Which means that either she threw it herself, and that would strike me as odd, or else the attacker was wearing gloves."

Aragona lazily completed the information, grinding his right pinky into the corresponding ear and staring with curiosity at the result on the fingertip.

"In any case, after the phone call from her brother, she received six other phone calls, all from the same number, between the hours of 6:34 P.M. and 9:13 P.M. She answered the first and the fourth call; the first time she talked for three minutes and fifteen seconds; the second time for two minutes and twenty-six seconds."

Romano turned to look at him again.

"You know, you really ought to compete on some TV quiz

show. I swear to you all, he only looked at it once, with me, and I can barely remember these things even when I read them."

Pisanelli snickered: "You can fit a lot into an empty jug. Who was the other phone registered to, if I may ask?"

Aragona blew a short mulberry in the general direction of the deputy captain.

"Carlo Cava. The guy from the modeling agency."

Everyone exchanged surprised glances. Aragona commented.

"What are you all making those faces for? It doesn't strike me as that odd that the guy should have been obsessed with the young woman. And after all, he's one of the potential supects, so I can't see why anyone's surprised."

"Agreed," said Lojacono, who didn't seem to move a muscle even while he was speaking. "What surprises me, really, is the time of night. If the phone doesn't get any bars in that building—and we saw that that was true ourselves the day that the bodies were found, because when Alex tried to call over to here, she was forced to go out into the street—then that means that the young woman was outside at 9:13 P.M."

Romano expanded on the information.

"They were able to determine in the forensic laboratory that the young woman's cell phone was playing music at top volume from a playlist when it was shattered. That must mean that she came in with her earbuds in, and if there was noise from a struggle or anything of the sort, she simply didn't hear it. Her house keys were in her purse, where they belonged. So she either opened the door herself and then put the keys away, or else she rang the doorbell."

"But the neighbors didn't hear any doorbell," said Alex.

Palma nodded: "Right, she must have used her keys."

A meditative silence descended over the room, until Lojacono said: "Did they find anything on his or her person? Anything odd, documents, letters, notes . . ."

Romano ran down a list.

"No, I don't think so. In Biagio's wallet there was his ID, the money I mentioned, his card for the university dining hall, his building badge, a receipt from a certified letter, a bus ticket, his driver's license, and a Padre Pio prayer card. In her purse, on the other hand . . . hold on . . . ah, here we are: one light-colored lipstick and another dark-colored one, eyeshadow, her house keys like we said, a paperback romance novel, one of those tiny fold-up umbrellas, her wallet with the bills and loose change, her ID card, a photograph of a woman who might be her mother, a note on which is written: 'This is for you. I love you,' which might have come with a gift, but which also doesn't look recent, at least at a first glance. Nothing much. Here are all the photocopies, if you want them."

"What about in the rooms, in the drawers?"

"On his desk, and on the sofa bed where he slept, there was just lots of stuff about biochemistry. For the computer, we're going to have to wait, they're still analyzing it, but they told me that he had no internet connection, which meant there was no email and no history of internet sites visited; he strictly used it for doing calculations and that sort of thing. In her bedroom, there were teddy bears and plush dolls and clothing, as well as the photographs on the wall, which I think you saw. There was also a copy of the release form she signed at Cava's agency for the photographs used in the advertising campaign. No mention of compensation, of course."

Once again, silence. Maybe somewhere in the sea of fragmentary information was the nugget that they needed. Maybe, well hidden, there was the piece of evidence that would allow them to figure out who had killed the two kids and why.

Or maybe not. Maybe nothing could explain such a deranged and desperate act.

Palma felt old and weary.

"All right. Let's give it some thought. If nobody comes up

with anything, and if nothing new happens, then tomorrow we'll hold one last meeting and then we'll hand the case off to the geniuses at police headquarters. That way, they can teach us the way police work is done. Have a good evening, everyone."

XLIV

Have a good evening, people.
Have fun, laugh, get excited, feel comforted. Do what you can to get the chill out of your bones from this long workday.

Rid yourself of the dirt and grime, try to be reborn. You can do it, if you make an effort and a little sacrifice; you can pry loose the icy fingers of ugly thoughts from your mind.

You can do it. Or, at least, you can try.

Lojacono was standing in front of the bathroom mirror, shaving, when Marinella walked in to get her makeup.

"Papà," she asked, "since when do you shave twice in a single day?"

The lieutenant replied vaguely.

"You know, he's an old friend, I haven't seen him in ages. I don't want him to see me looking shabby, he might think I'm aging badly."

The young woman burst out laughing.

"Do you know that all the girls in my class are in love with you? They saw you at the start of the school year, when you brought me to school, and they went nuts, they say you're a heartbreaker."

"Oh come on, I'm falling apart. But wait, what about you: are you getting made up to go eat a bite at Letizia's? Don't you think you're overdoing it a little?"

"Papà, a real woman never goes out of the house without

makeup on, you know what they say: a hint of makeup, a hint of high heels."

He gave her a sidelong glance in the mirror.

"A real woman? But you're just a little girl, and I don't want you to forget it. And listen, you stay in that restaurant until Letizia's done, then you go straight to bed. That way tomorrow you won't be exhausted for your math test."

The two faces in the mirror were incredibly similar, with narrow eyes upturned at the corners and high cheekbones, one face covered with shaving cream, the other half made-up.

"Don't worry, Papà. You don't have a thing to worry about. I love math, and you know that."

Have a good evening.

Or at least try to have one.

Make a serious effort, because for all you know it's an opportunity. Don't just think about how to kill a few hours.

It might seem like any old evening, and instead turn out to be "the" evening you've been waiting for.

An evening that, if you let it slip by, you'll never get a shot at again.

Alex pressed her ear against her bedroom door. She couldn't hear a thing.

She'd told them once again that, after the meeting, she was going out for a pizza with her colleagues. In a tone of annoyance, as if it were an almost intolerable burden, she'd explained to her parents that Commissario Palma cared deeply about team spirit, and that in order to indulge this fixation of his, she'd be obliged to go out to dinner, though she would have been just as happy to skip it: It's just that, you know, Papà, I'd be the only one to miss it.

She'd said goodnight and gone to change: you two go to bed, I've got the keys, I'll see you in the morning.

Rosaria in her head. Rosaria in her heart. Eagerly awaiting Rosaria on her flesh.

She'd chosen a pretty aggressive set of intimate wear, a thong and a push-up bra that she'd bought in a shop in another part of town, far from home and far from the police station, as well as a garter belt supporting a pair of fine-mesh fishnet stockings.

Then she had put on a dark dress, neither particularly short nor with a plunging neckline, but snug and close-fitting, which emphasized her lithe, petite figure. The dark makeup she'd applied made her cheeks look slightly gaunt and hollowed, giving her a feral look. Which is what she wanted.

I'm a she-wolf tonight, she thought, as she gazed into the mirror. Tonight I want you to know that you'll be devoured by my ferocious maw. Tonight, you're not in charge, Senior Director Martone. Tonight, I'm in charge.

Her overcoat, her purse, and out the door. Five brisk strides down the hallway, and she'd be gone.

Her father, in his dressing gown, was standing by the door, barring her way.

She felt as if she were about to die. She thanked God she was already wearing her overcoat, and she immediately clutched her collar tight to her throat to conceal the dress and the thin gold chain she wore around her neck.

"Papà, are you still up? You scared me."

Her father studied her. For the umpteenth time, she felt the same sensation she had when she was a little girl and she felt those empty eyes delve into her, bringing her darkest emotions up into the light.

"So you go to meetings at the office all dolled up? With all this makeup?"

Her heart was pounding in her ears. Now what am I supposed to do? What am I going to do?

"No, you know, Papà, it's just that . . . yes, it's a meeting, that's true, but afterward we're all going out to dinner and I just . . . "

Unexpectedly, the General broke into a smile.

"You're a big girl, now. Do you think that your mother and I don't know that? You don't have to tell me about it, I know that you're a shy, intensely private person and there are certain things you don't like talking about, but I do understand that there's someone you're sweet on, one of your colleagues from work. And I'm happy for you. I just hope he's a serious, respectable young man, because you deserve someone like that."

In some strange way, that sly conniving smile filled her with even greater horror than the severity that terrorized her on a daily basis.

"Come on, Papà, please, don't think that . . . there's no one, don't be silly, I . . . "

The man gave her a wink. That had never happened in her twenty-eight years here on earth. Oh my God, now I'm going to vomit on his slippers.

"Go on, go ahead. Maybe, if you feel like it, you can tell me all about it tomorrow morning. But not a word to your mother, or she'll start to worry. You know how apprehensive she can be. Have a good evening."

Have a good evening, that's right.

But instead, maybe, it's anything but a good evening.

Maybe it's just the umpteenth fake pearl in a necklace made up of evenings all the same and without a reason why.

Maybe this evening will come into existence and then die without a trace, if not for the usual wake of melancholy.

Maybe it would have been better if it had never come at all, the damned evening. Because at least during the daytime you can throw yourself into your work, seeking out problems and worries elsewhere, while instead, in the damned evening, you bump your nose up against the you that you're not.

Maybe it'll kill you, the good evening.

The effect of the car's heater took just two seconds to vanish when Romano shut the engine off. Too cold outside.
And likewise too cold inside, he thought.
He couldn't hold out for more than a couple of days at a time. Every time he swore to himself that he'd never go back there, but instead, not forty-eight hours later, here he was again.
Even when it was a thousand degrees below zero, like it was tonight. Even after a long day of working myself blind. Even when I could be cozy under a blanket, fast asleep.
Here I am, outside of Giorgia's place.
To be exact, he thought to himself, this is Giorgia's mother's place. Giorgia's place is the apartment I have the keys to in my pocket. Giorgia's place is the apartment I can't bring myself to come back to, now that she no longer lives there. Giorgia's place is the apartment she abandoned with a fucking letter.
He could just glimpse the dull glow of a television set on the fourth floor. Couldn't I offer you anything more than an evening in front of the TV? Wasn't it better to stay with me?
The temperature had dropped even further. The body of Francesco Romano, AKA Hulk, showed no sign of awareness: no shivering, no sneezing. Maybe it's true that rage makes me stronger, he thought to himself. Maybe I really do turn green and incredibly strong. I'm full of rage, you know that, my love? Jam-packed with it.
The irony was that if a woman had come into the police station and said: you know, Warrant Officer Francesco Romano, my husband, the one I broke up with because he hit me, that's right, just once, but hard, terribly hard, well, every other night he comes and parks downstairs from my mother's apartment, where I'm living now, and he sits there looking up at the windows, if anyone had come in to report such a thing,

then he himself, Warrant Officer Francesco Romano, would have gone straight out to pick him up, and he would have told him, look out, buddy, keep this up and you'll find yourself in deep trouble.

And instead it was none other than he, Warrant Officer Francesco Romano, sitting there doing it. Sitting in a car outside her house and watching. And waiting.

Waiting for what? He couldn't say. If someone had asked him, he wouldn't have been able to answer.

Maybe she's going out tonight. She certainly would have every right to do so. She's a free citizen of a free country. Maybe she feels like going dancing, who knows. She could do that. It would be her prerogative. Policemen like him were paid to ensure that people enjoyed their rights. What would he say, if he actually did see her go out, those spectacular legs, that thick head of chestnut hair, that generous, sensuous mouth, if he saw her leaving for a dinner out, followed by dancing and even, why not?, taking some strange man to bed?

What would he say?

What would he do?

He saw the light turn on in the narrow bathroom window. Maybe she's getting ready to go out. The light went off again almost immediately. No, she was just taking a pee.

He settled in to his seat to get more comfortable and raised the lapels of his overcoat. Then he put both hands under his armpits to keep them warm and got ready for the wait ahead.

Have a good evening, Warrant Officer Francesco Romano, he thought to himself.

Have a good evening.

XLV

There was something going on, thought Lojacono. There was definitely something going on.

Or more than just something.

It had been obvious from the beginning of the evening, from the instant he'd come face-to-face with her, made up and dressed to the nines—high heels and slit skirt under her short overcoat—in the parking lot of the Hall of Justice, as if she were leaving a beauty parlor, her hair perfectly coiffed, scarlet lipstick gleaming and long earrings glittering in the light of the streetlamp.

It had been obvious as well for three lawyers who'd crossed paths with her, elbowing each other as they turned to eye her from behind as she strode away, though only after greeting her respectfully when face-to-face with her, and equally obvious to a couple of young men loitering nearby, as they'd opened their big yaps to express their shameless and overt appreciation.

And it had been especially obvious when, climbing into his beat-up compact as if stepping into a Bentley, she'd brushed his lips with a rapid, surprising kiss.

Lojacono, wearing the only decent suit he owned, had immediately felt inadequate to the challenge. Because of his car, his shoes, his extremely ordinary aftershave; because he hadn't bothered to get a haircut, because he didn't have enough money to take her out to some stunning restaurant; because of the rudimentary conversation he could offer her, what you'd expect from a policeman, because of the Sicilian accent that he generally flaunted with pride, but which was so distant from the polished language that her drooling colleagues, the other assistant district attorneys, could bring to bear.

The sensation of inadequacy only worsened when, determined to park courteously and legally, and therefore spurning all the cheap and easy options, the sidewalks, the spots marked handicapped only, the no parking zones, the apartment building driveways and the pedestrian crosswalks, he was forced to leave the car several hundred yards from the restaurant's front door, forcing the woman to take an unexpected walk on her high heels. But she surprised him by resting her weight on his arm with a tender intimacy that he never would have dared to imagine.

The stroll to the restaurant was easygoing and cheerful, because Laura kept making fun of herself and the way she wobbled and swayed in her high heels on the uneven pavement; it was also intriguing and alluring because of the weight of the prosperous breast that he could feel swaying against his biceps. A distant but audible siren song, calling out to his senses, through the layers of cloth of the two overcoats, the two jackets, a bra and a blouse and a shirt. In spite of the terrible cold, he wished it would never end.

Lojacono had identified the restaurant during his anxious preparations for the evening out, focusing first and foremost on his determination not to run into anyone else who might happen to know them.

It was a discreet, cozy place, with a panoramic plate-glass window overlooking the sea, and the kitchen put a lively new spin on classic Neapolitan cooking; the reviews were excellent. Even though the table offered a breathtaking view, it was reasonably private, set off to one side from the center of the dining room.

For the lieutenant, the situation began to spin out of control the minute he had helped Laura out of her overcoat.

Piras had decided to weigh in with her heaviest armaments. The dress that she'd brought in to headquarters in her handbag, only to put it on in her own office, behind a locked door, was the fruit of a well considered choice made at the end of a long and, for her, highly unusual session of clothes shopping in the center of town. Up top, it presented a plunging neckline that only a woman with a remarkable bosom could dare to wear. Luckily she'd had the good sense to bring a silk shawl as well, so as to limit the spectacle somewhat. She'd put it on almost immediately, otherwise most of the customers and the male staff would have had a hard time directing their attention elsewhere, but for Lojacono the damage was already done. The wave of physical attraction that he'd felt steadily rising within him since the day they'd first met had now received an explicit visual confirmation, and the dinner became, in his head, a prelude to the moment when he'd finally hold the woman in his arms.

They had a wonderful night out. They talked about shared acquaintances and the city, that strange place, so difficult and yet so lovely, exotic to them both, yet which offered such alluring opportunities. Lojacono admitted that the fact that they'd met, for instance, gave him a more benevolent feeling toward the numerous negative characteristics that so annoyed him.

They tacitly chose not to talk about the past, even though they each would have been curious to know more about and better understand the other's loneliness: they didn't want to run the risk of letting sadness or melancholy cast a dark veil over that long-awaited evening out.

Laura ran her eyes over Lojacono's facial features, his shoulders, his broad, powerful hands. She sensed a surge of weakness growing beneath her sternum, and one part of her chastised the other part for having kept it so long under lock and key. She wanted him. She had wanted him the minute she met him, she was sure of that now. This was the first time such a thing had happened to her, at least since she had attained the consciousness of a real woman. Her mind went back to Carlo, her first boyfriend, the man she thought would be the only one in her life, dead so many years now, and the occasional flings of the years that followed, flings that had left not a trace on the surface of her heart. She compared those emotions with the wonderfully unsettled feelings that filled her now, as she ate and laughed her way through a dinner whose flavors she'd never remember, and she realized that she couldn't miss that opportunity.

Lojacono talked about Marinella, and as he did he sought, without finding it, any memory of Sonia, his daughter's mother. Ancient history now, belonging to another land and a different man. He had a chance to leave it all behind him, once and for all.

The dinner ended, and it was strange, because they both would have gladly gone on talking, drinking wine and shooting brief, enchanted glances at the array of lights wreathing the waterfront; but they also felt the overwhelming urgency to get away from there and be alone together.

Little by little, their words dwindled like drops of rain at the end of the night. Their eyes were locked. Laura laid her hand on Lojacono's and said, in a soft voice: Let's get out of here.

The drive to Piras's house was short and, at the same time, extremely long. As if she were afraid of losing the hard-won intimacy, the woman never once stopped caressing his thigh, though very gently. His desire was starting to verge on the painful. They went upstairs, each of them listening to their own heartbeat as it accelerated.

They hadn't uttered another word, after that "let's get out of here" whispered at the restaurant. Words weren't necessary.

In the little elevator they stood facing each other, Laura's breasts rising and falling as her breathing grew ever so faintly labored.

She opened the door and, once they were inside, leaned back against it, in the dim light that came in through the windows. He took off his overcoat and stepped toward her. He kissed her, gently and deeply, as their bodies pressed together and they became acquainted inch by inch. She stood on tiptoe and he leaned down to meet her. During that kiss, she emitted a brief moan of pleasure. He ran his hand over her back.

His cell phone and hers both started ringing at the same time.

XLVI

Alex's cell phone started ringing just as she started the car. It was Rosaria, who started talking without even bothering to say hello.

"How about you come to my place, instead of us going to some useless restaurant? I can make an excellent *penne al pomodoro*."

There was a smile quivering in Alex's reply: "My favorite dish, *penne al pomodoro*. It's what I would have ordered at the restaurant."

"Fine. Via Atri, number 8. You know the surname. You'll have to use the parking structure, because you can't find street parking to save your life."

When she got there, and after galloping up a narrow, twisting staircase, out of breath, Alex found the door open. She was greeted by her friend's voice coming from the kitchen.

"Come on in. I'll be there in a minute."

In the living room, the lights were low, the walls were lined with books and DVDs, a television set, a comfortable-looking sofa, a table set for two, lit by tall candles. The care for the details, comfort favored over elegance, and a heartwarming attention to knickknacks and curios, carpets, doilies, and tablecloths betrayed a feminine dedication that Alex would never have suspected. Rosaria's home seemed like that of a completely different person. She had expected a modern atmosphere, a setting of steel and glass, functional and cold. She was delighted to have been mistaken.

She took off her overcoat, breathing in a faint aroma of incense from a burner that sat on one of the bookshelves. She ran her eyes over the titles, discovering a tireless reader who roamed freely through all genres. Albert Camus, Bertolt Brecht, and Jorge Amado alternating with Rex Stout, Massimo Carlotto, Donato Carrisi, and Gianrico Carofiglio; the collected works of Gabriel García Márquez, Jorge Luis Borges, and Eduardo Galeano, along with Andrea De Carlo and Alessandro Baricco.

"When do you find the time to read all this stuff?" she murmured, as if talking to herself.

"I find it, I find it," a subdued voice replied from behind her.

She looked around and saw Rosaria's eyes over a pair of wineglasses full of red. Rosaria was wearing a cheerful-hued dressing gown, protected by an apron lightly spattered with sauce. Her smile was enchanting, veiled by a thin layer of makeup.

"God, you're so beautiful," she said.

Alex blushed slightly, picked up a wineglass, and clinked it against Rosaria's.

They drank in brief sips, all the while staring at each other. Only then did Alex notice that the speakers, hidden away amongst the books, were emitting the warm notes of a blues number being sung by a woman.

"Oh my God, the sauce!" Rosaria exclaimed.

She set her glass down on the table and hurried into the kitchen. When she came back, she was heaving a sigh of relief.

"*Mamma mia*, another second and—"

She never finished her sentence, but stopped, jaw hanging open. Alex had stripped off her dress and was curled up on the sofa.

"I'm not hungry. Not hungry for food, anyway," Alex said, looking at her.

Her voice, low-timbred, seemed like the voice of a cat purring with satisfaction.

Rosaria thought that she was going to have to guide her friend toward the world of the senses, unfolding her little by little like the petals of a flower, accustoming her to think of herself outside of social conventions and inhibitions. She didn't know that Alex had crossed those barriers years ago; there were radically different limitations that her complex psychology imposed upon her. Rosaria didn't know about the miles and miles driven, the mask she wore to induce a fleeting sense of bodily peace in dark private clubs. She didn't know about the frustration, the sacrifice, the fantasies that she cultivated in silence in her own bedroom while her jailer slept.

And most of all, she didn't know how hard she'd had to work to force herself to be there, that night, and how once she had achieved that determination, she had immediately passed on to imagine what was going to happen there.

For her part, Rosaria was willing and ready. She wanted to be involved and was fully intrigued, she was no longer satisfied by passing relationships sparked by chance meetings in bars with people seeking that and nothing else. She wanted someone to share tears and laughter with, someone with whom to share the emotional journey of enjoying a good film, someone to have a healthy argument with. She wanted someone she liked from top to bottom.

They made love for hours, in every way imaginable. They experimented with each other's bodies, rising to summits they'd never before attained. They understood why love between women is finer, deeper, and richer than anything men can imagine, because there is no end to it, it's never satiated, and once the anger and fury have passed, it offers gentleness, without ever establishing a difference between taking and giving.

Each read in the eyes of the other the fullness of pleasure and the incipience of renewed desire. They discovered how to play and how to find each other, how to lead the other by hand to a vantage point from which to observe the world from a happy distance.

Now, in the rich scent of the many orgasms they'd freely exchanged, Rosaria's hand was tracing the outlines of Alex's face, as if trying to impress into body memory something never to be forgotten.

"I want you," she told her. "I want you now, and I want you tomorrow and the next day. I can't stand to think of you far from me."

Alex listened to Rosaria's raucous voice the way she might have listened to a new and familiar piece of music. She couldn't think of anything quite so wonderful either.

"Yes, it's been beautiful for me, too."

Rosaria gently shook her head, continuing to caress her face.

"It's not just a matter of flesh, of chemistry. I want your life. And I want to give you mine."

Alex said nothing. She listened to her heart racing in her chest.

Rosaria went on.

"I know, this must seem absurd to you. You must be thinking: who is this woman, coming to talk about certain things with me, after we make love just once? But I recognized you. The minute I saw you, I recognized you. I knew who you were and I glimpsed the road we can travel together. I don't know if it's a phase of my life, if I've lost my mind or I'm just tired of battling against my own indifference. I only know that I love you, and that I want to share my time and my desires with you."

Alex listened, her eyes half closed, her blood pumping confusedly through her veins. I recognized you too, she wanted to tell her. I too believe that happiness lies here, in this bed, in your hands and in your mouth. I too am tired of keeping my skin and my soul rigorously separate . . .

"I'm certain you'd never disappoint me. Isn't that right?"
"Yes, Papà."

What can I say to make sure I don't lose her? To keep her from understanding that I'm not as brave as she is, that the chains holding me back are a thousand times more unbreakable?
"I'm not trying to scare you," Rosaria went on. "You're young, and your life is organized differently from mine. But if you don't feel the same way that I do, if you don't think the way that I do, please, tell me now. I need to know if there might be room for me in your heart."
Alex narrowed her eyes. In her mind, a terrible tempest was raging. She'd never thought, every time she'd made off with a moment of stolen pleasure in some furtive encounter, that she was doing anything wrong, anything in violation of her principles, even though the places those encounters took place were shady and meretricious.
But now, instead, she felt like a traitor, guilty and faithless. And happier than she'd ever been before.
She opened her mouth to reply, and her cell phone rang.

XLVII

They decided to go separately, each under their own power.

Piras, who had been summoned directly by the police chief, was expecting a car from the district attorney's office; Lojacono, who'd been alerted by Palma, had his own car.

When it had become clear to them that, for the second time, they were going to have to separate, just when things were about to turn especially nice, they'd indulged in one long last look. Then she had caressed his face and he had given her a fleeting smile.

"I'm right here," she had said, quietly. "I'm not going anywhere."

"Me either," Lojacono had replied. And now he was driving through the night toward police headquarters, where he knew Alex would be waiting for him.

He felt he was seething inside. His desire for Laura, the beauty of the evening, and, especially, the cheerfulness, the youthful enthusiasm he'd experienced, had taken him back in time, restoring hope: he could be happy again. But afterward he had been jerked roughly back into the reality of his work as a policeman, who found himself faced on a daily basis with murders and horrors: the big city was a difficult place, and now Marinella, too, was in the big city.

The thought of his daughter came naturally into his mind, as a logical consequence, any time a crime was especially horrific. Every time he found himself investigating the murder of an innocent victim. Every time he had to deal with the effects of madness and evil.

It was just as he was thinking about her that he actually spotted her.

At first, he thought it must be a trick of the mind: your eyes follow a thought and trick themselves that they're seeing something that's not there.

He was stuck in traffic at the beginning of the waterfront esplanade, where at that time of night the city's *movida* was in full fling and thousands of people were flowing toward the beachside "chalets," stands and kiosks selling iced beverages, even in the midst of that terrible cold snap. His compact car was inching along in the second of the four lanes, and she was walking toward him, in the opposite direction, about thirty feet away.

A more careful scrutiny, free of extraneous thoughts, confirmed that he wasn't suffering from a hallucination. It was Marinella, no doubt about it. She was laughing, her hair blowing free in the wind. She was laughing, joyous in a way he didn't remember ever having seen her. She was laughing, her happy tip-tilted eyes turned upward. Turned up toward the face, vaguely familiar suddenly, of a tall, taut young man who was gesticulating as he told who knows what story.

Behind Lojacono the car horns blared impatiently, and he was forced to put the car in motion.

He looked around in search of a place to park. He was going to run and grab his daughter by the lapels she was clutching close around her neck, he'd demand to know why on earth she was out wandering the streets in the middle of the night in the company of a potential rapist in a city swarming with potential rapists, instead of sleeping peacefully in a warm bed, her arms wrapped around her teddy bear. But there was nowhere to park, nor double-park, or even triple-park—not the tiniest nook or cranny to leave his car. And they were expecting him at police headquarters.

He pulled the cell phone out of his inside jacket pocket,

with some difficulty because his fingers were stiff with the cold, cursing under his breath as he fumbled with it. He dialed his daughter's number, only to find that that cunning little Lucrezia Borgia had turned off her phone. In the meantime the river of cars had swept him far away.

Bewilderment was giving way to rage. He'd entrusted his daughter to someone. He'd placed his trust in someone. Tapping feverishly at his phone, he found Letizia's number in his directory. He was moving forward in jerks and starts, urged along by an unfortunate automobile behind him occupied by four young men who were increasingly impatient with his distraction; they'd have much preferred someone with better reaction times in gobbling up the few yards of forward space that opened up from time to time.

It was the waiter who answered. From the music and the voices he understood that, in spite of the late hour, the trattoria was still buzzing.

Letizia came to the receiver. Her voice was upset, or at least so it seemed to Lojacono.

"Letizia? *Ciao*, it's me. How is everything, all right?"

"Ah, *ciao*. Yes, of course, everything's fine, why? And you, how are you? Are you having a good time?"

"Me? Yes, certainly, thanks. Could you pass me Marinella, please?"

"Marinella? Why? Has something happened?"

"No. I just want to speak to her. She's there, isn't she?"

"Here? Of course she's here. But she had a bit of a headache, so she decided to go to sleep. I wouldn't want to wake her up . . ."

Lojacono let a moment of thoughtful silence flow past, then he said: "I think trust is the foundation of any good friendship, don't you? I think that two friends need to know they can rely upon each other. If there's no trust, then there can't be any friendship, either."

The woman's voice was trembling with tears.

"Peppe, I never . . . believe me, I love Marinella as if she were my own daughter. I'd never do anything to hurt her, I wouldn't let her run risks. I—"

The lieutenant felt the anger surge into his brain.

"First, don't you ever call me Peppe again. Second, Marinella isn't your daughter, she's mine. And it's up to me to decide whether something's risky or not. I'm responsible for what might happen to her, and right now she's out on the street with someone I don't know, in the middle of the night, in a very dangerous city. And all of this is your fault, and my fault too, for thinking that you were different, somehow."

He hung up, and when not even a second later, Letizia tried to call back, he angrily rejected the call. He had to focus on his work, this fraud concocted behind his back by his daughter and his friend was getting in the way of his professional responsibility: another unforgivable betrayal.

He'd just parked in the courtyard of police headquarters when he received Marinella's call. In the background, he could hear the noise of traffic and people in the street: obviously the young woman had turned her phone back on and had quickly learned what had happened.

"Papà, *ciao*, it's me. I'm sorry . . . "

Standing, in the gusting wind and right before the eyes of the two policemen on duty at the front door, Lojacono hissed: "Go straight home. Now, do you understand?"

"But . . . Papà," she stammered, "I haven't done anything wrong, I went to the movies and got myself a sandwich! All my girlfriends at school go out at night, and—"

"I don't care what your girlfriends do. Go straight home. We'll talk later. And as soon as you get there, call me from the land line, that way I'll know you're really there."

"But if I tell you that I'm going, don't you trust me? You need to check up on me? I—"

"It was you who showed me that I can't trust you. And apparently I can't trust Letizia, either."

Now the strains of frustration could be heard in Marinella's voice.

"It's not Letizia's fault. I'm a woman, Papà, I'm not a little girl anymore, but you don't want to accept it. For fuck's sake, I just went out to see a movie! I didn't do anything wrong!"

Lojacono stared grimly at the two policemen, who turned their eyes away.

"I'm responsible for you, with respect to your mother as well. And I have work to do, I can't chase after you the way a girl your age needs to be chased after. I think it might be better if you pack your bags and head back to Sicily."

He pressed the red button, ended the call, and strode briskly through the front door.

XLVIII

He was of average height, broad-shouldered, with large, gnarled hands, splayed flat on the table. At first sight you'd take him for a bum. Raggedy whiskers, dirty gray hair hanging low over the nape of his neck, a heavy jacket, an oversized sweater from which projected the tattered collar of a shirt that might once have been sky blue, emanating a pungent odor of curdled vomit. His reddened eyes and the broken capillaries on his nose were hallmarks of a binge drinker.

Everything about him bespoke poverty and hard living.

What contrasted with that picture was the erect spine, and even more so, the expression on the face, the calm, proud gaze, almost defiant, the firm jaw and the straight line of the mouth.

Aside from Lojacono himself and two policemen in uniform standing by the door, there were five other people already in the room when he arrived. Piras, who had evidently found time to change out of her stunning outfit into a more sober-sided skirt suit; Palma, who in spite of the late hour appeared less rumpled than usual and actually looked as if he were in the throes of some strange euphoria; the police chief, a bald and corpulent man in his early sixties with a perennially irritated demeanor; a man in his early forties, extremely well dressed and with an off-putting manner, introduced to him as Francesco Gerardi, director of the mobile squad; last of all, an old acquaintance, Commissario Di Vincenzo, the man who had kicked Lojacono out of his old precinct, thereby actually doing him an enormous favor: he had in fact been assigned to the San

Gaetano police station upon his arrival in the city, and there he had been languishing without any assigned duties.

The lieutenant shot a questioning glance at Palma, who shrugged his shoulders.

It was the police chief who solved the mystery of that presence.

"Commissario Di Vincenzo is here because we've summoned him to lend Pizzofalcone a hand in case the investigation now under way proves not to be moving sufficiently expeditiously in the immediate short term."

"Which is the most likely outcome, I'd have to say," added Gerardi, immediately staking out his position.

The forces were deployed in fairly unambiguous fashion. Gerardi and Di Vincenzo represented the faction calling for the shutdown of the Pizzofalcone precinct; Laura and, perhaps, the police chief, the side trying to keep it alive.

"It ain't necessarily so that we need anyone else's help," Palma retorted, stung by the insinuation.

The door swung open and Alex came in; her overcoat was buttoned right up to the neck and there wasn't a trace of makeup on her face. She nodded a greeting and sat down, off to one side.

Palma went on, with greater equanimity now.

"Now we're all here. Lieutenant Lojacono and Officer Di Nardo are in charge of the investigation, so let me sum up for them. As you may have realized, in part because you've surely seen his photographs on the alerts that have been distributed widely in the past few days, the gentleman sitting here is Cosimo Varricchio, the father of the victims in the apartment on Vico Secondo Egiziaca. He turned himself in voluntarily at police headquarters forty-five minutes ago, and he has not yet been questioned."

Cosimo Varricchio let himself go a little and flashed a contemptuous smile.

"And with all the photographs you circulated, I still walked in on my own two feet. Nice work."

The head of the mobile squad snapped.

"Varricchio, keep your mouth shut unless you're asked a question. Keep in mind that your position—"

Varricchio didn't even bother to look around in his direction.

"My position, my good sir, is the position of a father who came to the police the instant he heard that his two children had been murdered. Or am I wrong?"

His voice sounded like metal scraping across ice. The tone was tranquil and the Calabrian accent was very strong.

The police chief tried to steer the interview back onto the tracks of formal procedure.

"No, Varricchio, you're not wrong. And before anything else, we'd like to express our condolences for your son and daughter. But you must admit, it's odd that you should appear out of thin air three days after the murder. And seeing that . . . "

" . . . and seeing that I'm Calabrian and an ex-convict, you put me at the top of the list of suspects. Isn't that right?"

This time it was Di Vincenzo who lost it.

"No, that's not right at all! You're a suspect because you vanished the same day as the murder and only surfaced now. It's absurd to claim that you heard nothing about it before this."

Piras gave Di Vincenzo a chilly glance; she'd never concealed her strong dislike of the man.

"Di Vincenzo, unless the rules have changed without my knowledge, the interview in these situations is conducted by the investigating magistrate. And unless you can show me otherwise, that magistrate would be me. Therefore, unless you have any pertinent questions to ask, keep your mouth shut or I'll ask you to leave the room, seeing that you are the one with the least legitimate grounds to be here. Agreed?"

The violent verbal attack surprised all those present, and Palma was unable to conceal a smirk of gratification.

Piras addressed Varricchio.

"Signor Varricchio, my name is Laura Piras, and as you just heard I'm the magistrate supervising the investigation into the murders of your children. Will you explain to us, to the satisfaction of Commissario Di Vincenzo and all the rest of us, just why we only have the good fortune of your visit three full days after the fact?"

"It's very simple. I got drunk, I went whoring, I slept, I got drunk again, I slept again, and then I finally woke up. And then I went down into the street and I went to get an espresso in a café; there was a television going and I heard about what had happened. I asked directions to get here and I made my fucking way right over."

Gerardi addressed Piras in mellifluous tones.

"Dottoressa, do we really have to put up with such language? This is—"

Laura waved her hand in his direction, annoyed, as if shooing away a fly.

"Just where did you spend all this time?"

"In a pensione over by the central station. It's called Da Lucia, I think. The whore took me there. I paid for three days. And I brought the alcohol with me."

Palma asked Piras for permission to put a question himself, and she agreed.

"Signor Varricchio, can you tell us whether the reason you came to town had anything to do with your children? Whether you met them and, if so, when?"

"I wanted to take Grazia back home and as you can see, she would certainly have been better off if she had come home with me. I went to the apartment where they live . . . where they *lived*, but she wasn't there. Only her brother, my son, was there."

Lojacono shot a glance at Piras and asked: "Can you remember what time that was?"

"The train got in at 5:35 in the afternoon, an hour late, and I went straight over to their house. It took me half an hour, I prefer to walk. So it must have been about six o'clock."

"How long did you stay?"

The man fell silent, furrowing his brow in thought. Then he answered: "Twenty minutes, maybe. I didn't check the time."

Alex studied him. A father, a daughter. Not love, but ownership.

"And what happened during that twenty minutes?" she asked him.

Varricchio turned to look at her.

"I hadn't seen him in a long, long time. He hadn't even come to visit his father. You know my story, don't you? Never once had he come to see me in prison, to look me in the face, never once had he come back to the village since I was released. I wouldn't have recognized him, if I'd seen him on the street. They say that blood has a voice. Then I must be a little bit deaf, because I never heard it."

The officer insisted.

"Let me ask you the question again: what happened in the apartment?"

"I told him: you do as you please. You're clearly ashamed of your father, you studied here, you've always done what was best for you. As far as you've been concerned, there never was such a thing as your family, so do whatever you like. But your sister is coming home, because that's where she belongs."

"And what was his answer?" Lojacono asked.

A leering grin flitted across Varrichio's face.

"That I'd broken the family by getting myself thrown into jail for killing a man. That I just needed to leave them alone, him and his sister. That Grazia was a good young woman, and she had every right to enjoy a good life. I asked him: just what does a good life mean to you? Being a slut in the city, or going to live with that useless idiot of a singer-songwriter of hers?"

His tone was distant, coldly descriptive. As if he were reading the transcription of a conversation. Piras broke in: "In short, you had an argument and the discussion degenerated from there."

"Dottore', I'm his father. It's not as if I'm going to hold in certain things. I gave him a smack in the face."

That admission caught everyone off balance.

"So you're saying you laid your hands on him."

"I'm saying I gave him a smack in the face. Can't a father give his son a smack in the face, or has the world turned completely upside down when it comes to that as well?"

The police chief coughed.

"Did he hit you back?"

Varricchio almost burst out laughing.

"Seriously. You actually think that sons can turn around and hit their fathers, nowadays. No, he didn't hit me back. He said that I needed to leave, that if I didn't, he'd call you, the police, and he'd have me arrested again, and that that's exactly where I belong, behind bars. He'd never go back there as long as he lived, and he didn't want his sister to go back either."

"What did you do then?"

"I laughed in his face. I asked him: if I refuse to leave, what are you going to do to me? Will you kick me out the door? At that point, he changed his tone. He asked me: Do you understand that your daughter is grown up now, that I'm a grown-up too, and that we're no longer the children you left behind when they put you behind bars? Then he actually offered me money."

"Money? What money?" Lojacono asked immediately.

Once again that same leering grin appeared on Varricchio's face.

"He said that he was going to earn enough to keep his

sister like a lady, and even enough to let me live comfortably back home without ever having to work another day in my life. At that point, I looked around at the pigsty they lived in, and I had another laugh and said to him: I see how much money you have, I see how nicely you're both living."

Lojacono was utterly focused now.

"Did he say anything else to you about the money? How was he planning to—"

Di Vincenzo, deciding that Piras's warning to remain silent had expired by now, impatiently addressed the police chief.

"I've had enough, Dottore, what's the purpose of all these questions? Are we or aren't we interested in understanding whether this man, an ex-convict with a criminal conviction for murder who's only been out of prison for less than a year, came expressly up here from his hometown to murder these two poor kids? I don't understand the purpose—"

Piras whipped around on him like a tiger, her upper lip bared to reveal her teeth.

"Di Vincenzo," she snarled, "I warned you. Get out of this room right now. You have no jurisdiction over this investigation."

Di Vincenzo turned beet red and stared at the police chief again.

"Dottore, we're in your office, not in the courthouse, and so, quite frankly, I don't see why I need to take orders from—"

The police chief leaned back in his chair.

"You're quite right, Di Vincenzo. So I find myself obliged to order you to do as Dottoressa Piras just requested. Go home, Di Vincenzo. If there's any need for you to be informed as to the outcome of this interview, I'll tell you all about it. *Buonanotte.*"

Di Vincenzo stood up with a taut, lurching motion and, shooting a glare charged with hatred at Lojacono, who didn't bat an eye, left the room. Palma hoped never to cross paths with him again: that wasn't a man likely to soon forget or forgive being humiliated.

Piras turned back to Varricchio.

"Answer the question, please. Did your son tell you how he planned to obtain that money?"

Varricchio shook his head.

"He said that he only needed a short time to get it and that it had to do with the work he did. Nonsense. Anyway, I just left."

Alex was dubious.

"Without any more fighting?"

Varricchio leaned toward her.

"What was I supposed to do, Signori'? Kill him?"

The wisecrack was so macabre that everyone was disconcerted.

That man was devoid of emotions, Palma decided. A man like that could kill his children.

Lojacono was the only one to maintain his composure.

"Listen carefully. I'd like to know how you got into the apartment. Also, when you left, did you meet anyone else?"

The questions astonished just about everyone, including Varricchio, who furrowed his brow, struggling to remember.

"I rang the doorbell and he came downstairs and opened the door for me. He recognized me immediately; just as well because, like I told you, I would never have recognized him. When I left . . . no, I didn't run into anyone. I slammed the door and left."

Palma looked at Piras meaningfully: the man had no alibi to ward off suspicion.

The prosecutor nodded and the commissario asked: "Then what did you do?"

Varricchio shrugged.

"I waited downstairs in the street for a while, to see if Grazia would arrive. Then I figured that maybe, slut that she was, she wouldn't come home at all, and standing out in the street like that was freezing me solid. And so I walked, at random, until I wound up in a bar. I had several drinks and then I went in search of a whore."

Palma persisted.

"What time did you pick up this prostitute?"

"I couldn't say. I'd had a lot to drink. I don't remember."

A moment of silence, then Alex spoke.

"So you're saying you just gave up. The first time he said no. You traveled miles and miles, hours and hours, and all your son had to say was no. You could have picked up the phone, you would have saved a lot of time and effort."

"No, I hadn't resigned myself. But they weren't children anymore, Signori'. I'd lost them. The wasted time wasn't the hours of that trip, it was the sixteen years I spent in prison thinking how nice it was going to be when I finally saw them again. By now they were just a couple of strangers. And I also found out what I had become, in those sixteen years: a useless man. The real shame, Signori', isn't the freedom they take away from you, it's the man that they kill. And I'm a deader man today than that poor soul I beat to death all those years ago, all because of one beer too many."

"Why didn't you just go back home, then? Why didn't you just go and catch the first train out?"

"And what was I supposed to tell the people back home? That not even my own children wanted to see me? At least I could let them think that I'd spent some time with them. That they'd taken me in for a few days. That they'd said: Papà, stay with us for a while, that way we can tell you what we've been up to in all these years."

The police chief ordered the two uniformed officers to take Varricchio to another room. The night was giving way to a chilly dawn.

Piras ran a hand over her tired eyes.

"What do you say? He has no alibi, he has a motive, and he had opportunity. He admits that he was there."

The police chief nodded.

"What's more, he's an ex-convict, with a notorious reputation for out-of-control bursts of rage. Even behind bars, he was involved in a couple of brawls."

Gerardi, the director of the mobile squad, who had kept his mouth shut up to that point, out of fear of winding up like Di Vincenzo, decided that his time had come.

"In any case, he wasn't captured as a result of the investigations undertaken by the Pizzofalcone police precinct. That at least should be made clear."

Palma snapped.

"Let's not talk nonsense, we were hot on his trail. And as far as that goes, we weren't likely to find him as long as he was shut up in a pensione over by the central train station."

Piras came to his aid.

"The commissario has a point. Let's order his arrest and go on home."

What Lojacono said next stunned everyone.

"But what if it wasn't him? Are we going to toss him behind bars on the basis of mere suppositions? Someone whose two children were just murdered?"

Palma stared at him aghast, as if his own dog had just bitten his hand while he was petting it.

"What . . . on earth are you talking about? He has no alibi . . . And did you hear the tone of voice he used? We're grieving about those kids more than he is! The Dottoressa, too, thinks—"

The lieutenant stood up.

"Everyone reacts to tragedies differently. Maybe it was the trauma that's causing him to act this way. In any case, boss, I'm not saying he's innocent, I'm just saying that there are matters that have yet to be looked into. Why would he have killed them? And how would he have done it?"

Piras stared at him, grim-faced. Only now, now that the shuttering of the Pizzofalcone police precinct seemed to have been warded off, he of all people was putting in his two cents.

"What do you mean, how would he have done it? First he killed his son, then he pretended to leave the apartment after the end of the screaming fight, and then waited for the young woman to return home, and murdered her, too."

Lojacono shook his head.

"I don't know about that, I'm not certain. It's just my opinion, nothing more."

The police chief stood up.

"All right then, let's all get a few hours of sleep and we'll all be able to think more clearly. In the meantime, let's hold him overnight, Laura. Let's see if he has a lawyer, and if he doesn't we'll make sure he has a court-assigned one and then we talk about logistics. We can convene a press conference and announce that we have a suspect. *Buonanotte*, everyone."

On their way out, Palma fell into step next to Lojacono.

"I don't know how the fuck you make certain decisions," he told him in a hard voice. "Tomorrow morning we'll have a general meeting in the office and decide on a common plan of action. Common, understood?"

The lieutenant nodded.

And went to his car.

XLIX

Aragona strolled through the front door of the police station whistling a little tune, very proud of himself. With an immense spirit of sacrifice, he'd forced himself to come into the police station monstrously early, and in fact it was a good solid half hour until the beginning of the shift. He was really savoring the looks he expected on everyone else's faces when they walked into the squad room and spotted their hardworking colleague already at his desk. What would they do then, deprived of their usual opportunity to mock and deride him?

What's more, he didn't want to set himself up for a brutal dressing down by Palma. The fear that the precinct under his command might soon be shut down because of an unsuccessful investigation into the double homicide had stoked his superior officer's hysterical tendencies. Better to avoid him.

He trotted up the stairs with a cheerful burst of energy, threw open the door, and found the entire team arrayed before him, immersed in a strange silence. He took off his glasses, checked the watch on his wrist, the clock on the wall, and then again the watch on his wrist, establishing beyond a doubt that they were perfectly synchronized. And at that point he threw both arms wide.

"Why, what the . . . Tell me the truth, you all sleep here, don't you? Are you a theatrical troupe on tour, prison convicts, or something else of that kind? It can't be: It's not even eight in the morning yet!"

"Arago', shut up, this morning isn't the time for it," Romano retorted, in a foul mood. "Didn't you read Palma's message summoning us all here at this time of the morning? It's a good thing for you that you came in earlier than usual, otherwise he would have skinned you alive."

The officer pulled his cell phone out of his pocket.

"No, I had it turned off. Is there some regulation that it always has to be turned on? Why, what's happened?"

Palma appeared. In a break with routine, he was neat and tidy, well turned out, tie knotted, jacket buttoned. Even his hair looked kempt, and he'd recently shaved. He was carrying a small stack of paper.

He checked to make sure that everyone was present, and then let his gaze linger briefly on Lojacono, seated at his desk with the documentation concerning the Vico Secondo Egiziaca case spread out in front of him.

"*Buongiorno*, thank you all for coming in early this morning," he began. "As some of you know, last night Cosimo Varricchio, the father of the two murdered kids, turned himself in of his own free will at police headquarters, and was questioned by Dottoressa Piras in the presence of the chief of police and a couple of high officials: the chief of the mobile squad Gerardi and Commissario Di Vincenzo, designated successor to be put in charge of the investigation in case we were judged to have failed. I am pleased to be able to tell you those of you who weren't present that Di Vincenzo was eventually ordered out of the room by Piras."

There was a stirring of triumphant surprise among all those present. Nearly all those present. Alex limited herself to returning Ottavia's smile, while Lojacono remained impassive.

Palma continued staring at him. He went on: "Given that the questioning of Varricchio was determined to be dispositive, later this morning there will be a press conference to inform the news media that we have finally made an arrest for the double homicide. I've been invited to attend, which means that the work done by the team in this police station has been fully recognized. It's a major achievement, and it chases away a number of our lingering phantoms. The danger of the precinct being mothballed hasn't been eliminated entirely, but if nothing else, we have shown that we know how to do our job."

A sense of uneasiness seeped through the room. Why was Palma speaking in such understated tones, at complete odds with the substance of his words?

Pisanelli gave voice to the general sense of bafflement.

"But listen, boss, if everything's going so well, why aren't you happy? Is there something that's bothering you?"

Palma replied without changing his expression.

"Yes, yes there is. Last night, at the end of the interview, and in the presence of Gerardi, one of our most relentless enemies, Lieutenant Lojacono expressed serious doubts about the theory of Varricchio's guilt. And by so doing, he made it clear that we don't all agree on just who it was that murdered the two kids."

What ensued was a moment of collective awkwardness. Lojacono didn't lower his gaze before Palma's hard-eyed glare.

"But what did the guy say?" asked Romano. "Because I'm starting to get the idea that he hasn't confessed."

At this point, Palma snapped.

"Because as we all know, guilty parties invariably confess, right? If we only sent people to prison who had made full confessions, then the whole problem of overcrowded prisons would be a thing of the past. Of course he hasn't confessed. But he has no alibi, he definitely has a motive, he admits that he was in the apartment and that he had an argument with his son, in fact, that he even laid hands on him. And he displays absolute indifference to what happened to the two kids. He hasn't even asked for a lawyer to be present."

Ottavia looked at Lojacono.

"Giuseppe, why don't you think that it was him?"

Lojacono continued staring at the commissario, who waved his hand to indicate he should speak.

"I'm not saying that it wasn't him. I'm just saying that we don't have any proof that clinches it. In practical terms, he's in the same position as the young woman's boyfriend, or anyone else who can't prove that they were somewhere else during the hours the double homicide took place. And the truth is that Varricchio has a point: since he's an ex-convict and a Calabrian, he's guilty until proven otherwise."

Palma raised his voice.

"How can you think that I'd base my actions on such flimsy prejudices? If that's the way I operated, none of you would even be here! He has no alibi and—"

Lojacono interrupted him, calmly.

"He could have denied having a fight with his son. He could have said that he'd been welcomed in affectionately and that he'd had nothing to do with the argument overheard by the neighbors. He could have pretended to be upset and in despair. He could have denied any disagreement with his daughter, and we would have had nothing to use against him."

Aragona broke in.

"Well, he's certainly not a relaxed individual, if he murdered someone with his bare hands. And those two kids were murdered with such a violent beating that—"

Romano hushed him.

"Arago', you never miss an opportunity to talk bullshit, do you? Because all that a guy has to do is make a mistake once, and then anything that happens in the radius of three hundred miles to anyone he's ever met is his fault? Lojacono is right: If we don't have solid evidence, then we have to go on searching."

Stung, Aragona shrugged his shoulders, grabbed a magazine off Lojacono's nearby desk, and from that point on feigned utter disinterest in the conversation.

Palma looked at Romano, in astonishment.

"And now you're putting in your two cents. Didn't you all hear me say that we're going to cease investigating? Of course we'll continue, but in the meantime, at least, we won't have the case taken away from us."

Alex spoke, as if to herself.

"And in the meantime, a man who may be innocent will sit in a jail cell, thinking over and over again about all the mistakes he made in his life, perhaps feeling indirectly responsible for the deaths of his children. Worse than hell."

Palma ran his hand through his hair.

"All right, then, let's do this: let's reverse the order of the process. Convince me that Varricchio isn't guilty. Give me one reason to believe that it wasn't him. You do realize that he vanished entirely for three days, and he didn't even know that we were looking for him? The minute we release him, I guarantee, that's the last we've seen of him. We'll never find him again."

Ottavia sensed the commissario's dismay and came to his assistance.

"That's right. We can continue the investigation all the same. If we identify another culprit he'll be set free, otherwise we'll go on sifting through the evidence. It's not as if the attorney general is going to indict just on the basis of suspicion and flimsy clues."

"There are still too many details that don't add up, as far as I'm concerned," said Lojacono. "A person doesn't have an outburst of rage, kill their son, pretend to leave, slamming the door behind them, and then wait for their daughter to come home and than assault her, simulating a rape. What's more . . . "—and here he searched through the sheets of paper on the desk in front of him—"there is this six-minute phone call between brother and sister at 6:32. What did he do, then, did he leave the building, make a call from his son's cell phone, talk to his daughter and tell her to come home with the intention of murdering her as well, and then go back inside?"

Palma shrugged his shoulders.

"Theoretically, it's possible. Just as it's possible that he simply came back later. In other words: it's conjectures that suggest we should arrest Varricchio and it's conjectures that lead us to think it might not have been him. But if the only way of keeping our hands on the investigation is to—"

"The money," Alex murmured. "There's still the matter of the money."

"What do you mean?" asked Pisanelli.

The young woman turned to look at him.

"I keep wondering: what became of the thirty-seven hundred euros that the young woman was paid for her photographs? She knew that she could have earned a great deal more, Cava had told her so and I believe him, because he was obsessed with her, as is proved by the phone calls. So why did Grazia want that exact sum of money, and why did she want it so urgently?"

Lojacono filled in the point that his partner had raised.

"And that's not all. Biagio promised Foti that he would help him record a CD. And Cosimo Varricchio, too, told us that his son was certain that he'd be able to ensure financial security for himself and his sister, and even for him, the father, if he would just leave them alone. It's clear that he expected a significant cash influx, before long. Something much bigger than just thirty-seven hundred euros."

Palma stubbornly shook his head.

"Maybe he was just talking nonsense to get rid of his father and maintain good relations with his sister's boyfriend. Or else he'd invented a scientific system for betting on horse races. Let's not talk nonsense, if you please."

Aragona was leafing through the magazine, sprawled in his chair.

"Certainly this obsession with the thirty-seven hundred euros was a family trait," he said in an offhanded tone, as if he were having a conversation at the bar.

Palma turned beet-red with fury.

"Aragona, don't you understand that when we're having a serious conversation nobody wants to hear your wisecracks? I don't—"

Lojacono had turned toward his colleague, his curiosity piqued.

"Why do you say that?"

"Didn't you read the article about this business over at the university?" Aragona replied. "Or do you just look at the pictures?"

Lojacono exchanged a glance with Alex.

"But it's just an interview, Professor Forgione mentioned it to us, there isn't any—"

Aragona tapped his finger on a page.

"Lookie here."

Lojacono read aloud.

"Question: 'Dottor Varricchio, you are considered one of the most promising young scientists in the country. Tell us something that might encourage other young people to enter the world of research.' Answer: 'Many people assume that this is a sterile world, where there are no opportunities to make any real money. That's not true. A patent, which costs more or less thirty-seven hundred euros, can allow you to sell the results of your research to a manufacturer, and in some cases, it can even make you rich. Young people today can think of research as a significant source of revenue.'"

A sense of bafflement was seeping through the room.

"Well?" asked Romano. "What's so odd about that? All right, it was a reference to a sum that—"

Alex leapt to her feet, her eyes glittering as she stared at Lojacono.

"A patent. She paid for her brother's patent. And that's why Biagio preferred working at home over the past few months, in spite of the fact that he had no internet, forcing himself to put up with a great deal of inconvenience with the laboratory at the university."

Palma was confused.

"So . . . what does all this mean? It doesn't have anything to do with the father's visit and—"

Lojacono was rummaging through the files on his desk.

"Romano, on that list . . . where the heck is it . . . I clearly remember, among the things he had in his wallet there was . . . Here it is!" He raised a xerox triumphantly into the air. "A return receipt from a registered letter. You can clearly read the addresss of the recipient, see, boss: 'Trademark and Patent Office, Rome.' This is it!"

Palma turned to look at Ottavia, as if seeking help.

"I don't understand, what does this have to do with anything? . . . We're investigating the fact that Varricchio worked at home instead of going to the laboratory. So he submitted a request for a patent, what of it?"

As if Alex hadn't heard him, she said to Lojacono: "The key. He didn't even have to knock to get in."

The lieutenant nodded.

"He went to demand an explanation. An explanation for everything, and he thought he had a right to demand it."

"Certainly. He was paying, and that meant, in his head, that he was buying."

By this point, Alex and Lojacono were just talking directly to each other, as if there was no one else in the room but them. Romano had the impression he was watching a ping-pong match.

The lieutenant added: "And, of course, nobody knew anything. That was in both their interests."

A smile spread across Alex's face: "Until the sister arrived.

That's when everything went to hell, when it all slipped out of control."

Aragona was sick and tired of that call-and-response.

"Listen, if you'd be kind enough to explain it to us, too, you'd be doing us a favor."

Lojacono stood up and grabbed his overcoat.

"Boss, I'd recommend you postpone the press conference. I have a feeling you'll be announcing a very different piece of news, by the time the morning's over. And please, trust me, sell it as well as you can, because you're absolutely right: Your team is on top of things. The very best. Come on, Alex, let's go."

Before heading out, in front of the appalled eyes of the whole officeful of officers, Di Nardo planted a kiss on Aragona's cheek, telling him: "Officer Marco Aragona, you're a goddamned genius."

He swept off his eyeglasses with a self-conscious gesture.

"You're right about that. But later you'll explain exactly why, right?"

Alex was already chasing Lojacono down the stairs.

L

To get there, they had to ask directions. They were absolutely unable to remember how they had gotten there the previous time.

In words of one syllable and choked off phrases, they'd done their best to put together a strategy. It was no easy matter. They possessed no incontrovertible proof that could put their target with his back to the wall, and they had no doubt that he possessed the knowledge and the tools to upset their plan. They needed to rely on his lack of cold-blooded confidence, the intrinsic instability of his personality, the tension that had built up deep inside him over the past few days.

His remorse.

They had very little in hand and only one opportunity before his mind started cooking up alibis and erecting defensive walls. Only one chance to ensure that the one who paid wasn't an innocent man, a man who had just lost both his children.

That an ancient transgression not cast a shadow of guilt over an entire lifetime.

Alex carried in her heart a deep well of regret for having attributed, in her own personal mental process, the scarlet letter of guilt to Varricchio at the very instant she'd heard him speak, the night before. Transferring to the Calabrian family the subterranean injustices and secret dynamics of her own family, she had judged him guilty of murdering his own flesh and blood, by first depriving them of their happy adolescence, and then actually cutting off their lives, root and branch. Now that she knew what had actually happened, she was more determined than ever to see justice done.

Lojacono, too, was driven by a similar degree of determination. He was not willing to renounce, for his own advancement, the principles that had first convinced him to become a policeman, and truth be told, he'd never really been persuaded of the idea that Varricchio had killed his children. Sadly, it was something that happened: financial interests, sheer pettiness, and abject ignorance did sometimes lead to that sort of murder. But the man had left his home to ask his daughter to come back and live with him, because he didn't want to grow old all alone in an open-air prison all too similar to the one in which he had been confined far too long. He simply couldn't have committed such a cold-blooded murder.

In the very few hours he'd spent lying in bed staring at the ceiling, listening to the restless sleep of Marinella, who had dropped off fully dressed, the lieutenant had plumbed the depths of his own immense love as a father, and he had realized that there was no room in it for any hypothesis of hatred, no matter what might happen. And his doubts about Cosimo's guilt had only emerged reinforced, along with the determination to oppose a deduction that was too simplistic to be plausible, namely that the man had murdered Biagio and Grazia, the son in a fit of rage, the daughter out of premeditated animus.

Then Aragona had read the interview and the pieces of the jigsaw puzzle had fallen into place. The overall picture had come into focus in all its tragic harmony, explaining all the hows but especially the whys and wherefores. A picture that made perfect sense from square one but which was only fully visible now, and which supplied an answer to each and every question.

That however did nothing to solve the problem.

Before anyone noticed their presence, they observed the everyday activity of the laboratory through a soundproof plate glass window, which gave them the impression that they were watching a silent movie. The researchers moved back and forth around and through the instruments with skill and dexterity; it seemed impossible that they never bumped each other or broke anything. Every so often one of them would make a wisecrack and the others would laugh, or else they'd limit themselves to a brief exchange of glances; from time to time they'd exchange data that they read aloud off computer screens. Alex and Lojacono decided that, all things considered, collective workplaces tended to look the same everywhere, that in terms of human interactions, there was no difference between that laboratory and the squad room at the police station.

Renato Forgione was sitting off to one side. He was ashen-faced, and his eyes were wandering without concentration. No one was speaking to him, as if his colleagues were intentionally avoiding him.

Then the young man looked up and saw them. His eyelids fluttered as if he were trying to ward off a horrible hallucination, and Lojacono thought he'd detected a slight slumping of his shoulders underneath his lab coat, almost a reaction of dismay.

He emerged from the laboratory, walked over to them, and spoke to them in a monotone.

"*Buongiorno*. Did you need me? Is there any news?"

At first, the two policemen said nothing. Then Lojacono pulled several sheets of paper out of his overcoat pocket.

"Let me come straight to the point, Dr. Forgione. Were you aware of the fact that, last October 21st, Biagio Varricchio had submitted a request to the Trademark and Patent Office of Rome in his own name?"

Forgione shut his eyes and then opened them again, as if he'd just been slapped in the face.

"Me? No, how could I have—"

Alex drilled in.

"Isn't that what you went to talk to Dr. Varricchio about after reading the interview with him in the university magazine?"

Renato took a step back.

"What are you talking about? I couldn't have known anything about that. And when do you think I went to see Biagio, anyway?"

Lojacono dealt the blow.

"We happen to know that you were at his apartment late on Monday evening. You came in through the downstairs entrance using your own key, which you have because your father is the owner of several apartments in the building, and then you left several minutes after Grazia Varricchio's return home, listening to music in the earbuds of her cell phone. There was no one else there, which means that the double homicide was committed in your presence. We've also found the murder weapon, and we're in the process of taking fingerprints from it now."

Alex held her breath.

Forgione replied instinctively, albeit with a shaking voice: "What are you saying? The statuette is at my house and—"

Alex breathed again. It was over.

Lojacono leveled his almond-shaped eyes into Renato Forgione's.

"Stay calm," he said. "It's all going to be much easier, now. Please come with us."

LI

You don't know my father. You have no idea what he's like.

My whole life, I've felt that damned pressure crushing down on me. If he'd demanded something, if he'd hammered at me, maybe I would have been capable of defending myself, of living my life. But he never did. He just looks at you, nothing more.

He has a gaze, you know, that stings the flesh worse than ten cracks of a bullwhip. A bitter, pained, sorrowful gaze. A gaze that tells you: I understand, you hate me. You have it in for me. That's why you don't excel, that's why you're not the best.

I'm the only son of a great man. I've never had anyone else to share the burden with me. In that, Biagio was luckier.

Seems ridiculous, doesn't it? To call someone lucky who practically never even knew his father just because he had a sister. And yet I'm sure of it, he was the lucky one. He actually had a family.

My father isn't a family, he's a great man. He's a genius. Did you know that he was shortlisted for a Nobel Prize a few years ago? They informed us of the fact privately. He's world-famous in a sector as small and restricted as ours. That's right, in our sector, because there was never the slightest doubt that I was bound to follow in his footsteps.

I liked music, do you know that? When I was a kid, I played the guitar, strictly self-taught; it might have been the only thing

I felt I was really good at. I asked him if I could take a few lessons. He told me that he wouldn't tolerate the slightest distraction from my studies. He had a look on his face, when he said it, that I wish I could show you. The face of someone who'd just been stabbed in the back. And so from then on, no more guitar lessons, Renato. Nothing at all.

I met Biagio in my second year at the university. Let me tell you one thing: I know how to study. When it comes to memorizing things, spending time with my nose in a book, staying up all night to prepare for an exam, I'm outstanding. But I don't have a speck of intuition. No. I have no imagination, I don't get special or innovative ideas, I don't see things that other people miss. Biagio did. He'd understand things in a flash, then he'd reconstruct them with proofs: and they were identical to the ones in the book.

Like nearly everyone, he would have liked to be a doctor, but he didn't even bother to take the admission test. I have no doubt he would have pulverized that test, he would have gotten the highest score in the whole country, but he couldn't afford to study medicine. It took too long, you had to buy too many books, the fees were too high. Biagio didn't have a cent to his name.

He chose to major in Biotechnology because he thought that meant he could start working earlier. To make ends meet, he did any work he could get. He was even a moving man, can you believe it? He transported furniture and boxes. And he managed to send some money home to his sister.

We met at a final exam. We talked a while and decided to study for the next exam together. And since then we remained fast friends.

Until Grazia arrived.

It was all going great, you know?

I gave him money, true. In fact, I paid for everything.

We're pretty wealthy. The great man earns a good salary,

but he doesn't care about that: he works for the glory of it, there are certain things he pays no mind. So I could just take all the money I wanted and give it to Biagio. To make sure he didn't have to go find a job, to keep him from going away and stranding me here.

We were a team, you understand? A team. He would intuit things, establish the overall guidelines, and then I would follow up on them stubbornly. We signed our articles jointly. Every so often I'd sign them alone; he'd let me do it, for money. That way, the great man could be proud of his genius son and forgive him his eccentric notion of hauling along a little bit of extra Calabrian ballast on his journey. He had no idea that things were actually the other way round. In the end, it turns out that the great man makes mistakes, sometime.

We'd have gone on like that for years. I'd have undertaken my university career, and once I had built a foundation, with a teaching position somewhere, Biagio would be able to choose whether or not to follow the same path or instead look for a job in manufacturing. In the meantime, the great man would enjoy his retirement, and we would be free. Yes, we'd have gone on like that.

Then his sister arrived.

She had won the statuette at a beauty contest when she was sixteen, at the beach. And she'd given it to her brother. Biagio was prouder of her than of our publications. He was subjugated by Grazia, who was like a cross between daughter, sister, and girlfriend. When he introduced her to me, you should have seen him, he seemed out of his mind with joy. What an asshole.

Then he started telling me about her idiot boyfriend who wanted to become a reggae singer; and his father, the murderer, who sooner or later was bound to show up to take her back home. Which is what happened, isn't it? In the end, that's what happened.

He'd got it into his head that he needed to straighten out

his sister's life. He didn't know how, but he was going to straighten it out. I certainly couldn't finance the dreams of glory that he had for her. Even the great man would have gotten mad about that, if I'd spent too much money. I told him to be patient, the academic competition for the position would take place in a year or so, he'd help me to win it, and after that he'd be free to choose more remunerative activities.

But he wasn't willing to wait.

I should have figured out that he'd started working on his own. I should have figured it out. He had an old idea about an industrial yeast, something that, if it had worked, would be able to almost double the output of ethanol, with the same energy output. He'd come in to the laboratory, stay until late, gather up his data, and then go home to work on them further. And I, idiot that I was, believed that he just wanted to be able to keep an eye on his sister.

I wonder where he got the money for the patent. It costs, you know. You need almost four thousand euros, and he didn't have anything like that amount of cash. She must have got her hands on it; maybe she worked as a whore. No doubt about it, she was pretty. That's a fact. Biagio said that she looked exactly like his mother as a young woman.

Then that interview came out, and I understood. You know when the veil falls off your eyes? Everything was suddenly clear. The photograph, what he was saying about patents. The possibility of earning through research, and so on and so forth. I understood why he'd stopped coming to the university, why he was no longer working on new articles, or on our joint projects. He was dumping me. He was leaving, ready to earn his own money.

So I went to talk to him. That was my apartment, you understand? My own home. He was robbing me of my future, my prospects, out of my own apartment. I went there and I asked him to tell me honestly what he was doing.

He didn't deny a thing. He didn't even dream of it. He told me that he'd had no choice, that his sister's life was at stake. That there was no time to spare, otherwise Grazia would go off with that guy and she'd ruin her chances. That's what he said: she'd ruin her chances. And his father had arrived, too. The only way he had to resolve that impasse was the patent for his yeast.

His yeast.

He had discovered it and formulated it in my father's laboratory, with the resources and tools I'd put at his disposal, while living in my apartment, eating the food that I brought him, and yet he insisted that the yeast belonged to him.

I couldn't even bring myself to speak. I just looked at him and said nothing. And at a certain point, he turned away from me and started checking an equation as if nothing had happened.

I think I lost my mind there. But I was cold. I could see myself from outside, as if in some movie. I turned around and took the statuette off its shelf. One blow. Then more. I don't remember exactly.

I'd just finished, I would have left the place calmly, and she would have survived. She was as guilty as he was, but she would have made it out alive. Instead, the door swings open and in she comes.

I realized I was done for when you said that she had the earbuds in her ears. How could you have known that? Did you see her? Some outside security camera, is that it? You always read about that in the newspapers.

I put my hands over her face, I was wearing gloves; with the brutal cold we've been having, my hands go numb. Then I choked her, and I only stopped once I was certain that she could no longer scream. I put her on the bed: maybe it would look like someone had come in and had tried to rape her. It's full of immigrants around here, and she is so pretty. She was so pretty.

I'm not sorry for what I did. He was a damned thief. I thought he was my friend, my best friend, but I was wrong. He was a backstabber.

A weasel, a goddamned traitor. Say so, to the great man, tell him that it wasn't my fault. I'm innocent.

I miss him, actually, though. After each exam, after each journal article, after every success, you know what we would do? We'd hug. I never hugged anyone, but he and I would hug. Damn him.

Damn him.

LII

You need to look out for the cold. Because, over time, the cold will seep into your bones and insinuate itself into your soul.

And when it insinuates itself into souls, it changes them; it dries up the source of a smile, it fills with ice the gaps that once made it possible to stroll along the brink of sentiments and emotion, enchanting you with the sight of the panorama.

Look out for the cold.

Giorgio Pisanelli set out once again on foot for the park outside the National Library.

Once again, he was running late. The news of the arrest of Renato Forgione had thrown not only the police station into a state of frantic disarray, but the entire city. There'd been a cavalcade of reporters and television news crews in Pizzofalcone, eager to dig into every nook and cranny of an investigation that promised to be sensational, in the best possible way, luckily: the police had broken the case of the two murdered siblings in less than five days. And just think, it had been none other than the Bastards who had pulled off that coup.

In spite of that, the deputy captain felt weighed down by an enormous burden. His chat with Leonardo had undermined all his certainties: What if the monk was right? What if actually this whole idea of a murderer of the desperate, the lonely, and the depressed was just something he needed for himself? A fantasy built especially to avoid drifting helplessly downstream?

Once he reached the deserted, frost-ridden flower beds, as he watched his breath steam before him, Pisanelli saw himself for what he really was: an old, sick man, close to the end. A man toying with his own madness, someone who spent his evenings talking with his dead wife. Dead. Carmen was dead, and he was refusing to accept that simple reality.

Maybe he himself ought to step aside from life.

He looked around. Agnese wasn't there.

Are you dead, too, Agnese? he wondered. And he asked the question aloud, in the lunar landscape of the park, empty of the shouts of children, the stern voices of mothers, and the melodious notes of birdsong. Of spring, which might never return.

He let himself collapse on the bench, indifferent to the freezing cold that stabbed into him through his clothing. He was tired. The idea of giving up, of yielding once and for all to the silence, didn't frighten him; if anything, it comforted him. He decided that it might perhaps be time to shuffle offstage, because the emptiness of the performance he was staging day after day now struck him as unbearable.

A little bird hopped toward his feet. Lazily, poking through the icy fog that veiled his heart, he greeted the bird and, through it, his poor friend, who might perhaps be dangling now from a knotted sheet, or lying in her bed, stuffed with pills, no longer breathing. I'm sorry, Agnese. I'm so sorry. I couldn't manage to save you. And I can't even manage to save myself.

He lay down. The cold was terrible. Even the pale afternoon sun had abandoned that patch of park in defeat. He shut his eyes.

Ciao, Leonardo, old friend of mine. At this time of day you must be preparing for your spiritual exercises. Don't feel guilty about not being there when I left this world.

Ciao, Carmen, my darling love. How I wish I could believe that we're going to see each other soon, and then spend the rest of eternity together. How I wish it were true, so that I'd be about to caress your sweet face once again.

Ciao, Agnese. I hope you can find peace. And I hope I can find it, too.

"*Ciao*, Giorgio."

The synchronicity between his last thought and the arrival of that voice had been so perfect that he didn't even start at the sound. Pisanelli felt a hand gently touching him, and he sat up.

"Thanks for holding a place for me. I hope that Raimondo didn't think that his Mamma had forgotten about him. You see him? He was waiting for me."

Agnese sat down and started scattering breadcrumbs for the sparrow, which set to pecking happily.

"You know, I'd dozed off. And in my dream he was saying to me: Come on, Mamma, don't you see how late it is? Giorgio must be getting worried. I jumped out of bed and I hurried over. How are you?"

Pisanelli looked at her for an instant. Then he put his arm around her shoulder and said: "Fine, Agnese. I'm fine."

Beware of the cold, because the cold can change you.

The cold is capable of whispering horrible stories in your ear, sad stories that will turn your mood gray.

You see the cold out your window, as it extends fingers of fog and ice throughout the night, slowly and inexorably invading the streets and your thoughts.

There is no army that can withstand the invasion of the cold. It arrives like a death sentence, and there is nothing you can do.

You can only wait, and pray to survive a little longer.

Without letting the cold change you too much.

Ottavia stuck her head into Palma's office to bid him goodnight. The commissario was standing by the window, with his back turned. His arms were crossed and his back was bowed.

"Everything all right, boss?" the woman asked softly.

He replied without turning around.

"Ah, Ottavia. Yes, have a good evening."

His chilly tone hit her like a rough shove.

"What's wrong?" she whispered. "We broke the case, didn't we?"

Palma turned and gave her a tight smile. His face was tired, marked by deep circles under his eyes.

"Certainly, of course. You were outstanding. And you in particular, standing up to the onslaught of the journalists and maintaining total confidence, letting nothing slip. I saw the news reports here, on the office television set. They're so good at trading in mere conjecture."

Ottavia was worried.

"Boss, what's the matter? You don't look happy to me. We've caught the murderer, everyone's talking about us: now there's no way anyone will call for the precinct to be shuttered. It's what we wanted, isn't it?"

The commissario sprawled in his chair.

"Yes. It's exactly what we wanted. But I wasn't up to the task. And I just can't figure out why not."

"What are you talking about? You were in charge of us, you were in constant contact with police headquarters, clearing the way so that we could do our work and come to the right solution. Without you, sir, this place would no longer even exist."

"No, Ottavia. You're very kind, but that's not the way it is. In order to score a point in this depressing rivalry that I've let myself be drawn into, I would have sent an innocent man to jail. A father, ravaged by remorse, a man who had already paid dearly, all too dearly, for a moment of blind rage. Just to win the match, just to keep the police station open, I would have taken a cheap shot, indifferent to the repercussions."

"But you really believed that Varricchio was guilty. We all did."

"Lojacono didn't, and he was right. I'd forgotten the reason I chose this profession in the first place: to find the truth. Maybe I'm not suited for the position I occupy. Maybe I should step aside."

Ottavia felt her heart tug. She walked around the desk and stepped close to him.

"Don't you say such a thing, not even in jest. Without you, we would be nothing, don't you understand that? We need a guide, a reference point, because we can't do it on our own. It's no accident that no one else wanted us. Only thanks to you have we rediscovered the strength that we thought we'd lost forever."

Palma looked up. They were extremely close.

"Maybe someone else could handle it better. Someone else wouldn't have forgotten that we have to be certain before we—"

Ottavia put her hand over his mouth.

"Hush now, hush. That's enough. I don't want to hear any more of this nonsense. I told you that we need you. That *I* need you."

Palma's eyes welled up with tears. Slowly, he lifted his arm from the desk and caressed Ottavia's hand.

She sensed his smile as it spread under the skin. Almost without realizing she was doing it, she started running the tips of her fingers over his face.

Then she turned and hurried away.

It's dangerous, the cold.

After you get over the first, stinging sensation, your flesh gets used to it and it all seems to be finished, but it's not.

The cold is a treacherous, sneaky enemy, it knows how to stage a torpor that seems like nothing more than ordinary somnolence, but is actually a bellwether of death.

The cold is treacherous, it knows how to work its way into the chinks of your armor, and once it's penetrated it's hard to get rid of it.

The cold knows how to kill with the weapon of silence.

Lojacono turned the key in the lock, heaved a sigh, and entered the apartment. Marinella was sitting at the dining room table, waiting for him.

As soon as she saw him, the young woman burst into tears.

"Papà, I'm so sorry. I didn't want to disappoint you."

He stood there, motionless, like a statue made of ice.

"Believe me, Papà. It was just a childish escapade, I wanted . . . you know, all my classmates go out with boys. He . . . he's a good person, he lives here in this building. I met him on the stairs. He's a university student."

Lojacono said nothing. He didn't even seem to be breathing.

"It's not Letizia's fault, I pushed her into it. She's so sweet and kind, she cares for me, like a mother. I just wanted it so much, I begged her, and in the end we agreed that I'd be back before the restaurant's closing time."

Silence. A cold silence.

"Papà, I'm begging you, answer me! I didn't do anything wrong, I swear to you. We went to the movies, we ate a hot dog, we laughed and we talked. I didn't do anything wrong."

Little by little, the tears streaked her cheeks, as her sobs shattered her phrases.

"Papà, I'm begging you, don't send me away. I'm happy here. Don't send me back to Mamma. I want to live here with you. I'll never lie to you again, I swear it, just don't do this to me. Don't leave me alone again. Please."

Lojacono's expression never altered. He headed off to his own bedroom. At the door, without turning around, he said: "It's been a long day. I'm hungry. Make dinner, please."

The cold, be careful, you might not even feel it.
Distracted by the humdrum events of your life, caught up in the pointless daily grind, you might not notice the cold.
We might not even stop to think, we miss the signals that come from outside.
We might continue gazing at our belly button as if it were the center of the solar system, all the while failing to notice that the cold is all around us.
That's when the cold envelops us, catching us off-guard.
And that's when the cold wins.

"Hello? Alex? *Ciao*, it's me. Congratulations, you're a superstar."

"Oh, come on, what are you talking about? I didn't do anything."

"Oh yes you did. Everyone's talking about it: Did you see what the Bastards managed to pull off? And it would seem that, if it hadn't been for you, the two victims' father—"

"Rosaria, the investigation wasn't over, that's all. Then the right evidence surfaced and we just drew the logical conclusions."

"I love it when you act all modest. You're even sexier. But I know exactly what's there, behind all that delicious shyness."

"Hey, cut that out! What if someone hears you?"

"So what? Are you ashamed of me?"

"No, I'm not ashamed. But you know as well as I do, we have to be careful, this isn't a relaxed work environment."

"I don't give a damn about the work environment. I already told you, this isn't just some ordinary thing. I'm not kidding around, Alex. And I want to see you again, right away."

"Rosaria, I . . . today I can't do it, I have to have dinner with my folks."

"What about tomorrow?"

"Please, let's let a few days go by. If it were up to me, I'd already be there at your side, you know that, but . . . "

"Do you mind if I ask what the problem is? If the two of us are happy together and if—"

"It's not just that. I . . . my folks don't know that . . . I mean to say, they don't know about me. They don't know that . . . "

"Do you understand that this just doesn't make sense? Do you really think this is possible? You're the wonderful woman that I know and you hide behind a—"

"That's not the way it is, you can't talk about things you don't understand. I . . . it isn't easy. It's not easy at all."

"Okay. I get it. Well, I'm not interested in—"

"No, Rosaria, don't be like that, please: it's not that I feel—"

"I'm not interested in a woman who doesn't have the strength to look at herself in the mirror: much less the strength to have a genuine love affair in defiance of all conventions. So just cling to your—"

"Rosaria, I'm begging you—"

" . . . cling to your little life. If you make up your mind to be yourself one day, give me a call. Even though I can't promise you that I'll be here waiting for you."

"I'm begging you, don't do this. Please."

. . .

"Please."

Because the cold has this effect.

It's only just arrived but it seems as if it's always been here. That it's never made way for sunlight, laughter, and the desire to be together.

The cold makes you want to shut yourself up indoors, never to see another soul.

Everything seems threatening in the cold. Everything seems terrible and dark.

The cold erases the future.

Francesco Romano was back in his car. Once again the cold was numbing his limbs, his nose, his ears.

Once again he was looking up at the windows of Giorgia's mother's apartment, unable to tear his eyes away.

He was turning an opened envelope over and over again in his hands, and inside that envelope was a sheet of paper. A single sheet of paper, and it wasn't even fully covered with writing: a scant half page of type.

More powerful than an air conditioner, that half page of type. More powerful than an air conditioner running full blast. Chilling, freezing.

A light blinked on. Romano visualized the guest room in his mind, where right now Giorgia would surely be staying. Who knew what his wife was doing. His wife? Yes, his wife. She was still his wife.

He hefted the envelope, as if the bulk of that fraction of an ounce of paper somehow corresponded to the words written on it. *Mamma mia*, how light it was.

He shifted in the seat, to keep his muscles from going to sleep. You'll have to come out at some point, he thought. You'll have to come out, sooner or later.

And you'll have to speak to me. You'll have to confront me and tell me to my face what's written on this piece of paper. And you'll have to convince me that it's true.

Because marriage is a serious matter, and you know that yourself. If someone agrees to live with someone, with no other commitment, they can leave whenever they like, and no one can say a thing. You don't stand up and make any promises to anybody, when you're just living together. You just set up housekeeping together, and that's that; all you need is a suitcase, to put an end to things. Holy matrimony, on the other hand, is a binding together of two hearts before man and God. You can't unravel that bond with a misguided backhand smack.

I don't believe it, Giorgia. I don't believe that you only want to see me again in front of a lawyer to hammer out the terms of our divorce.

I don't want a divorce, understood? I don't want that. I'm not ready to live without you.

He looked up at the window with the light burning behind it once again.

Sooner or later, you'll have to come out. And talk to me. Without any fucking lawyer between us.

You'll have to tell me, looking me right in the eye, that you no longer love me.

And yet, sooner or later, the cold ends.

Just when you least expect it, a morning dawns with a different gust of wind, a wind that smacks of the sea, for a change.

A special feel to the air, slipping under your skin, numbed by the cold, a strange lust for life. A feel that makes you think, after this long winter, that tomorrow may come after all, and that it may not be so bad.

The cold ends because that's how the world works. There's no real reason, but it ends.

And everything starts over again.

Aragona pretended to look out the plate-glass window that in the winter protected the roof garden of the Hotel Mediterraneo from the chilly north wind.

He'd spent a long time making his preparations. His expression was supposed to be the dreamy gaze of a man remembering extraordinary adventures, experienced in faraway lands, and who at the same time scans the horizon in search of new exploits and a brighter future. The gaze of someone who sees beyond the wall and beyond the present day, the gaze of someone who shoulders the responsibility for other people's safety.

Unfortunately, no one was looking at that gaze.

The other tables were all occupied by businessmen just passing through or conference attendees busy reading reports and newspapers, and typing on their cell phones; but Aragona's expression of a superhero wasn't meant for them.

It had only one target.

Irina, the waitress he was in love with, pirouetted light-footed and discreet from one table to the next, serving the various distracted guests. Aragona wondered how it could be that they didn't all get up en masse to give her a standing ovation when she emerged from the kitchen carrying a trayful of cappuccinos. She was beautiful, her blonde hair pulled up and gathered beneath her white cap, her eyes bright blue and sparkling, her body lithe and appealing, and her accent exotic and thrilling.

She had already approached him once, and he, his voice warm and overbrimming with ulterior meanings—he hoped that she would catch them, those ulterior meanings—had addressed her with his usual, loving phrase: a double-shot espresso, ristretto, in a large mug, thanks. He suspected that the young woman was merely pretending not to remember what he ordered every morning just to give herself the opportunity to listen to the words anew, those loving words of his, the way you do with your favorite song on a record. He, too, he had to admit, even though he had carefully tracked out of the corner of his eye her every step, acted as if he hadn't even noticed her approaching, so that he could hear her ask, once again: Can I bring you something hot to drink, Signore?

Now he was waiting, scanning the horizon through his blue-tinted eyeglasses. It took the time that it had to take, he mused. A double-shot espresso, ristretto, in a large mug, after all, was no simple thing to make. The mug, for starters, had to be just the right temperature, and the espresso needed to be ristretto, of course, which means that it had to drawn in just the right amount and with just the right interval. But eventually Irina would return, and when she did, she would find him in that alluring posture, painstakingly perfected right down to the tiniest detail.

He heard the clinking of the cup and the woman's sensual voice uttering the long-awaited words: "Here you are."

He pretended to emerge from his important thoughts, gave her a distracted but enchanting half-smile, and replied as he always did: "Thanks."

There, it was all over. Now he'd have to wait until tomorrow for another intense exchange with the woman who had taken possession of his heart. The day, he mused, was nothing more than this: an interlude between a "thanks" and a "here you are."

Then the unbelievable came to pass. Irina stopped, turned around, and came back to his table just as he was shoving a cookie into his mouth. She was luminous as a summer day.

"I saw the gentleman on television, yes?" she asked.

She had seen him! She'd seen him smiling like a fool, behind Ottavia as she read the press release drawn up in coordination with police headquarters, along with old man Pisanelli, beaming with pride, and Hulk as he looked around grim-faced, and Alex, who seemed to want to stand off to one side, and the Chinaman, expressionless as always. She had noticed him!

"*Mmmpfff*," he replied, spraying cookie crumbs into the air and all over the table.

Irina nodded, and moved on.

Aragona drank a sip of water, which allowed him to gag down the cookie and save his life.

Once he had resumed a normal rate of respiration, he turned his eyes, streaming with tears, to the horizon.

It turns out, he thought, that the weather was getting nicer after all.

Acknowledgments

The Bastards grow with the fundamental help of a number of wonderful people.

Fabiola Mancone, Valeria Moffa, Gigi Bonagura, Paolo Cortis: the angels of the city, and my own personal guardians.

Giulio Di Mizio, for everything that concerns the job of the medical examiner and our conversations about death and life.

Sister Rosa from the Convent of the Thirty-Three (*Monastero delle Trentatre*), for her patient efforts to instruct a perfect ignoramus on religious topics.

Roberto de Giovanni, for leading me through the mysteries of biotechnology, and Giovanni de Giovanni, for having kept me company during the writing.

Stefania Negro, who stitches one book to the other with extraordinary care.

I Corpi Freddi, who are inside every one of my stories.

Severino Cesari, Francesco Colombo, Paolo Repetti, Valentina Pattavina, Rosella Postorino. This and other novels belong to them more than to the author.

Maria Cristina Guerra, for her heroic support.

The late Gigi Guidotti: I don't know how I'll travel this road without him.

And once again, she who is at the source of all my writing and who lets me wander off, since I know she will be there to greet me with a smile once the river stops flowing: my Paola.

About the Author

Maurizio de Giovanni's Commissario Ricciardi books are bestsellers across Europe, with sales of the series approaching 1 million copies. De Giovanni is also the author of the contemporary Neapolitan thriller, *The Crocodile*, and three installments of the Bastards of Pizzolfalcone series. He lives in Naples with his family.